Wenyu Lake

John H. Zane

Copyright © 2024 John H. Zane

All rights reserved. No part of this book may be reproduced or transmitted in any form or by any means, electronic or mechanical, including photocopying, recording or by any information storage and retrieval system without permission in writing from the publisher.

Bedford Street Books—New Bedford, MA
Paperback ISBN: 979-8-218-49528-2
eBook ISBN: 979-8-3303-9136-3
Library of Congress Control Number: 2024917727
Title: *Wenyu Lake*
Author: John H. Zane
Digital distribution | 2024
Paperback | 2024

This is a work of fiction. The characters, names, incidents, places, and dialogue are products of the author's imagination, and are not to be construed as real.

Published in the United States by New Book Authors Publishing

Dedication

For my wife, Petra, and our son, Tobias, and for our time together in China.

"When man's spirit is in chains, he loses all respect for nature."

Ma Jian, <u>Red Dust</u>

"So does the eye of Heaven itself become an evil eye, when incapable or sordid hands are interposed between it and the things it looks upon to bless."

Charles Dickens, <u>Hard Times</u>

"A love of nature keeps no factories busy. It was decided to abolish a love of nature...."

Aldous Huxley, <u>Brave New World</u>

In Chinese, family names appear first.

Chapter 1

The lake was best seen from, well, nowhere, shrouded as it was in a thick cloud of smog. The sun could not penetrate the greyness; the surface of the water was a dull black. What little land was distinguishable slipped in and out of shadows, along with the buildings and factories crowding the shore. Along the banks, the water was muddy brown turning to brackish green where a long line of rowboats rested, long disused, rotting and partly filled with rank, oil-stained sludge. In the brown and yellow reeds that dotted the shore, a carpet of algae, capped by a greyish white foam, bobbed and bounced in the slight breeze.

The sounds of the town seemed distant and muffled by the haze, and there was no discernable movement on the lake until a man in heavy waders appeared, waist deep and working his way deliberately through the weeds: a tall man, with his hair shaved short on the sides and a thick black mop on top speckled with silver, high cheekbones, and intense dark eyes. His many-pocketed vest held rows of thin glass beakers arrayed against his chest like strange ammunition as he pushed aside plastic bags and food wrappers, orange peels and soggy bits of cardboard; a few minutes earlier, he had banged his shin on a completely submerged refrigerator.

With each step, a palpable, chemical stench rose in bubbles around him. Periodically, he lowered a glass beaker into the water in order to capture a sample at the bottom. He had been in the lake for many hours and he could feel where new leaks were forming in his patched and cracked waders but he disregarded the unpleasant squishing of his feet as he used a waterproof pen to write on the label of the beakers: date, time, place, depth. He held one up to the smog obscured sunlight in the hope of seeing some sign of aquatic life but there were only particles of pollution slowly descending to the bottom. There were dangerous levels of chemicals and chemical fertilizers permeating the lake, and they were increasing, creating excessive growth of algae and a subsequent lack of oxygen. No fish, let alone any spoors, could live in such an environment. The lake was dying, and not slowly but rapidly. Even wild fowl, if they landed on the water at all, quickly departed.

It was not difficult for Tao Lin to locate the immediate source for the putrid smell. From where he stood, he could make out through the smog a concrete pipe spewing industrial waste less than a hundred yards away. And behind that, on the bank of the lake, a massive factory complete with smoking chimneys, large warehouses and office buildings, and a long row of industrial silos each the size of a 10-story building. The silos contained tons of fermenting corn and sugar beets mixed with specialized bacteria for the making of monosodium glutamate. Surrounding the tanks were unloading docks bringing in raw material and loading docks for bags and boxes of finished product. Conveyers crisscrossed between the tanks and the warehouses. The Golden Prosper Spice Seasoning Works, owned and operated by his former childhood friend, Gao Bing, was the pride and joy of the town. It provided jobs for hundreds and much needed tax revenue, was one of the biggest employers, the single biggest taxpayer, its Golden Prosper Spice Seasoning a provincial champion brand, and Bing the richest man in town.

But money was not what Lin wished to think about. Money was a constant source of trouble in his life or, in fact, his lack of it. Only this morning, as he collected his specimen beakers and his much-patched waders, did he hear his wife, Chen, lamenting his lack of what, it seemed, everyone in the town was acquiring: a better car, a maid, vacations to foreign destinations, a bigger gift to hand to the local schoolteacher for special treatment of their 9-year-old daughter.

"And, you know, Gao Bing has offered—" Chen began but he cut her off, gulping his tea and shoving some pork filled buns into his pocket. "Enough. I am not my friend, or ex-friend. I do not own and operate an MSG plant. I am a scientist. I work for the protection of the environment of this country. I don't do business. You can be the business person in the family."

"Yes, of course. And I am. But you could do a bit as well. Everyone else is making money. Why not you?"

Lin sighed. "You know, Chen, it's not a real choice, being poor. It's not something anyone likes. The fact is, scientists who work for the State Environmental Protection Administration don't make much money."

"Then the offer from Bing?"

"The offer from Bing is a bribe. You know it, and I know it."

So started his morning, the heavy shoulders of his daughter as she made her way out the door to school, anticipating the taunts of the other children. "Melon head, melon head. Your father has a melon head."

Ever since he brought up the degradation of the quality of the water in the lake at a planning meeting for Communist Party cadre and the non-Party business community, having previously saved his criticisms for formal and private complaints to his higherups at the provincial level State Environmental Protection Administration, the taunts and jeers began. He knew it was a risky business, going so public with his concerns and grievances, bringing the weight of the town down on his shoulders, but, with the lake possibly beyond redemption, he saw no alternative. His suggestion that businesses close down if they did not either install proper environmental equipment or utilize already installed environmental equipment *at maximum capacity* was met not only with incredulity but with outright laughter. He felt sorry for his daughter, Xiaoyu, but his job, his duty as he clearly saw it, was to show people that the environmental degradation of China was a runaway train, that the lake was dying, that it was at a tipping point; once passed, it was a point of no return. They needed to realize that the demise of the lake was important, that it would change their lives and the lives of their children and grandchildren. They all needed to work together, to make sacrifices, and unfortunately that included his poor daughter being cruelly teased by her classmates.

He stood in the water, staring at the wastewater pouring into the lake from the factory: it was loaded with ammonium, sulphate, suspended solids, and an astronomical chemical oxygen demand of almost 30,000 milligrams per liter. It was the biggest polluter of any number of factories surrounding the lake, choking it, starving it of oxygen. In Lin's previous environmental report, he had suggested that the Golden Prosper Spice Seasoning factory introduce an activated sludge system to treat its wastewater. It was expensive, he knew, and used an inordinate amount of energy. It was not lost on Lin that the energy needed was produced by outdated, inefficient coal-fired plants, resulting in yet another pollution dilemma, but there was always compromise involved in the weighing of lesser evils. In any event, his plan was ridiculed by Bing as a direct assault on the economic viability of his business. Simply put: it would adversely affect his bottom line. SEPA was not a Ministry, at least not yet, and any directives by its field agents were subordinate to all other Ministry directives. There was no business incentive to treat wastewater, and certainly no ethical considerations by the factory owners that Lin had ever encountered. Until they passed higher level laws, increased enforcement, and controlled the rampant corruption within the bureaucracy, his reports would continue to be a source of great amusement before being added to the mounds of garbage that were strewn upon the bed of the lake.

He finished collecting his samples and waded ashore, considering whether to head up the northwest tributary early next morning, one of the three main waterways which fed the lake. Not that the lake needed any more problems but it seemed that sources of pollution from the tributaries were getting worse. Certainly, he was finding the usual high levels of pesticides and phosphorus and nitrogen from farming communities overusing chemical fertilizers upstream but there seemed to be increasing, and alarming, quantities of heavy metals and carcinogens as well arsenic, cadmium, cyanide, and mercury. They were concentrated in the northwest corner of the lake. Yes. He would ride up the tributary tomorrow and take samples, he decided, as he mounted his solid, ancient, reliable flying pigeon bicycle and, having loaded his sample beakers into the wooden cages strapped like paniers to the back, set out for the town and his laboratory. The muffled tinkling of the glass against the soft, worn wood sounded like wind chimes.

Chapter 2

Gao Bing stood staring out the window from his glass office tower high above the monosodium glutamate factory. Behind him loomed the towering fermentation silos, before him the vague outlines of the lake shrouded in heavy smog. He was nodding his head contentedly having just finished a meeting with his chief sales representatives: a very satisfactory meeting. Not only were sales booming but he had discovered more and more opportunities to introduce MSG into the food chain from nuts to cooking oils to dried fish, even to toothpaste (although labelling requirements had made this somewhat problematic for western export). The possibilities were endless. One of his greatest successes had been introducing MSG into dog and cat food destined for the foreign market: the animals loved it, and since China now controlled almost half the pet food market, he was supplying an ever-growing portion of MSG to it.

There had been some setbacks, of course. There always were for entrepreneurs like himself. Uncooked fruit was not agreeable to doses of flavor enhancers. Nor were uncooked vegetables. Although he had been instrumental in introducing large quantities of MSG into animal feed, which increased the appetite and water retention and therefore the weight of the animals, his attempt at injecting MSG directly under the skin of living pigs had not turned out so well. All agreed that the meat tasted much better because of the infusion, at least with those pigs that had managed to live long enough to make it to the slaughterhouse. Unfortunately, most had died from hypertension and dehydration and had been dumped unceremoniously into the lake under cover of darkness. Ah well. Live and learn, was his motto. He was not easily discouraged; in fact, he was excited to hear from a friend who had just returned from a business trip to Africa that the Africans used prodigious amounts of MSG; in fact, they rolled their meat directly in the powder before cooking. He was elated at the thought of all those potential millions of new customers, at the thought of muscling his way into foreign markets, undercutting the price of whatever competition was out there for however long it took, and then sitting back and enjoying the profits. Of course, he couldn't compete directly with the COFCOs and the Ajinimotos of the world but he knew how to set up small scale sales forces' skilled at keeping customers happy. It had succeeded beyond all expectation here in the province and he saw no reason to believe that he could not replicate such success in the outside world.

He glanced at the wall beside the floor to ceiling window; on prominent display, surrounded by the ubiquitous framed photos of high-level cadre officials shaking Bing's hand, was a portrait of Misuhara Kanagawa, his idol and shining example. It was Kanagawa-san himself who had discovered the fermentation process for MSG in the late 50's, experimenting with various formulas which enhanced the taste sensation in human beings. His factory on the outskirts of Yokohama was the first, and biggest, manufacturing plant for MSG, a place Bing had visited, as he would a shrine, a few years earlier. He had taken very careful notes in his head (no phones, cameras, or pens and paper allowed, naturally) of the processes and equipment in the factory and implemented many of them in his own. Although the Japanese were universally hated by the Chinese, Nanjing being a knee-jerk battle cry for most of his fellow citizens, Bing held no such prejudice: he was more than willing to learn from a race of people who had proved themselves so exceptionally capable. And at least the Japanese devils shared a common Asian culture and history with China. They even looked a bit like us, he thought, unlike, say, the round-eyed, big-nosed foreign devils he met on his travels with their wispy straw-like hair, cold, gleaming eyes, braying laughter and big teeth. Westerners were the ones you had to be especially careful of, was his opinion.

In any event, he was proud of how he became a manufacturer of such an essential product as MSG, such a worthwhile contribution to the clear superiority of Chinese cuisine. In the early 80's, after the chaos of culture revolution, on a train ride back from the provincial capital and an unsuccessful trip to secure financing for a fish farm he had wished to build on the shores of Wenyu Lake, he had sat next to a young Taiwanese businessman. They had struck up a conversation, the man explaining that he too had failed to find enough investors for an umbrella factory he wanted to open in Jiangsu province. As they talked, he pulled a package of instant dried noodles from his bag and, with a thermos of boiled water, mixed the noodles, a package of dried vegetables and peppers, and a mysterious red and white powder together in a tin cup with a lid. He closed the lid tightly.

As he waited, a crowd gathered. Most had never seen instant noodles although some said they had seen them in the far south and in the capital city. They pressed around him, asking about how they were made and whether they tasted like the real thing. The Taiwanese explained to them that instant noodles were common in his home country. He pulled out two more packages to share with them. Tin cups with lids appeared and he prepared the two packages as he did the first. After a few minutes, he opened the lids and the passengers dipped in their chopsticks. There was general astonishment at the quality and taste and, of course, convenience of the noodles. While the others ate, Bing studied the discarded noodle package which he had picked up off the floor of the train carriage. He knew that in no time there would be thousands of factories throughout China making these noodles, all trying to desperately push their way to the top of the consumer food chain with good taste and cheap prices. But Bing thought if he could find out what was the most important ingredient involved in the production, then he could become a supplier to the producers. He asked the Taiwanese about the ingredients, about which one was perhaps the most important. The man looked carefully at Bing who was studying the noodle wrapper.

"You want to know what is most important?" he asked, leaning in closely towards Bing. "Monosodium glutamate. Flavor enhancer. Without it, the noodles would be bland. You saw how people reacted to the taste. That would not have happened without MSG. We use it on a lot of our food in Taiwan. It's plentiful and, as far as anyone knows, has no ill effects on people."

Bing, rumbling along on a dark night in a hard sleep carriage on a Chinese rail line, had found his calling.

He had started his MSG fermentation production with no more than a dozen open vats, his workers mixing by hand the corn and sugar beets used as raw material, then the bacteria for the fermentation. It had been hard work to get the process down correctly, but he had persevered; two years to get a viable sample, two years to develop his sales force, reinvesting his profits into upgrading and modernizing the plant, until a decade later he was unbeatable. It helped that Deng Xiaoping had decided that to be rich was glorious, so that after his initial success he had access to an almost endless supply of low to no-interest loans from the local Construction Bank and support from the town cadre. These people looked after Bing, and he, in turn, took very good care of them, never missing a chance to give a lavish gift at Spring Festival, never failing to remember a birthday. Sometimes even a key to a new automobile was stuck inside a red envelope in the case of a very important favor needing to be granted. And look at the factory now: a long row of fermentation silos each 100 feet high; acres of warehouses and offices and loading docks and lifts and conveyers. It was a joyous sight.

Bing turned away from the factory to look at the lake, noticing movement among the thrushes along the bank a hundred yards or so from the factory. It was a typically murky day, with smog rolling in from the factories as well as the coal plants and steel works to the west of Wenyu Lake, but he could just make out the tall figure of his ex-schoolmate and former friend, Tao Lin, as he pushed his bicycle up onto the dirt road above the lake, shuffling awkwardly in his rubber waders, climbing carefully onto his bike, and heading toward town. Melon head, he thought with disgust. Making trouble for businesses, constantly writing negative reports about the water quality and the factory discharges around the lake. It was a mystery to Bing why the man could not just shut up and get rich like everyone else. They had grown up together, gone to school where they had both excelled. Lin had gone on to university, no easy feat for a country boy, and become a member of the Chinese Communist Party, also no easy feat considering his family background.

Bing, meanwhile, had rejected university and pursued a life in business while Lin began by studying medicine, had then turned to biology and chemistry, and environmental studies, whatever in hell's name that was, Bing thought. The man had held a relatively high-level position with the State Environmental Protection Administration in Beijing and was attached in some way to the prestigious Chinese Academy of Social Sciences, Bing knew. Then, suddenly, Lin had decided to return to his hometown. He had heard it was because his mother was getting old and feeble, and that he had grown tired of the chaos of the capital city. Whatever. All Bing knew was that now Lin spent his days pushing around a rusted old flying pigeon with a bunch of glass beakers on the back, digging in the mud of the lake and the dirt of the fields, measuring unknown things in the air and water, and not only making trouble for everyone but at the same time making a pathetic, mid-level bureaucrat salary. He was a pariah, hated by the business community and mistrusted by most everyone else. An idealist is what he was. Although ideals were a complete mystery to Bing, they were clearly something to avoid at all costs.

Bing had even offered Lin a job at one point: factory chemist in charge of production quality, something he had thought up. Great pay, hardly any hours, benefits. But he had not only declined, in his most recent report to SEPA, he had singled out the Golden Prosper Spice Seasoning Company as one of the biggest polluters in the entire lake. He had the gall to suggest that Bing treat his wastewater with activated sludge and bacteria, a system that, even considering the expense of installing it, would have increased his energy cost by close to forty percent. Luckily the idea was so absurd that no one took it seriously. Why just last winter, Lin had personally accompanied one of the chief environmental inspectors from the provincial capital when he visited the factory, pointing out the wastewater and its lack of treatment in great detail. It had taken political resources and funds to take care of that headache, and he resented Lin's creating such trouble.

But enough: time to think about growing his business and the profits it would bring him. He was currently experimenting with MSG in candy and soft drinks which showed some promise. He was also thinking of branching out into new businesses; he was already, like most successful Chinese businessmen, dabbling in real estate. Beer had caught his fancy: seemed like a good side business and not so far removed from the fermentation process required to make MSG. Bing liked the high-profile possibilities with beer: the advertisements, the sponsorships, the sports events.

As he stared out at the smoggy lake and the hazy shore, he could picture clearly the flashy label on millions of beer bottles, red lettering on a green background, an outline of the mythical, crystal-clear waters of Wenyu Lake, maybe one or two anthropomorphist carp jumping from the water. He could see his own ubiquitous smiling face staring out from endless television commercials as he shook hands with track stars, swimmers, badminton and table tennis players. Oh yes. He could see it now. Picking up his office phone, he punched a button for the corporate development office. He wanted a draft business plan on his desk first thing Friday morning on the potential production of a Wenyu Lake beer.

Chapter 3

Lin set out early knowing that it would take most of the morning and part of the afternoon to arrive at the upper reaches of the northwest tributary. He gulped some green tea, packed a lunch of pancakes filled with pork, slung a small overnight bag over his shoulder as in all likelihood he would need to find a room in a farmhouse for the night, and tiptoed out of the apartment. Setting out so early had the advantage of not hearing complaints from his wife or to suffer the disheartened looks of his daughter. He stood in front of the elevator as the door opened. The old neighborhood committee woman operating the lift sat on her three-legged stool in her droopy, faded blue-cloth uniform with the red armband pinned to her sleeve.

As Lin entered, she frowned at the row of numbered buttons, at the battered metal walls, at the ceiling, deliberately avoiding making eye contact. He sighed, amazed that his conduct at the Party meeting had reached even the neighborhood committees, meaning that his outcast status was unanimous and assured. He shook his head as the lift descended fitfully and shuttered to a halt not quite on a level with the ground floor. With a frown and a glare at the little woman, he stepped down and made his way through the entranceway's scarred, metal door, and around the building to the bicycle shed that ran along the entire side of the building. He unloaded his equipment and overnight bag to the back of his bike before leaning his hands against the side of the building in order to stretch his calve muscles. He took a few minutes for each leg, before climbing onto his bike and pedaling out the gate and into the northbound traffic.

There was the usual chaos, cars careening from one lane to another, the bleating of horns, bicycles forced on to dirt sidewalks by the motorized traffic, mixing dangerously with pedestrians and with the wares of shops which spilled onto the street. He passed a small park on his right, one of the few remaining on the outskirts of the city. Already businesses were encroaching around the perimeter of the park: restaurants, massage parlors, VIP clubs where, on the weekends, the new and young rich filled the parking lots with their shiny foreign automobiles. The park was supposed to be reserved for the people but the police leased off land to businesses and no one had the courage, or stupidity, to complain. It was a beneficial relationship for everyone but the poor. Lin weaved his bike between lines of parked and moving automobiles on what was once a bicycle lane but was now just another spur for traffic. He passed the south gate of the park where a flock of old women were practicing Tai chi, their arms raised in unison, balanced on one foot, their hands rotating gracefully. Behind them were the usual bright red banners hanging from the walls of the park encouraging citizens to conform to family planning laws, to support the work of the local communist government, to show pride at the chance for China to showcase its wonders at the upcoming Olympic games in Beijing.

At the east gate of the park, barbers set up their stools in a row in the open, all wearing soiled white coats and rounded hats, chattering constantly to potential customers passing by, snapping their scissors and motioning to the stools. Tables beside the stools held towels and scissors and assorted hair products, creams and oils and, of course, the ubiquitous black hair dyes that were essential to all aging Chinese men. Lin, stalled between a three wheeled farm vehicle and a massive SUV, watched as one barber turned from his customer and, with his thumb and forefinger delicately holding the bridge of his nose, let a stream of mucus fly from both nostrils. He cleared his clogged throat, gave a rattling cough, and returned to his customer. Advanced bronchial congestion, Lin thought, with corresponding Viral Rhinitis or common cold, which he will pass on to his customers today and, by the sound of it, the next day and the next. His customers will carry it home with them to share with their families, however many generations living under one roof, who will then pass it on further, until, in a few short weeks, it will have reached the majority of the population of the town. For just that reason, Lin didn't trust barbers. He cut his own hair with his own clippers, despite his wife's protests. Shaved short on the sides with a flop of salt and pepper on top, it was somewhat bizarre, he knew; it certainly attracted curious glances from people. But he rarely, if ever, caught a cold.

A mile or so past the park, the traffic thinned and Lin could stop concentrating on obstacles on the road and enjoy the warm fall day as he pedaled along a causeway and a bridge which separated the last, pure stretch of marshland from the lake. Fed from springs and with little development around it, the marshland contained relatively clean water, serving as a filter for the water running into the lake. Lin had found myriad signs of microbic life in the marsh, larvae in the grass and the spoor of fish eggs in the water, although whatever was swept into the lake during rain and high water soon died from lack of oxygen. Past the causeway, another mile farther on, he reached the northwest tributary and was greeted by the acrid smell of chemicals, the water pouring from its mouth the color of light chocolate. Just upstream was a tannery and shoe factory, and Lin concluded that today must be a brown-shoe tanning day: the colors varied from bright red to a dull yellow depending on what dyes were being used. Although the tannery was required to filter its runoff before dumping it in the tributary, there was little enforcement. Lin had cited the factory to the provincial government, along with Bing's, of course, and a number of others surrounding the lake, but, after issuing citations and recommending wastewater treatment solutions, nothing seemed to happen. Inspectors were paid off; invited to banquets in the provincial capital under the guise of better understanding the recommended environmental initiatives, where the food would be exquisite, sharks fin soup and abalone and sea cucumber, with bottles of the best rice wine liquor. Red Envelopes containing cash or vouchers were distributed, and the wastewater flowed unimpeded.

As Lin passed the factory, and the giant cement sculpture of a shoe next to the gates, he had no doubt that behind the office windows, there would be eyes upon him; he well knew that he had, as usual, made enemies with his latest report to the provincial SEPA, and that there were people who would be happy to see him and his flying pigeon disappear forever into the murky toxic water of Wenyu Lake.

He continued up the winding road towards the headwaters of the northwest tributary and considered the new heavy metals, mostly cyanide and mercury, that had begun to appear in the lake. He knew all about the shoe factory, the lead-based dyes and acid heavy runoff, the chlorinated phenols and chlorinated paraffins, but the new chemicals were disturbing. He knew of no other new industries along the banks of the tributary but something was happening at the headwaters and he aimed to find out just what it was.

As he rode, he studied the landscape around him. The rains had been good in late summer but the countryside, although at first glance covered in green flora, was denuded in many places. Quarries had slashed the hillsides and there were no shade trees to be seen, no dove trees or willows, only scrub pines and locusts and clumps of bamboo doted the hillsides and little else. Along the banks of the tributary were spindly poplar trees, genetically modified and planted a decade back. Other than the poplars, there were no other tall trees to be seen, and certainly no forests. This small mountain range and its denuded landscape had been like this for over a half century. Nothing had recovered from the Great Famine and the Great Leap Forward of the 1950s; no tree was left standing, fed into backyard blast furnaces that melted down lumps of worthless, low-grade iron. There had been some effort at replanting but always with the same modified trees. And since all the trees had the same genetic code, it meant that, once a blight came, and it inevitably would, there would be no diversification and nothing would survive, and they would be back where they started from.

On the steeper grades of the road, Lin shifted down to a climbing sprocket which he had had specially built into his bike although he still needed to dismount and push on the steepest grades. He paused every few miles to take water samples from the cloudy, rust colored water of the tributary. He would not be able to analyze the true content of the water until he got back to his laboratory, but he could clearly see that the sediment was loaded with unnatural colors. He had never investigated this far from the lake and assumed he was technically reaching the limits of his jurisdiction despite having petitioned the State Environmental Protection Administration for permission to explore sources of pollution far from the lake. Obviously, went his argument, the lake could not be brought back to life if the sources of its water were not investigated and cured. He had heard back from SEPA recently, and been assured that, in fact, permission was forthcoming.

As he climbed steadily, at such an altitude, even in the early afternoon heat of a September day, the air was fresh and the riding pleasant. He passed innumerable fields of corn and sweet potatoes and peanuts with villages of faded red and yellow brick partly hidden behind the spindly poplars and locust trees. An occasional donkey grazed along the bank of the wide stream amid plastic bags, waterlogged cardboard, and abandoned appliances. Lin calculated that in another hour or two he would reach the last village and that the headwaters would probably be another hour past that. He wasn't sure he would get as far as that today but he expected to find out most of what he needed to know from the villagers. It was their source of drinking water, and from what he had seen downstream, he could imagine that they would have much to tell him.

By mid-afternoon, he was entering the village, following a sharp curve in the stream that ran along the brick and cinder block houses. Corn stalks and dead branches culled from the nut trees that dotted the hillsides were stacked outside the doors of each house, ready to fuel the fires beneath the Kong beds when the cold winter season, thankfully short, arrived. It was a poor farm village of maybe a few thousand, subsisting on rice, nuts, corn, wheat and perhaps sweet potatoes, and nothing else that Lin could see. He was surprised by how deserted the village was: at this time of day there should be children playing and women sweeping the streets and men coming and going from the fields. Occasionally he caught sight of a shadow in a window, a furtive figure peering from a doorway, as he made his way along the main street. He reached the village square, with the usual bright red banners hanging on the walls, exhorting the villagers to work for the common good, to achieve the glorious goals of the communist party's latest five-year plan, and to always follow family planning guidelines. Although the village had long ago installed piping to bring water to each of the neighborhoods, the original village well still stood in the middle of the square. Lin parked his bike nearby and took a seat on a stone bench that circled the well.

Inevitably, children began to appear, curious about the stranger and his bicycle with the wooden racks of specimen bottles. As they gathered round, Lin spoke with them, told them where he was from and about his work. They were all dressed in hand-me-down clothes with logos from famous American and European sports teams; skinny as they were, Lin observed that they were by no means suffering from malnutrition. There was, however, something about the eyes of some of them, something confused and slow in their movements and in the few words they uttered, maybe something thyroidal, that they shared in common.

He asked after their parents.

"My father is sick," said one of the older children. "Are you a doctor?" he asked hopefully. "He has a bump and he shakes. He needs a doctor but there isn't one here. We would have to go to the lake and we cannot afford it."

"I am not a medical doctor but a doctor of science," said Lin. "But I know about sicknesses. I would like to see him."

"He does not want to be seen. He is ashamed."

"Tell him that I come from the government and that I am here to help."

He ran to a nearby house and entered through a doorway covered by a curtain of thin, hanging strips of brightly colored plastic. The curtain closed like water behind him as Lin and the other children waited.

"And you all?" Lin asked. "Do you also have parents who are sick?"

They looked at their feet, rubbed their noses, but no one spoke. Some shook their heads no, some yes. He heard the curtain part and the older boy returned.

"They said they will see you because you are from the government and maybe you can help."

Lin followed the boy through the curtain and entered a simply furnished room which held a sofa and chair on one side and a large, fire heated Kong bed on the other. The boy's father lay in the bed, too sick to even move to the sofa. The first thing Lin noticed were his hands which paddled in a palsied motion, as if they were scrambling eggs with a pair of chopsticks, round and round, steadily, with no pause. His chin moved jerkily left and right, and Lin saw that he had a lump on his neck the size of a small melon. It pulled at the skin of his face so that his right eye was almost closed and the right side of his mouth was drawn down. Lin took one of the man's whirling hands and held it in his own. He touched the growth on the man's neck and found it hard as glass. "I'm sorry to see you so sick, comrade. Can you tell me when this began?"

His wife answered. "He is having difficulty speaking. He understands but he trembles when he talks. The lump began last year in winter, and the shaking soon after. We think it's the water: the color, the smell, have all changed these last few years. There are men and machines up above the village at the headwaters. We see them on occasion but they keep away from the village as much as possible." She looked furtively about, lowering her voice to a whisper. "Whatever it is, there must be money in it. The police and the village party secretary are driving new cars and building new houses." She paused, staring helplessly at her husband, and then looked warily at Lin. She cast her eyes down, ashamed, full of regret at having given him so much information.

Lin smiled reassuringly. "My name is Tao Lin. I am from the State Environmental Protection Administration from Meiyu Town and I am testing the water here and downstream. Once I know what's in the water, I will report to the provincial authorities and see what can be done. Meanwhile, boil as much as you can of what you drink and use to cook. There is not much else I can do until I find the source of the problem. Are there others who are suffering like your husband in the village?"

"Many," she answered. "But no one wants to talk about it. And no one wants to complain. The Party Secretary and the police have told us that the sickness is coming from the air and not from the water. The air is bad, yes, from the steel works in Xishan but it has been bad for years and no one has developed such a sickness. They also say that only the weak are getting sick but my husband has worked many years harvesting nuts and growing corn. He was always strong and has never been sick before."

Lin stood, holding the man's hand in both of his, and gave him a sympathetic look. "I -the Administration - will do what we can." He turned to the woman. "We will try and get a doctor up here as soon as possible." He left the house, thanking the boy for his kindness, and pushed his bike through the gaggle of children, through the square and up the main road of the village. He had not gone more than fifty yards, wondering just exactly how far it might be to the headwaters, before a policeman, driving a small Lifan motorcycle, pulled up in front of him, blocking his progress. His weight and size dwarfed the 125cc machine. It seemed impossible that the bike could hold such a person but he dismounted with a practiced, and somewhat elegant swing of his leg. Lin stood beside his bicycle, not all that surprised to see the police. After all, it was a small village. The big cop, a cigarette dangling from his lips, eyes covered by mirrored sunglasses, inspected the bicycle carefully, picking up and replacing a number of samples from their wooden cages.

"You are from the government?" he asked, after noisily clearing his throat and spitting into the middle of the dirt street.

"That's right. I am a deputy inspector with the State Environmental Protection Administration. From Meiyu." He handed the policemen his card with the Agency seal on it.

"So why are you here? This is not Meiyu."

"I am inspecting tributaries around the lake, and this is one of them."

"I don't think you have the authority to inspect so far from Meiyu. In fact, I'm sure you don't. Report to the police station immediately and we will find out under what authority you are working. It's just around the bend on the right. I will be waiting for you."

Lin sighed and watched the big man mount his comically small motorcycle and disappear in a cloud of exhaust.

As he continued up the road, he noticed that a few of the old brick and cement block houses had built second floors of bluish white tiles and aluminum framed windows which stood out against the dull red and yellow of the traditional brick walls. He noticed a new, black Hyundai sedan in front of one of the renovated houses. Well, someone was making money somewhere around here, he thought, and he suspected he knew who and where.

Chapter 4

The police station was the newest building in the village with the same ubiquitous style of bluish-white tiles and aluminum framed windows. Although the building could not have been very old, the outside was rust stained and marked with soot and dust. He entered and stood before a desk now occupied by the fat cop who held a lighter in one hand and was spinning a pack of triple 5 cigarettes on top of the desk with the other. He had not removed his sunglasses. Behind him stood a small, thin man with large glasses and short, cropped hair, undoubtedly the local communist party official. The man sported a large mole on his chin which sprouted a single, long hair.

"I am Fang Shu, Party Secretary in this village, and you have no authority to be here," he stated immediately. "I have called the provincial authorities and your jurisdiction ends many miles below the village. I don't know why you are here and I don't care. You must go."

Lin asked if he could sit, pointing to a metal chair in front of the desk. He sat before they could respond, stretched his long legs, and sighed. His eyes scanned the room, took note of the large, 5-gallon mineral-water bottle on its white plastic dispenser, and of the table with tea thermoses of gaudy colors and two clear-plastic water pitchers with filters. In one corner was a collection of full and empty mineral water bottles, and in another were stacked cardboard cartons of small bottles of carbonated Lao Shan spring water. If you worked at the police station, you didn't have to worry about drinking the local water, he thought.

"You are right that I have no authority here in your village, although I am told that permission is forthcoming. I have, in fact, found some chemicals in water samples in the lake that seem to come from this tributary, and I came to investigate."

"Whatever it is you found, it's not from this tributary and certainly not from this village. I suggest you investigate elsewhere," said the Party Secretary, pushing his oversize glasses up on his nose.

"I will be writing a report on the chemicals I have found below this village and submitting it to the Environmental Protection Bureau. I am sure they will send a chief inspector to investigate and determine if there are violations taking place," Lin said.

The cadre shrugged indifferently. "There are no violations here. The inspector is welcome to come see for himself."

Studying him closely, he seemed truly unconcerned, Lin thought. He must be supremely confident that he can bribe his way out of the situation, or that the cumbersome bureaucracy would never get around to investigating. Both were certainly plausible. In any event, there was nothing more for Lin to do. "It's late and it's not possible to get back to the lake this evening. If you could tell me where I could find a farmhouse that will let me a room for the night, I would be most grateful."

The two frowned, then mumbled quietly together for a minute before answering. "There is a farmhouse a few miles down the road that will give you room and board for the evening," said the fat cop. "I will call them now to make sure that you are welcome. Someone will be waiting on the road for you when you pass."

He paused, lit one of the triple 5s, and leaned back in his chair. "And since this is not your jurisdiction, your water samples do not belong to you. We have taken the opportunity to empty them."

He knew it was fruitless to object or to argue; that they were going to such lengths to keep the contents of the water secret merely confirmed his suspicions. In the end, they could not hide what was in the water nor what was happening to the villagers. He had only to take more samples farther south of the village, and this he would do in the morning.

With that, he stood, nodded his head goodbye, and stepped outside to find his samples emptied, the sullied water mixing with the dust of the street on both sides of his bicycle. A small man, even small for a province of small people, with a red Chicago Bulls ballcap pulled down low over his face leaned against a wall nearby, watching him closely. They stared at each other in silence before Lin mounted the bike and rode slowly back down the main street, the man following closely behind. Again, he could see shadows of people disappearing into doorways and alleyways, feel eyes peering from windows as they followed his progress out of town. Despite riding at an inviting walking pace, no one tried to speak with him. As he passed through the square and the old well, some of the children were still there and waved to him. But when they saw the Bulls cap man, they stopped playing and stood very still.

He shadowed Lin at an easy trot for another half mile out of town until Lin lost sight of him in the fading light. A few miles farther on, he made out the figure of a woman by the side of the road. She motioned for him to stop and showed him the way to the side of her decrepit farmhouse. She spoke little, was obviously displeased at this sudden inconvenience, but Lin was happy to enter a clean room with a brick Kong bed, a small table, and a not too battered armchair.

The woman held out her hand, and Lin counted small bills into it until she was satisfied. "I will bring dinner in an hour," she stated, and left.

Outside chickens scratched in the yard, and behind him he could hear a pig grunt in its stall as cicadas hummed in the stunted trees, the steady pitched noise rising and falling. Lin sat in the armchair, thought of unpacking his bag and taking some notes on the day, but he found it very pleasant to just sit and listen to the sounds of the farmhouse all around him. He could hear the water rippling in the stream; he pictured the water as clear and sparkling, with wild cress growing in the small pools, bugs playing on the surface, even minnows swimming with their darting, upstream motion. He wished the water was as it once was, not so long ago, maybe half a century before, before it all went to ruin, before it filled with poison and before it got to the point of no return.

At sunrise, having washed his face in a basin full of water, Lin sat at the small desk. The farmer woman had brought him a bowl of porridge with pickled vegetables and preserved eggs and the empty bowl lay next to his notebook, along with a portable, micro-filter kit which he used to first filter the water from the tea thermos before making his tea. He began writing a draft of a report about the northwest tributary. Obviously, such high levels of mercury and cyanide could only mean an illegal, and possibly substantial, gold mining operation, and the woman he met yesterday confirmed that there were workers and machines above the village. The hills above the tributary were known for abandoned mines, once worked with the backs of peasants welding pickaxes and shovels and little else. Whoever was working the mine shaft now must have hit an ore deposit with a worthwhile mixture of gold. With a few jackhammers run by generators, trommels to crush the ore, barrels and barrels of liquid mercury to separate the gold from the crushed ore, and a cyanide sluice, which the stream at the headwaters would feed to recover whatever the mercury was unable to recover, they could be mining 5 or 10 ounces of gold a day. A lot of money in today's market. At first, they may have tried creating a tailings pond to contain the pollution, or possibly just to mix with more cyanide in order to squeeze whatever fragments of gold where still left in the discarded mercury and ore, but eventually it all washed down the stream and into the tributary and the village below. A few short years later, he figured, was all it took before the sicknesses appeared.

The village Party Secretary would be in on it, of course, as well as the police. Whatever percentage they were taking from the operation, or even if they owned the operation outright, whatever percentage they kept after expenses would buy a lot of shiny, new Hyundai and second story extensions on a cinderblock house. Lin knew that when money was involved, or when the possibility of losing money was involved, he needed to be very, very careful.

There was no sign of the farmer woman when Lin stepped out of his room, just some scrawny chickens scratching the dust. He strapped his bag to the back of the bike and headed out, the farmhouse and village fading in the distance. He turned his head constantly to see if he was being followed but saw no one. He stopped to collect samples every mile or so, hurrying back to his bicycle in case someone from the village police station appeared, but the road was deserted. Eventually, as he sped effortlessly downhill, he was back within his jurisdiction, and, in what seemed no time at all, found himself approaching the walls of the shoe factory and the giant cement shoe sculpture. Trucks were racing in, unloading animal hides, barrels of dye and glue, and great spools of string; others were racing out, loaded with pallets of finished products destined for the international market. Yet another successful business contributing to the economic health of the town and to the ruination of its water. Why was their no balance in this country? Lin wondered. It seemed so easy to do the worst things and so difficult to do anything good. He shook his head sadly, but then concentrated on the samples he was carrying, on his scanning electron microscope, his spectroscopy and the other equipment back at the lab, and at the certainty that he would soon be able to confirm his suspicions.

Chapter 5

Xi Peng stood on the loading platform of the tannery, nodding his head appreciatively at the half dozen container trucks pulled up to the bays and the beehive of activity from the workers who were unloading raw materials and loading finished goods. He thought back to the days when the factory was just starting, how the 20-foot and 40-foot containers had been scattered about the yard in disarray, with twice as many workers hoisting raw materials and boxes on their backs, all dressed uniformly in dusty blue Mao-suits. What a difference a decade could make. He remembered when he got his first order with a Big Box store in the U.S., how carefully they had packed the 40-footer and how proud they were when they shut the doors and it was loaded on a flatbed and sent off. Unfortunately for Peng, the branches from an enormous willow tree, wet from the monsoon rains and unobserved by anyone, had caught in the top of the doors of the container. When the 40-footer arrived in Long Beach, having sworn that it contained no agricultural material, a spot inspection found the pile of twigs and willow leaves. It was quarantined for weeks and fumigated at great cost to Peng. The Big Box store was furious, ruining its spring sale of boating shoes, and threatened to never do business with him again. The stress of those days, Peng thought. But all had been forgotten; the Big Box was back, enamored with his products, one of his best and most enthusiastic customers.

He gazed out the gate at the traffic passing on the street, catching a glimpse of a bicycle with a strange set of wooden paniers speeding by. Son of a bitch didn't fall off his bike and break his neck, he said to himself. It would have saved everyone a lot of trouble. He frowned, left the loading dock and made his way down a wide corridor with forklifts whirring here and there, up a metal set of stairs to his wall-to-wall carpeted office. Just the sight of that son-of-bitch Tao Lin made his heart race. Peng sat at his desk, lit a cigarette and ran a hand over his flat-top haircut, feeling the thick hair spring back between his fingers. Here I am, working hard to bring jobs and money to the town, creating an excellent business producing top quality goods for not only the domestic market but the North American market, and that bastard wants to shut me down. Lin's last report to the provincial State Environmental Protection Administration wanted me to install a filter system that would have killed the business. Simply killed it. There was no way he, Xi Peng, was going to let that sanctimonious bureaucrat ruin his business. He worked hard to get where he was, had started from nothing, a simple shoe salesman selling wholesale Chinese shoes to low end department stores and supermarkets. Junk shoes of the lowest quality, utterly worthless: inferior stitching, lousy leather, low-grade glue that lost strength with the least change of weather. The only thing he made a good margin on was Mao slippers: so easy to make and such a simple design. But then they had gone out of style and he was forced to sell whatever garbage he could find.

    He thought back on the day that changed the course of his life, a day in the provincial capital when he had gone to an upscale "friendship" department store and found a pair of American made, leather boating shoes that were outrageously expensive. He bought a pair, counting out his money carefully, painfully, and took them home to dissect. The stitching was made of thick leather string of strong quality. The soles were heavy and durable, and no glue oozed out between the sole and the leather. The leather itself was soft, pliable, in a rich, dark color. This was nothing like the inferior shoes he was selling. This was an altogether superior product and Peng was determined to introduce them to a wider market, and to hopefully become their sales representative. He did some research, made some phone calls, and found out the company was located in the backwoods somewhere in the northeast of the United: as far as he could tell by thumbing through his daughter's grade school atlas, somewhere near Canada and north of Boston. He found out they had a rep office in Beijing and called them and left a message, asking whether he could represent them and introduce their line of products to a wider range of clients, not just upscale "friendship" department stores. They got back to him immediately, saying they were not happy with their current sales rep and that they would be very happy to meet with him in Beijing the following month when their CEO was planning a visit.

He puffed on his cigarette, thought about all that had happened since that fateful meeting in the Capitol City when he introduced himself to the CEO of the Androscoggin Leather Works company of Pine Tree Point, Maine. Eventually, he had signed an exclusive contract for all of south China with a minimum sales requirement and a non-compete clause. He never did meet the minimum sales, and he paid no attention to the non-compete. What he realized, after months and months of pushing the product in dozens of cities, was that most Chinese simply would not pay such a price. No matter that the product was vastly superior to anything produced locally, no matter that they lasted ten times as long and were aesthetically pleasing. He begged the Androscoggin Leather Works company to lower their price but they refused. Their operating costs were high, especially their labor costs; good raw materials cost money; they had upgraded machinery the previous year; and complied with some very stringent environmental regulations. The margin was already razor thin in the Chinese market, they told Peng. It was the best they could offer. Now, they told him, he needed to do the selling that he had promised to do.

It was then that Peng saw the simple, and obvious, solution; if he could make shoes of a similar quality in China he would save on the cost of shipping, save on the cost of labor, and introduce a more reasonably priced, upscale Chinese brand of shoe to a specifically Chinese market, a Chinese market that was becoming more and more affluent and more and more discerning. Maybe, he dared think, after he had perfected his production, he could even sell his own shoes into the North American market. He accepted a standing invitation to visit the factory in Maine. Oh, those very large, big nosed, big hearted, strange looking, not so smart Americans. They proudly showed him everything from raw material purchase to design to production to labor management to marketing, even to wastewater treatment and environmental regulations compliance (the only thing he had absolutely zero interest in). He couldn't believe his good fortune. Immediately upon returning to Meiyu town, he went to work drawing up a detailed business plan which he introduced to the town Party Secretary, the mayor, and the local Construction Bank. It was received with great enthusiasm. Reams of papers were signed, a banquet followed with fine food and excellent rice wine, and after Peng had sobered up the next day, he began, with relentless energy, building his business.

Naturally, in a matter of five or six years, and after dominating the domestic niche market for quality footwear, he drove the Androscoggin Leather Works Company out of business. It was comically easy. His shoes were of the same quality at half the price. All the Big Box stores in North America were thrilled to buy his product, to sign long term contracts, to pass on savings to their deal crazy customers and to pocket a hefty margin for themselves. Oh, there had been some threats from Androscoggin about the non-compete clause in his original sales contract but luckily the Dispute Resolution clause required all disputes to be settled in a Chinese court. As far as Peng and his advisors knew, no non-compete clause had ever been enforced in China. Most courts either did not recognize the principle or had never heard of it. Besides, what Chinese court would possibly side with a foreign devil over one of their own? The threats simply died away.

And the Androscoggin Leather Works Company of Pine Tree Point, Maine? Bankrupt, of course. Unable to control the ridiculous demands of their workers, unable to get around government regulations, environmental regulations, and unable to significantly lower their overall costs, Peng and other Chinese companies put them out of business. Now their sixty or so workers were unemployed, roaming the streets of that deadbeat town making disparaging remarks about China, the *Government*, and big retail Box stores in general. Meanwhile, as they grumbled, they continued to buy all their Chinese made goods at the Big Box retailers outside town. And in a last ironic and satisfying twist, Peng had sent an agent to Pine Tree Point to bid on the equipment in the bankrupt Androscoggin Leather Works Company which he picked up for next to nothing. It was loaded on a freighter out of Portland that was bound for Shanghai after dropping off its cargo of Chinese made goods. The freight cost was negligible as very little freight was heading in the other direction and the shipping company was happy to have something to put in its hold. It was gratifying for Peng to know that the equipment was now installed in his own factory and helping his bottom line.

And speaking of satisfying, he had just hired a new design assistant for his design department. Very young. Very good looking. Very grateful for the job. He had a sofa in the back room of his office which always came in handy. A colleague once, on seeing the sofa, had told him he should put a sign on the ceiling saying *you got the job*. But what was really exciting was that on a table next to the sofa was a two foot long, whitish-gray, glistening ivory elephant tusk. A friend had brought a dozen back from a government delegation trip to Africa. The entire delegation had taken advantage of their diplomatic immunity to pack in as much ivory and rhino horn as possible, not to mention other exotic wildlife. Peng was pleased to get the tusk, had no illusion that he would get a rhino horn but he did manage to get some powder. He took a pinch now from the drawer of his desk and stirred it in his tea before making a call to the design department. Perhaps after the trip to the sofa they would take a ride in his new car.

Chapter 6

Lin had spent the afternoon in his tiny lab attached to the municipal town building, a building that consisted of the usual aluminum frame windows, dirty white-blue tiles, and the brown steaks of leaking fluid from the myriad air conditioning units. Having unlocked two locks and a padlock on the sturdy steel door, he switched on the fluorescent lights in the windowless room before unloading the samples from his bicycle, placing the samples in beaker holders on the tall work bench built so that he could work standing up. Along the walls of the twenty square foot room were rows and rows of shelves containing a virtual aquatic history of the lake in the last ten years: formaldehyde filled mason jars with various species of fish. At least, these were the fish he had found years ago. Some of the jars contained aberrations like two-headed carp and three eyed perch. These were scary enough but, even worse, it had been almost a year since he had actually found any fish at all to put into one of his jars, deformed or otherwise.

 He stood at the work bench and loaded his electron microscope with a water sample. He would see what sort of free radicals were roaming about, and then use chemical analysis to check levels of cyanide as well as the usual excessive levels of pesticides and fertilizers. For the mercury, it would require reflection spectroscopy to measure. That he had such equipment and instruments in his tiny lab was a source of pride. The State Environmental Protection Administration allowed a part of his budget to be spent on transportation, normally a Xiali or Geely or another inexpensive Chinese made automobile, but Lin used the allotted money to buy a used, somewhat outdated, electron microscope from the technical university at the provincial capital and the rest to update his lab equipment. As he read the initial measurement, it confirmed his suspicions: large quantities of mercury, certainly capable of causing the sickness he had seen in the village, and especially heavy quantities farther upstream and closer to the illegal mining activity.

He would need to send samples to the main lab in the provincial capital to get a more precise analysis but he had enough evidence to write his report which he proceeded to spend the afternoon doing.

Lin quit work at six and, weaving in and out of the barely controlled chaotic traffic, pedaled his bike to the market, a narrow, tin-roofed, open-sided warehouse with dozens of stalls on each side, produce spilling into the crowded aisle. He stopped at a fishmonger where he bought a small carp which the man pulled from a tank behind him. He let Lin inspect the gills and the eyes before unceremoniously bringing the steel end of his brush down upon the head of the carp, which went limp immediately, and then gutting and scrapping the scales expertly from the body. This he deposited in a plastic bag and they exchanged crumpled bills. Lin moved down the row of stalls, buying some flat sheets of tofu at one, then ginger, spring onions, celery, and mushrooms at another. The round-faced farmer woman threw a bundle of coriander into his bag before handing it to him over the mound of vegetables and he thanked her and smiled. Once outside, he loaded the groceries on the back of his bike and rode through town, past the few remaining one story brick houses with courtyards which were dwarfed by five and six story buildings of the usual metal framed windows, bluish-white tiles, and leaking air conditioners. He and his wife, Chen, and Xiaoyu had lived downtown when they were first married but, it seemed along with everyone else, had moved to the outskirts, to a neighborhood of row upon row of modern, high-rise apartments located in what was once a rice paddy. Lin disliked living outside of town in such a sterile environment, in a building that, after only a half dozen years, was beginning to show distressing signs of wear and tear but the units were all owned by the government and his work unit provided the apartment to him free of charge. Besides, Chen loved the updated appliances and the comfortable bathroom and the ability to stay cool through the long summer and warm through the two months of winter. And Xiaoyu attended an excellent school only a short walk away.

Lin managed to cross the street with only a minimal clamor of squealing breaks and raised fists as he rode his bike through the gate of their compound, past the small shed housing the security guard, through a courtyard, and parked his bike under the rusted iron roof of the bicycle shed. He stuffed his groceries into his bag which he slung over his shoulder, walked around the building, through the front door, and pushed the button for the lift. He watched it descend from the 8th floor. It was an even floor day, when the lift only stopped on the even numbers in order to save on maintenance and electricity. This odd/even system, in fact, saved little energy but appeared to be a means in which to give the many tiny, indistinguishable residence committee women who operated the lift the ability to discriminate between their passengers: if they approved of you – Chen and Xiaoyu, for example – then they would be kind enough to drop you on the floor above your apartment so you could walk down one floor and not up. (And heaven forbid they just dropped you on your odd floor on an even day, an unthinkable concept.) If they disapproved, you were left on the floor below to make your way up the stairs to the next landing, something that always happened to Lin.

As the door to the lift opened, Lin nodded to the neighborhood committee woman with her blue jacket and red armband who barely nodded in return. He didn't have to say which floor to go to: she knew where he lived, knew where everyone lived, knew most everything about everyone. The door closed and started up with a jerk and a screech of a cable. Just before reaching the 4th floor, the lift stopped well short of the landing and he was forced to climb out of the lift, using his free hand to pull himself up. He turned to glare at the residence committee woman, who kept her eyes fixed on the ceiling, before walking to the staircase and ascending the stairs to his apartment on the 5th floor.

He opened the aluminum door, and then the aluminum screened door, and entered the kitchen, the first room in the apartment. "Hey there, Xiaoyu," he said, putting the groceries down on the only part of the table that was not covered by school books. "How are you?"

"Good," she answered, not looking up from a large notebook over which a cramped hand was copying Chinese characters. Her thick black hair was tied back in a ponytail, and her small nose almost touched the page.

"I've bought a carp we can steam for dinner. And some tofu. I suppose your mother will be working late tonight?"

Xiaoyu shrugged. Lin refrained from telling her to sit up and to hold her fingers straighter when copying characters. Maybe she needed glasses, he thought, making a note to talk to Chen about the last time she had had an eye test.

"How was your day?" he asked.

"It was ok. I have a lot of homework. My friend Xi Jin told me her father has a new car. It's German."

"Well. Jin's father has a lot of money." From selling shoes and treating his workers badly and dumping poisonous chemicals into the lake, he added to himself.

"And she has a music player that's only this big." She spread her thumb and forefinger apart.

"Incredible what they can do with microchips these days," Lin said as he unloaded the groceries onto the small kitchen counter, placing the fish in the sink and the vegetables on a cutting board and rinsing some rice which he loaded into the rice cooker. He then went into the small living room, sat in a chair by the window, and picked up an Advanced English Conversation Workbook. He was supposed to attend an Environmental Equipment Manufacturers Trade Show in Shanghai next month and he needed to refresh his decent, but rusty, English. He let the book rest in his lap, however, and stared out the window, wishing he could be more spontaneous with Xiaoyu but, the fact was, he was really too old to be a father. He was in his mid-50s; still relatively young looking, he thought, tall and thin, and without the flabby belly and arms of most Chinese men his age, and still with plenty of energy and a full head of natural salt and pepper hair. But when it came to talking to his child, he tended to feel old and out of touch.

He and Chen had met late in life, on his return from many years in Beijing, when he had been sure that he would remain a bachelor for the rest of his days. She was a widow, in her late 30s. Her husband had been a supervisor for a construction battalion and had been crushed one day by a light pole that a careless worker had backed into with his truck, just like the famous Mao-era model worker Lei Feng who had met the exact same fate. In any event, they had not had children, had assumed that Chen was the problem for their inability to procreate. But it must certainly have been her husband for after meeting Chen at a Party Planning Meeting, and dating for a few weeks, the lonely, older, not particularly exciting couple found that they were relatively compatible and began spending almost all their time together. They did share a common background, having both grown up poor in Meiyu when it was a much quieter town, not the small city it now was, and they had acquaintances in common.

When they finally slipped into bed one evening, she assured him that she wasn't able to get pregnant and was too old anyhow but he impregnated her almost immediately. It seemed her modern-day Lei Feng husband, whose picture Chen still kept in a bookshelf, a big barrel-chested man with simian arms and springy hair and pox scars on his cheeks, had been impotent. So they had gotten married, with minimal emotional attachment but a strong desire to raise their child. They were both members of the Chinese Communist Party, Chen working with the Party Planning Commission on land distribution issues which involved, Lin knew but tried not to know, the local government buying once collectively owned but recently privately owned farmland for a cheap price and then selling at a huge profit to land developers. The methods used were not strictly illegal; immoral, for sure, but that had never stopped anyone in the CCP from making a profit. All over town, you could see farmers in shiny new automobiles driving down the street, driving erratically as their driver's license would be, like the car, only a few days or weeks old. They would have traded their land for the car and a sack of money, a fraction of the true value. Chen didn't seem to find anything wrong with the arrangement: the farmers were happy, the developers were happy, and she was very good at the work. She was a local, from a farm family herself, who knew the farmers personally and could talk easily with them. She was paid relatively well, had already invested in some land of her own outside town that was perfect for future development. And Lin knew that she had probably purchased the land by simply offering a shiny new car and a sack of money.

He heard the distinctive click as the rice cooker turned off, lay the English book beside his chair, and went into the kitchen to prepare dinner. He liked to cook, had gotten pretty good at it while living alone for so many years. People often said they didn't like cooking just for themselves but Lin had no such complaint: you could cook whatever you pleased without worrying about the likes or dislikes of others. Of course, with Xiaoyu he had no such worries. She ate whatever was put in front of her, just as she always cleaned up after herself, cared for her clothes, always woke up on time, never missed appointments. He worried that she was already grownup and that she would one day wonder what had become of her childhood. He worried but, as always, didn't see what could be done about it.

He laid the carp on the small kitchen counter. It looked fresh with clear eyes and pink gills so Lin tried not to think about all that he knew about what a farm-raised carp contained: the PCBs, dioxins, antibiotics, pesticides, and the ever-present traces of mercury. The fishmeal they fed the carp was toxic; the water they floated in was toxic; the whole production process was toxic, and no telling what was in the water in the tank in the market. How they managed to make them look good after all that was a mystery. Something involving bleach, he believed, but it was just another of a multitude of environmental issues he would rather not think about at the moment. People had to eat, even when they knew too much about the corrupted food chain. At times, it made it difficult to sit down and enjoy a meal but at least he did not share this information with his family. He saved all of that for his official environmental reports.

The kitchen was small with only a two-burner stove but he moved easily around the cramped space as he cut up celery, ginger, spring onions, mushrooms, garlic and coriander. When the water from the steamer was boiling, he put in the fish, heated oil in a wok, and put more oil in a small frying pan. He tied each sheet of tofu into a knot and put them in the boiling oil in the wok along with the celery and mushrooms and garlic. When it was ready, he took the steamed fish out of the pot and placed it onto an oval plate, then heated the small frying pan of oil until it was almost smoking. This he poured over the fish, which made a very satisfying crackling sound, then put the ginger, spring onions, and coriander over it.

Xiaoyu cleared the table as he added a splash of soy sauce and sesame oil to the fish and another handful of chopped coriander. She spooned two bowls of rice from the rice cooker and put them on the table beside the fish and tofu and they sat, picking up their chopsticks, before Lin said: "Let's eat."

They ate in silence, accompanied by the loud sound of their chewing. The carp was good, despite what he knew it contained.

"Are you visiting your grandmother this week?" Lin asked when they had finished.

"Yes," said Xiaoyu. "She's going to tell me more stories."

"She's got a lot of stories," Lin said with a smile as he pushed his chair back from the table and began to clean up. "Since she started losing her eyesight, all she has are her stories." Xiaoyu nodded and went back to her homework, as Lin grabbed a broom from the closet and began to sweep the floor. It was kitchen cleaning day and Lin used a dustpan to pick up the dirt before running hot water over a mop in the corner sink. He had a system for cleaning the house which was quite efficient: a strict schedule for each day and for each chore. He did laundry twice a week, and Chen was responsible for hanging the clothes in the tiny glassed-in balcony and for the ironing. Naturally when he travelled or worked late, he needed to adjust his schedule but for the most part it worked well. Chen wanted to hire an Ayi, an Auntie, to come clean three times a week but he was adamantly opposed. Once, when she had brought someone by to interview, there had been an uncomfortable argument with the woman listening in from the kitchen. "I don't want a stranger in the house," Lin had said. "It makes me uncomfortable. What's wrong with the system we have? Why waste money on an Ayi? Besides, I bring work home; I have research material here. I don't want someone snooping around." Chen had sighed. Like other discussions about money or new cars or foreign holidays, she knew when to concede.

Xiaoyu had seated herself on the table, her feet dangling down, her eyes still buried in her book, as Lin collected the three chairs and stacked them in the corner. He ran the steaming mop first by the stove where the grease had sputtered on the floor, then under the kitchen table and Xiaoyu's dangling feet. He made quick work of it, never mistaking a chip in the tiles for a spot of dirt—he knew exactly where the chips were and never wasted energy scrubbing a spot that needed no additional scrubbing—and checking his watch to see that he was done, as usual, in just under 5 minutes. He rested the mop against the doorway to the living room, turned on the lights, and returned to his armchair and his English grammar.

As he was studying a particularly difficult example of the subjunctive, Lin smiled at the recollection of one of his colleagues in Beijing who, whenever there was a delegation of foreign English speakers visiting, would recite: *I would if I could, but I can't so I shan't.* This always solicited a good laugh from the delegation and, although Lin had heard it dozens of times, he, too, had laughed. It really was a perfect phrase to describe English: a deceptive language, easy to learn at first but impossible to master grammatically.

"I'm going to bed now," said Xiaoyu as she poked her head into the living room.

"Is it time?" said Lin with his brow furrowed. "My how time flies when you are studying English grammar. I'll come tuck you in in a minute."

Once Xiaoyu was done in the bathroom, Lin went into her bedroom and sat on the edge of the bed. "Thanks for taking care of your grandmother," he said, gently patting her foot. "It means a lot to her."

"Well," said Xiaoyu, "actually, I don't always listen to Grandma. Sometimes I play games on my mobile with the sound off because I know she can't see me and because I've heard the stories before."

"Actually, I do the same. Well, I don't play games but I catch up on work while your grandmother tells her tales. I'm going to see her at lunch tomorrow, and you are going to see her after school the next day?" Lin asked.

"Yes."

"Well, even if you're playing games and I'm working, the point is that we are keeping her company."

"Sure," she said with a shrug of her shoulders, arranging her pillow and turning on her side. Lin, with nothing more to say, patted her foot again and left the room.

He had been reading in bed and had just turned out the light to go to sleep, punching his pillow and sighing contentedly, when Chen got home. He could smell cigarettes when she entered, which he hated, and, for the thousandth time, wished she would give it up.

"Do you have to smoke?" he asked from the darkness. She turned on the small reading lamp, sat heavily on the bed and began removing her shoes. "I mostly only smoke when I have these meetings at night and everyone else is smoking. I never buy my own. I don't smoke here in the apartment."

"Yes, but the air pollution is bad enough for your lungs without making it worse with cigarettes. Do you know what kind of free radicals it lets loose in your body?" It was a rhetorical question so she simply sighed and shuffled off to the bathroom. He heard the water run and listened to her brush her teeth and then flush the toilet. She returned and took off her clothes and slipped on an old t-shirt that had once belonged to him and fell past her knees. She stood combing her long hair and staring at nothing. Still a fairly good-looking woman, he thought, with a straight back and sturdy legs. Her peasant features—a flat face and wide nose and crooked teeth—had been smoothed out by face creams and avoiding the sun, braces and teeth whiteners, and driving a car instead of a bicycle. She set the brush down and climbed into bed beside him.

"It's just that I worry about your health," he whispered.

"Don't," she answered. "I have many things to worry about and my health is not one of them. Farm family Liu on tract 109 is holding out for much more money. I don't know who they've been talking to but it's going to make for a very tricky negotiation. And my own land needs investment and that means partners and a significant loss of control." She ground her teeth and stretched out on the bed. Lin said nothing, had no desire to talk about money, his least favorite topic, especially late at night. And, of course, it was anathema to the idea of sex which they hadn't had for many months. When they did, it was functional, a type of need that became too great and sought release as they rolled into each other's arms and, after a series of quiet grunts, rolled out. None of it induced what Lin would call desire.

"Get some rest," he said, patting her arm before punching and shaping his pillow.

"Yes," she said. "I have an early meeting across town. I need some rest." She also rolled over facing away from Lin. It was some time before they fell asleep.

Chapter 7

"I know it's difficult for you to understand why I did what I did, Lin," his mother said.

Lin looked down at the wraith-like woman in the bed, her milky eyes staring at nothing, her greyish-white hair fanned out on the pillow, her club foot exposed to the air, and an array of medicine bottles and packages crowding the small table beside her head.

"I understand, mother, under the circumstances. Really, there's no reason to keep thinking about it all these years later." Lin sat on a wooden chair beside the bed and took her hand in his, papery and lined with pale blue veins. "You did what you had to do, for yourself and for me. It seems it worked out for the best."

"Well not for your father," she said with a frown. "You can't say it worked out for him at all."

No, Lin thought, he was murdered by your husband, my stepfather.

"He was an opportunist, your stepfather," she continued, which was a polite way to put it, Lin thought. "Pragmatic. Cold, I know, but he never abandoned us, and he supported your membership in the Party."

That was always a bit of a mystery, exactly why he would have allowed Lin to go so far after what he had done to Lin's father. Maybe he had plans to expose Lin at some point but a massive heart attack at the age of 42 when Lin was half way through his university studies in the provincial capital put an end to that.

"Maybe it's because he loved you and needed to support me because of it," Lin mused, although throughout his life he had seen no outward sign of love.

"I think so. He and your father were very competitive, especially about me. I told you all this before," she said dreamily, closing her eyes and rolling over so that she was face to face with Lin in his chair.

"Yes, you did. Many times," Lin said, shifting in his chair.

"Well, I'm going to tell you again, because that's all I have these days are these memories and nothing else to do but think about them and speak about them." Lin didn't need to wait for his mother to start murmuring; the stories were imbedded in his brain, and they played like a movie reel in front of him.

There was Lin's father, just returned from Shanghai before the start of the war with Japan. He was tall and thin and pale and tired after so many days on the road, having to hide not only from the Japanese but from General Chiang Kai-shek and the Nationalists who would have taken him into the army as a common soldier and that would have been the end of him. "Or maybe he would have been lucky and landed in Taiwan," Lin heard his mother whisper, frowning at the thought of Taiwan, of all that would have not happened in her life and all that would have happened differently.

"But he made it," Lin said.

"Yes. Made it back to Meiyu town, where he went to the Chief Magistrate to look for work, back to the big house, crossing the stone bridge and past the beautiful, tall front gate with the life-sized lion dogs on either side. Gone now, as you well know, the house, the gates, the wall, the gardens. Torn down so they could build the fertilizer factory." She shook her head, her white-grey hair swaying on the pillow. "I especially remember the lion dogs, the one with a paw resting on a cub and the other on a small globe.

"In any event, your grandfather came around to the servant's entrance and was almost chased off by that hag, Ms. Yuan, the head of the kitchen, who used to beat us with a broom handle to the back of the legs whenever she felt the need. I saw him through the window in the kitchen, standing there with his hands at his side, a straight back and tall but eyes downcast while that horrible woman told him what she thought of him, which was very little. He never moved. Just gave her his name, said he had lived here before, and was looking for work. Patient as a mule, until she finally went to get the overseer. I peeked out at him occasionally as he stood there, head bowed, for what seemed like hours, like a statue, until overseer Zhang finally appeared in front of him."

"So, Tao Shanshan. You have returned from the big city." Overseer Zhang looked him over carefully. "How many years now? Six, seven?"

Shanshan nodded, keeping his eyes downcast.

"And now you are looking for work?"

Shanshan nodded again.

"Well, you look strong enough. There aren't many men left since the General came through this summer. I believe you worked with the carp when you were a boy."

"Yes," Shanshan said, brightening at the thought of the fish. "I fed them when others were busy and could not do it."

"Well, good. None of the old men want to do it anymore, and that's all there are around here: old men afraid of the water and of climbing the pole and feeding the fish." He had Shanshan show him his hands and he could tell that he was used to hard work and the handle of a shovel.

"Ms. Yuan," he yelled over his shoulder. She appeared in the doorway, glaring at Shanshan. "This man needs some food." She disappeared back into the kitchen.

"You can stay in number 15 to the north of the Great House wall. I believe you know your way around."

Ms. Yuan arrived with a bowl of porridge and a long piece of garlic wrapped in leavened breed. "I suppose you will need a spoon and chopsticks," she said with disgust, disappearing once again into the kitchen.

"Go eat," said Zhang. "I will come fetch you, and you can begin with the feeding of the fish."

Overseer Zhang appeared at the doorway to Shanshan's room in the early afternoon. He presented Shanshan with a shovel, its handle smooth as glass, the point shiny and sharp. "After you finish with the fish, you can assist the men shoring up the northern wall of fishpond three."

Shanshan took the shovel and followed Zhang past the rooms of cracked mud and plaster, all of them without doors, all with holes in the corner for chimneys, all empty this time of day.

"Little has changed since you left for the city," Zhang said as they walked along the grey-brick, serpentine wall of the great house, through a stand of poplars with the lake shimmering on their right, and skirted the earthen wall of the first fish pond. They stood in front of a weathered, wooden shack with a door half off its hinges. "We still fatten our famous Wenyu Lake carp with grain and grass pellets," Zhang said, sidling through the doorway. "I think you remember all this." Shanshan remembered, moving quietly into the shack and around the overseer, grabbing the large, rough burlap sack on the ground with its sturdy leather strap on the top which could be buckled together. Shanshan looked around for the tin scoop that was used to fill the sack, and Zhang nodded to the side wall where it was hanging by a string. He filled the bag with the rough, fragrant pellets, and headed out to the set of wooden stairs leading to the first of three ponds, hoisting the bag on his shoulder and staggering to the top. "Just remember," Zhang said from below, "do not feed the pellets to the carp until you are at the end of the pole so that all the fish have room and a better chance of eating. If you feed them near the bank only the big fish will feed. Do you understand?" he asked. Shanshan nodded, and Zhang turned and disappeared around the corner of the wall.

Shanshan lowered the bag to his feet and stared at the long, curved, smooth wooden pole that stretched out 30 feet into the middle of the pond. He buckled the sack onto the pole, pushing it free of the bank so that its weight made the pole spring up and down as it dangled above the water. Shanshan pushed the strap ahead of him and then straddled the pole with his legs hooked under. He pushed the strap holding the sack ahead, and then pulled himself along behind. By this time, the carp were roiling the water, following his progress with their perfectly round mouths gasping open, their prehistoric grey backs all but out of the water, the red tint around their gills flashing in the sun. Once Shanshan reached the end, he rested his chin on the pole and began to toss the pellets in great sweeping arches with both hands. It seemed to take an eternity to reach the bottom of the sack but when he did, he edged his way backwards, dragging the sack with him. He recalled in his youth being able to swivel around for the return journey but, as he looked down at the water, he thought he would wait before trying such a maneuver. Back on the bank, Shanshan descended the stairs to refill the sack, and made his way to the second pond. By the time he was crawling out on the third pond, he was faster, even confident enough to turn around on the pole and return going forwards. At the shed, he dropped the leather bag on the pile of feed, grabbed his shovel and went to find the work party.

On the eastern wall of fish pond number three, stood the work crew of four older men shoring up the bank. They were mixing lime and sand and clay in hollowed out mounds of dirt with their shovels and applying it to the wall. They paused as Shanshan stood before them, and then made a space for him to join in with the shoveling. No one spoke, and Shanshan did as the others did until Overseer Zhang showed up and inspected the wall.

"Fine," Zhang said, rubbing the toe of his cloth shoe along the newly repaired wall. "That will do. Now off to the lake. The weirs need more work if we are going to trap any wild carp this season." The men frowned, thinking of the hours in the water, the mud up to their waists, the leeches, the back-breaking effort of repairing underwater bamboo poles and nets. "And if you don't do a proper job, you'll be back in the lake until it's done right." They shouldered their shovels, headed single-file towards the lake, only Shanshan showing excitement at the thought of submerging himself in the crystal-clear waters of Wenyu Lake.

Chapter 8

Chen had been out late for four nights this week. Lin did not seem to care, she thought, always buried in a book or writing reports that were sure to get everyone in the town upset. He took her explanation of working late without question, and she *was* working late but not always. Sometimes she was with Bing in his luxurious top floor office of the massive MSG factory, who was also working but not always. She didn't care that much for Bing and his bragging and his rice wine breath and his pot belly and, although she hadn't had the experience, his undoubtedly microscopic manhood but it was business. When he tried to get too close to her after endless glasses of maotai, it was tolerable because, while he was pawing her and she was gently but firmly pushing him away, she thought about her land and what an excellent business partner he would make. With his money she would not just sell the land like some peasant farmer but work side by side with the developer, oversee the clearing and the infrastructure, approve designs for the buildings, budget the construction, and then they would sell the apartments at an immense profit. Oh, Bing would get his cut and then some, as would all the others with their hand out: the mayor, the local cadre, the land agent, the land registry, lawyers, municipal officials, fire regulation officials, building inspectors, even police. And, of course, the environmental inspector, although this was a sensitive subject as Chen would be certain to avoid having her husband anywhere near the site in case he found some minnow or grasshopper or lizard or snail that needed to be saved and a percentage of the land put aside for its well-being. She knew just which inspector she would use, one from south of the lake, the fat, oily one with the long pinky fingernails and the combover hairdo, who could be bought for less than 50,000 Yuan, she was told, no questions asked.

But she was getting ahead of herself. She rolled down the window of her car, letting the warm autumn air in, and fought her way through the stop-go traffic in the town on her way to the outskirts in the north and a visit with farm family Liu. She frowned behind her dark glasses, thinking how to settle the problem on tract 109, the one key piece of farmland that was holding up the town's most recent development. And Liu was not the only problem; now there was farm family Fei, Fu, and Kan and a dozen others who had already signed and settled and received compensation but who were now demanding additional compensation. She suspected that some troublemaker, probably a child of one of the farm families who had managed to get into the law university in the provincial capital, was now advising the family and friends. And now that everyone had a mobile phone and internet, it was so much easier to share information, to compare notes, and to complain. It made her job that much more difficult. She felt for the first time, as the town melted away behind her, just a bit anxious. These were people she grew up with, who knew her as a child, knew her lately deceased parents, who were relatives and acquaintances, and she had always found it easy to talk to them, to find common ground and build an easy rapport. But things were different know; money was involved, lots of money, and there was no better way to tear apart relationships then by introducing a profit motive.

    She turned off the main road and began bumping along a dirt track that ran between rice paddies. Water buffaloes raised their rubbery, water-dripping snouts to watch her pass; farmers with shovels and hoes balanced on their shoulders walked between the paddies in bare feet. She tried not to think of the mud collecting on her just washed car as she climbed a small hill covered in orchards and corn fields and turned into the brick-and-mortar farm house on tract 109, surprised to see that there was a crowd gathered in the yard. She hadn't removed the key from the ignition before faces appeared in the windows and she had to push the door hard in order to climb out.

    "What is going on now?" she asked, staring at the first face in front of her.

    "No one here is happy with the negotiations," said a flat faced, broad nosed farmer woman whose name Chen should have been able to recall but couldn't. "We know that farm family Liu is demanding twice as much as we got and that they will probably get it."

    Well, three times more, thought Chen, shaking her head. In fact, she was authorized to go as high as five times. "She not only has more land," Chen said, pushing her way through the crowd, using the large bag on her shoulder to keep people at a distance, "but it's dry land, better land, not rice paddies which require a lot more work to clear. Anyway, who told you that it's twice as much?"

"Her husband," another woman answered. "After a few rice wines with my man, he boasted about the amount of money he was going to receive."

"Well, you can't trust what people with too much rice wine in their bellies have to say." She had reached the door of farmer Liu's house. "Now, please. Let me talk with Mrs. Liu."

She knocked on the flimsy wooden door and Mrs. Liu appeared immediately. She let Chen in, and shut the door quickly. "I know my husband has been foolish."

"Very foolish, Mrs. Liu, to discuss our private negotiations. It's going to be difficult for us to give you more than the people outside were given."

Mrs. Liu sighed. "We deserve more. The people outside deserve more. We are being taken advantage of." She motioned Chen to a seat at the rough kitchen table.

"Just exactly who has been telling you such things?" Chen asked impatiently.

"We are not so ignorant as you think, Chen," she said, sitting down opposite her. "We have mobiles now, and even internet, and we can talk to people all over China who are facing the same situation."

"I never accused you of being ignorant. As I explained, everyone gets approximately the same compensation depending on certain circumstances. It's true that you have taken longer to settle but it's also true that your land is more valuable than the others. Part of the deal was that you would not disclose what the terms of your settlement would be." Here she gave Mrs. Liu a sharp look. "As for that husband of yours…"

"Oh, it would get out anyway. You know what it's like, such a small community and everybody knowing everyone's business."

They sat in silence until Mrs. Liu asked, "And what if I don't agree to the settlement?"

"Then we go ahead without you. Did you see the picture in the papers and on the internet of the house in the middle of a massive construction site in Guangzhou? That tiny house stuck on a point of land with a ladder reaching down fifty feet so the people could come and go?" Chen asked. "I don't think that's the kind of attention you want, not to mention the inconvenience."

"I saw the photo. I felt sorry for the people. I admired them"

Chen sighed. "You can't stop progress, Mrs. Liu. Look at how fast and how far the town is growing. It will soon be designated a small city. When you were young, there were plenty of farms between you and the town but now it's you."

"When does it end?" she asked wearily. "And what are we to do? I only know farming and this land, and I'm too old to start something new."

"You have seen the terms of the settlement. We provide you with an apartment in a municipal housing complex closer to town, you have the money from the settlement, and you have a pension."

"Small apartment, small settlement, small pension. I don't want to live in town in some strange building surrounded by people we don't know."

"Your neighbors will be there. All the people outside in the yard will be there," said Chen, waving a hand towards the front door. Mrs. Liu did not look convinced.

"So, I am to sign over everything while you and the developers and the mayor and the Party all get rich."

"I am hardly getting rich, Mrs. Liu. I'm just doing my job. And rich is relative: the developers have to take the risk of financing all the construction, the infrastructure, the roads, and eventually the buildings and making sure it's profitable."

"And the Party?"

"Well, yes. They lease the land and that's how they raise revenue in order to provide for services like your apartment in town and your pension, and of course for roads and electricity, hospitals and schools, and police."

"Those are not services for the poor, Chen. Everyone knows that hospitals and schools cost a lot of money. And no one wants anything to do with the police. And I don't want the apartment. I just want to stay here."

"Not an option, I'm afraid. It's progress, and you can't fight it."

Mrs. Liu let out a sigh, scratched her sun-browned, mottled arm. "I'll sign," she said, suddenly deflated. "Not because I want to, and not because I don't want to keep fighting but because my husband wants us to. He'll be happy in town, sitting playing mahjong in the park all day, drinking and smoking and not working in the fields anymore."

Chen hid the fact that she was elated, that one of the last prime pieces of the fifty-acre site was just about to settle, that all the others would have to accept what they had once they knew that Mrs. Liu had settled. Chen would be toasted when she got back to the office, and there would be a substantial bonus and perhaps a promotion. She had seen the survey maps in the planning office, and the architect's drawings, the neat rows of eight story houses with playgrounds and two parking spaces for every resident.

She solemnly laid the documents out on the table. "The terms are as we discussed last time although you have broken the disclosure agreement. No matter," she said, waving her hand magnanimously. "Your husband can tell people that the reason you settled for a higher amount is because of the quality of the land."

Mrs. Liu nodded her head, and signed where she was told to sign. Chen left a copy of the papers on the table and placed the others in her bag. "Thank you, Mrs. Liu. You will like it in town. There's Tai Chi every morning and lots of people your age and good markets. And all modern appliances and conveniences in the apartment."

Mrs. Liu just stared at her blankly, not bothering to answer, before shuffling off to the interior of the house. After a brief spell of sadness for the old lady, the elation resurfaced. At least until she stepped outside to face the dozen or so angry farmers who were waiting for her.

"We want to settle on the same terms as her," one shouted, shaking his fist.

"You have cheated us," said another, as they crowded around. Once again Chen held her handbag in front of her to fend them off as she made her way to the car, key ready.

"We've been through all this. You all received substantial compensation: money, apartments, pensions. If Mrs. Liu received more, it was only because of the quality of the land. Now please." She wrenched open the car door and climbed in but when she tried to close it, an angry farmer grabbed it. He leaned in close to Chen, his brown tobacco-stained teeth barred. "We are going to the municipal building soon, maybe next week, all of us, to file a complaint against these settlements." He turned and spat in the mud beside the car.

"We are going to demand justice."

"You can demand all you want but you're probably just going to find trouble," Chen said as she jerked the door closed, and drove slowly past the angry faces.

Once she was off the muddy road and on the paved road back to town, her feeling of euphoria returned as she rolled the window down and reveled in the rich-smelling, late fall breeze and the few bright, golden colors she could make out through the ever-present haze. She popped in a CD, her favorite K-pop, humming along to the melody and rummaging under the seat for a package of cigarettes she hid for just such an occasion. She took a long satisfying drag and let the smoke drift lazily from her mouth as she calculated what she would demand as a reasonable bonus, and what sort of promotion she could expect.

Chapter 9

A few days later, Lin was back in his lab finishing the report on the extreme mercury and cyanide levels from the northwest tributary. He could not put in a direct assumption about the operation he suspected on the headwaters since he had not personally seen it, but he could describe factual cases where similar operations in other parts of the province and country had produced such levels of toxic chemicals. It would then be up to the provincial SEPA to either investigate what was happening, shuffle it off to the enforcement bureau, or simply stuff his report in a filing cabinet somewhere. He couldn't waste his energy on trying to guess what the agency might do, or try to influence them beyond his lengthy and frequent reports, but he did highlight the case of the farm worker with palsy and whatever type of lymphoma the poor man certainly had and recommended medical personnel be deployed. He ended by proposing immediate investigative action, emphasizing strongly the dire health consequences for anyone living along the banks of the tributary who were reliant on the water.

He printed two copies of the 7-page report, stamped it with his field agent seal, and slipped it into a secure government envelope which he sealed again with the State Environmental Protection Administration stamp. He then dropped it off at the municipal post for official correspondence which was in the building attached to his lab. He could not help but notice, in fact was supposed to notice, the sigh and visible shake of the head from the clerk who took the envelope. Word would certainly get around that he had filed yet another report. He couldn't say whether the town officials actually broke the seals to look at the details of his report although he suspected they might. In any event, he always used multiple means of delivery and checked with the provincial office to see that the report got to where it was supposed to go. Really, though, it was disheartening to know that his simply submitting a report was enough to have a clerk shaking his head and to send a buzz through the local bureaucracy.

He climbed aboard his bike, already loaded up with beakers and measuring equipment for another field trip, and made his way out of town and back to the lake. A monitoring station set up near the State-Owned cement plant in the southeast corner of the lake had again recorded alarming levels of $Co2$, ash, dust, nitrogen dioxide and sulfur dioxide as well as other particle pollutants, and this despite the plant having recently built a new horizontal kiln and installed scrubbers in their stacks. He would check the air quality and take some soil samples to see what changes might have occurred since he was last out there in the spring. He knew he would find the usual traces of metals, dioxins, and dibenzofurans in the topsoil but he had a duty to at least see if the quantity had increased. He would ride out and visit the plant and see if he could meet with Assistant General Manager Hu again and find out exactly what was happening. AGM Hu was a reasonable man who at least treated Lin with respect rather than the contempt he got most elsewhere.

It was, as usual, a smog-filled day and Lin could not see the far shore of the lake through the haze as he pedaled along the unpaved side road running beside the bank. He could barely make out the towering silos of the MSG factory that loomed above him on his right, the glass tower office of his ex-friend Bing enveloped in a cloud of smog. A slight northwesterly breeze brought the smoke from the gigantic stacks of the steel works down to the lake which accounted for the haze that blanketed the area, although the works were almost thirty miles away. Still, it was a pleasant day to ride, the summer heat having given way to the coolness of late autumn. He enjoyed feeling the muscles of his legs burn as he pedaled, loved the knowledge that this was the most ideal transportation imaginable: it provided exercise, improved your health, and produced zero $Co2$ emissions. He was sorry to see the country moving farther and farther away from bicycles and into automobiles. Unfortunately, there was no going back. He always remembered when a delegation of European politicians had visited Beijing when he was there. They had pleaded with the city government to keep their bicycle lanes open and free of cars and not make the mistake they had made in Europe of closing their bike lanes in the 60s only to have to rebuild them in the 90s. This proposal was met with stony silence by a city government that, after having torn down their ancient city walls, looked to Los Angeles freeways as the apex of civilization.

He swerved around a wagon loaded with cabbage and pulled by a donkey, the driver reaching back rhythmically to snatch a handful from the nearest cabbage which he chewed with an open mouth. He passed fields of corn and wheat and soybeans and peanuts and, as he got closer to the southeast tributary which flowed into the lake, terraced rice paddies. Farmers with rakes and shovels worked the fields, others had their tools balanced on their shoulders as they walked along the road, and many were crammed into the beds of small three wheeled tractors with their small diesel motors whining as they went past, shooting great puffs of black exhaust into the air. All the workers smoked and stared at him as they went by, always curious about the strange paniers on his bicycle which carried his sample cases and beakers. An occasional truck or a cement mixer rumbled by but the side road was relatively quiet and he was able to pedal without having to concentrate too much on the traffic.

After an hour or so, the silos and smokestacks of the cement plant, along with the conveyers that carried the raw materials and the finished clinker from the loading and unloading platforms, came into view. He stopped his bike and parked it under a tree as he extracted a beaker from its wooden cage and walked to a field where a farmer was hoeing soybeans.

"Hello," Lin said in greeting. The man stopped his work and stared at him but did not return his greeting. "I'm from the State Environmental Protection Administration, here to check the soil quality in the area. I'm going to take a sample of the soil to analyze."

The man continued to stare at him and Lin feared he might be mentally deficient. Eventually, the farmer spat between the rows of beans and grinned, showing a mouth of sparse brown teeth.

"You can take all the soil you want. You can take the whole field for all I care. Nothing will grow in it anyway. Look at the beans," he said. Lin squatted in the field, took the stunted soybeans and the small, yellowed leaves between his fingers, and examined the dark grey dust on his fingertips. It was harvest season. The rains had been good this year. There was only one reason why the field would look the way it did.

"Since when did the dust start to appear?" he asked, using a small metal spoon to shovel topsoil into the beaker.

"Early or middle summer," the farmer answered. "Hard to say

exactly but I noticed the dust on the leaves around then. The sun can't get through. The beans can't grow. I tried spraying the leaves but I can't spray the whole field every day. And it's not like I don't know it's coming from the cement plant. I've been up there, fat lot of good it did. They say it's not their problem. They got orders to fill that are more important than a bunch of soybeans and peanuts."

"Yes. Well. I am going to the plant myself to see what can be done."

The farmer mumbled something Lin could not make out as he continued his uninspired hoeing of the stunted soybeans.

"Where'd you say you were from again?" the man suddenly shouted just as Lin had reached his bicycle.

"Meiyu town. The State Environmental Protection Administration."

"And you think you can fix this?"

"I can try," Lin answered as he climbed on his bike and pedaled towards the factory.

Lin continued down the road, noting that the corn and wheat, the vertical plants, looked healthy enough, although he stopped periodically to collect soil samples from them as well, but the leafy, ground-level crops like soybeans and peanuts were seriously underdeveloped. As he got closer to the cement plant, he saw clearly what the problem was: the vertical kiln was back in operation and spewing out a steady stream of filthy grey smoke. The kiln was ancient and was supposed to be mothballed after the horizontal kiln came on line but that was obviously not the case. He pedaled to the entrance of the plant and parked his bike with a hundred other bikes under a tin roof and went to register at the office beside the gate.

"I'm here to see AGM Hu. My name is Tao Lin from the State Environmental Protection Administration," he told the guard, who looked him over and then picked up a phone. After a few minutes of mumbled conversation, the man handed the phone to Lin.

"Hello?"

"Hello Tao Lin. I am very busy today but I can see you briefly in my office. I'm sorry I can't come to the gate to greet you but you know how to get here, I believe. Building 3, just past the main office building. 2nd floor."

"Yes. Thanks. I will see you shortly."

The guard gave him a badge to wear around his neck and had him sign his name in a log book and Lin headed through the gate and into the grounds of the cement plant. The dust was everywhere, thick and grey and powdered. It rose up from his feet to his ankles, almost to his knees as he walked. When a truck went by, he had to pull the neck of his shirt up over his mouth until the dust settled. Normally they sprayed water each hour to keep the dust down but obviously they had other more pressing concerns. Lin found the building, climbed the stairs, and knocked on the door of AGM Hu's office.

"Come in," he yelled, getting up when Lin entered and giving him a warm smile. "Tao Lin. It is good to see you. I hear you are keeping everyone very busy around the lake."

"Just doing my job, Lao Hu," Lin said, using the term "old" as a form of respect. AGM Hu was the oldest manager at the plant and, year after year, succeeded in dodging retirement. "But no one seems to appreciate my hard work," Lin added sarcastically.

"Well, I appreciate your hard work," he said, sitting back down in his chair. "I also know why you are here so I won't waste your time or mine. The vertical kiln is back in use because the horizontal is at full capacity. We have been designated an emergency production plant to manufacture specialty cement for the hydropower plant at the Three Gorges Dam and we are under a very difficult production schedule. Not to mention we are having some difficulties with the production," he muttered, looking suddenly tired. "Obviously, we still have backlogs for orders of Portland Cement from our existing customers so we are obligated to produce this with the vertical."

Lin thought about the last time he had seen the vertical kiln in operation. AGM Hu had given him a tour just before it was supposed to be mothballed. They had entered a brick warehouse surrounding the kiln which contained piles of broken and crushed limestone and coal, not large, crystal chunks of anthracite coal but coal of the lowest quality almost as fine as sand. These raw materials were placed on conveyers and loaded into the base of the kiln. Lin and AGM Hu had climbed a small ladder to a platform ten feet above the ground that circled the kiln. The limestone and coal mix were fired until it reached a temperature high enough to turn the limestone into clinker. There were holes spaced periodically along the walls of the kiln wide enough for a long metal pole to be inserted. They watched as three men, covered in soot and stripped to the waist in the heat, used the poles to stir the mixture by hand. It was clinker production of the most rudimentary sort, and the level of pollution it produced was astronomical.

"You know that the soybean and peanut crops are failing because they can't photosynthesize," Lin said.

"Yes. We offered wagons of water with spray nozzles but it didn't do any good. I'm afraid it just comes back." AGM Hu shrugged his shoulders. "I am well aware that you will write a report about our failure to comply with the air quality guidelines and failure to shut down our vertical kiln. That is as it should be. That is your job. Unfortunately, I have my job as well. And, Tao Lin," he paused, sighed, "your directive comes from the State Environmental Protection Administration and my directive comes from the Ministry of Commerce of the People's Republic of China. So, write your report, as you should, but it will make no difference as I will continue to operate the kiln until we have met our production requirements and MOFCOM is happy, and then we can go back to trying to comply with your SEPA directive."

That was the simple truth, and Lin bowed his head in acceptance of it. "And there is nothing to be done for the farmers? No compensation?"

"Farmers always complain," AGM Hu said with a shake of his head. "It's drought or floods or blight or locusts. I'm afraid this year it's dust. But take heart my friend," he said, standing and extending his hand. "We should be back on schedule by Spring Festival and the soybean and peanut farmers will be happy as will a certain SEPA Deputy Inspector."

Lin shook AGM Hu's hand. "I appreciate your honesty, Lao Hu. Let's hope you can meet that production schedule."

"We will do our best," he said with a not altogether convincing smile. "Now if you will excuse me, Tao Lin, I must be at the laboratory for an inspection. I will see you to the gate."

"No, no. I can find my own way out. I've taken enough of your time already."

"No. I insist."

As they left the office and went down the stairs, continuing to argue good naturedly about just how far AGM Hu would escort Lin to the gate of the plant with Lin insisting that the front steps of the building were more than enough. This inevitable, essential, ritualistic courtesy having been satisfied on both sides, they shook hands and parted ways, AGM Hu to the laboratory and Lin to his bike.

When AGM Hu entered the laboratory, the conversation stopped abruptly. The half dozen men, all in dirty white lab coats, gave him a nervous greeting.

"So," he said, leaning against the edge of a table, "where are the latest test results? And don't tell me that they look like the last batch of test results."

The chief engineer cleared his throat. "There have been some improvements in the tensile strength. We all agree that the cement will be more than capable of enforcing the rebar." Which is good, AGM Hu thought, since I'm sure the rebar will fail to be produced to the required specifications.

"And the saturation?"

There was a general shuffling of feet among the men. "That, unfortunately, has not improved as we had hoped. It's still far above what is required for Portland Cement but not quite at the expected level."

"And what do you plan to do?" he asked. "We are behind schedule. Our first shipment is due next week."

"It's unrealistic," interrupted another engineer. "The requirements are ridiculous. They must have copied them from a blueprint, probably a foreign blueprint, without taking into consideration the difficulties our plants might have here in China. Besides," he said incredulously, "they expect the structure to withstand a category 5 storm with a flood of epic proportions. In which case, in my opinion, not only would the structure crumble but the world would come to an end as well."

"Yes, yes," AGM Hu said wearily. "We've been through this before. The question is, what do we intend to do about it? It's too late to request a review of the specifications. How close are we to meeting the specs?" This was the question that he, as Assistant General Manager in charge of quality, would need to answer but he wanted to hear from his engineers, from their own mouths, what he must, in the end, be responsible for and propose.

"Very close," said the chief. "So close, that it is our shared opinion that there is no danger in reporting that we have reached our goal and can begin shipments."

AGM Hu took a deep breath amid the long silence. "Good." He

clapped his hands. "That is what we will do. I will draw up the report to send to the Central Authorities. In the meantime," here he gave them all a piercing look, "I want everyone to work overtime in order to improve future shipments. There is no reason that we cannot get closer to the specifications as we proceed." There was general nodding of heads at this proposal.

"Comrades," AGM Hu said, drawing himself up and throwing his shoulders back, "I don't have to keep reminding you that this is the power station at the three gorges we are talking about. The greatest engineering project ever undertaken by the People's Republic. We must not be remiss in our duty." As AGM Hu made his way out of the room, they all gave a general cheer of agreement, some saluting, forgetting for a moment that they were not soldiers but highly-educated engineers.

Chapter 10

When Lin returned to his lab late that afternoon, he was surprised to find the wife of the sick village farmer sitting on the steps. She stood up slowly, rubbing her backside and brushing the dust from her thick, blue cotton work pants. They bowed slightly to one another.

"I am sorry to bother you," she said, lowering her eyes. "I remembered that you worked for the State Environmental Protection Administration and so I asked around town and they said to wait for you here,"

"I hope you have not been waiting long," he said. "And your husband? He is better?"

"He is much worse. I came to town to buy medicine, traditional medicine. He is too sick to be moved but I am hoping the medicine will help." She looked away, a fierceness in her gaze, and then caught Lin's eye. "I thought I would stop to ask if there was any news from the authorities about our water problem."

"It is much too early to expect an answer. Much too early. The government works very slowly, I'm afraid."

"Yes, and we have no time to wait," she said bitterly. "But you are doing what you can and I am grateful," she sighed and handed Lin a many times folded piece of lined paper that looked torn from a child's notebook. "This is the number of a store in the village that has a phone and will take a message for me, for Wan Xie."

"I will certainly call, Mrs. Wan, as soon as I have news."

She thanked him and set off up the road with a heavy tread, a small bag of medicine clutched in her hand. Poor woman, she would be walking most of the night, Lin thought. As he turned to enter his laboratory, he noticed movement at the 2nd floor window of the municipal building above him and a man's face, enveloped in a cloud of smoke, slipped back into the shadows. My dear half-brother, he thought sarcastically, or one of his underlings, before turning and opening the metal door to his lab.

He lined his beakers up in their wooden stands along the back of his work bench but did not yet start the work of analyzing the soil. There would be time for that at the end of the week so he began to prepare for his trip the following day. First thing in the morning, he would visit the northeast tributary of the lake where he had received a scribbled note about possible lead poisoning which someone had slipped under the door of his lab. It contained a detailed description of a used lead-battery recycling warehouse and furnace in a small village a few miles from the lake along with some observations about the young children who were unable to focus and were behaving in peculiar and violent ways. This was the first time such a thing had happened to Lin, receiving a note directly from a citizen, and he was somewhat nervous about exactly what he should do about it. After all, he was a scientist who was in the business of investigating potential environmental infractions, infractions he mostly learned about by analyzing data from monitoring stations and from samples he collected of water and the earth itself. He was not a social worker, out to cure all the myriad and multitudinous injustices visited upon the local population. The citizen could have submitted a petition to the petition bureau, a lengthy and likely futile option but much more common than to approach Lin directly. Of course, now that he had the note, he couldn't exactly ignore it. Besides, he was due for a visit to the northeast tributary. He prepared some chemical analysis kits and beakers so that he could leave directly from his apartment and then closed up the lab and climbed aboard his trusty flying pigeon. He would visit the bathhouse before heading home, he thought. A long sweat and a good soak are just what he needed to wash away the futility of the day.

Early the next morning, his pockets stuffed with pork buns, Lin loaded his bicycle with his supplies, and headed north out of the village and then due east on a relatively quiet side road to the end of the lake. A steady wind had developed overnight and blown away some of the smog, turning it into a surprisingly pleasant fall day. The leaves of the poplar trees lining the road were golden and flashing in the sunlight. The long leaves of willows danced in the breeze and the nut trees in the distant mountains shown a deep red. Only the blanket of bright green algae carpeting the lake on Lin's right, spitting up a greyish foam along its banks, spoiled the sight. He rode contentedly along the packed dirt road, dodging the ubiquitous three wheeled farm vehicles, the drivers all dressed in the same muddy blue suits and blue caps, cigarettes dangling from their lips, the engines, mounted directly in front of the drivers, emitting a sputtering white cloud of exhaust. A few small trucks passed Lin, loaded with corn or melons, or pigs, which he smelled long before they reached him, but mostly the traffic was thin and he enjoyed the ride.

At the northeast tributary, he joined a paved road heading north along the bank of a small river. A few miles up the road, he began looking out for telltale signs of the grey acrid smoke normally produced by backyard blast furnaces and smelters used to melt secondary lead. He spotted a beaten-up MAW truck overloaded with used lead-batteries and listing dangerously to one side as it turned into the village ahead. As he made the turn himself, he saw, at the top of the village beneath the blasted-out side of a hill, two short smokestacks spewing clouds of smoke which descended upon the roofs of the houses. Lin followed the river that ran beside the town, the water the color of copper and rust, and, parking his bike, collected a number of samples of water and soil. He did a quick chemical reaction test on the water for lead content, a test that although not completely accurate in terms of the micrograms of lead per gram—this would have to wait until he returned to the lab— would certainly confirm that lead was in the water. From the looks of the two smokestacks, Lin had no doubt whatsoever that lead was blanketing the village.

As he proceeded up the main road to the far side of the village, people stopped on the road or in their doorways to watch him pass, his paniers full of beakers and gauges and testing equipment always attracting attention. A man sitting outside a small store hailed him as he passed. "Hello. Where are you from? What are you looking for?" he asked.

"I am from Meiyu town, from the State Environmental Protection Administration, and come to see about the smoke above your village," Lin answered over his shoulder as he pedaled past. He reached the end of the town where a large gate guarded a brick warehouse that housed the smokestacks. Two men were unloading used car batteries from the back of the truck that Lin had seen earlier. They paused to stare at him as he parked his bike against the wall of the warehouse and began to inspect the soil and a garbage choked moat that surrounded the building. The men went back to work unloading the truck as he collected a sample of soil and water, marking each beaker carefully with his waterproof ink pen. After returning the beakers to their wooden holders, he slipped quietly through the gate. Inside were piles and piles of used car batteries scattered about the yard of the warehouse, and a mountain of old, rusted electric scooters and motorcycles. A half dozen men squatted on the ground with clawed hammers, pounding on the old batteries to loosen first the metal bands and then the plastic casings that housed the lead. Battery acid leaked into the earth around them as they tossed the metal into one pile and the plastic into another. Other men came with wheelbarrows to collect the lead and transport it into the building housing the smokestacks. Lin followed one of the wheelbarrows, grateful that no one had tried as yet to stop him. Inside the building, he was immediately struck by the heat and by the roar. Men shoveled coal into an air furnace which provided refractory heat to the attached smelter. The lead was thrown directly into the smelter which was then stirred into a thick liquid by men with long iron poles. The flue, which sent the smoke up the stacks, leaked and the air was thick with smoke. The whooshing sound of the furnace was deafening. No one had a mask let alone any protection for their ears. Almost all had cigarettes dangling from their lips.

"What the hell do you think you are doing here?" a voice shouted at the back of Lin's head. He turned to encounter a small, compact, wide shouldered, and very angry man, obviously the owner or manager. Lin said nothing but handed the man his card with the seal of the Agency. The man looked at the card and motioned for Lin to step outside. He was yelling something above the noise of the furnace although Lin could not make out a word of what he said. Once they had stepped outside of the smelter building, the man turned on Lin with clenched fists, his face menacingly close. "This is a private plant. You have no right to be here. Get out." Lin stood his ground, feeling his own anger rising. The clawed hammers of the workers, raised above the used batteries, paused in mid-air as they all turned and stared at the two men.

"I am from the State Environmental Protection Administration. I am reporting what I have seen here to the Environmental Protection Bureau in the provincial capital. Are you the owner here? Do you have a license to run this operation?"

"I am the owner. I have permission from the village party secretary, and that's all you need to know. Now get out." He pointed to the gate, but Lin was not finished. "I will be writing an environmental assessment report. You are in clear violation of the Environmental Regulation Laws of the People's Republic of China concerning Wastewater Discharge Standards, and Air Pollutant Emission Standards. You will receive a citation shortly from the provincial capital. If you have a license to operate, you will be given one month to conform to the Standards. If you have no license, you will be shut down immediately. Do you understand?" Lin was a good head taller than the man, and he glared down at him.

"You can bring it up with the village Party Secretary. I have nothing more to say."

"I will gladly have a word with him," Lin said. He paused after walking through the gate. "But I also have a few more words for you. You are polluting this village; you are harming the children. The worker's conditions are abhorrent. At this rate, if they haven't already, they will develop lead paralysis or toxic encephalopathy from exposure." Lin found he was raising his voice and shaking with barely controlled anger. "It is criminal." As he turned, he noticed that a knot of people from the village had gathered at the gate and were looking at him hopefully.

"He should be put in prison," a woman shouted. "My son is sick. He cannot sit still, cannot read or write, and bangs his head against the wall."

"Mine also cannot read and write and cannot sit still," another shouted.

"Mine is aggressive and cannot be controlled," said another. They pressed around Lin as the owner took a few steps back towards the gate.

"I am a doctor of science, not of medicine," Lin said to the villagers, "but I will ask the provincial government to send someone to check your Blood Lead Levels. In the meantime, I will see what can be done about shutting this operation down."

The owner spoke up. "And you can see about what can be done with the people who are employed here, and at a good wage." A number of villagers scoffed at this. Just then, a shiny black sedan pulled up next to the crowd and a round man in a cheap beige suit, the label stitched to the sleeve, stepped out of the back. His thinning hair was slicked over his scalp, his eyes wary, an insincere smile on his round face. He carried a small, black plastic purse on a strap around his wrist and sported an enormous, shiny gold wristwatch.

"Now, what have we here?" the man asked, as Lin extended a card to him. He studied it carefully, then reached into his purse and produced a card for Lin. "I am Comrade Fei, Party Secretary of the village. I am pleased to meet you, Comrade Tao." They shook hands, Lin somewhat reluctantly.

"There is an office just around the corner. Shall we go and have a cup of tea and discuss the situation?" Comrade Fei asked with a forced smile.

"I see no reason to go anywhere to discuss anything. As I have said to the owner, this recycling plant is in violation of air and water quality standards under GB 8978 and GB 16297, which, *Comrade*," Lin said, twisting the word sarcastically, "I am sure you are aware of."

"Yes. Well, as you are aware, Comrade Tao, the recycling of used lead-batteries is an encouraged enterprise in the MOFCOM directives of the most recent 5-year plan. We are simply doing our part to promote the economic success of the village and the province and the PRC. We are balancing our need to meet our production goals and our need to comply with any relevant environmental regulations."

"You are doing no such thing," Lin answered. The villagers pressed in closer. "This plant is shameful. It complies with no environmental regulations whatsoever, and this is what I intend to state when I write my report to the provincial authorities. I also intend to request that a doctor come to measure the Blood Lead Levels of the villagers, especially the children and the people employed in the plant. Anyone showing a ug/dl level above 30 will be given immediate medical treatment at the cost of the plant."

They stared at one another for a long moment, Comrade Fei snapping the gold band of his wristwatch and eyeing Lin warily. "I am sure we can come to an understanding, Comrade Tao," he said finally. "Won't you join me for a cup of tea in the office?"

Lin sighed. "No. I do not want to have a cup of tea and we will not come to an understanding. You will hear from authorities in the provincial capital as to what will be done here. In the meantime, I would suggest that you at least improve the ventilation in the furnace room, and have the workers wear masks, and the children should not be downwind of the smokestacks and should not play in the topsoil. The topsoil is where the lead settles and it should not be stirred up." He walked to the wall next to the gate and retrieved his bike. "Oh, and as to the water, boiling does not help with lead but there are gravity filters and pitcher filters available that work. Perhaps you could see to it in your budget to purchase some of these for your fellow citizens."

"We keep our fellow citizens in mind with all that we do, Comrade Tao," Comrade Fei answered, to the audible jeers of the villagers.

As Lin mounted his bike and began to ride away, the villagers followed along beside him, walking quickly to keep up. "Where do we buy these filters?" they asked. "We will not get them from him. Are they available in Meiyu?" Lin stopped his bike and took out a small notebook. He wrote down the name of a department store in Meiyu town that sold filters. He knew that many could not afford them but perhaps they could pool their money. He gave the note to the closest person and got back on his bike.

They continued to follow him. "Is it safe for our children to play outside?" they asked.

"Will my child get better if they close the plant?"

"Does lead affect the child in my belly?"

"Not downwind." "Maybe." "Hopefully not," he answered, picking up speed as he rolled down the street and the villagers began to fall behind. "I need to get back to work but I will do what I can," he shouted over his shoulder.

As he descended the main street of the village, the last question he heard in a high-pitched voice was, "When will you return?"

Chapter 11

"So he went back to living in the servant's quarters of the great house when he got back from Shanghai," said Lin's mother. She was sitting up in bed, propped up by pillows. Her clubfoot was outside the covers, exposed, it's small, curled and rounded toes balled up and buried in the red and swollen foot. Beside the bed was the table full of vials of pills and packages of traditional Chinese medicines. She had just woken from a long nap and her almost unseeing eyes were clearer, not as they would be later after she had consumed the pain killers and the anti-inflammatory and steroid medication for her rheumatic arthritis.

"In the northern room of house 15. It was a hovel, really, with no doorway but it had a brick Kong bed and a straw mattress, and a table and chair and a fireplace with a cooking pot." She looked out the window at the hazy smog. "He said he still remembered the porridge Ms. Tan gave him, the old, bent, unpleasant woman who ran the kitchen. He had not eaten for days."

"And she was your boss as well," Lin said. This would be the hundredth time that his mother had mentioned Ms. Tan, as if he had not heard her name each time she told her story.

"Yes," his mother answered. "An evil old woman who would beat us with the handle of a broom if we did not move quickly enough. But she could cook. Even something as simple as porridge somehow became magical in her kitchen." Again, she gazed out the window at the haze. "Your father never got near the kitchen, he being a field hand. He answered to Overseer Zhang, who your father thought a decent sort, a fair man of few words."

During Shanshan's time in house 15, Zhang heard little from him and even less about him. Shanshan had become adept at feeding the carp, had even begun to feel a certain affinity for the scaly creatures, a feeling he was sure they returned considering he feed them. He could almost sense them smile as he shinnied his way onto the pole each day with his bag of pellets. His was a simply regulated life:

each day he woke just before sunrise, lit a small fire under the iron pot from leaves and stalks which he had scavenged the day before, boiled water and, if there was anything left of his hoarded tea, dropped in two or three leaves. He would watch the leaves shrivel and the water turn a yellowish green before gulping it down. He then grabbed his shovel, which stood beside his bed, and went out to see Overseer Zhang about his daily duties. Work was over at sunset, when he returned to his room to find food on the table left by someone from the kitchen of the great house: usually a piece of tofu and some vegetables to put in his iron pot but sometimes just a piece of unleavened bread wrapped around a long stalk of garlic. And then a deep sleep before rising again just before the sun.

For his labor, he was given room and board, a blanket, a cloth jacket to use for the two cold months of winter, and a sewing kit and a piece of old cloth with which to patch his ragged clothes. He had been told that once these items were paid off, presumably sometime in the spring, then he could begin to receive a few copper pennies or paper yuan for his work, enough to buy tea leaves, perhaps a piece of pork once a month. When he finally began to receive money, he was careful with it, never spending it as others did on cheap bottles of rice wine and tobacco and the occasional prostitute. He kept it in a small tin box he had found in the trash heap of the great house, and behind the fireplace of House 15, Shanshan had removed a loose brick and it was there that he concealed the tin. He dreamt of saving enough to buy tools of his own in order to work a piece of the Chief Magistrate's land, perhaps to have a few good harvests, to sell what excess he managed to save after paying off his master, even dreaming of buying some land for himself. The tin danced in Shanshan's dreams, jingling and overflowing: it was his last thought each evening, and his first each morning.

One day in mid-summer, he arrived as usual at Overseer Zhang's house with his shovel and waited with the others. As the sun rose above the banks of the fish ponds, the heat was instantly overpowering, damp and relentless. Overseer Zhang appeared; you could barely see his eyes in his round face and he was already sweating.

"As of yesterday, we are officially at war with Japan," he announced. "The Chief Magistrate has heard it on the wireless."

The men murmured among themselves and lit the cigarette butts behind their ears. "It is no great surprise since we have been fighting them for years," said Zhang. "The only question is whether they will come this far south. For now, it is unlikely. We are just a town off the main trading lines. The General is busy defending the cities and they say the communists are active in the countryside although not nearby. Certainly, we have seen no sign of them but we must keep an eye out for any and all of these people. The Chief Magistrate cannot afford to lose any more workers, old and broken as most of you may be, so he has posted guards on the roads to the village to warn us of any strangers approaching. If they come, you will need to hide in the hills and be quick about it and not return until you hear three gongs from the drum tower in quick succession. Do you understand?"

"Understood," they muttered, not pleased at the thought of spending long nights in the woods in order to keep themselves in basic servitude to the Chief Magistrate. The alternative, however, was the unknown which might, or might not, be worse than what they had. Some had heard about the communists and their promise of land reform and were sympathetic, although too old to imagine a world without the authority of a Chief Magistrate and endless hard labor. In the end, none were eager to give up what little food and money they received in tough times and so clung to their shovels and followed the orders of Overseer Zhang.

And so the seasons swept by, one after another, with the war raging elsewhere and the inconsequential town protected from the carnage. Mostly Shanshan schemed and plotted to increase his small tin of coins and paper yuan, always prepared for any opportunity that might come his way: having sewed pockets on the inside thighs of his pants, there were always nuts to hide away when he was working on the nut harvest, or rice when he was at work separating the husks from the rice, or corn kernels when they were being brought to the mill to be ground. And these he would collect over time in small sacks to sell to the hungry villagers. But his most lucrative scheme involved the carp which by now, at the mere sight of Shanshan, crowded the shore in a heaving mass whenever he came close to the fishpond. On moonless nights, Shanshan would sneak to the edge of the pond and simply hook his fingers into two large carp who were almost out of the water in their excitement at seeing him. These he would slip into a burlap sack and carry along a trail bordering the lake to a neighboring village where a fishmonger was happy to pay for the fish at a discount, no questions asked. In this way, Shanshan slowly increased his hoard of money, and his dreams became sweeter.

Chapter 12

Some days later, after finishing and submitting his report on the Lead Battery Recycling facility, Lin made a trip to the textile mill located south of the town on the only large tributary running out of the lake and down to the fertile plains below. Theoretically, because the water flowed south and southeast away from the lake, the deputy inspector for the next county should be filing reports on the water quality. Lin knew this inspector, an oily, pox-faced cadre with long pinky nails and a combover hairdo, driving around in the usual shiny, black sedan. He had been spotted around Meiyu town doing Environmental Assessment Reports for development projects despite being from the next county, a practice that was not technically illegal but was nevertheless unscrupulous. He had not once paid his respects to Lin during these somewhat clandestine visits, nor, for that matter, had he ever filed a negative assessment. Lin was certainly disappointed by the lack of support from a colleague but he was not about to start denouncing fellow party members to the provincial authorities. He had enough to do without taking on that bureaucratic headache.

In any event, the water flowing out of the textile mill was well within Lin's jurisdiction. He had been there once before to take water samples and submitted a report to the provincial bureau on the results, but he had left it up to their office to cite the factory or not. The reason for this current visit was his receiving a call from the Party Secretary in a village just downstream complaining of the water quality. Lin was surprised and quite pleased to actually hear an environmental complaint from a village Party Secretary; it meant that he actually cared about an environmental hazard and for the welfare of his citizens. It was either that, or he had failed to get a substantial enough pay off from the management of the mill. Lin tried not to be cynical as he headed south out of Meiyu town, past the ever-present towering silos of the MSG plant on his left, gliding down the gentle sloping road through rice paddies and waving fields of corn and wheat, towards the textile mill. He was to meet the Party Secretary outside the gates of the mill at 10:00 a.m. which gave him time to collect some samples downstream before the meeting.

At a quarter to ten, Lin pedaled past the mill which sat imposingly on the east side of the river. A bridge led to the gates which were open to allow for the passing of numerous trucks. Inside, he could see the stacks of 500-pound bales of cotton waiting to be processed and hear the clacking of the hundreds of combing and spinning machines and the whirring of the looms. Beside the gate a massive concrete signpost advertised the mill, The Splendid Paradise Textile Works, in gaudy red letters with a flowery background. Under the name was a long list of the foreign brands that contracted with the mill to manufacture their goods with their colorful logos in English. Lin studied the famous brands thinking that these people were indifferent to the effects of such manufacturing on the environment and on the people of the village downstream despite the fact that such environmental conditions in their own country would be unthinkable. What they cared about was simply getting their inexpensive products made with cheap Chinese labor and relishing their fat margin.

Lin parked his bike fifty yards below the gates of the factory, took his shoes and socks off, rolled up his pant legs, and stepped into the slow-moving river. The water was the color of rust and warm, which surprised him. The factory discharge pipes must be pumping at full volume as he filled his beakers, sealed them with cork stoppers, wiped them dry, and labeled them.

"How's the water?" said a man standing on the bank. He was average height, athletically built and with a powerful torso, wearing a polo shirt, khaki trousers and running shoes, probably a decade younger than Lin. His bright smile showed a row of gleaming white teeth. Could this possibly be the party secretary, Lin wondered? He was not a smoker, judging by his teeth, had no beer belly, and, like Lin, his hair was streaked with grey and not dyed black. And, incredibly, it appeared that the man had actually arrived on a bicycle which was parked directly behind him.

Lin waded out of the stream and gave the man his outstretched hand. "Tao Lin, from SEPA. We spoke on the phone."

"Party Secretary Ling Yang. Nice to meet you in person, Comrade Tao," he said as they shook hands firmly, looked into one another's eyes and finding an instant liking. "I am sorry to have troubled you with this visit," Ling Yang said apologetically. "I know that our village is not your responsibility. I contacted our SEPA deputy inspector a number of times but he was, well, how shall I say, unresponsive."

"Worthless would be a better description."

Ling Yang bowed slightly and smiled, watched as Lin stepped to his bike and placed his beakers of water samples in the paniers with their wooden racks, and dried his feet off with a small towel.

"Interesting arrangement," said Comrade Ling, bending to inspect Lin's bicycle. "You've had a climbing sprocket built in, I see. Very practical."

"Very practical when I am fighting a headwind or spending time in the northern hills. You are also a bicyclist." Lin nodded to the Giant model mountain bike behind him.

"Always," Comrade Ling said. "It really is the best way to get around, is it not?" he asked rhetorically as Lin nodded his head in agreement. "These Chinese made Giant bikes are excellent quality. And very popular with foreigners."

"Yes. I am thinking of buying one for weekend riding." They both stared at one another's bikes for a moment.

"You don't happen to be a badminton player, do you?" Lin asked suddenly.

"Yes, I am." answered Comrade Ling, surprised by the question.

"You have the build of a badminton player, and an overdeveloped right wrist and forearm."

"Of course." He looked sheepishly at his right arm. "I play three or four times a week. And you?"

"Once a week, at my daughter's school, the parents and some teachers and an administrator get together to play. I am an ok player. I suspect not on your level."

"I did play first squad at the Party School. And I travelled around the country a bit with a team, semi-professionally; I even went once to Malaysia."

"Well, I know the rule is that you should never ask someone much better than you to play but perhaps we could have a game someday."

"I would like that."

"So, Comrade Ling," said Lin, "shall we see what we can find out from the mill director? I am sure you have paid him a visit already."

They pushed their bikes up the road toward the gates of the factory.

"Twice, so far," Comrade Ling said. "He produced his business license from the provincial authorities giving him permission to operate the mill and told me there was nothing more to say. The fact is, Comrade Tao, people are getting sick in the village. The cancer cases are skyrocketing. I have tried to install a main filter system but I don't have the budget for such a project. The villagers are trying to use pitcher filters as much as they can but they are expensive and the filters need to be changed quite often."

"And not always effective, I'm afraid," said Lin. "Not from what's spewing out of this mill. You're dealing with synthetic and residual dyes that contain extremely hazardous chemicals: tributyltin, pentabromodiphenyl ether, phthalates, perfluorooctane sulphonate, aniline. All cancer inducing. Even natural dyes, once you give them a vivid color, contain chrome, tin, copper sulfate and iron sulfate. These metals you can mostly manage to filter out of water but not the others."

"And the solution is a wastewater treatment facility at the source," concluded Ling Yang.

"Yes. That's exactly what the mill needs to do, and as soon as possible so that relatively clean water reaches the village. Long term? The entire textile industry needs to change. People talk about natural dyes as a solution but producing enough to cover every textile factory in the world would bankrupt the food supply. Natural dyes are just that: natural. Which means they derive from things we eat. People are experimenting with alternative cloth made from wood and recycled waste but we won't see that sort of change in our lifetimes."

Comrade Ling sighed, ran a hand through his hair.

"I am just giving you the facts," Lin said. "I am often accused of being far too negative. It comes with knowing a bit too much about chemistry and biology. And maybe human nature as well," he added with a shrug.

"Anyway," he said, pulling himself up to his full height. "Let's go see this director."

They were met at the gate by an assistant to the manager who was pacing just inside and talking on his phone. He quickly hung up, gave a slight bow, then looked completely taken back by the bicycles.

"You do have a bicycle parking lot, do you not?" asked Lin impatiently.

"They usually send me around the back, to the worker's entrance," said Ling Yang with an annoyed shake of his head.

"Yes, yes" said the young assistant with a confused nod. "But no need to go to the back gate. Please leave them by the doorway there and I will have someone look after them." He made a quick call on his mobile phone and a worker soon appeared, lit a cigarette, and squatted beside the bikes.

"This way, please." They passed one warehouse after another, containing machinery involved in breaking down the great bales of cotton: machines for carding, combing, drawing and spinning. Then there were warehouses for checking, folding, twisting and gassing the textiles, the result being a cacophony of clacking and whirring and wheezing machines and a great rush of noise escaping from the open doors as they passed. They took this all in, often with their hands held over their ears, before finally stepping into a massive building where, at rows and rows of worktables, women sat at sewing machines, surrounded by mounds of cloth, creating the finished product. Floor managers, all men, wandered the aisles between the rows, occasionally stopping to have a few sharp words with the women. At a set of steep, iron stairs, they climbed to a landing that overlooked the worktables, and entered a carpeted office. When the young assistant shut the door, the silence was deafening.

"Please have a seat," he said. "The director and the Party Representative will see you shortly."

They nodded. A young woman appeared with two paper cups of tea. They thanked her, started blowing into the green tea leaves that floated on the surface of the hot water. After slurping the tea gratefully, Lin held the cup up in front of him, rotated it, and looked at Comrade Ling with an ironic glimmer in his eye.

"For this cup, first a tree is cutdown, a tree whose purpose in life is to not only house all manner of entomological and ornithological creatures but to capture and store carbon dioxide. The unfortunate tree is turned into wood chips and then into wood pulp which is then mashed into paper. The paper is bleached. A thin coat of polyethylene is added to make it waterproof. It is then transported to a manufacturer who might use a synthetic ink to print a label on the cup like this with The Splendid Paradise Textile Works logo. It is then transported to this factory, and to a thousand, perhaps a hundred thousand just like it, where we will drink from it once, and throw it in the wastebin."

"It must be hell to be a scientist," Comrade Ling said with a smile and a shake of his head.

"And don't think that a paper cup is that much worse than a plastic one, or even a ceramic one. When you take into consideration the fact of the energy used to make the ceramic cup, the raw materials needed, the kiln, the glazing—" The young assistant appeared before them.

"This way, please." He led them down a long, carpeted hallway past a great number of cubicles until they reached the end, stepping into an office covered on one side by floor to ceiling windows that seemed to hang over the rows of cutting and sewing tables beneath them. On the other walled side of the office hung dozens of gold-framed pictures: high ranking Communist Party officials shaking hands with a well-dressed, well-groomed director; model workers accepting awards from the same director; the director again posing on various fashion show runways around the globe; even a picture of him posing with a European leader. In one corner, Lin noticed a set of golf clubs in a shiny bag with a sports logo on it. The director himself they found sitting comfortably behind a massive desk made of what looked like a single piece of rosewood, beside him in a dark, ill-fitting suit sat the Communist Party Representative.

"Gentlemen," said the director, standing up and extended a name card which he presented with two hands and a slight bow. They all exchanged cards in the same manner before he motioned for them to sit in the chairs opposite his desk. The chairs were low but Lin with his height was still able to be at eye level with the men behind the desk. The director and the Party Rep laid the business cards in front of them.

"Comrade Tao and Comrade Ling. What exactly can we do for you?" asked the director.

"Director Jiang," began Comrade Ling, "as you are well aware, this is the third time that I have paid a visit to the factory. Nothing has changed in the village. In fact, things are getting worse. People are getting sick and the reason is the quality of the water."

"Do you know that for a fact?" interrupted the Party Rep,

thrusting his jaw out. As he spoke, he rolled two walnut shells in his right hand which made un unpleasant grating sound.

"Well. Yes. We do know that for a fact," interrupted Lin. "The river is full of dangerous chemicals which are downstream from this mill. I wrote a report on the water quality in March of this year which I submitted to the provincial SEPA. I am sure that they provided you a copy." He paused, looking at them closely. They remained expressionless, although he was sure his report was somewhere in the office.

"There are many sources of pollution in the river, Comrade Tao," said the Party Rep, "and in the lake itself. Certainly, it cannot all be attributed to this factory."

"I am quite aware of the sources of pollution in the lake, and in the rivers and streams surrounding it," Lin said bitingly. "However, you are dumping great quantities of synthetic and natural dyes into the water that can only come from the production of textiles. These are carcinogenic and people are getting sick."

"I doubt very much that you can pinpoint the source to this factory."

The director jumped in, his hand raised in the air. "And your proposal, Gentlemen?" he asked. "And before you answer, I am sure you are aware that textiles are an encouraged industry under the current MOFCOM directives in the most recent 5-year plan and that we enjoy very high-level support from the provincial government and even the central government in Beijing."

Lin, ignoring the reference to high-level support, answered. "As I reported in March, the wastewater needs to be treated before reaching the river, which is the only way to mitigate the worst of the pollution. I realize that this comes at a cost to the factory but, as you well know, you are currently in violation of the Environmental Regulation Laws of the People's Republic of China regarding Wastewater Discharge Standards."

"Cost?" interrupted the Party Rep, his walnut shells clacking irritably away. "The cost would be outrageous. To put in such a treatment system would bankrupt the company."

Doubtful, Lin thought, although it would certainly hurt your bottom line.

"Do you have any idea how many people are employed in this mill?" the Party Rep continued, fuming.

"Quite a few, I suspect."

"Eight hundred and seventy-seven. And that is directly. There are thousands employed peripherally through the business of the mill. Do you know how much the factory contributes in tax each year?" the Party Rep said, almost shouting, the blood rising in his face.

"Yes. We know all that," Lin said, holding his hands palm up in front of him. "We are not asking that you bankrupt your factory. We are asking that you put in place a system in order to protect the environment and the people who live downstream of the factory. That is our proposal. Now what is your proposal?"

"Comrade Tao, Comrade Ling," came the smooth voice of the director, a slight smile on his lips. "We intend to immediately request a copy of your report and to instigate, also immediately, a feasibility study on the installation of a treatment system for our wastewater." He smiled broadly. "You understand, of course, that this will take time and the work of the factory must go on."

Lin and Ling Yang nodded grudgingly.

"In the meantime," said the director, "I will order one hundred pitcher filters with a thousand extra filters to be delivered to your headquarters, Comrade Ling, no later than..." he turned, leaned back in his chair, and stared at a calendar hanging on the wall, "the 12th of the month. So, no later than the end of next week." He clapped his hands together softly, satisfactorily.

"Is there no way to lessen the amount of pollutants being discharged?" Comrade Ling asked.

"What?" spat the Party Rep. "And re-configure our entire industrial output?" He shook his head, as if someone had just asked what it would take to bring the moon closer to the earth.

"My report," Lin said, bowing slightly to the director, "contains a detailed proposal on the implementation of a wastewater treatment plan. I am grateful that you will study the plan, and perhaps, in, say, three months you will give me a report of your own on your progress?"

"Most assuredly," answered the director with a smile and a nod of his head. The Party Rep's walnut shells clacked even louder.

"And now if you will excuse me," said the director. "Some buyers from the United States are coming through with a delegation in a few minutes."

Lin and Ling Yang stood. They shook hands and the Party Rep

ushered them out of the door and into the arms of the young assistant who returned them through the mind-numbing whirring and banging of the mill to their bicycles. As they pushed the bikes out the gate and across the bridge, a minibus full of foreigners passed, a flash of heads with strangely colored hair, round eyes, big noses, and mobile phones held in front of their odd faces to snap photos of the mill. They would never get out of the bus and look at the river, Lin thought, never see the strange color of the water or understand the deadly chemicals floating downstream that people were forced to drink. They would never meet any of the woman sitting at those sewing machines attaching their labels to their designer clothes. They would be wined and dined by the director, speak to the design team, be impressed by the quality and orderliness and efficiency of the mill, place their orders and get back in their bus to the hotel and the airport, having seen as much of China as they wished to see.

Across the bridge, the two men paused. "It was my understanding that the Party Rep was supposed to be at least somewhat sympathetic to our side," said Ling Yang, shaking his head. "He was more capitalist than the director. He looked like he wanted to kill us, especially you," he added with a concerned look at Lin.

"I'm sure he and the director have come to a very beneficial arrangement," Lin said smiling.

"Listen, I really appreciate your making the trip out here, Comrade Tao. We will get the filters, I believe, which is more than I got the last two visits."

"I am happy to help. I wish there was more that we could do," he added wistfully. "In any event, please come to Meiyu town, Comrade Ling, and we will see about that game of badminton."

"I certainly will." As he mounted his bike and pointed it down the road, he turned his head. "You must make a lot of enemies in your line of work."

"More than I like to think about," he answered.

"Well, you've got a friend in me but you better watch your back." Ling Yang pedaled off, the downhill slope taking him quickly out of sight.

Yes, Lin thought. Although he never quite understood, both figuratively and literally, how a person went about that.

Chapter 13

Lin was waiting by the front door of the apartment for Xiaoyu to fetch her school bag. Chen was sipping coffee, a drink she had suddenly found a taste for, at the dining table and rifling through an official document, occasionally making a note in the margins.

"You know there is another Planning Meeting with Party and non-Party comrades this afternoon."

"I haven't forgotten," she answered, not looking up.

"I am supposed to present an environmental assessment report," he said.

"That should be fun," she said sarcastically.

"Well, I know it's not what people want to hear but there's not much I can do about it." She gave him a weary look that contained all that she thought Lin *could* do about it.

"Maybe you should skip this one," he suggested.

"I can't miss another meeting, Lin, or they will make me write yet another silly self-criticism. I will sit in the back and do my best to ignore it. I'm afraid you can't expect any support from me. I've got too much going on to stick my neck out in a meeting."

"No no," he said with a sigh. "Just try not to pay too much attention."

Xiaoyu appeared with her pink, mini mouse school backpack. She said goodbye to her mother who gave her a smile and a wave of her hand. She and Lin headed for the elevator. It was an odd day for the lift so they did not have to walk up or down a flight to catch it. When the doors opened, the usual old residence committee woman operating the lift with her officious red armband was sitting on her three-legged stool. She frowned at Lin but gave Xiaoyu a big smile.

"Aren't we the pretty girl this morning," she said.

"Thank you, Mrs. Xi," Xiaoyu mumbled, squeezing herself into the corner although she couldn't get far because of the backpack.

"And what are we studying today? I hope the selfless sacrifices of the Communist Party leaders who do so much to improve our lives." She gave Lin a sharp look before settling in for the ride down.

Lin had no idea why he was singled out by people in the town as a troublemaker and malcontent. He was a party member in good standing, was passionate about his work, aware of his responsibility, had even held a fairly prestigious position in the nation's capital for over a decade, but his refusal to make money, and his criticism of those who did so at the expense of the environment, made him out to be some sort of counter revolutionary. Once again, he was confronted with how bad his reputation was when all the old ladies of the residence committee were glaring at him.

He said goodbye to Xiaoyu at the gate to the compound, she turning right to her school and he turning left to get his bike and pedal into town to his lab. Once he got settled at his desk, he found he could not concentrate much that day with thinking about the meeting that would take place later that afternoon.

A little before 5:00 p.m., the Committee Room that took up most of the 3rd floor of the local government building where Lin's lab was located, began to fill up. Lin picked a seat close to a window because as soon as everyone filed in, finished saying hello and putting hot water and tea in their thermos cups, they lit up. A cloud of smoke soon enveloped the room, despite its size, so that Lin could barely make out the photographs of this month's model workers prominently displayed along one wall. On another hung announcements for work unit requirements and quotas and tax collection initiatives and employment targets, with the back wall taken up entirely with framed photos of the leadership in Beijing, right down to the Provincial Party and the leaders of the town. Other than that, the bare spaces of the walls consisted of scuffed concrete with pieces of tape and glue and wires dangling from them in a typical show of communist aesthetics. Lin shifted uncomfortably in the wooden chair, when he caught a glimpse of Chen who had just entered and taken a seat in the back. They nodded to one another before she unpacked a satchel full of documents which she immediately became engrossed in. About two dozen party members were present, a decent turnout, he thought, as well as some younger Municipal Party Youth members, the usual residence committee busybodies, secretaries, minor functionaries, and, bunched together on the far side of the room, a dozen non-Party comrade business community members, including Gao Bing, who, when he made the mistake of catching Lin's eye, frowned. On a raised platform at the front of the room sat the mayor, Cao Xiaoping, and two of his deputy mayors on either side of him. Xiaoping rapped his knuckles on the wooden table to bring the meeting to order.

"Welcome, comrades, welcome. This is the 17th Planning Meeting of this calendar year and the 5th meeting to include non-cadre. As you know, we encourage the business community to participate in our town planning; the business community is no longer just an official consultative committee but our welcome as members of the Chinese Communist Party." He smiled broadly at the businessmen on the far side of the room, who greeted him with short, and uniform, applause.

"Before we begin with a report on the tax collection numbers, employment, and the progress of our infrastructure projects," Xiaoping paused theatrically, holding up an official document with stamped red seals, "a new directive has been published regarding the state of the youth of this country. Many of you may have thought that the campaign against spiritual pollution was a thing of the past but it is not."

He glared at the room as the half dozen representatives of the residence committees rapped their knuckles on their tables supportively. "Western influences are sneaking into the fabric of our society with their glorified depiction of sex and prostitution and licentious music."

A few mumbles of assent could be heard.

"We must be vigilant. Satellite dishes are popping up all over the town. These are forbidden and must be reported. Some citizens are intercepting cable television carrying channels from the U.S., Europe, Australia, and the Philippines that do not conform to our standards. These cable boxes must be banned."

There was an uncomfortable shifting of eyes as a many in the crowd thought of just how they might hide their boxes.

"Some magazines with questionable content have also been appearing at our kiosks. These must be confiscated. This is a war. I expect all party members and concerned citizens to be vocal in their support of a new campaign to keep the ideals and morals of the PRC pure and resolute. This is no time for half measures. Once society is contaminated, it is very hard to turn back. So, remember, in the words of Chairman Mao Zedong," here everyone sat up slightly in their chairs, "*'Grasp firmly. For not to grasp firmly, is not to grasp at all.'*" Another mumble of approval.

The great thing about declaring a war, Xiaoping thought, was that inevitably you had to declare victory. Once enough satellite dishes and cable boxes and magazines had been collected and displayed prominently in the front hall of the Municipal Headquarters, then the superfluous campaign would be over and they could go back to their main task of supporting the businesses in the town and making a name for themselves in the province. Xiaoping turned to his left. "Now, if you would all please give your attention to Comrade Pei, who will begin with his reports on our overall budget, end of the year financial projection, and current tax revenue. Please begin, Comrade Pei."

The deputy mayor extinguished his cigarette, cleared his throat and began an interminable monologue in an inflectionless voice which put half the room to sleep. In the middle of the tax revenue figures, Xiaoping finally interrupted and brought the presentation to an end.

"Many thanks for your hard work on that, Comrade. We are all very grateful, and grateful to hear that our tax revenues and employment numbers are the envy of the province." More uniform applause, followed by the sound of teacup tops being removed from their cups and a great slurping of tea.

"I would now like to introduce a new initiative that we have been working on the last few months. Mr. Shu, if you could please stand up." In the back of the room, between the businessmen and the party members, stood Comrade Shu, dressed in a well-tailored suit with a haircut that looked like it did not come from paying 50 cents to sit on a stool on the barber street outside the town's public park. He bowed to everyone, then inspected his well-manicured nails.

"Mr. Shu is now heading our Economic Development Bureau. He has been working for many years throughout China on attracting foreign, and domestic, investment to towns and small cities of our size. His proposal for an economic development zone in the northwest of our soon to be designated small city has been accepted by the provincial authorities and they have promised to assist with 50% of the funding." More applause, only this time with enthusiasm, especially from the business contingent.

Lin raised his hand. Xiaoping pointed to him reluctantly. "Northwest of this town is a wetland area which has been designated as such. Is this zone going to affect the wetlands?"

"It has been approved, Comrade Tao," said Xiaoping impatiently. "A part of the wetlands will be developed and a part kept as they are."

"Was SEPA aware of this decision? I can't imagine that they would approve of taking the last unspoiled marshland around the lake and turning it into a development zone. This was discussed at a provincial plenary level meeting and it was determined that the marshland should be preserved. Surely you aware that they are the equivalent of lungs for the lake."

There was a general impatient movement from the crowd, and some of the businessmen openly scoffed.

"Of course SEPA was consulted. As I said, it has all been approved. You are welcome at any time to review the documents at the planning office. Not all the marshland is to be developed, just the western half."

Lin sighed, rubbed a hand hard over his forehead.

"Now," continued Xiaoping. "We would very much like to hear from Mr. Shu himself on the efforts he has made to attract investors to the town."

Mr. Shu, who had never sat down, stopped inspecting his fingernails, and walked regally to the front of the room. He bowed slightly to the crowd before stepping to a whiteboard which had been wheeled to the front of the room by a secretary, and, in red and green markers, drew the outline of the zone, marking the designated areas of industries they were hoping to attract. "Of course, everyone wants high tech industries in their zone, but the competition is intense. We offer good tax incentives and excellent lease contracts and construction packages but so does everyone else. What makes us stand out from the crowd?" He looked around. No one answered. Well, Lin thought bitterly, we offered some outstanding marshland before it was sold off. At that moment, the back door of the Committee Room creaked open and two men in black pants, white shirts, windbreakers and flattop haircuts entered and stood against the wall looking carefully at the crowd.

Mr. Shu continued. "What we offer is an infrastructure of highly successful businesses throughout the lake region." Here he gave a nod to the non-Party cadres who puffed up their chests in approval. "Like businesses attract like businesses. We have food manufacturing, textiles, tanneries, some heavy construction industries. All of these would find a welcome home here."

At this, Bing stood up, a palm pressed to the middle of his chest. "If I may, Mr. Shu."

"By all means." Mr. Shu put a cap on one of his markers and stood with his arms crossed on his chest.

"I would like to announce that I intend to go into the production of a malt beverage, a malt beverage that I hope will carry the name of our town and a picture of our lake and be famous around the province and hopefully the country. The beer production facility will be established in the new economic zone of Meiyu City." There was thunderous applause, and Bing bowed three times to the crowd.

"This is exactly what we need," said Mr. Shu with an approving nod of his head. "Such entrepreneurial spirit. I suggest we make Mr. Gao head of the board of overseers of the zone." More thunderous applause.

Mr. Shu continued with his presentation, listing the various investment opportunities, drawing graphs of construction costs in relation to land sales and tax receipts, and ending with an extremely optimistic outlook for the development zone. Again, there was loud applause as he moved to the back of the room and took his seat. Everyone then shifted forward and looked impatiently at their watches. Dinner time was upon them.

Xiaoping rose and thanked everyone for their attendance and participation. He put on a pair of glasses and looked absently around him. "Our next meeting," he paused as a secretary in a short skirt and white blouse appeared beside him with a piece of paper which he held close to his face, "is scheduled for the 9th of November." He looked quickly around. "If there is no further business, then I propose we adjourn until November 9th." Lin's hand shot up. An audible sigh escaped from Xiaoping.

"Yes, Comrade Tao."

"I have prepared the General Environmental Assessment Report as you requested," Lin said.

"Yes, yes. Well, since we are out of time," he motioned to the secretary who stepped forward again, "Comrade Liu here will have your report mimeographed and distributed to everyone as soon as possible."

Reluctantly, Lin handed over the report to Comrade Liu. Just so much more trash to litter the bottom of the lake, Lin thought.

"And Comrade Tao," Xiaoping said. "If I might have a word with you before you go." He stood by the main door of the Committee room to bow and shake hands and see everyone off.

Lin stayed behind as the room emptied. Chen stopped and leaned towards him. "I'll get some dinner together for Xiaoyu. See you soon."

The two men who had come in at the end of the meeting were the last to reach the door of the committee room. They spent a few minutes whispering with Xiaoping, heads close together, occasionally glancing at Lin, before leaving.

Soon it was just Xiaoping and himself, Xiaoping standing in front of the podium with his feet spread apart and Lin sprawled in the wooden chair.

"Listen, Lin, I'm not going to beat about," Xiaoping started in a low growl. "I had a call from the village Party Secretary in the northern district who said you were snooping around the other day stirring up trouble."

Lin sighed, looked out the window to see a stream of black sedans leaving the compound and entering the main road to the town, a uniformed policeman holding up traffic to let them through. Only the mayor's sedan was left, the driver leaning against the door and lighting a cigarette, no doubt grumbling about the time and his late dinner.

"I'm just doing my job, Xiaoping, which to everyone at this committee meeting and in this town appears to think consists of snooping and making trouble."

"Well, that's the thing, you see. You have no jurisdiction in that district and you know it. That, in fact, is not your job. Your job is the lake district and I suggest you stick to that."

"Do you know what is going on at the headwaters of the northwest tributary?"

"No, and I don't want to know. I have enough to worry about here."

Lin shrugged. "Fine. But as you are aware, I filed a report on the water quality in the tributary which *is* my jurisdiction and I hope that someone from the provincial capital will act upon it."

Xiaoping stood staring down at Lin. "I think the saying is: it's better to be reasonable and join the winning side than to be unreasonable and lose. Why are you so stubborn? Why can't you find a middle way to accommodate everyone's interest?"

"That's exactly my question to you. The lake is dying. The entire ecosystem will be beyond repair in, I calculate, less than a decade. Why can't the businesses around the lake find a middle way to accommodate the interests of the environment?"

"Ok. Never mind. We are, as usual, at an impasse and there's no need arguing. Just one more thing, Lin. We have noticed that people are approaching you about issues which may not be a part of your job as a scientist. You should be careful how you handle these issues."

"I don't ask people to come to me. It appears that the system has given them nowhere else to go which is a sad commentary, actually, on the ability of the Chinese Communist Party to provide for its people." Lin paused, then stared hard at Xiaoping. "Are you having me watched? Were those Public Security Bureau goons who just left?"

"Everyone is watched. I thought you would have known that by now, *Comrade*," he said ironically. "And obviously it's not just me who is watching."

"Thanks for the head's up. I will remain ever vigilant in the service of the Party, for we must grasp firmly," Lin said laughing but Xiaoping only frowned.

"Is that all, Mayor?"

"Yes. Have a good evening."

"You as well."

As Lin left the building and climbed onto his bicycle for the ride to his apartment, he knew he should have been nervous about what Xiaoping had just told him and at the appearance of the PSB officers, but all he could think about was the marshland and how it was soon to be cut in two, drained and paved over, and lost forever.

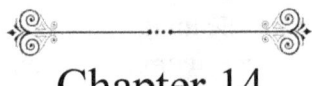

Chapter 14

Lin, changing into his sweatpants and sweat shirt and lacing his sneakers, looked forward to his Thursday night badminton game. In a very pleasant surprise, he had gotten a call from Comrade Ling Yang at the beginning of the week to see about a game and Lin had proposed that he join him on this evening at his daughter's school. The fact was that he had no friends to speak of; mostly he had acquaintances or colleagues he corresponded with in distant towns and cities, so he liked the idea of not only having a badminton partner but possibly making a friend, especially with a man who appeared to have views similar to his own. He checked his racket bag: two Yonex uniformly strung rackets, tape for his fingers, chalk to dry his hands, two oversized sweat bands, and a long thin towel and a few smaller ones. He was not in charge of bringing the shuttlecocks today but he put a can in just in case someone forgot. He shouldered the bag and stepped into the kitchen where Chen and Xiaoyu sat at the table, Chen pouring over official documents and Xiaoyu laboring over an exercise book.

"I'm off."

"Have fun," Chen said with a wave of her hand.

"I might have a beer afterwards with Comrade Ling but I shouldn't be home too late."

"Don't tell me you have actually found a friend," Chen said caustically.

"Hey. I'm a friendly man. It's not my fault no one in this town wants to be friends with me."

"I wonder why," she mumbled with another wave of her hand.

He closed the metal door behind him, thinking that he might need a jacket with the late autumn nights getting cooler but continued to the stairs anyway. He could always wrap a towel around his neck if it got too cool. Today was an even number day for the lift but instead of pausing on the 4th floor and pushing the button, he continued down the stairs, stretching out his calves by taking two steps at a time. On each landing, Lin snaked his way through the clutter of old furniture, rugs, tables stacked with magazines and electrical appliances, and bundles of cleaning rags and plastic wash buckets. Every month, the residence committee made people clear the stairways, with a stern lecture about fire hazards, but the junk always returned. On the ground floor, Lin burst out into the night, jogging the short distance to the gate of the compound and out to the street. There was the usual haze of coal and industry-produced smog in the air but otherwise a perfect evening.

He turned right and walked quickly down the street, dodging bicycles and three wheeled bicycle carts and motorized carts loaded with everything from fruit and vegetables, furniture, stacks of boxes, farm equipment, and people. He weaved his way past a slow-moving truck and arrived at the gate of the school a little before six and just as Comrade Ling pulled up on his bicycle. He was unhooking the clip on his helmet, his badminton bag strapped to his bike rack.

"Comrade Ling," said Lin. "I am very pleased that you could come."

"Comrade Tao." They shook hands warmly. "It is my pleasure. And please," he said with a smile, "call me Yang."

"Excellent. And please call me Lin. Now," he made a sweeping gesture through the gate, "let me show you where the bike park is."

They walked shoulder to shoulder through the gate and Yang parked his bike with a hundred others under a rusted tin shed beside the courtyard and the dusty outside sports ground. Before shouldering his bag, Yang attached a heavy lock to the frame of the bike and the frame of the bike rack.

"Nice lock," Lin said, nodding impressively.

"Swiss. Kryptonite. Cost about a third of what the bike cost but worth it," said Yang with a laugh.

"In Beijing, I once had three bikes stolen in a month."

"Even our village has problems with bicycle theft," said Yang with a sad shake of his head. "Now you either need a lock like this, or you need to ride something no one would bother to steal."

They went around to the back of the main building, past stacks of discarded school desks and chairs piled against the walls, and entered the indoor sports hall which housed a basketball court now transformed into 3 badminton courts. There was the usual thrill at the first glimpse of bright lights and the smell of athletic energy that made Lin smile and brought a bounce to his step. The other players were milling about, parents of students and a few athletic-minded teachers and one administrator, making up a rather thin crowd. Lin and Yang stopped before them and Lin gave a slight bow as he introduced Yang.

"Everyone, this is my friend, Comrade Ling."

They waved their hands in greeting and Yang gave a bow. "Very nice to meet you all," he said, "and I appreciate your allowing me to join you. I am looking forward to it."

The administrator stepped forward officiously and extended his hand. "Welcome, welcome, Comrade Ling. It's a pleasure to have you. You should know that we are not exactly top-tier players but we are pretty good and we are, above all, enthusiastic, so I hope you will not be bored." He smiled slyly. He, and Lin, were by far the best players in the group, and you could tell that he was sizing Ling Yang up and looking forward to testing his skills against him. "So," the administrator clapped his hands. "There are ten of us tonight. I suggest we let Comrade Tao and Comrade Ling start with singles on court one and the rest of us with doubles." Everyone made their way to their respective courts and began unpacking bags and stretching out. Yang was whirling his arms about and raising first one leg up almost to his chin and then the next. Lin leaned against a wall and stretched his calve muscles, touched his toes a few times, then shouted to Yang above the sudden noise of the hall. "Shall we get started?"

"All ready," Yang answered, picking out one of what appeared to be a multitude of rackets from his bag and stepping into position on the court. They warmed up slowly, taking lazy steps back to return a high shuttlecock and short steps in to counter a drop. Lin sensed an almost total control from Yang whose motions were sinuous like a cat with never a wasted step. He practically danced around the court, exerting little effort although Lin was soon sweating profusely and they had not even begun to play a game. He knew he was in for a very difficult time.

"Shall we start?" asked Lin.

"Certainly. Up or down?" Yang asked as he spun his racket.

"Up." Yang held the grip out for Lin to see that the "Y" was right side up. "Your serve."

"Ok. Best of luck," said Lin as he retreated to the service line and hit a hard serve to the back corner. Yang stepped back two paces, leapt into the air, and shot the shuttlecock to his backhand. Lin returned it, just barely, but with no pace so that Yang's next shot, easy and graceful and perfectly placed, slipped past Lin's outstretched forehand. This was to be the rhythm of the game, Lin returning a number of shots before Yang put the shuttlecock out of reach. Lin was happy each time that he made Yang work for a shot but he could tell that Yang was holding back, that he was missing some winners in order to keep the rallies going. Thankfully, he did it with grace, with the best of intentions, and Lin, rather than feeling patronized, was grateful. As they became more familiar with one another's shots, the rallies extended to an exhilarating degree. So focused was Lin that he failed to notice that the doubles games had come to a stop and the other players were now standing beside court number one and watching. At one point Yang hit a feathery drop shot from an impossible angle, which Lin could only lunge for and miss, and the crowd clapped appreciatively.

"Game," Lin said, walking to his bag, breathing heavily, and grabbing a towel to wipe his dripping face. "Too good, Yang. I am nowhere near your level but I hope you at least had some exercise."

"I certainly did. An excellent game, Lin. I enjoyed it very much." Yang said extending his hand. He was sweating but barely breathing hard.

The administrator stepped forward. "May I try my luck?" he asked. Lin waved his hand at him. "By all means."

This time, Yang did not hold back but proceeded to trounce the administrator, landing extraordinary shots into every corner of the court and with every conceivable degree of speed. The administrator lunged, stumbled, cursed, and eventually collapsed as Yang extended his hand and thanked him for the game. The administrator had barely the energy to return his handshake.

Meanwhile, someone must have made a phone call to the younger crowd of badminton players who played in the Thursday evening time slot just after them. The sidelines of the court were suddenly filled with young athletes, all having raced over at the news of Yang's prowess and eager to have a try. One by one, they flexed their muscles, stepped out on the court, before being taken systematically apart by Yang. No one came close to beating him although a few gave him a game. Lin and the others eventually drifted away and played some doubles. Lin could not help but notice that the others were eyeing him with a certain amount of admiration, something he had never experienced before, a sudden gain of face through the introduction of his talented friend.

At 7:30 a gong sounded and they all began to pack up their bags to get ready to depart. The younger players pleaded with Yang to stay for the next session but he declined. "I am here with my friend, Comrade Tao, and we are going to get ourselves a well-deserved beer." He looked at Lin with raised eyebrows, who nodded his head affirmatively. "Besides," Yang added, "I am too old to hope that my luck could hold out for another hour or so." The youngsters surrounding him all burst out with incredulous laughter, then gave him their hands and told him to come back anytime. Again, Lin received some curiously respectful looks which he tried not to be too pleased about.

As they stepped out to the cool, early evening, Lin wrapped a towel around his neck and Yang dug a warm-up jacket from his bag.

"There's a place right around the corner where we can get a beer and some small dishes, if that sounds ok to you," Lin said, directing Yang towards the gate. "Probably easiest to leave your bike here."

They strolled past the walls of the school and turned right at a crowded alleyway too small for cars. The wares of the countless small shops poured into the street, an assortment of plastic buckets, plastic wash basins, mops, brooms, toys, and clothes of every sort hanging from hangers attached to wire racks on the walls. Each and every shop appeared to carry the exact same merchandise. Restaurants were dispersed between the shops with cheap plastic chairs and stools and rickety tables. They came upon a row of green grocers, with vegetables and fruit displayed on blankets, clogging the pavement. Next a row of hair saloons sporting piles of black hair outside their doors and laundry racks draped with thin towels. Why the great mounds of hair were kept in a pile and not thrown away had always been a mystery to Lin until he had read that it was often recycled, sold to manufacturers of soy sauce who used it to increase the level of protein in their product.

They weaved their way through the pedestrians and bicycles that snaked through the narrow lane, bells ringing, and the children who sat, crawled, and ran in and out of the traffic, miraculously avoiding injury. They stopped at a small restaurant and found two plastic stools and a table outside. They placed their bags between them, their backs against the wall, and stretched their legs out almost into the street. Each let out a breath of air.

"That was great fun, Yang," Lin said smiling. "You said you were an experienced player but you didn't say just how good you were. How did you manage that?"

"Ah, well," Yang answered modestly. "At the Party School, I did travel with the first team around the province, as I mentioned, even to Beijing and once to Malaysia. But you know how it works when you are in primary school, Lin. The Party Sports Authorities came to our school one day for tryouts when I was nine years old. We were lined up on the sports ground, first 100 meters, then 200, then 400. A bit of ball handling to see if you have hand-eye coordination. Some discus throwing or shotput tossing."

"Ah yes," said Lin with quiet laughter. "I remember that day well. They didn't like my height for running although they had me catch and throw a bit to see if basketball might be an option. Of course, once they saw me run, that was it. I didn't come in dead last but I wasn't far from it." He smiled, before adding: "Not that it would have made much difference. I would never have been a protégé. Like you."

"Well, it didn't start out well for me," said Yang. "My legs were too short to be any good at sprinting. My only chance was the 400, and I was determined. I loved athletics. I knew I could be good but you only had that one chance, that one day, to impress the provincial Party sports people.

"Anyway, I lined up for the 400 and started out slow, as usual, but about the 3rd lap I was gaining on the ones in front. At the 4th lap, I passed the 2nd boy and had my sights on the 1st when a foot reached out, clipped my back foot, which collided with my other foot, and I went flying." He chuckled at the memory. "I landed on all fours, my knees and my palms were bleeding, I had rocks and dirt stuck in my skin, but I jumped up and chased after the boy who'd tripped me, jumped on his back and began to beat him on both ears."

Lin laughed loudly. "What a sight that must have been."

"As it turned out, it saved me, I believe. They liked my spirit even though they were skeptical of my short legs. I'm not sure I would have caught that 1st runner but I certainly caught the one who tripped me."

Lin shook his head in admiration. "So, you Went to a Party Sports School."

"Yes indeed. From the age of 10, I was in the provincial capital. Seven hours of badminton per day. Seven hours of school and homework, an hour of television, the rest for eating and sleeping."

"No wonder you play the way you do."

"Well," said Yang with a sigh, "I might have gone farther with the game but—" he hesitated. "It's a typical sports story. Not in any way special." He raised his pant leg up almost to his thigh and exposed two long, pink, raised scars on his left knee. "You can't play 7 hours a day for that many years, on a surface that hard, and not have knee problems. Unfortunately, they botched the first operation and had to do a second, which worked, thank the heavens. After the operations, it wasn't possible to play at the level I used to. But at least I can still play now, as an old man."

"Ha," Lin snorted. "Hardly an old man's performance tonight. Anyway, I'm very glad you came. It gave me face with my colleagues."

Yang shrugged. "Happy to have been of help." An old woman appeared with a dirty rag and gave the table a half-hearted wipe. She stared at them with vacant eyes.

"Two cold beers, please," said Lin. "And bring some chicken in spicy oil, peanuts with peppers, and smashed cucumber, enough for two." She blinked her eyes, and then disappeared. "The food here is good, despite the service. Northern style. I tend not to eat too much after badminton," he said. "We can always order more if you like."

"No. Cold dishes are good after sport," said Yang.

"Hey," Lin rapped his knuckle on the table. "I've been meaning to ask: did you actually get the pitcher filters from the mill?"

"We did, thanks to you. They came in a truck, right on time. The villagers were quite happy. I didn't take all the credit for myself. I let them know about you and about the meeting at the mill."

"Well, if you wouldn't mind, I wouldn't mention me. I seem to be getting an unexpected, and frankly unwanted, reputation as someone who can right the wrongs of the excesses of the business community, and," here he gave Yang a careful look, "the wrongs of the Communist Party. I am certain that I am on a list of those that have deviated from the Party line, and that I am being watched, all of which has to do with this new reputation of mine."

"Unwanted or not, Lin, it is your reputation." He paused, stared at Lin. "Let's face it; there is much lacking in what the Party offers its most vulnerable citizens."

Lin nodded. "That certainly is the truth, Yang. I know that I don't know you that well, but it seems to me that we are dedicated Party members who are at least aware of the, well, of the failings of the CCP."

The old woman appeared with the beers, the small plates of food, and chopsticks which she set down with a clatter on the semi-clean table. "No hot dishes?" she asked. They both shook their heads and she went away with an incredulous sigh. When she had shuffled through the doorway, Lin continued. "Frankly, I get so tired of being surrounded by Party members who refuse to criticize, who constantly cheer the economy and trade and commerce and the GDP, and never once stop to reflect on where all the cheering will lead. And don't get me wrong, it's incredible what the people have been able to achieve since the opening up, and I say people because I think the Party takes a bit too much credit for simply allowing the Chinese people the freedom to be productive, but I find so little balance within the Party. It's either all good news and numbers, or it's nothing."

He paused, held the beer up. "Cheers, Yang."

"Cheers." They clinked the tops of their bottles together, each took a long swig, Yang burped contentedly and Lin smacked his lips.

"I'm at odds with the Party, as you can see, and not trusted," Lin said with a shrug of his shoulders, using his chopsticks to lift a peanut to his mouth.

"That's a shame," said Yang with a shake of his head. "I am certainly aware of how difficult it is to try and balance the needs of over a billion people but I agree that the emphasis seems to be more on those that have and not so much on those that have not."

"And now we need to find a way to change the emphasis. Well, here's to the two Party members who agree that maybe more balance is better than more GDP."

"Hear, hear," said Yang, as they clinked their bottles together again and drank deeply.

"Enough Party talk," Lin said, first digging into the spicy chicken, then tasting the tangy chunks of garlic and sesame oil that coated the smashed cucumber. "Let's stick to sports."

The discussion turned to whether they thought the badminton star Lin Dan would take gold at the next Olympics set to take place in Beijing in less than two years' time, conceding that the Chinese Malaysian, Lee Chong Wei, would be tough to beat. They agreed that Li Na was a wonder and great for the sport of tennis in China: it was only a matter of time before she won a grand slam. "Also, they don't push the women tennis players so hard," said Yang. "You notice there aren't any Chinese men tennis players on the circuit. That's because they push them too hard, train them too hard, and burn them out before they can even get there." Lin shook his head sympathetically. They concentrated on finishing their beer and food before emphatically denouncing the game of golf, agreeing that it had no place in China, that it was not only the epitome of petite bourgeoise but environmentally unsound.

"Did you get enough to drink? To eat?" Lin asked.

"Absolutely. Now," they both began fumbling in their bags for money, "please let me get this."

"Certainly not," Lin said, indignantly. "You are my guest."

"No, no. You were kind enough to host me for badminton. The least I can do..." Yang held his wallet up triumphantly but Lin was a step ahead of him, on his feet and yelling for the old woman. Yang tried to stand but Lin held him in his seat by his shoulder, laughing, as the woman appeared and took the money from him. "Ha," he said. "I finally beat you at something this evening even if it was only in settling the bill."

"I will not let it happen again," Yang said with a smile as they shouldered their bags and weaved their way through the crowded lane. At the gate of the school, Yang held out his hand. "No need to walk in with me. Thank you for a very pleasant evening. I enjoyed myself."

"And I as well," said Lin, as they shook hands. "Let's do it again."

"Certainly." Yang paused before turning. "And if there is anything I can help you with, Lin, just let me know. Anything."

"Thank you. I hope I don't have to call on your help, but I am grateful for the offer."

As he walked home, a few moments later Yang sped by on his bike, a strong light beaming in front and a red-light blinking behind, waving his arm.

"Be safe," Lin yelled; my friend, he added to himself.

Chapter 15

From what little news Shanshan could get from Zhang, the war was still raging across the country. It seemed the Nationalists and the General had lost their strongholds in the cities of the north and were now being pushed back even from Shanghai and Nanjing. The Chief Magistrate was on the verge of flight: there were fully loaded wagons in the stables ready for teams of oxen to move them at short notice. Thinking of his tin box of money, Shanshan thought it was possibly a good buying opportunity. Wealthy villagers and tradesmen were undecided as to whether to stay or flee south with the General, and this uncertainty would surely affect the price of goods, and eventually of land. But absolute chaos was never good for business. The Nationalists had retreated from the north and the west, they and the General, his downtrodden soldiers and a stream of refuges, fleeing southeast through Fujian Province until they found themselves with their backs against the Straits of Taiwan and only the island left as a refuge. The Chief Magistrate and his ox carts and family and a few of his servants, including Zhang, finally fled along with the retreating army. The economics of the village collapsed with the defeat of the Nationalists and the disappearance of the Chief Magistrate. Meanwhile, the workers now tended the fields and orchards and fishponds as best they could although in no time at all nature had begun to reclaim great swaths of gardens, gates, fields, out buildings, courtyards, and the many sagging walls of the great house. For Shanshan and the workers, it was a free for all to get as much from the abandoned land as possible in order to avoid starvation. There were very few carp left in the ponds which had failed to be re-stocked, although Shanshan was still able to attract the few fish that remained.

The crops suffered the same fate as there was very little seed left to replant and they harvested what they could from the depleted fields. The nuts and the orchards continued to do well but there was fierce competition among the villagers and most everything was pilfered: apples and peaches picked before they were ripe to feed empty bellies. There was food coming in from the countryside but the farmers were asking higher and higher prices, and some had begun to hoard their wheat and rice and beans and corn in the hope of even higher prices to come, or, in the event of a complete collapse, to feed themselves through hard times.

The worker's hovels behind the great house were soon empty, wooden door and window frames taken for firewood, even some of the roofs dismantled to be burned during the few cold months of winter. Shanshan stayed on, having had no desire to join the fleeing Nationalists and having no knowledge and, therefore, no real fear of the Communists. He continued to work from dawn to dusk only this time just to keep alive. The great house was empty save for the few servants who were too old to make the journey southwest, and the two kitchen maids who had been left behind and had claimed the courtyard just off the kitchen for themselves. Shanshan had never seen the kitchen maids before: as a common laborer he had little, if any, contact with the people serving inside the great house, but now he observed them stepping timidly out of the courtyard with baskets to collect whatever they could find to eat. He watched them from a distance, noticing that one was very pretty, clear-skinned with a round face, rounded eyes, and long plaited hair. She moved awkwardly, however, and sometimes carried a crutch, her foot turned inward and dragging along the ground, malformed and almost useless. Her companion was the complete opposite: short and squat, with a pockmarked face and a hair lip. No wonder they had been left behind, Shanshan thought, such damaged goods. He felt sorry for them. They could not possibly have much success scavenging so close to the house. Shanshan himself walked miles to find food; watercress in the northwest tributary, frogs in the shallows of the lake, snakes in the hills, and the occasional partridge egg, he had even repaired a few of the weirs and nets in the lake, all of which required hours of hard hiking or sloshing through cold water. Surely the clubfooted maid could go no farther than a few hundred yards from the great house.

He began to leave food on the doorstep of their courtyard house: carp when he was lucky enough to catch some, fresh cress from the streams around the lake, handfuls of nuts, some corn to grind into meal. Once he had even left a handful of honey wrapped in a large gingko leaf that he had managed to snatch from a hive that he had found in the forest, his hand and arm having been stung badly. He would lay the food down, knock on the door, and then step back a dozen paces. He was always disappointed when the hair lip answered although she was jolly enough and thanked him in a loud voice. But when the clubfoot answered, he was enthralled, her rounded eyes downcast, a shy smile upon her lips, a slight bow of thanks. She is lovely, Shanshan thought, despite her deformity. Each time, he took fewer steps backwards until one day he remained on the doorstep with the food in his hands, an actual carp which he had freshly caught in his nets, a small carp but he knew they would appreciate it. The door, thank heaven, was opened by the clubfoot.

"I have brought a fish," said Shanshan, thrusting it with both hands from his breast awkwardly. He felt the blood rush to his face. "I caught it this morning."

She bowed and turned her eyes to him. "You are very kind. I do not know what we would do without you. And your name?" she asked after hooking her finger through the gill of the fish and letting it hang by her side.

"I am Tao Shanshan."

"I am Jiang Nan. As you can see, the Chief Magistrate would not take us with him to the coast, though we pleaded, so we have been abandoned."

"There are many who have been abandoned." Shanshan ran his hand through his hair, looked thoughtful. "I will do what I can for you, Jiang Nan. I have good days and bad days finding food but I will share what I can with you. I am the last worker left in the north houses, house 15. If you need anything, you can find me there."

"Again, you are very kind, Tao Shanshan. I hope to see you again soon." She gave him a smile which made even more blood rush to his face. He turned quickly, stumbling over his own feet as he left the courtyard.

His dreams now turned from his hidden tin of money to Jiang Nan, which did not disturb his sleep at all.

Chapter 16

The following Monday morning, Lin arrived at his lab to a circus like scene: people were milling about the municipal town building as well as the door to his lab. There were police moving among the crowd, questioning people, and the Public Security Bureau officers were leaning against their black sedans watching closely through their dark glasses. It appeared that half the crowd were gathered to protest some recent landgrabs made by the municipal government, shouting about the injustice of having lost their land for so little compensation and raising their fists in the air. The other half of the crowd had congregated near Lin's lab. As he snaked his way through, he noticed the woman with the sick husband from the village in the northeast hills who appeared to have brought some friends with her. They were squatting beside the door and stood up as he approached.

"Ah, Mrs. Wan," said Lin with a bow. "I hope that your husband is better?"

"I am sad to say that he is dead, Comrade Tao." He could see the anger in her eyes and the set of her mouth. "The village Party Secretary has told me it is unfortunate but that it has nothing to do with the water."

"He is a liar, and corrupt," spat one of Mrs. Wan's friends. "The water is filthy. We have gone to the headwaters of the stream and we saw men with lots of equipment working an old mineshaft, before we were chased away. The Party Secretary and the police have denied everything but they are rich now. It is obvious." Her anger also flashed in her eyes.

"And your husband is also sick?" Lin asked.

"Yes."

"And mine as well," said the other friend. "We have come here because there is no one who will do anything in our village. We thought perhaps you could help."

Lin sighed, fingered the keys to the front door of his lab. "I have made my report. I expect that I will get an answer this week as to whether someone will be sent out from the provincial capital. Unfortunately, there is not much more I can do. Your town is outside our jurisdiction. Have you tried Taoshan town to the north of you?"

"There is no one there who will listen to us either," Mrs. Wan said resignedly.

At that point three farmers stepped forward. "Comrade," one farmer said, removing a bent cigarette from his mouth. "Perhaps you do not remember me but you came to my field a few weeks ago to take samples of the soil."

"Ah yes. I remember." Lin looked around nervously as the people started crowding in on him.

"The ash and soot and smoke from the cement plant has gotten no better. My peanuts and soybeans are a complete loss this year."

"And mine," said the farmer next to him.

Another farmer nodded his head in affirmation.

Lin took another step back, wondering why they had all decided that this Monday morning was the time to come air their grievances and seek a remedy. More people approached, this time the knot of villagers who had spoken to him in front of the used lead battery recycling plant. One of them, a small man in a blue Mao jacket, stepped forward. "Comrade Tao," he said with a bow. "We thank you for your recent visit to our town. We have taken your advice and purchased pitcher filters, at least as many as we could afford. The pollution from the recycling plant has not improved. We are afraid to let our children play outside."

"Yes, yes," Lin said, taking yet another step backward until his back was against the door of his lab. "Listen, everyone," he said in a loud voice. "I have sent my reports about your situations. Citations from the provincial SEPA have been issued and, hopefully, within a few weeks, there will be a visit from a deputy inspector as well as a doctor for those of you and your family and friends who are sick. More, I'm afraid, I cannot tell you." He noticed a black sedan pull up in front of the municipal building and Xiaoping stepped out along with his driver. The crowd surged around them, the driver lashing out with clenched fists, and the police moved in and began to shove people back, pushing an old farmer so hard that he landed on all fours in the dust. The PSB officers began to stir, conferring among themselves and pointing out certain people before disbursing among the crowd. Just then Lin noticed two young men approaching him, athletically dressed and looking out of place. What now, he thought?

"Comrade Tao," they said, gazing about confusedly.

"Ah," Lin said with a smile of recognition. "Badminton players!"

"Yes," they answered. "We came to ask you how we can get in touch with Comrade Ling. We are organizing a tournament in the next—"

"Now is not a good time to talk. As you can see, things are a bit hectic this morning." He was groping with his keys. "He lives in Shunyi village below the mill." Just as he was about to fit one of the keys in the door, a PSB officer appeared at his elbow, his dark glasses making him look like some predatory life-sized insect.

"Why are these people here, Comrade Tao?" he asked in a low, threatening voice.

"I have not invited them here, if that's what you're asking. They have come to see about the progress of reports I have written, that's all."

"Those reports are not their business," he said, reaching out and holding Lin by the elbow. "You should have told these people to mind their own business."

"I told you," Lin said, shaking off the man's hand. "I did not invite these people here. But as to whether it's their business or not," here he felt the anger rise up, "it certainly is their business. And I intend to keep them advised of what is, or is not, going on."

The man took Lin's arm again, only this time in a vice like grip. Lin noticed that another PSB officer had a hold of Mrs. Wan and he was leading her towards the municipal building, and others were marching those they assumed to be ringleaders into the building. The farmer who had been pushed to the ground had moved to a sitting position in the dust and was confusedly rubbing his wrists. Lin shook his head as if he could shake the scene in front of him from his eyes. He turned to the PSB officer and asked, incredulously, "What are you going to do, arrest me?"

With his free hand, the man pulled his jacket back to expose a shoulder holster and pistol and then proceeded to march Lin through the crowd, many of whom shouted after him, up the stairs, into the lobby, and down to the cellar to what could only be the municipal lockup. They passed Xiaoping on the landing in close consultation with his vice-Mayors and looking exasperated. If he noticed Lin being led down the stairs, he gave no indication of it.

"What are you charging me with?" Lin asked. "I would like to know," he spaced each word out carefully, "what - are - you - charging - me - with." The man didn't answer, simply dragged him across the rough concrete floor until he was standing in front of a small desk where a fat cop told him to empty his pockets into a plastic basket with a number on it. "Phone, wristwatch, belt, shoelaces."

"Shoelaces?" Lin asked in disbelief.

The cop shot up, punched him in the chest hard, and shook a finger in his face. "Empty your pockets. Phone, wristwatch, belt, shoelaces," he shouted. Lin, shocked, did as he was told, fumbling with shaking fingers to undo his laces. The officer behind him took him by the arm again as the cop at the desk got up and opened the large metal door which led down a hallway with rows of narrow doors on both sides. At the end on the left, the officer opened the heavy, metal door and shoved Lin in; it closed behind him and the key was turned in the lock. He listened to the footsteps fade away.

The cell was no more than twelve feet long and maybe half as wide, with a narrow metal bed bolted to the floor taking up half the space. In place of a mattress was a piece of plywood, a worn blanket folded at the foot. There was a tiny sink in one corner and a squat toilet in the other, just a porcelain hole at floor level with a footrest on either side. There was no window although Lin could see high up on the wall an opening covered with metal bars which led to a grate on the street. He sat on the plywood bed, rubbed his chest where the cop's fist had struck him, rubbed his forehead with the palms of both hands, and then stared at nothing for what seemed like hours but could have been minutes. He was totally helpless, unable to contact anyone, unable to plead his case. He let out what he thought was a scream but turned out to be a pitiable groan. At one point, he jumped up and began pacing, three short steps between the door and the wall, the last step landing on the footrest of the toilet, spinning around, back again, and back again. He could hear muffled sounds through the grate from the street: cars, voices, someone moving a wheelbarrow or a cart, grunting and cursing. Eventually, he fell onto the plywood bed, exhausted. He must have slept until he heard the key turning in the lock of the cell door, and Xiaoping stepped in, leaned against the tiny washbasin, a cigarette in his hand. From the fading light, he assumed it was late afternoon.

"Must you smoke?" Lin asked, blinking his eyes slowly.

"That's all you have to say?" Xiaoping said with a sneer as he ground his cigarette out on the floor.

"What do you want me to say? I want you to get me out of here; that's what I want."

"It's not that easy, Lin, now the PSB are involved. I don't think you understand the trouble you're in."

"Yes. Once again, I'm in trouble for doing my job. What exactly are they accusing me of?"

"Incitement of a crowd. Stirring up trouble. Plotting against the state."

Lin shook his head. "And you're not telling them otherwise."

"I agree with them, although not with the last charge," Xiaoping said with a shrug.

"Like father, like son."

"Exactly. Your father was a fool, and so are you."

"And your father was a corrupt party official and a—"

"Don't say it, Lin. It doesn't do any good. He was a pragmatist. And neither of us would be here if he didn't do what he did."

This time it was Lin's turn to shrug.

"So, can you get me out of here or what?" he asked after a long silence.

"No. No I can't. The PSB want to keep you here until they finish questioning all the people involved in the incident this morning. Once they have completed their investigation, they will probably let you go with a warning. That is my guess."

"How long will that be?"

"A few days, maybe," said Xiaoping.

"Can I talk to Chen at least?"

"You cannot talk to anyone but I told Chen what happened and she is going to bring you a change of clothes and some toiletries."

"So that's it, then."

Xiaoping nodded his head.

"Ok. Go away, please, brother," Lin said turning his head to the wall and wrapping the blanket around his shoulders. Xiaoping shook his head in disgust, swinging the heavy door open, almost hitting the policeman standing on the other side. Their steps echoed down the hallway until Lin heard the key turn in the lock. He pulled his legs under him in a lotus position and lifted the blanket up over his head.

Chapter 17

Lin barely slept that night; each time he woke, he wondered why he was not in his own bed and then the events of the day before crashed in on him and kept him awake. Thankfully the morning finally came and the door was opened by a policeman who set a bowl of rice porridge with pickled vegetables and preserved egg on the floor along with a bucket of water to pour down the barely functioning drain of the toilet. Lin ate the porridge slowly, then began his pacing, three steps, turn, three steps, turn, until he was tired and then sat cross-legged on the plywood bed and again pulled the blanket over his head. He thought about Madame Sun and how he might get ahold of her. Chen would certainly try to do it, he thought, despite hearing Xiaoping's explanation about the PSB investigation and his assurance that Lin would be released in a few days. When a paper bag arrived later in the morning with a change of clothes and a toothbrush and toothpaste, he was hoping there might be a note inside from Chen but obviously the PSB would have searched the bag. He took his clothes off, used the water dripping from the tiny sink to give himself as much of a bath as possible, and brushed his teeth. While he was changing into his clothes, he heard shouting from the other end of the hallway. He put his ear to the small, barred window of the door and could distinctly hear Comrade Ling Yang's voice raised in anger.

"I am here to see Comrade Tao Lin and I am not leaving until I do so," Yang shouted. "It is outrageous that you are keeping a Party member in jail and not allowing him to contact anyone. I have talked to your supervisor this morning, who is a colleague of mine. Call him now, and then open this door immediately."

The cop guarding the jail fumbled with his phone, punched in the number, then gave his name. There was a pause. "Yes," he said. Another pause. "Yes. I will." The policemen put the phone down and stood, warily eyeing Yang, as he reached for the keys hanging on his belt. "You have ten minutes," he said to Yang.

"I am a Party Secretary," Yang growled, stepping toward the guard, fists clenched. "And I am visiting a Party member and deputy inspector of SEPA and I will take as much time as I think necessary."

"I will need to search you," the guard said carefully but not before retreating behind his desk. "No phones allowed. No sharp objects. Those are the rules," he added, his voice, at the end, almost apologetic.

Yang looked at him with contempt, wondering whether to continue the battle, before quietly acquiescing and depositing his phone and the contents of his pockets into a plastic tray. The policeman swung the door open and they proceeded down the hall to Lin's cell. He opened the door, hesitated, before Yang yelled. "Go. I will call for you when I am done."

When the main door had closed, Yang shook his head and put his hand out. Lin smiled, taking his outstretched hand.

"Thank you, Yang. You don't know how good it is to see you. How did you know I was here?"

"Some badminton players reached me this morning and said they'd seen you being led into the municipal building by the PSB. Luckily, I have a colleague on the Security Committee who works closely with them. He has authorized my visit."

"Well, I'm awfully glad you managed it. I've never been in this situation before." Lin shook his head. "It's not pleasant."

"It's outrageous, Lin. The power of the PSB is out of all proportion. I did have a discussion with my colleague who said that, as far as he knew, they intended to release you as soon as they complete their investigation, probably by tomorrow evening. I'm not sure whether that's the case or not," Yang said, leaning against the sink. "The fact that you are in jail at all does not give me confidence." He ran a hand through his hair. "You know, Lin, these PSB goons and these cops are the worst, so arrogant, how they demean you. Like that cop at the door, trying to make me feel like a nobody. How I wanted to crush his fat skull." Yang raised his shaking clenched hands and made as if to strangle something.

"Unfortunately, in this situation, it's me against the police state. In any event," Lin said with a somewhat weak show of bravado, "I suspect they will release me soon, even sooner then they like if the head of the SEPA in Beijing, Madame Sun, gets involved. And afterwards, of course, they will keep me under a tight watch. I've made too many enemies in this town to be left alone to simply go about my business." Lin leaned towards Yang. "I need to use my connections in Beijing, Yang. I need you to get in touch with Madame Sun. I am pretty sure that my wife, Chen, has already managed to reach her but, just to be safe, I would really appreciate if you could contact someone in her office, hopefully her secretary, who knows me. Just leave my name and tell them the situation. I am sure that she will help."

"Leave it with me, my friend. I will do whatever it takes to reach her. In the meantime," he looked around the cell with disgust, "if there is anything I can bring you."

"No, thank you. I've had a change of clothes from my wife, and now that I have talked to you, I am feeling much better."

"Well, let me get to work on getting in touch with Madame Sun. Hopefully you will be out of here by nightfall but it may involve another night." Again, he surveyed the cell with distaste.

"I am very grateful, Yang. Another night won't kill me. More than that, though, and I might start beating my head against the wall."

"We'll get you out before then." They shook hands, and Yang stepped into the hallway. "Guard," he growled in a threatening voice. The main door opened immediately and the cop hurried down the hallway.

"We will talk soon. Tomorrow at the latest," Yang said over his shoulder.

"Many thanks again."

The door was closed in Lin's face. The footsteps faded down the hall until he heard the dreaded clang of the main door slamming shut and the key scraping in the lock.

Madam Sun sat behind a large desk piled with folders and reports and documents. A heavy woman with greying hair and dark circles under her piercingly sharp eyes, she gazed out the window of her 7th floor corner office at the traffic on the 3rd ring road. An endless stream of automobiles and buses and scooters, headlights glaring, stretched out in both directions, barely moving, a swirl of smog drifting up from the road. Every night she looked out on this scene and thought of how Beijing had been built backwards: they tore down the city walls and started with highways and ring roads and flyovers instead of subways and elevated trains and pedestrian walkways. Even the famous Beijing bike lanes were clogged with automobiles, or being squeezed out of existence altogether, fallen prey to the power of the combustible engine. The city is an environmental disaster, she thought, and anyone with the power to change it had their heads buried in the sand. Madame Sun's secretary knocked lightly on the half open door and bustled in, a folder held tightly against his chest. He took a seat in front of the desk.

"What have you got for me, Dawei," she said, talking her eyes from the window. The man shifted in his seat, pushed his glasses off his nose with a delicate finger, and sighed. "Since we received word from Tao Lin's wife and from a Party Secretary Ling Yang, I have spoken with the PSB official in charge of Meiyu town and the lake district. He says the charges against Tao Lin are serious, that he has been responsible for subverting the power of the state, picking quarrels and making trouble, and undermining public order by creating a disturbance in a public place."

"Yes, yes," said Madame Sun wearily. "Of course that is what he says, Dawei. He is the head of the provincial PSB. That is what they always say because they are dull, ordinary, power-drunk gangsters. Tao Lin is no more guilty of those charges than I. What did this whatshisname say about his release?"

"First Lieutenant Zhu. He says it is pending the outcome of their investigation."

"Get him on the phone. Now." She pushed the phone towards her secretary, a hard edge to her voice. Dawei shuffled through the folder, found the number, and dialed.

"Put it on speakerphone," Madame Sun ordered.

It was minutes before a voice answered, "Yes?"

"First Lieutenant Zhu?" asked Madame Sun.

"I am First Lieutenant Zhu."

"And I am Madame Sun, head of SEPA, calling from Beijing. You spoke with my secretary, Dawei, earlier."

"Yes, Madame Tao. And I explained to your secretary—"

She cut him off sharply. "It is not you who are going to explain anything, Comrade Zhu. It is I who is going to do the explaining. Tao Lin is a Deputy Inspector with SEPA and one of my most trusted workers. He has never before been involved in the nonsense that you are charging him with and I want him released immediately." She paused, a glint in her alert eyes. "You may find getting a call from the head of an important administration in Beijing uncomfortable, but, as you are no doubt aware, we are due to be designated a Ministry by the President himself in the coming months, and then you will find a call like this more than just uncomfortable." Another pause, in which they could hear Comrade Zhu breathing rather heavily, and fiercely exhaling smoke from a cigarette.

"We are completing our investigation into the matter concerning Tao Lin," came the heavy voice of First Lieutenant Zhu.

"When you complete your investigation is of no interest to me," said Madame Tao. "Nor does it matter whether Deputy Inspector Tao Lin is in jail during your investigation or not. He is a Communist Party Member in good standing and has served the party faithfully and at a very high level for many years."

There was more heavy exhaling on the line.

"Comrade Zhu," said Madame Sun, clear exasperation in her voice. "It would be a mistake to make me spend my evening contacting certain members of the Central Committee."

"I will see what can be done."

"Excellent," she said with a lift in her voice. "His immediate release is what can, and will, be done."

There was no response from First Lieutenant Zhu.

Madame Sun continued. "One other thing which might be of interest. Tao Lin is due to be in Beijing very soon to receive the People's Model Worker Award, the highest award given for government service at the State Environmental Protection Administration. It would be most unfortunate, Comrade Zhu, if people in Beijing found out that a future model worker recipient was improperly jailed by the Public Security Bureau shortly before receiving the award."

Dawei looked up quizzically at Madame Sun when he heard this, and she smiled slightly.

Officer Zhu began mumbling something about there being nothing improper about the investigation when Madame Sun leaned in towards the telephone, a grimace on her lips. "I want it done now." Before he could answer, she snapped. "My secretary will follow up this evening to make sure that it has been done." She punched the disconnect button.

Dawei was still giving her a quizzical look. "I thought about it this afternoon," she said. "After all, it is in my power to give Tao Lin the award, and he certainly deserves it. Plus, I like the irony of it: it will completely confuse the tiny minds of the bureaucrats in that provincial little backwater he chose to return to. And hopefully, it will protect him in the future."

Chapter 18

A few hours after Lin had received his bowl of rice porridge for dinner, and just as he was wondering how he would get through another long evening on the plywood bed of his cell, he heard footsteps from the hallway. The key scraped in the lock and a guard appeared in the doorway and gestured for him to come out.

"Bring all your belongings," the guard said. Lin shoved his dirty clothes and toothbrush and toothpaste into the paper bag and followed the guard down the hallway and out into the spaciousness of the hall. He felt himself stretching to his full height and breathing deeply as the plastic tray holding his belongings appeared in front of him and he stuffed everything in his pockets, threaded the belt through his pants and laced his shoes. "Am I free to go?" he asked.

"There are people waiting for you in the mayor's office. I am to take you there immediately," said the guard.

Lin went up the stairs behind the sweating, panting guard, through the foyer, past the large reception desk of the municipal government building, and down the hall to the first office, its door wide open. Inside Xiaoping sat at his desk flanked by two PSB officers standing one on each side who were unfamiliar to Lin, no doubt down from the provincial capital. All had cigarettes in their hands and mobile telephones pressed to their ears when the guard led Lin to the center of the room. Xiaoping motioned for him to sit as he snapped the phone shut and stubbed out his cigarette. The two PSB officers slowly ended their conversations, closed their phones, and turned to stare at Lin.

"You appear to have friends in high places, Comrade Tao," said Xiaoping.

"More friends than I have around here, Mr. Mayor," Lin said, giving Xiaoping a hard look.

"You have no friends here because all you do is make enemies, as we have discussed many times before."

One of the PSB officers cleared his throat. "Comrade Tao. There is a possibility that you will be charged with the following crimes: organizing an illegal demonstration, inciting a crowd, stirring up trouble, and plotting against the state. Are you aware what the penalties may be for these charges?"

Lin leaned back in his chair and stretched out his long legs. "I'm sure it's any number of years in prison, Comrade, but thankfully I am not guilty of the charges: I did not organize the demonstration; it was spontaneous and completely out of my control. Nor did I incite the crowd. On the contrary, I told them to wait until there was a response from my reports and I would speak to them then. The only trouble I cause, and the only plotting I do, is when I do my job, reporting on the environmental degradation in my jurisdiction and exposing the people responsible for it. If that is a crime than, yes, I am guilty."

The other officer stepped around Xiaoping, parked half of his heavy backside on the edge of the desk, and leaned in very close to Lin. His breath was putrid. "You are not liked here, Comrade Tao. You do not appear to understand the rules of the game and how to play it. I suggest you study the rules closely because if you fail to play the game properly, there will be serious consequences." He gave Lin a dangerous stare before adding, "and you need not ask me if that is a threat: it is." He leaned back, removed his weight from the desk and returned to his place next to Xiaoping.

The other officer chimed in. "You will be watched closely, Comrade Tao. Your movements will be watched and your reports will be monitored to ensure they are not being used to plot against the state."

"So, are you telling me that I should stop doing my job? That I should suddenly agree with everyone in this town that it's fine to destroy the lake and everything around it?" He paused, glaring at the three of them, before asking, "Have I got that right?"

They did not even bother to answer, simply looked at him as they might look at something unpleasant stuck to the bottom of their shoe.

"You may go," Xiaoping said wearily as he lit another cigarette and pulled a pile of folders towards him. Lin grabbed his bag and left without looking back. Once outside, he breathed deeply, grateful to be outside and to feel the sky above him as he climbed onto his bike and pedaled to his apartment.

Chen was waiting for Lin when he got home, Xiaoyu fast asleep with her head cradled in Chen's lap. She gave Lin a look of weary relief that he was home as she slipped out from under Xiaoyu's head and stood. They hugged quickly before moving quietly into the kitchen and sat at the table.

"I'm glad you're out," Chen said. "I suppose because of Madame Sun. It took forever to get ahold of someone in her office."

"Yes. Thank you for that. Have we got any beer?" Lin suddenly asked, feeling a great thirst. Chen got up and rummaged in the back of the fridge and found a bottle. She opened it and set it in front of him and then sat down heavily. Lin took a long, satisfying swig. "It was not my fault, Chen," he explained. "Everything conspired against me. Why all those people had to turn up at the same time on a Monday morning is a total mystery. Even some badminton players showed up to ask how to get in touch with Ling Yang. Not only that, there happened to be a bunch of farmers demonstrating against a government land grab." Here he looked closely at Chen. "Maybe that's something you know about."

How was she to know that it would be on that same Monday morning, she thought, feeling slightly guilty, but she straightened up, brushing aside the comment. "It's not a mystery, Lin, why these people show up. They come because you give them hope, false hope in fact. I can't see how it's your job to be making promises to people."

"My job involves trying to prevent and solve environmental disasters. If that gives people hope, so be it."

"Oh, Lin," she said, looking completely dejected. He wished so much that he could make her feel otherwise as she continued. "The real point is that you've made too many enemies in this town. They were just waiting for something, some excuse, to put you in jail and they found it yesterday morning. But if not yesterday, then they would have found something else."

"But here I am. I'm not in jail."

"Only because of Madame Sun." Chen stared at the table while Lin slowly turned his bottle in a circle. She finally broke the uncomfortable silence. "I don't think it's a good idea to depend entirely on Madame Sun. You need to try and find some middle ground between your job and your high ideals and the people of the town. Otherwise, they are going to lock you up again, and for much, much longer."

"You know that SEPA will be designated a Ministry in a short time."

"Yes." Chen shook her head sadly. "And don't you know what that means?"

"It means," Lin said triumphantly, "that I will soon issue Ministry level reports that will demand action. Don't you see, Chen? Xiaoping and Bing and Xi Peng and the SOEs and all the rest will have to comply and we can start to save the lake. Even the President said that environmental issues are going to be a high priority in the next 5-year plan." There was a fire in his eyes.

"Your being naïve, Lin. It means that they will do all they can to put you away before you ever get that power."

"There's always Madame Sun," he said with a bright smile.

"Hopefully," Chen said frowning.

"Be more positive, Chen, for heaven's sake. I'm positive and I just spent a night in jail."

At that, she had to smile, but it was not long before the frown returned.

Chapter 19

At 7:30 a.m., as Lin was preparing breakfast for himself and Xiaoyu, his phone rang. He noticed the Beijing number on the screen, looked at his daughter and put a finger to his lips, and stepped into the living room.

"Madame Sun," he said with affection. "I can't thank you enough for all you've done."

"Forget that, Lin," she said, a gruff warmth in her voice. "I do not let PSB goons put any of my workers in jail. I hope that you have survived the experience."

"Yes. It was not pleasant, though, and quite unnecessary."

"We can go into the specifics when we meet: soon, hopefully. You see, you have been recommended for the SEPA Model Worker Award and I am almost certain that you will win it. I will know for sure by the end of the day once the votes are counted." She paused, said something to someone in a fierce whisper. Already in the office, Lin thought, giving orders and making people jump. "In two weeks," she continued, "you will fly up to Beijing for the ceremony, which is on a weekend so you shouldn't miss any work appointments. I hope that is amenable to you."

"I don't know what to say," Lin stuttered. "I'm shocked. Flattered. Embarrassed," he added with a laugh.

"Well, it's what you deserve. I will send a notice to the provincial SEPA, and they will send someone down to meet with you and take you to the airport. Oh, and just for fun I will have Dawei inform the Party Secretary and Mayor of whatever the name of that town you live in and they will have to put your picture up on the Committee Room wall."

"Meiyu town, soon-to-be-designated small city. Yes, thank you. That would, indeed, be fun."

"Well, I have much to do today so take care of yourself, Lin, and I look forward to seeing you here in the Capitol City in a few weeks."

"Thank you again, Madame Sun, I can't begin to tell—" The ring tone buzzed in his ear. A busy woman, he thought, and grinned, and no nonsense. For many people, she could be abrupt and off putting unless you knew her ways.

Lin returned to the kitchen where Xiaoyu was finishing her rice porridge and he joined her at the table. He blew on his tea and took a loud slurp, staring at nothing and smiling at the thought of his picture up on the wall of the Committee Room for everyone to see. His phone rang again and he noticed the number of a chief inspector at the provincial SEPA office as he punched the receiver button. "Comrade Bei," he said. "What can I do for you this morning."

"Comrade Lin," said Bei. "I hope I am not disturbing you so early."

"Not at all. I have just gotten off the phone with Madame Sun."

"As have I," he answered. "First, a congratulations on your Model Worker award."

"Well, thank you. I don't believe it's official yet."

"I don't believe Madame Sun would announce anything unless she was sure of the outcome." There was a pause. "She wants me to come down to see you at the end of next week, and to meet with the mayor, and, of course to deliver a copy of your Model Worker award for the Committee Meeting room." Here he gave a small snort of what sounded like sarcastic approval. "I also thought we could pay a visit to the village above the northwest tributary that you mentioned in your report, the one with the suspected illegal mining operation at the headwaters. It would be good to confirm what you have already surmised in your report. I know that Taoshan town was supposed to investigate but they appear to have no interest. As you know, that's Comrade Tang's territory so he has more than likely come to a beneficial arrangement with the village Party Secretary." He paused before continuing. "By the way, we have extended your jurisdiction to include the village and the headwaters, as you requested."

"I thank you for that," said Lin.

"Well, you may not be so thankful once you see what is going on up there. It sounds wild and not exactly safe. We will have to be careful."

"I'll be happy to have your company for such an investigation."

"Good. On Friday we can travel back together and I will drop you off at the airport. Your flight is scheduled for 15:00. It has all been arranged here."

"Excellent," answered Lin. "I look forward to seeing you next week."

"Yes," said Comrade Bei. "Until then."

As the line went dead, Lin was already thinking about what they were sure to discover at the headwaters and the logistics of issuing what would hopefully be a final and immediate cease and desist on the mining operation. He also considered whether there would be time to visit the lead battery recycling plant at some point. He had not had a visit from someone from the provincial capital since early summer and he might as well take advantage of it. If a short time in prison and threats from the PSB were intended to dampen Lin's enthusiasm, it appeared to be having the opposite effect.

He stayed close to his lab that week and the next, aware that the PSB were keeping an eye on him, always an officer with dark sunglasses leaning against a black sedan when he left the apartment for work and when he left the lab. He filed a number of reports, sure that they would be opened and read, but he was hopeful that eventually they would be delivered to the provincial SEPA. After all, there was nothing in the least revolutionary, or counter-revolutionary, about them. To be safe, though, he filed multiple reports by various means, both electronic and mail, including having the reports posted by colleagues in other towns. The PSB were powerful, well-funded and well-manned, but like all unruly bureaucracies, they were not always coordinated and they were inherently lazy.

He had thought about contacting Mrs. Wan in the village before they paid their visit. After making some inquiries, he had learned that she had been released from jail some days ago, but he decided that perhaps she had had enough of dealing with the police. She would be under surveillance, undoubtedly, and threatened with jail at the least provocation so best to leave her be.

On Thursday morning at 9 a.m., Comrade Bei was waiting beside his car when Lin arrived at his lab. He was a small thin man with dark, dyed hair which made him look younger than his fifty or so years, and wire-rimmed spectacles which gave him the look of an intellectual. The few times that Lin had met Comrade Bei, he had admired him for his seriousness of purpose, his scientific knowledge, and his surprising sense of humor, although he was unsure as to where exactly he stood on the corruption meter. They shook hands and Comrade Bei nodded towards the black sedan parked on the side of the street, a heavy, plainclothes PSB man with the inevitable dark glasses and a cigarette dangling from his mouth watching them closely.

"You've made knew friends." he said with a smile.

"And what good friends we've become," Lin laughed, giving a wave to the officer who watched with a stony expression. "They are outside my apartment each and every morning and evening, and here outside my lab all day. What a waste of time and energy," Lin said, shaking his head in disbelief.

"Waste is what the PSB does best, I believe." Comrade Bei said. "Shall we get started?"

"Of course. Let me just get a case of beakers. We can collect samples in the village and at the headwaters, which I wasn't able to do before, although the samples below the village were a pretty good indication." Lin undid the two key locks and the outside padlock, switched on the lights, and located the beakers. He thought about bringing something heavy and easy to swing in case there was trouble but then put such thoughts out of his mind; he was a deputy inspector with SEPA here with a chief inspector from the provincial capital and anything out of the ordinary was not something he wanted to consider.

Lin closed up the lab, placed the beakers in the back seat, and climbed in beside Comrade Bei. The car, a new model Chinese Xiali, was all shiny plastic and smelling of air freshener, with a character for luck woven in bright red string hanging from the mirror. Lin found the seat not particularly comfortable, his knees up around his chest until he could figure out how to adjust it.

"Pretty new, is it?" Lin asked as they made their way north out of town, the PSB officer following leisurely behind.

"As you know, we got budgeted for a Chinese automobile so this is it."

"And? Are you happy with it?"

"Four wheels and a roof in case it rains," said Comrade Bei. "That's about all I care to know when it comes to cars."

"Same," Lin replied as they dodged the heavy morning traffic through the town. "Although I am curious about the quality of Chinese automobiles. I mean, why is it that the Japanese and the Koreans can manufacture good, solid automobiles for the international market and we can barely manufacture a few cars domestically."

"It's the joint venture model," Comrade Bei answered confidently. "There's no incentive and no reason to innovate. By law, all our manufacturers are in bed with foreign companies, and that makes them less than energetic and unmotivated. All they have to do is sit back and collect fifty percent of the profits for basically doing nothing."

"Yes. I've heard that side of the argument. The other is that we are just not developed enough to produce an internationally marketable car. I think we will only manufacture something decent when the technology changes, not with a conventional gasoline combustion engine. Electric, or hydrogen, maybe. Something where we can get ahead of the foreigners."

Comrade Bei shrugged his shoulders, swerved around a three wheeled tractor loaded with farmworkers, and checked in his rearview window for the PSB. "Do you think he is going to follow us all day?"

"Looks like it," said Lin as they passed outside of town and approached the causeway and the last of the wetlands on their left.

"Ah yes, that reminds me," said Lin with a wave of his hand at the acres of cattails and sawgrass waving in the wind. "Whose idea was it to let the town develop half of the wetlands? I thought it had been decided definitively to keep it as a nature preserve."

"Someone had some influence over our deputy head although I don't know the specifics. You know what they say, Comrade Tao, about SEPA deputy heads, don't you?" Comrade Bei asked with a grin. "The only honest deputy head is one who is bribed and stays bribed."

Lin let out a barking laugh as they reached the road that ran along the northwest tributary, turned left, and came up to the tannery and shoe factory. The water today was a bright, coppery red so it must be red leather coloring day at the tannery.

"I see there hasn't been any improvement at the shoe factory," said Comrade Bei, nodding to the unreal color of the water.

"What can we do?" asked Lin. "I write my reports, you issue your citations, and we are generally ignored."

"That will change, Comrade, that will change. Hopefully before the end of winter we will be designated a Ministry and then we will no longer be ignored."

"Yes. I am optimistic," Lin sighed, "but I can also see the usual enforcement difficulties, a lack of manpower, and mayors and Party Secretaries still siding with business. Not to mention," he said with a grin, "deputy heads staying bribed."

Comrade Bei smiled. "Things will change. It has to, or the country will sink under the weight of all this pollution."

"I hope you're right," said Lin with some conviction. He turned and looked behind them, gave a wave to the PSB man on their tail, before settling in for the drive and a companiable silence.

Chapter 20

After a few hours, they reached the farmhouse below the village where Lin had spent the night. It had taken them about a fifth of the time it took Lin when he was riding his bike; he did not dispute the convenience and efficiency of the combustion engine, just the sustainability. Also, he was sure that his bicycle seat was quite a bit more comfortable than the passenger seat of a Xiali.

"Now," said Lin, all business. "You've read my report so you know what to expect at the headwaters. You should also know that the village Party Secretary, Fang Shu, is a slippery character, along with his policeman co-conspirator and his goons. They were the ones who spilled my samples on the ground and kicked me out of town." Comrade Bei nodded, then turned to Lin with a serious expression.

"What do you think, Comrade Tao? Will they use force to stop us? I suppose it depends on the size of the operation but I suspect we should be prepared."

"There's money involved," said Lin, "so there's always the possibility that they will. We'll get no support from the police, of course. In fact, just the opposite."

They had reached the village square, and Comrade Bei parked the car. "I have told our agent in Taoshan where we are," he said, switching off the ignition and setting the parking brake. "One call, and he will be here."

"Good," Lin said, reaching into the back for his sample case and his bag. "Now. I suggest we make our way through town slowly before heading up the trail to the headwaters. If some of the villagers want to talk to us, well, we can listen. But considering our company," here he nodded behind him to the PSB officer who had parked on the other side of the square, "and the reception we will get from Fang Shu and his policeman and his goons, probably best not to attract too much attention from the villagers."

"Agreed."

Lin stepped out of the car, stretched and rolled his neck back and forth a few times before slipping the strap of the bag over his head and onto the small of his back. Comrade Bei locked the car and hoisted a small knapsack on his shoulder which Lin assumed contained the paperwork and the chops for issuing the citation to the village Party Secretary. The day was cool and relatively clear, and the muddy red and yellow walls of the village houses looked positively pretty in the sunshine. Lin took a last glance at the black sedan. The PSB officer had tilted the seat back and appeared to be preparing himself for a long nap.

Before they had gotten halfway across the square, some children began to appear, shyly poking their heads out of alleyways and doorways. Lin recognized Mrs. Wan's son, who stuck his head between the strips of plastic hanging in front of his door as Lin nodded to him. The boy looked down before shuffling out to the square.

"I am sorry about your father," Lin said. The boy continued to look at the ground but shrugged his shoulders slightly.

"And how is your mother?" Just then Mrs. Wan rushed through the doorway to greet Lin.

"You have come," she said gratefully.

"We have come," said Lin with a smile, then turned to introduce Comrade Bei.

"I am very pleased to meet you," she said. "I take it you will inspect the headwaters today. I could show you the way, if you like."

"Considering what happened last week and our little adventure in jail, it may be best for you to avoid being with us," Lin said.

Mrs. Wan looked at them, then at her son. "My husband is gone and, of course, I need to look after my son. His grandparents are too old to be of much help and mine died long ago. Perhaps you are right," she said resignedly. "In any event, there is a trail through the nut trees at the top of the village which is well marked. If you follow it and keep close to the stream, you should have no difficulties. You should reach the mining site in under an hour."

"Thank you," said Lin kindly. "I am sure we can find our way." He noticed from the corner of his eye the man in the red Chicago Bulls ballcap who had poured out his beakers and followed him last time he was here. He was watching them carefully and whispering into his mobile phone before walking hastily towards the main street.

As they made their way out of the square, the many children who had suddenly appeared tagged along beside them. Occasionally, a man or woman would appear and ask them if they were doctors.

"We are with the State Environmental Protection Administration," answered Lin patiently. "We are going to do some tests on the water in the village and at the headwaters."

They all answered that the water was filthy and that it was making them sick.

"Once we have made our inspection, we will see about getting a doctor here to help," said Lin. As they came to the police station, the gaggle of children fell timidly away when Party Secretary Fang Shu appeared on the front steps.

"Comrades from the State Environmental Protection Administration," he said with a magnanimous wave of his hand and a forced smile. "Welcome to our village. And Comrade Tao, welcome again to our village. Won't you come in and join me for a cup of tea?"

Lin heard the sound of a motorcycle start up, the engine revving mercilessly, the clutch popping and the tires squealing before the noise faded as it climbed out of town. He turned to face Fang Shu. "We are not interested in tea. We are interested in seeing the operation at the headwaters and finding the source of the water contamination," he said.

"There is no operation that I know of. And as to contamination, I said before it must be coming from elsewhere."

"We will soon find out, and then I will be back for that cup of tea," said Comrade Bei with a nod of his chin. Fang Shu merely lit a cigarette and pushed his thick glasses up on his nose with a nicotine-stained finger.

They made their way through the village and into fields of flinty soil full of corn and sweet potatoes. There were mules tethered along the banks of the stream and farmers working the fields with hoes and shovels, and others with rickety ladders pruning the orchards and nut trees. The farmers stopped to watch them as they wound their way up the hill to the trail at the top and disappeared into a tangle of woods. Lin noticed tire tracks on the trail and there was a faint smell of exhaust hanging in the air.

"The policeman is ahead of us," he said to Comrade Bei. "No doubt trying to clean up the operation before we get there. He won't be able to do much other than hide the workers and perhaps some of the equipment."

The trial was rutted and rocky, thick with locust trees, scrub pine and gorse, none of it tall enough to keep out the strong sunlight. They were soon sweating, Comrade Bei struggling with the uneven ground on his short legs. They could hear the murmur of the stream to their right, and to their left the sound of someone in the woods following them, not trying terribly hard to be inconspicuous. Occasionally, Lin could make out the bright red flash of a ballcap. He tapped Comrade Bei on the shoulder, nodding his head in the direction of the sound, to which Comrade Bei nodded acknowledgment. After almost an hour of steady climbing, they came to a clearing on the side of a hill with a wide tunnel entrance shored up by uncut logs. The cop was in front of the tunnel, leaning his ample backside against the seat of the bike and smoking a cigarette. They looked around at the trampled earth, at the wheel tracks of heavily loaded carts running towards the stream, but they saw no sign of life.

"Well, well. What have we here? Inspectors from the State Environmental Protection Administration. What a pleasant surprise." They stood in front of him, catching their breath and looking around.

"As you can see," the policeman said, "this is an abandoned site. We have never seen or heard of anyone here."

"I'm sure you haven't," said Lin sarcastically. "But we'll have a look around anyway." He started taking pictures of the site with his mobile as he stepped towards the tunnel entrance, noticing a large six-cylinder generator on a four wheeled trailer parked just inside along the wall. They must have had a hell of a time wrestling that up the trail, he thought.

"I wouldn't go too deep into that shaft," the cop said as he spat in the dirt. "Probably not safe after all these years."

"I don't have to go far," said Lin, "to see that people have been working this shaft very recently." He stepped into the darkness, clicked the light from his mobile on. From the generator he could make out a tangle of electrical lines running down into the mine as well as the tracks where the cart was wheeled in and out. There were even piles of fresh-looking refuse along the walls containing instant noodle wrappers and wooden chopsticks and bottles and tins. He was sure the workers were down there, directed to keep quiet by the cop, but how far down Lin didn't know. Nor did he particularly want to find out. There was not much more the workers could tell him that wasn't already in evidence all around him.

Lin left the tunnel, stepped out into the sunlight, skirted the cop who continued to lean on his motorcycle while leisurely inspecting his fingernails, and followed the tracks around the hill towards the stream. There he found Comrade Bei examining a set of trommels used to crush the ore and taking photos with his mobile; the grinding wheels were shiny with recent use. Again, they followed the well-worn trail until they came to a wooden shed which was locked but between the wooden slats they could see clearly marked blue and white plastic barrels containing supplies of mercury and cyanide. Past the shed was a shallow concrete pool of mercury where the crushed ore was dumped and the mercury allowed to separate the gold from the ore. Lin took a sample from the pool, using rubber gloves from his bag before dipping in the beaker. From the pool, the mercury flowed into a wooden sluice gate where cyanide was washed over the remainder of the tailings in order to retrieve whatever gold might be left over after the mercury treatment. As they followed the sluice to the stream, Lin taking samples along the way and marking them, Comrade Bei taking photos, they came to a large tailing pond, the stream having been dammed with a makeshift stone and cement wall. The water was a sickly silver-blue, iridescent, and shiny with mercury and rainbow-colored streaks of cyanide. There was a drainage pipe at the far end of the dam which could be opened and closed. The pond was not designed to actually contain the polluted water but more than likely to squeeze the last bits of gold from the crushed and discarded iron ore. The wastewater was indiscriminately dumped downstream and to the village below, and onward through fields to the lake. Lin, continuing to take samples, following the stream for a hundred yards before climbing back up to join Comrade Bei.

"Well, just as I suspected," said Lin, working his rubber gloves off and stuffing them into his bag. "A decent sized operation, I believe. Looks like there's plenty of money being made here."

Comrade Bei nodded his head. "Enough to make things difficult. The village Party Secretary will claim to know nothing about it, just like the cop. Until we send enforcement up here to confiscate the equipment and scare the workers off, they will keep on operating."

He shrugged. "You can write a report to that effect, and I will issue a final citation."

"And we get a doctor to have a look at the villagers. A medical person will be of some benefit, although unless they stop drinking this water all together, I'm not sure what advice they could give. In any event, they can at least document the diseases."

"Yes," said Comrade Bei. "I will make sure that happens."

They made their way back from the tailing pond up past the sluice gate and the shed and the trommels, to the mouth of the mineshaft. The cop was still there, still leaning on the seat of his motorcycle. They paused directly in front of him.

"Pretty big operation," said Lin.

"I guess it was long ago," said the cop. "As I said, we haven't seen or heard of anyone working this mine."

They turned their backs on the man and started toward the trail.

"Enjoy your walk back," he shouted as they disappeared into the woods.

At the police station, Comrade Bei started up the stairs for his meeting with the village Party Secretary.

"I will leave you to deal with him," Lin said. "I still have samples to collect from the village water. I'll be back in a quarter of an hour."

As Comrade Bei disappeared through the door, Lin caught a glimpse of Fang Shu sitting casually at a table in the entrance, a teacup in front of him and a cloud of smoke settled around his head.

Lin worked his way along the stream through the eerily quiet village, stepping on rocks and discarded cinder blocks in order to collect the samples, then writing his data on the sides of the beakers with his practiced hand, all the while keeping a careful eye out for the man in the Bulls cap. When he returned to the police station, he found Fang Shu and Comrade Bei sipping tea and talking amicably of some political intrigue that had occurred recently in the provincial capital. The citation with the red seal of the provincial SEPA lay between them. Comrade Bei stood and bowed slightly to Fang Shu. "Please see to it that when the doctor comes, he has a chance to meet with the villagers. And you will be seeing the enforcement team here soon."

"I'm sure," said Fang Shu without the least conviction.

They stepped out of the police station, shouldering their bags as they walked down the main street. The man in the red ballcap appeared from an alley and followed twenty feet behind them.

"Our shadow," said Lin contemptuously giving the man an evil glare. "Anyway, how long do you think it will take to get enforcement up here?" he asked.

"Oh, months. Many months. You know how busy these people are. And when they do finally show up, the Party Secretary may have connections with someone from enforcement and they will tip him off as to their movements."

"So, basically, the operation goes on until the vein of gold ore is depleted."

"Yes," said Comrade Bei with a shrug. "Hopefully that happens soon."

"In the meantime—"

"In the meantime, there's nothing more to be done other than getting a doctor up here to look at the villagers."

"That's something," Lin said, trying to sound as if it really was something, as if it were anywhere near enough.

When they reached the square, the villagers began to appear, one by one at first, but then in a large crowd. They pressed upon them, asking whether they had fixed the water, whether there was medical help available, whether their sicknesses would get better, whether they would come see this or that sick person bedridden in their house. A few of them sported large tumors which stretched the skin on their necks and shoulders. Some had nervous ticks and hands that would not be still.

"We will make sure that a doctor comes to have a look at you all," Lin said, his hands raised in the air. "You should boil the water before drinking it. Hopefully, the operation at the headwaters will be closed shortly and the water will get better."

They continued to shoot questions at them which Comrade Bei and Lin tried to answer, doing their best to assure them that they would get help. The crowd had grown bigger. The man in the red ballcap appeared from the main street carrying a short, black truncheon. He approached the crowd, waving it menacingly.

"Go back to your houses," he growled, smacking an old man across the shoulders, and whacking a woman hard on the back of her legs. They let out a cry.

"What in heaven's name are you doing?" asked Lin angrily,

pushing his way through the crowd to confront him. "Put that thing away and leave these people alone." He towered over the little man who refused to back down and did not lower the truncheon. On the contrary, he proceeded to take a swipe at Lin, barely missing his hip. Lin reached out and with one hand held the head of the man firmly away from him. He continued to swing the truncheon ineffectually a half dozen times, unable to reach Lin. It must have looked comical for the crowd was pointing, laughing, and jeering. The man's face was purple with rage, and, as he made one final lunge, Lin simply pushed him onto the seat of his pants, his head snapping back on the packed dirt road with an audible knock. Just then the little motorcycle appeared in the square, the cop screeching to a halt in front of the crowd. He dismounted and surveyed the scene, unholstering his pistol, holding it in his hand and letting it hang by his side. The crowd took a collective step back. The cop spat on the ground, told the little man on the ground, who was rubbing the back of his head and looking dazed, to get up and get out.

He then turned to Lin. "You have assaulted an employee of the police department, Comrade."

"If you want to call defending myself against that little piece of garbage an assault, go ahead."

He was tapping the barrel of the pistol against his thigh. His dark glasses hid any emotion he might be showing although his mouth was a taut line. He turned to the crowd. "That's it. Off you go," waving them away with his free hand. "Don't do or say anything you will regret. These people," he pointed at Lin and Comrade Bei, "are done here and they're leaving now. Isn't that right?"

"Yes," Lin said, and then added loudly. "For now. Remember, a doctor will be here shortly, and boil the water."

The crowd melted away, grumbling and muttering, as Lin and Comrade Bei reached the car. The cop continued to watch them, as did the PSB officer in his black sedan who was fully awake and observing everything through his dark sunglasses. They climbed in, sitting in glum silence for a few minutes before starting the engine and driving slowly out of town.

"Well," said Lin with a shake of his head. "That was a bit tense."

"Yes. Not a good situation," answered Comrade Bei. "I didn't like the look of that gun," he said, exhaling his breath.

"No," Lin replied, "but I wasn't that nervous. It seemed like more of a show for the villagers than a threat against us. You've got to feel sorry for those people to be in the hands of such tyrants."

They traveled for some miles and many minutes without speaking until Comrade Bei suddenly brightened and asked, "What about some of that famous Wenyu Lake carp for dinner tonight?"

"Well," Lin frowned, "it's not exactly from the lake anymore. In fact, it's farmed nearby." He stopped, hearing the negativity in his voice, then threw back his shoulders and put his chin in the air. "But it's good," he said loudly. "Yes. It's not bad at all. We will do that. We will have a feast of Wenyu Lake carp tonight." He smiled, turning to wave wildly at the PSB officer on their tail, then settling into the passenger seat for the journey back to the lake.

Chapter 21

After their early dinner of tainted but nevertheless tasty Wenyu Lake carp, they agreed to set out the next morning to visit the used lead battery recycling plant which was not far out of the way to the provincial capital. It was again a situation where enforcement would be required but the plant getting yet another visit from SEPA, and this time with a Chief Inspector from the capital, would hopefully make the village Party Secretary and the owner think twice about continuing to run the operation as it was. When they arrived in the village that morning, they could see the two short smokestacks spewing thick black fumes that blanketed the rooftops of the houses. They parked at the gate just as an empty truck was departing, the last of what must have been a great pile of used batteries being stacked in pyramids in wheelbarrows and pushed into the plant. Comrade Bei shouldered his rucksack as they climbed out of the car and began inspecting the moat surrounding the plant's brick wall. The water was the color of rust, clogged with plastic waste and old battery parts. They craned their necks, watching as the smoke drifted out from the stacks towards the village, before they headed for the gate. As soon as they stepped inside, the owner was there, a phone pressed to his ear. He glared at them for some minutes before finally ending the call.

"I can see there's been no improvements since I was last here," Lin said, looking around at the piles of batteries, battery parts, used scooters and motorcycles, and the workers squatting in the dirt in puddles of battery acid.

"And why should there be," answered the owner. "We have a license to operate."

"You don't have a license to violate the clean air and water laws of the PRC," said Comrade Bei simply, handing the man his card. "I am here to issue a final order to cease and desist, and to request enforcement to ensure that you do."

The man shrugged. "The village Party Secretary will be here

shortly. You can discuss it with him."

As if on cue, Party Secretary Fei appeared, purse dangling from a wrist which sported his enormous gold watch.

"Ah, Comrade Tao," he purred. Lin bowed slightly, backing off from a half proffered, rather limp handshake. "And you are?" he asked, turning away from Lin.

"I am Comrade Bei, a Chief Inspector at the provincial SEPA." He held his card out to the man with two hands. "I am here in support of Deputy Inspector Tao and to issue you a final citation regarding the violation of the clean air and water laws of the PRC."

"Yes, yes. We have discussed this with Comrade Tao—well, in fact, Comrade Tao lectured us but did not allow for much of a discussion. Have you time, Comrade Bei, to have a cup of tea? There is an office nearby." Party Secretary Fei waved his hand towards the back of the plant.

"A cup of tea would be fine. I will issue the citation and you can tell me exactly how you plan to remedy the situation."

"Excellent. Right this way," he said.

Comrade Bei glanced quickly at Lin who shook his head. "I will have a look around the village, and we can meet at the car in a half hour."

Comrade Bei nodded and the two disappeared into the shadowed and smoky interior of the plant.

Lin turned and walked slowly down the road to the first houses, all a uniform dull yellow or grey cinder block with bundles of sticks leaning against doorways and piles of grain and onions drying on the roofs. He walked on one side of the main street as the other half was strewn with stalks of rice, taking advantage of the tires of passing trucks and cars to break the rice from its husk and avoid the cost of taking it to a milling and separation plant. It seemed a somewhat unsanitary operation but it was an environmentally efficient secondary use of road transport, Lin thought, as he turned into a small alleyway in the village and bought a bottle of yoghurt at the window of a tiny kiosk. He watched the silky smoke from the twin stacks settle on the roofs and courtyards and school playgrounds as he sipped the yoghurt noisily through a straw. He had analyzed the soil in his lab, recording an astronomical 40 micrograms of lead per gram, which meant that children playing outside were breathing it and the water would be filled with it. He noticed a child perhaps 12 or 13 years old sitting on the steps of a doorway staring blankly at the street. There was a disturbing vacancy in his look, his mouth open and a pool of drool gathered between his lower lip and his gums. He approached the boy, waving and smiling but getting no response.

"Hello," said Lin, squatting in front of the child who looked through him. "What's your name? How old are you?"

"He won't answer," said a woman who appeared suddenly in the doorway. She gave Lin a distrustful look.

"Has he ever had the power of speech?"

"He used to speak, slowly and not clearly, but now he is mute."

"I'm sorry to hear it. My name is Tao Lin," he said with a bow. "I've been inspecting the lead situation in the village—"

"You are the one from the Environmental Administration."

"Yes."

"We are using the pitcher filters for drinking water. I share one with some neighbors. But we cannot filter our cooking water."

"No, but the drinking water is the most important." Lin paused, glancing again at the child.

"He was always slow," she said, following his gaze. "Never bright but good natured and alert. Now," she shook her head, "since a few years ago, he just stares into space."

"Well, it would be hard to say whether this is because of the smoke from the plant. Lead poisoning affects the cognitive skills in children, that's for sure. A doctor is scheduled to come here in a few weeks. If you give me your name, I can make sure that he has a look at your son."

She disappeared for a minute and appeared with a torn scrap of paper. "Thank you," she said gratefully. "I suppose there will be no improvement for the village until the plant is shut down." They both glanced at the twin stacks spewing their thick plumes of smoke.

"The plant needs to filter the smoke and make serious changes to its production. I don't know when that will happen but I know that they have been told to shut down immediately."

"But they won't," she said resignedly. "There are so few businesses in the village; we're mostly just poor farmers. The Party Secretary has invested in the plant. He and the owner are thick as thieves."

"We have an enforcement bureau that will be here, hopefully

soon. They will have the power to shut down the plant."

"Even if they show up, as soon as they turn their back, it will start up again. Those in power are only concerned with money and profits and not what happens to poor people."

What could Lin answer to that? She was right, and he was getting very tired of introducing false optimism to the desperate hopes of the downtrodden masses. "A doctor will be here shortly. That I can guarantee you," he said with as much conviction as he could muster.

The woman rubbed the hair on her son's head and he looked up with a smile. "I wonder," she said pensively, "if I would be just like the Party Secretary if I was in his place. I want money just like everyone else, probably more than anyone else, since I have none and never will."

"The idea," Lin answered, "is to try and make money without hurting anyone."

"Ha," the woman snorted, turning to enter her doorway before giving Lin one more definitive "Ha."

When Lin returned to the plant, Comrade Bei was shaking hands with Party Secretary Fei outside the gate, the both of them smiling as they walked to their cars. Comrade Fei's driver, the moment the rear door closed, roared onto the street, leaving Lin and Comrade Bei in a cloud of dust. They climbed into their car and proceeded slowly through the town once the dust had cleared.

"So, how did it go?" asked Lin.

"Oh, the usual. Empty promises of compliance and my hopefully not completely empty threats of enforcement." He paused. "He's in a tough spot, you know. There is almost no tax income generated in the village other than from the recycling plant and he's under pressure from the district to show income. He can't afford to upgrade the plant to the specifications SEPA requires."

They were out on the main highway leading north to the provincial capital, their windows rolled up in order to hear one another and the air inside close. Has he come to some sort of arrangement with the Party Secretary? Lin wondered, depressed that he had to wonder at all, but all too aware that their minimal salaries were barely sufficient and that arrangements were the norm.

"I told him," Comrade Bei continued, "that he would have to do something to comply and he agreed to start with fixing the chimney from the air furnace to the smelter which should at least help the workers."

"So that's how you left it?"

Comrade Bei nodded, his eyes fixed on the road. They travelled in silence for many minutes until he turned to Lin with a smile. "And you are heading to the Capital City to get your award."

"Yes," Lin answered with an incredulous shake of his head. "To get my award."

Chapter 22

A number of refugees had taken over the rooms of the Great House in the year since it had been empty, most of them woman and children but some old men. They camped out in the myriad rooms and corridors and courtyards, building cooking fires on the floors with old bricks, defecating beside the walls of the compound and leaving mounds of trash everywhere. They had little to do but scrounge for food and scheme against one another, most lamenting their having not left with the Nationalists and fearing what would become of them under the Communists. They managed to survive on whatever could be collected from the fields and the orchids and the nut trees, and the occasional fish they managed to catch in the lake but mostly they sat around lethargically awaiting their fate.

One day a young man named Cao Chu appeared among them. He was gaunt and dressed in the same ragged clothes as they but there was something about the way he carried himself, very quiet with a superior way of looking at people, that made him stand out. Cao Chu did think himself superior, as well as observant and careful, looking with disdain at the way the refugees lived in the great house, noting the filth accumulating everywhere and the dangerous lack of sanitation. He found a back courtyard that must have once belonged to the kitchen but was now abandoned and began to build a hut with bricks he scavenged from the gardens and thatch which he took from the roofs of the laborers' houses. He felt secure being near the great house, surrounded by high walls and the lake with towering trees and gardens. It was not so very different from the house in the French Concession on the Mao Ming Nan Lu that he had just left two weeks ago in Shanghai, except that outside there was no big city chaos and noise. He was supposed to be on the boat with his parents and sister and the Kwang family that employed them. They had boarded a steamer late one night and Chu, arriving at the house from his 14-hour workday storing and sorting cotton at the Kwang family warehouse on the river, found old Song, a crippled ancient servant, at the front door.

"They have all gone, Cao Chu. Off to the south and to Taipei. They have left instructions for you to go to the ship docked at wharf 9 on the Huang Pu. The Communists will be here in a matter of days, maybe sooner. It is all the same to me," he said, shuffling back into house. "I am too old to care one way or another."

Chu followed him into the house. "I will pack some things," he told the old man as he went through the house to the servant's quarters at the back but not before first noting that the rooms had been completely stripped bare. He had seen quiet preparations for a month but he was still shocked by the sight of the empty rooms and naked walls. In his room, which consisted of a curtained space with a bed at the back of the kitchen with another curtain separating him from and his parent's and sister's bed, he put his other set of clothes in a canvas bag. Under a loose stone beneath the bed, he dug out a small sack containing coins and a few hundred crumpled gold yuan notes, almost worthless with the endless rise of inflation. He then sat on the bed and stared at the curtain. What sort of life would he have if he boarded the steamer and continued a servant to the Kwang family? A life just like his father's, becoming bent and unsmiling and subservient and grateful for any scrap that came his way, sitting at night with vacant eyes and a bent cigarette in his hand. Maybe the Communists would be better, he thought, as he leaned back on the bed and closed his eyes. There was talk of land reform, of the death of landlords and the moneyed class and the rise of the poor. Now that was something to believe in. He closed his eyes and fell into a deep sleep.

When he awoke, a hint of a pink dawn was showing in the sky. He slung his bag over his shoulder and walked slowly through the house where he had grown up. He felt no need to hurry, unsure whether he wanted to board the steamer or not, so he dragged his feet, remembering how he had crawled, then tottered, then run along these floors, hiding under furniture and stairways, playing with the Kwang family children until he became too old and the class distinction was established and he went back to his place in the back of the house. But the Kwang family had been relatively good to him, had taught him to do sums and enough characters so that he had the basics to read and write, had employed him in their warehouse, had even promised to make him a clerk once he had learned enough of the business. Maybe there were opportunities in Taiwan, he thought, shifting his bag to his other shoulder and heading out the front door for good.

He was surprised by the crowds that had congregated on the river: thousands and thousands of refugees carrying bundles and suitcases, pushing carts loaded with furniture with children clinging to the top. Some carts pulled by shabby looking mules had been abandoned by the side of the road and were being plundered by thieves with large knives shoved in their belts and scowls on their faces. Chu eventually made his way through the throng to Wharf 9 only to find the crowd being pushed back by armed Nationalist troops pointing rifles at them and sweeping their bayonets menacingly from side to side.

"No more passengers," an officer screamed. "These soldiers will be the last to board. Stand back or you will be shot." He fired a pistol in the air, and the soldiers began to march up the gangplank, the ones farthest out from the left and the right turning smartly while their fellow soldiers covered their retreat. The officer fired again and the crowd cowered as the last soldier boarded and the gangplank was raised. A man managed to catch on to the gangplank, dangling from the end before the officer crawled out and smashed his fingers with the butt of his pistol and he dropped unceremoniously into the filthy river. The bow and stern lines were cut rather than risk the time it took to cast off. Chu stood on the wharf as the steamer drifted slowly away. He spotted his sister on the lower deck waving a straw hat. He waved back.

"Go south," she yelled. "We will meet in Taipei. You—" Just then the steamers engines revved as the bow of the ship caught the current and began to pick up speed. They waved to each other until they were out of sight.

How he ended up at Wenyu Lake was pure chance: the stream of refugees heading southeast scavenged most of the food as they went. They also attracted bands of thieves who picked at the edges of the crowd, taking away carts and dray animals and even kidnapping children. Chu thought it best to go it alone, and headed southwest away from the stream of refugees, where there was more of a possibility of finding food. He had found just enough to forage but he had also met farmers who would feed him in exchange for a day's worth of labor. Along the way, he had heard of a not-so-distant lake called Wenyu with an abundance of fish and forests of orchards and nut trees, and so he had come upon the lake. He thought himself fortunate to have found an abandoned Great House to live beside and a dry hut to live in, a lake with fat carp if you were patient enough to catch them, and food to forage if you made the effort.

It wasn't long before Chu observed that the courtyard was not completely abandoned. Two young women poked their heads out of a doorway on the far side and peered at him before quickly withdrawing. He also noticed a tall man who came almost every afternoon to chat with one of the girls, the pretty one, pretty even though she appeared to have a crippled foot—she moved awkwardly, and a crutch leaned against the wall near the door. The man always brought food of some sort, and often sat on the stone steps in the late afternoon sun. Chu felt a growing sense of envy for the tall man and the pretty cripple, at how they in their shy way so clearly cared for one another. The other girl, short, squat, hair lipped, joined them sometimes, interrupting their bliss as she joked and slapped her hands against her thighs. Chu could not make out what she said but it always made the other two blush and look embarrassedly at the ground. When the tall man took his leave, he held the crippled woman's hand and whispering in her ear. As the weeks went by, Chu noticed the tall man tapping on a window of the kitchen in the darkness and then waiting at the door when it was unbolted and opened just wide enough for him to slip through.

One day, Chu and Shanshan met by chance beside the lake. Each was carrying a carp and they were eyeing one another's catch.

"You've had some luck," Shanshan said carefully, brushing the hair from his forehead.

"And you as well," answered Chu as they held their fish up for inspection, two very nice specimens of equal size.

"Where did you get yours?" asked Shanshan. Chu waved noncommittedly to the northwest shores of the lake. "Near the tributary there. And you?"

Shanshan hesitated. "Actually, I have repaired some of the nets and weirs in the lake. I find trapped carp there sometimes but quite often they escape. I cannot repair all the nets by myself."

"Perhaps we can work together," suggested Chu. He stepped forward and gave a slight nod of his head. "I am Cao Chu, formerly of Shanghai but now a refugee."

"Well, Cao Chu. I am Tao Shanshan, also formerly of Shanghai, but originally from this village." Shanshan bowed slightly. "Indeed, perhaps we can catch more fish in the nets and weirs if we work together."

From then on, they formed a team, trapping carp in their nets and feeding them what they could forage from the fields. It was true that two were more productive than one, but still there were days when they could forage nothing. Even then, Chu noticed that Shanshan would disappear in the early evening and return with a bit of food, which he would share with Chu and the kitchen maids, saying simply that he had begged food from shopkeepers he knew in town. But shopkeepers had no food to spare, and Chu was convinced that Shanshan was hoarding money. The next day, another day of having no luck finding food, Shanshan had returned to his quarters and Chu followed, hiding behind a broken wall as he watched Shanshan through the doorless entrance remove a brick from the back of the chimney and take a few coins from a tin box. Chu guarded the secret, knowing that if times got even worse, he could always grab the box and run.

One morning, they found their nets empty, having been discovered by someone and picked clean. It was then necessary, once they had painstakingly filled the nets again, for them to take turns sitting up half the night to guard against thieves. The night before, Chu had successfully scared off two men he discovered climbing into the weirs. He had jumped and shouted and made enough noise so that they ran off but he was nervous that they would see that he was alone and return perhaps with more men.

"We need to defend ourselves, Shanshan," Chu said the next day sitting in the doorway of Shanshan's house. "I have noticed a few old shovel handles in the corner of the kitchen courtyard that no one has used for firewood yet. They would make good weapons. Let's take them with us when we guard the nets tonight. I am sure that they will return and they will be in for a surprise."

So it was that at midnight the thieves returned with two more men, all thin and starving and undernourished and desperate and hardly able to withstand the surprise assault by Shanshan and Chu as they leapt from the banks of the lake and began swinging their sticks. The men cried out and stumbled up the banks, their hands held beside their heads to ward off the blows. One man slipped and lay prostrate on the ground as Chu beat him mercilessly about the head and arms. Shanshan could see that he had broken the man's wrist.

"Enough," he said, stepping between them. The man rose whimpering, cradling an arm, and disappeared into the night. Chu was breathing deeply, a wild gleeful look in his eyes.

"They are just poor and starving like all of us, Chu," said Shanshan as they walked towards the water to inspect the nets. "You needn't have beaten him so badly."

"Yes, my friend, but we will not see the likes of them anymore, I guarantee it. And word will get around that the two fierce warriors guarding the nets behind the Great House are not to be trifled with." He was elated, slapping Shanshan on the shoulder and then demonstrating how he had swung his stick this way and that, leaping about, laughing until Shanshan was forced to laugh along with him.

Chapter 23

The award ceremony took place on Saturday morning at 11:00 a.m. in the large conference room at the SEPA headquarters. There was a lunch to follow, which was very kind of Madame Sun, Lin thought, as the offer of a free lunch would ensure that at least some people would show up. As it was, from his seat on the stage Lin looked out at a rather sparse crowd of maybe twenty-five people, very few of whom he recognized. They were all wrapped in their winter jackets despite it being warm in the room, with phones pressed to their ears, rifling through plastic bags, and noisily eating fruit which, along with paper cups of tea, had been laid out on a long table in the back. Beside Lin was Deputy Director Bo, who Lin knew slightly, and Madame Sun's ubiquitous secretary, Dawei, who was telling Lin the schedule of events.

"Deputy Director Bo will give a few words of introduction," he said quietly to Lin with a nod of his head to the D.D., "mostly concerning our new designation as a ministry. Then Madame Sun will say a few words about the award and about you. You will receive the medal around your neck so it's important that you stay below the podium when she presents it. Not only does she not want to appear smaller than you, even though she is, but one time a recipient bowed his head to receive the medal and knocked her in the nose." That would have been a sight, Lin thought.

"You can take the podium after that if you like." He did not seem all that enthusiastic, and, as Lin eyed the crowd of strangers, he politely declined the offer.

"Excellent," Dawei said, closing his notebook. "Lunch should begin no later than 11:45 a.m. and everyone will be free to leave after that." He nodded his head satisfactorily. "Madame Sun has an appointment at Zhongnanhai at 1:30 p.m. so she will only be able to lunch with you for a half hour." It was Lin's turn to nod his head. What would these people do without their secretaries, he wondered?

D.D. Bo stepped to the podium, cleared his throat and, although the crowd quieted, their eyes continued to be transfixed on their mobile phones, fingers flashing in a flurry of text messages. He then proceeded systematically, pedantically, to outline what changes would be made when SEPA become a Ministry, explaining in great detail what would take place at the district and provincial level. The crowd's eyes glazed and there were some audible snores which did little to deter the droning of D.D. Bo who soldiered on with little concern as to the state of his audience. After a half hour, Dawei drew a flat palm across his throat. D.D. Bo wrapped up almost mid-sentence and the doors opened to the regal entrance of Madame Sun as the crowd put their phones away and sat up primly in their seats. She took the podium and nodded, smiling, to Lin.

"As you well know, we are here today to honor District Deputy Inspector Lin Tao for his outstanding contribution to SEPA and to the protection of the environment in this country." She tilted her chin at the crowd and, on cue, they followed with polite applause. She proceeded to list his accomplishments, beginning with his work in chemical analysis at Beijing University during Cultural Revolution and the impact his studies had on regenerating the mineral content of the depleted farmland in northeast China. Lin appreciated the hyperbole from Madame Sun but, in fact, he was one of a team of hundreds who performed chemical analysis in the laboratories of Beijing University and in the countryside. It had kept him safe from the alarming and unpredictable purges of Cultural Revolution and allowed him to move freely between the city and the countryside, unlike many of his colleagues who were stuck for years working on farms in villages, scrabbling for food from resentful villagers.

"The most noticeable attribute of Tao Lin's service to SEPA," continued Madam Sun, "has been his ability to avoid corruption of any sort." This had the audience squirming in their seats; corruption was something Madame Sun did not tolerate but the truth was that each and every employee considered it to be a perfectly reasonable fringe benefit. In fact, they considered it a requisite for supplementing a pitiful government salary. As the presentation-now-turned-lecture continued, most everyone's eyes were glued firmly to the floor. "Corruption is what is destroying the environment of this great country just as much as the polluting factories and plants and mills. Arrangements," she fairly spat the word, "between SEPA officials and businesses, between SEPA officials and Party Officials, undermine the laws of this country and tip the environment toward a point of no return. Beware of arrangements, comrades." Here she stared at the audience with its downcast eyes, the only contact she was able to make was with Lin and her Secretary, before she sighed and came to her conclusion. "Stay true to yourselves and to your profession, be proud of your role as the protector of the environment, and look to Tao Lin as a model to follow." More polite applause as Lin saw the signal from Dawei and stepped to a spot just below the podium. He bowed his head as Madame Sun slipped a red and yellow ribbon with one large and four smaller gold stars around his neck.

As Lin felt the weight of the medal land against his chest, he caught a glimpse of the front with the shiny brass bust of Lei Feng in his red star military cap with earmuffs, a machinegun resting against his chest. Lin stepped back and shook the proffered hand of Madame Sun and there was a noticeably louder round of applause, everyone holding their hands close together in front of their face and rapidly clapping, before Madame Sun stepped down from the stage and a great murmur of voices rose in the room. There was a general scanning of mobile screens, some putting phones to their ears but most pecking out messages with one hand as they packed up their belongings, smiling and chatting in happy expectation of a substantial free lunch.

They moved down the corridor to the banquet hall, Lin staying close to Madame Sun's elbow. She parried numerous queries, people desperate to have a word, a whisper in her ear, or stopping her for photo opportunities, all of this with Dawei using his voice, and often his arms, to keep people at a distance. Eventually they reached the enormous, windowless banquet hall, three of its walls covered in gold drapes and the other in a massive national flag. As they took their seats at the head table, people continued to approach Madame Sun, at least those that Dawei allowed, and she turned a polite ear to their murmured voices until she gave a slight nod of her chin to Dawei signaling the end of the audience. She then turned smiling to Lin.

"Now, Lin," she said in English with only a slight hint of an accent, "we can discuss anything we like without the least concern of being overheard. Dawei has made sure that no one at this table is an English speaker. Comrade Pei is fluent in Japanese. "They glanced at a slightly built woman with a shiny forehead and wire rimmed glasses sitting next to her non-descript husband. "And Comrade Fu is a German speaker." A heavy-set man was popping pieces of cubed and marinated radishes into his mouth with his chopsticks, beside him a very descript wife with a bouffant hairdo, lacquered nails of varied colors, and a bright red down jacket zipped up to her chin. "You see, we are free to speak our mind," Madame Sun said with a wan smile.

"Well," said Lin. "I would like to start by thanking you again for your help."

"Never mind that. What you need to know now is that I will not be able to give such help in the future."

"But—" Lin said with a startled look.

"This is between the two of us as the official announcement will not be made until next month but I will not be heading the new Ministry. Nor will I be made a deputy minister. They have passed me over for someone less controversial, someone who has done their time in Xinjiang or Heilongjiang and who will return gratefully to Beijing and do as they are told. I," she said with a slight shake of her head, "have made too many enemies over the years. Just like you, only at a higher level."

"I don't know what to say. You are obviously the most qualified, the only one capable of making the Ministry what it should be."

"Not everyone thinks so or wants it so."

"What will you do?" Lin asked.

"Retire gracefully," she said with an unhappy smile. "There is a tennis center not so far from my hutong that is open exclusively to retired cadre during the day. I can improve my very rusty game. And my hutong has not been torn down to make space for a high-rise, at least not yet, and it has an excellent corner for a garden. So you see, Lin," she said with a shrug, "gardening and tennis are my future. No more politics. You, I am afraid, are on your own. I can do no more for you. If you find yourself in trouble, there is no one left at SEPA who will step in on your behalf. I don't know what your options would be, frankly, and it worries me. Escape to somewhere safe, perhaps," she mumbled. "Although I hope it won't come to that."

Dawei appeared quietly at her elbow and whispered the time in her ear.

"I am due in Zhongnanhai for a meeting and, no doubt, a polite thanks before my farewell next month. Be careful, Lin," she said, leaning close to him. "As you know, there are many who would like to take the teeth out of not only the new Ministry but also one of its most dedicated and principled deputy inspectors."

He stood as she did, and they shook hands. Before they turned to leave the table, Dawei said to Lin: "There is a Caijing journalist who wants to talk to you, and she's brought along a laowai. American, I think. Don't give them much of anything, especially not to the foreigner."

Lin nodded, still shocked by the news Madame Sun had given him, as he watched her leave the room. People still jumped up to approach her for favors, petitions, the endless requests made of the powerful, only none of them yet knew that her power was a thing of the past.

"Hello," said a voice behind him. He stood and faced a young and very pretty woman in dark grey pants and jacket with a silk blouse. Beside her stood a foreigner, short with shockingly red hair, freckles across his entire face, and a nose as sharp and pointed as a knife. Lin had plenty of experience dealing with foreigners but he had to concentrate to keep from wincing at the strange look of this one. "I'm Ling Su from Caijing Magazine." She extended a business card with both hands and a slight bow. "And this is Andrew McMillan from the Chicago Tribune." He also produced a business card before shaking Lin's hand.

"Very nice to meet you," the American said in flat, non-tonal Chinese.

"Nice to meet you both," Lin answered, and motioning to the empty chairs beside him. "What, exactly, can I do for you?"

"Well," said Ling Su, "we would first like to congratulate you on your award. We understand that you are a very dedicated environmentalist, and that when SEPA becomes a Ministry, they will need a lot more people like you."

"I guess I'm an environmentalist," Lin said, with a shake of his head. "But really, I'm just trying to enforce the environmental laws of the country with the resources we have. Hopefully they will increase substantially when we are a Ministry."

The foreigner cut in. "I understand that there is a lot of resistance to your work, that SEPA is full of corrupt officials who are only interested in co-operating with the business community, and that there is no real enforcement of the environmental laws."

Well, Lin thought, he gets right to the point, this bizarre looking man in his strange, monotonous Chinese. But he had no intention of falling into any of those rabbit holes. "SEPA does an excellent job with the resources it has, and will do an even better job when those resources are increased. We work closely with the business community to assure that, uh, that compromises can be made. By both sides."

The piercing blue eyes of Andrew McMillan gave Lin an ironic twinkle as he scribbled in his notebook, then looked at Ling Su and shrugged.

"Actually," Ling Su said, "we understand quite the contrary. We at Caijing are very interested in finding out just exactly how SEPA works on a provincial and local level, and not how the bureaucracy in Beijing sees it. You know we are quite well known for our in-depth reporting on sometimes sensitive subjects." Here she paused and gave Lin a hard look. "And that, naturally, we are accredited by the State Council Information Office and approved by the Central Propaganda Department."

Lin merely nodded and looked at his watch.

"Perhaps," she continued, "we could make a visit to your town and see for ourselves how SEPA works at your level."

"Certainly," Lin said, rising. "You will need to clear it with the provincial and local party officials, the local information office, and, of course, the Public Security Bureau at all levels. But after that, I would have no objection to meeting with you."

"Of course," she answered with a wry smile. "We would do all of those things and, hopefully, we will be able to meet in the next few months."

"Best of luck." Lin held out his hand to the two of them. "Again, very nice to meet you," he said as he gathered his jacket from behind the chair, checked the pockets for gloves, scarf and hat, and headed for the door. He planned to go to Beijing University, Beida, to walk the grounds and poke around the library before visiting the apartment of his good friend, Professor Huang Hengda. There they would sit in his book-lined study and slurp tea and talk of old times and what projects Hengda was working on while his sweet wife of forty years would be preparing Mapodofu and Yuxiangrousi and Jiaozi and setting out bottles of cold beer.

Chapter 24

Lin spent the rest of the afternoon at Beida walking the grounds in the monochromatic landscape of a deep winter Beijing day. The grass was brittle and brown, clouds of fine dust billowing about his legs as he walked, the buildings dull, the trees leafless, and the air thick with smog. It held the possibility of being a pretty campus in the summer but now it was simply depressing. Cold and shivering, he walked quickly to the science library where he sat in a cushioned chair as close to a heater as he could get and read various scientific journals that were unavailable to him in the province. Just as it was getting dark, he stood and stretched, hoisted his backpack, left the library and the university and headed to Professor Huang Hengda's which was a few miles to the southwest of the campus.

He hurried through the narrow streets crowded with returning workers scurrying in and out of overflowing shops, toting grocery bags and packages, ears and eyes glued to mobile phones. The cars, busses and scooters added their ubiquitous cacophony of blaring horns and screeching brakes. From the corner of his eye, Lin watched a small man slipping flyers under the windshield wipers of the immovable cars. At one point a driver, seemingly irate at having someone touch the windscreen of what looked to Lin to be an especially fancy car, jumped from the driver's seat. Cursing and yelling, he proceeded to beat the poor man on the back of the head who quickly fled, abandoning a stack of flyers in the middle of the street. These the driver kicked with rage as they flew up in a great cloud of paper before he climbed back in behind the wheel of his shiny new car. Despite the years Lin had spent in Beijing, he was always shocked by the level of violence living just below the surface of so many of the inhabitants. He was also dismayed by the lack of any empathy, or even sympathy, for the poor and indigent who made up a large minority of the city's citizens, those who were simply doing their best to earn a living. He had once been riding a bike through one of the endlessly clogged bicycle lanes of the city at midday during a sudden windstorm when the dust from the Gobi Desert darkened the sky in an eerie yellowish orange cloud. People were being blown off their bikes right and left. One man, dressed in ragged clothes and pedaling an ancient flying pigeon bike, was blown against a passing automobile and, bouncing off the passenger side, landed in a pile on the ground. While Lin stopped to see how badly the man was injured, the driver proceeded to get out and inspect a scratch on his automobile and to berate the man for having hit his car.

He was relieved to finally reach the gate of his friend's compound, turning away from the chaotic street and stopping at the guardhouse beside the gate to give the guard his name who then called Professor Huang on an internal line before waving Lin through. He walked among the dusty, dull-red, six-story brick apartment buildings, all in a shabby state of disrepair, with abandoned bicycles and scooters and furniture piled up against the walls. The compound had formerly belonged to Beida but with the Zhu Rongji reforms, the apartments were now owned by the professors and administrators who were employed at the university. Despite the outward appearance of the communal grounds and public space, inside the apartments were large and spacious by Beijing standards and the location close to the university and in a leafy neighborhood was a realtor's dream.

These intellectuals who had all been, in varying degrees, abused by Red Guards during Cultural Revolution, badly paid and for many years badly treated, now sat on real estate worth much more than they had ever earned in their entire lifetimes. It might not have begun to compensate for what many had experienced at that time, but it did help. Professor Huang himself carried the scars, literal scars, of the Cultural Revolution in the form of a pronounced limp. He had badly torn the ligaments and cartilage in his right knee while being hounded by red guards carrying little red books and shouting slogans. They had chased him up the small hill by the pagoda in the park in Beida and he had fallen between the rocks, laying there exhausted and breathing heavily. Luckily, they had lost interest after deriding him as a capitalist roader and a revisionist and he was able to limp back to his office hours later. He never received treatment for the knee and, although his limp was distinct, it did not particularly limit his mobility.

Lin found the building, stepped into the elevator and gave the neighborhood committee woman, with her ubiquitous red armband and blue Mao coat, the number. It was an odd day so he was let off on the 7th floor to make his way to the 6th. He knocked on the iron gated door in front of the main door which was opened immediately by Qianlu.

"Why, Lin, you've made it," she said with a warm smile and giving him a hug. Her head barely reached his chest and he could see the skin on her scalp through her thinning black-grey hair. "It is such a long time since we've seen you," she said, stepping back and leading him into the kitchen.

"I should come visit more often," he said, following her, "but it's such a long trip, and I'm not used to Beijing anymore."

"Yes," she said. "It gets more and more crowded, more cars and noise. You know what it was like here in the old days: nothing but rice paddies and wheat and corn and donkeys and an occasional truck. Now we are surrounded by development as far as the eye can see."

"I thought I heard something," Hengda said, storming into the room and swinging his bad leg wildly in front of him, a big smile on his oval face. "How good to see you, my friend, after all these years." He clasped Lin's hand and rested the other on his shoulder. "It seems the only way we get to see you is if you win a model worker award at SEPA."

"I have been terrible about visiting, I admit. But as I was saying to Qianlu, I am not used to the big city anymore. It makes me confused and tired."

"Ha. As it does to us all. And it only gets worse, especially when you are a decade older like us."

"But you both look good, in excellent health despite Beijing." The last was more of a question than a statement.

"We cannot complain about our health. Of course, good health at our age means nothing hurts too much," Hengda said with an ironic smile.

"Can I get you a cup of tea, Lin?" Qianlu asked. "A beer, perhaps? I know you have a fondness for Beijing Beer, something you don't get where you come from."

"Very true," Lin said, "and a Beijing Beer would be wonderful."

She put two beers and two small glasses on a tray on the kitchen table along with a bowl of spicy peanuts and another of tiny dried fish. "Off with you to the study while I get some dinner together." She put the tray in Lin's hands, and gently pushed him out of the kitchen in the direction of the fast-moving Hengda who was propelling himself down a long corridor lined with exquisite Chinese scrolls and framed calligraphy until they reached Hengda's study. The walls of the study were covered with sagging bookshelves stuffed with books, and contained a small desk, also piled with books, two hardbacked chairs, a small coffee table, and in the corner between more books stacked along the floor, a cot with a down blanket folded at its foot. They sat in the chairs, filled their glasses with beer, and, with a bottom's up and clink, drained them in one swallow.

"So," Lin said with a satisfied burp, "what are you working on now, my friend?"

"I am wrestling with a new translation of Huckleberry Finn," which he pronounced as He ke bei re Fen. "I am not satisfied with the way Zhu Wei portrayed the slave Jim's dialogue." He poured himself and Lin another glass of beer. "I was thinking of having him speak with an Anhui dialect but, you know, Jim is not speaking in dialect. It's still basic English with a thick accent and full of vernacular. I thought of having him speak with a Beijing accent, or maybe Harbin but it seems incongruous since he is black and comes from a southern climate." He shook his head at the complexity. "The problem with the south of China is they all speak dialects and not with accents."

"I can see your dilemma," Lin said raising his glass to Hengda. "But what a nice dilemma to have, thinking about interesting academic problems as opposed to thinking about hopeless environmental problems. Especially my personal problems," Lin said with a shake of his head as Hengda gave him a quizzical look.

"I've made too many enemies, my friend. The entire business community is against me as well as the town government. The PSB are watching my every move." Lin did not mention his night in jail chiefly out of embarrassment, and also the pain, of the memory.

"There's your award, though, and there's always Madame Sun." Hengda said.

"Well, maybe and maybe not." He didn't go into detail, keeping his promise to Madame Sun despite completely trusting Hengda with the secret. "As Chen has always warned me, I shouldn't rely exclusively on her patronage."

"And what would Chen have you do, exactly? If you stop doing your job properly, then you are in the pocket of the business community."

"Frankly, Hengda, it's hopeless. I can't compromise on the environmental laws, and they can't conform. My only hope is to try and hang on until SEPA becomes a ministry." They sat in silence for a time.

"Well," Hengda said. "I don't envy your position. The fact is, the environmental problems of this country are a runaway train. Hard to imagine how, or if, they will ever be fixed."

"For now, for this evening, I will try not to think about it," Lin said with a smile, draining his glass.

"Here, here," answered Hengda. "Let's talk about my recent trip to Princeton University, where I not only got to deliver a series of lectures about my translation of Moby Dick into Chinese, but I got to spend time with our daughter Min at Columbia." Hengda's translation had made him somewhat famous among academic circles considering that the work had taken him a decade and a half and was unlikely to be undertaken again, no matter how ambitious an academic might be. It was also during the time that he was doing the translation that Hengda had been hounded up the steps of the pagoda by the red guards who knew of his affinity for western ideas and his petite bourgeois studies.

"How is Min?" Lin asked. "She must be almost finished with her pre-med studies."

"One more year, and then med school, and then a residency, and then a specialty or a practice. I think she will spend the rest of her life in America," he said with a shrug. "Qianlu is very sad about it but I am pragmatic: much better that she has a busy, healthy, successful, and hopefully happy life in America than what she could expect here in China."

"A difficult decision," Lin said as they sipped their beers and ate the peanuts and the delicate fish, "but she has been in America for so many years, perhaps she feels more American than Chinese."

"Exactly, and that is an asset. America is not an easy place to feel comfortable; it takes time. Yes, they are friendly and polite but, for the most part, they are not exactly worldly, if you know what I mean." Lin looked at him quizzically. "For example, I have travelled to America a half dozen times, almost always to Princeton, and half the people I see there, the same people time and time again, are unable to pronounce my name."

"I suppose they expect you to adopt an American one, like Henry."

"Oh well. I solve that problem by telling them to 'Call me Ishmael.'" They had a good laugh at that as they poured some more beer and turned the topic to certain acquaintances they had in common from Beida and from CASS. The beer bottles were empty, the peanuts and fish long gone, when they gratefully heard Qianlu calling them into the kitchen for dinner.

Chapter 25

After rumblings and rumors, after fearful and sometimes hopeful whispers, the Communists finally arrived, descended on the village like a thunderbolt in two U.S. Army trucks, a dozen soldiers with rifles in the back of each along with a handful of prisoners. Up front sat the officers and the commander, Little Deng, who sat next to the driver of the first truck on a folded-up blanket so that he could see over the dash, clutching a cigarette in his nicotine-stained fingers. The trucks were solid and well built, compliments of the Nationalist Army who abandoned all the American equipment as they ran towards the coast. The Communists were now better equipped than General Chiang and they were using their advantage to spread out and take control of the remaining countryside. It was unusual to see a high-ranking comrade such as Little Deng in such an out of the way village but he often strayed from the beaten path in order to witness firsthand the implementation of the Directives from Beijing. They were here to win the hearts and minds of the countryside but he knew, from his long years of subjugating the countryside, that this was done not with love or compassion but with fear, and fear was what they were here to apply. Besides, he had heard many stories of the wonders of the sweet tasting carp of Wenyu Lake which he was looking forward to tasting for himself.

As the trucks rolled to a stop at the well in the village square, a soldier leapt from the back to place a stool beneath the passenger side door for Little Deng who descended with great dignity. He was pleased to see that there was no need to give orders or shout instructions; the soldiers had been through hundreds of villages and small towns and knew well how to implement the directives. At a minimum, 1.6 of every thousand citizens were to be executed for crimes such as hoarding, having capitalist or petite bourgeoise tendencies, having ties to the Kuomintang, or being landlords. In Meiyu village, according to Little Deng's intelligence report, this meant a few dozen were to be executed, although he could use his discretion if he found a particularly recalcitrant village or town. He was aware, of course, that the village population was likely half what his intelligence report told him what with those who had left with the Nationalists and those who had simply fled into the countryside. The villagers who stayed would have to pay the price for the traitors and cowards who had deserted, Little Deng thought.

A few soldiers dragged tables from a nearby house to set up in the square as a tribunal which they festooned with red banners and black characters proclaiming death to landlords and hoarders and glory to the liberation. As the rest of the soldiers fanned out, rifles at the ready, going door to door, searching for signs of hoarding or for signs of a bourgeoise lifestyle, an officer, using a portable megaphone, blasted out a message to the inhabitants. "Comrades of Meiyu village. The great Chinese Communist Party has now liberated this village. No longer will you be controlled by the moneyed class and landowners who have sucked the blood from Chinese peasants for centuries. You are now free, now members of the great proletariat where you yourselves will rule the land and control the levers of production. Able bodied men and women come assemble in the village square to witness what the great revolution has wrought, to celebrate your liberation, and to understand the goals of the Party and your duties."

Once the village square was full of the able-bodied adults, they proceeded with the weeding out of the bad elements. Those stupid enough to be dressed in bourgeoise clothing were singled out; Shanshan, standing at the edge of the crowd, saw a scribe with his greasy black-red robe, groaning and weeping as he stumbled from a push from behind and landed against the wall, his yellow slippers torn and muddied. Anyone with soft, smooth, and supple hands was dragged out and also thrown up against the wall. Then came the general denunciation as villager turned upon villager, hurling insults and accusations, pleading with the Communists to believe them over the others. Accused men and women were seated on a wooden stool in front of the tribunal where Little Deng and two officers sat. Sorting out the truth among the fear and shouting and weeping took a bit more time, although often the truth was irrelevant. Eventually those who served with, or even aided, the Kuomintang, and those who were suspected of doing so, were pushed into the corner against the wall. Those accused of Nationalist sympathies, if corroborated by many, were charged and sentenced, again whether true or not.

Often it was simply a matter of settling a petty grievance against a neighbor, and the louder and more vocal one shrieked a denouncement, the more successful they were.

One man was shoved forward who had fought with the Kuomintang but had chosen not to follow the General to the coast but to return to the village. On his knees in front of the tribunal, he gnashed his teeth and let out a piercing howl. "I fought the Japanese," he cried. "I killed them, many of them, with my bare hands I strangled them. I shot them. I gutted them with my bayonet. I am not a Nationalist," he sobbed. "I am a Japanese devil killer." The crowd was silent, watching. No one contradicted him.

"Well," Little Deng declared, "the Party is merciful. This man will not be executed but will go to a labor camp where he will work for the Party and be educated in Party ways." If he survives that long, he thought.

The man groveled in front of the tribunal, bowing his head to the ground in thanks before being carried off to one of the trucks.

Finally, there appeared to be no one else for the villagers to denounce so the prisoners from the trucks, a half dozen farmers from the countryside found guilty of hoarding grains and beans, were the last to be shoved against the wall and sentenced to death.

The knot of unlucky souls stood or dropped to their knees, shaking and pleading and pulling their hair while others simply stood in silence and stared with empty expressions. Little Deng was pleased to see that he would easily make the quota and an officer gave the order to have the prisoners' hands tied behind their backs. "Has anyone else knowledge of capitalist activity in the village," shouted Deng to the crowd.

There was silence before a voice rose up. "There is one who occupies house 15 of the workers quarters of the ex-Chief Magistrate."

Shanshan felt a tremor run through his body. He recognized the voice of Cao Chu as he pressed himself back into the crowd, trying to make himself small.

"It is that man there, the tall one," said Chu confidently, holding himself erect and staring at the table where the communists sat. "His name is Tao Shanshan and he lives in house 15. Behind a loose brick in the fireplace you will find a tin full of money which he has been hoarding."

Shanshan felt hands pressing against his back as he was thrust out of the crowd to stand bowing before the officer.

"Is it true that you have been hoarding, Tao Shanshan?"

Shanshan hung his head and did not answer. A soldier stepped forward and gave him a fist to the chest. He staggered back. "I have saved my wages, is all," he mumbled, gasping.

"You have hoarded money, Tao Shanshan, and that is a crime," said the officer.

Shanshan shouted, "That man over there," pointing at Cao Chu, "is a liar and a thief. His family—" An officer gave a barely perceptible nod to a soldier who stepped forward, and with the butt of his rifle, struck Shanshan a blow to the side of his head. He felt some teeth come loose as his mouth filled with blood. His knees buckled and he let out an audible groan as he spat blood and bits of broken teeth on the ground.

"Go and find the tin," shouted Chu. "You will see."

An officer gave a signal and a soldier departed. Little Deng turned and motioned to one of the officers. "How goes the preparations for lunch? Have they brought the carp? I would like to eat as soon as we are done here."

"All is being prepared," said the officer.

"Excellent."

Within ten minutes the soldier returned with the tin which he placed on the table. Little Deng swept the tin to the ground where all eyes watched it fly open and coins and bills scatter in the dust. "So, Tao Shanshan," he said, strolling in front of the tribunal, chest puffed out, a cigarette burning in his hand. Shanshan, on his knees before him, hung his head, a thin line of blood dripping from his mouth. "You are a capitalist and a petite bourgeoise hiding in peasant clothing. It is you and types like you that are a cancer on society and must be eliminated so that the new and glorious proletariat can rise up." He glanced at the villagers who stood with eyes wide and mouths open. "I hate to waste a bullet on this capitalist scum. Best to bury him alive but as I am impatient to try the famous fish of Wenyu Lake, and we have three more villages to visit this afternoon," he raised his hand in the air, and the soldiers began lining up the prisoners five at a time against the high wall of the square. Little Deng left and entered a dining room that had been prepared for him. He sat down just as the first shots rang out and beckoned to an officer. "Bring me the man who denounced the money hoarder. He will be useful to us in the future."

Chapter 26

Lin returned from Beijing the following day, faced with a work situation that was increasingly untenable. He would need to keep his head down, avoid any situation that involved confronting social dilemmas rather than scientific ones. Certainly, he continued to do his job, to make inspections, both planned and surprise, and to file his reports but he was still under surveillance and he was sure that his reports were being intercepted by the PSB. Without Madame Sun, his options were now limited. There was no one of the higher ups who would listen if he made a complaint. In fact, any complaint could be turned against him, accused of being a renegade and a roader who had lost touch with the Party. What was certain was that he would no longer be in contact with ordinary citizens; no longer would he give advice to workers, farmers, or villagers, or answer inquiries and follow up on notes slid under his door. This is what had contributed greatly to his imprisonment, and to theirs.

Mrs. Wan had been held in jail for a week; her friends had been released after a few days of psychological and physical abuse; the three farmers had been interrogated and released with bruises in places not visible, as were the two leaders of the delegation from the used battery recycling town. Even the two badminton players had been brought in for questioning, taken to a windowless room in the basement and verbally abused. They were so terrified that one had urinated all over his counterfeit Ralph Lauren chinos before they were allowed to return to their polytechnical university. He never did find out what happened to the badly compensated farmers who were upset about the loss of their land but he could imagine the pressure they received at the hands of their interrogators. The ring leaders were most likely still languishing in jail.

So Lin determined that it was best to target companies, factories, mills, and the local government without getting involved with individuals. His new focus was the marshland north of town where he spent much time ensuring that the planned Economic Development Zone stuck to its allotted land and did not encroach further on what was left of the marsh, and that it followed environmental regulations. He stood in front of bulldozers and steam shovels and dump trucks with a blueprint of the zone until the boundary was firmly fixed and the architects and engineers and investors could not try and squeeze however many more square feet beyond what was theirs. He discussed drainage and runoff and sewage and filters with architects who gave him wary, furrowed looks and stood back from him as if he was contagious. They shot furtive glances at their superiors, wondering who exactly he was and how much of what he demanded needed to be taken seriously. Cost overruns were a part of the business but they had encountered nothing quite like this. Environmental considerations, like landscaping, were always the tail end of the budget, and often neglected entirely, but here was a man who thought they were a priority. Naturally, he made many enemies this way, some new but mostly the same ones: the usual cabal of greedy businessmen who had made great piles of profits by poisoning the lake and had now moved into the marshland to do the same.

Meanwhile, high above the MSG factory, almost level with the giant silos, in the sumptuous conference room of President Gao Bing, a dozen men sat around a teak table containing tiny glasses of shiny, viscous rice wine of the most expensive sort. They popped spicy peanuts and small dried fish into their mouths with their chopsticks, and peeled apples and oranges and shouted to one another in the privileged voices of those who rule. The mood was boisterous, almost unruly, until Gao Bing tapped a bottle of rice wine with one of his silver chopsticks and brought the men to attention.

"Despite our illustrious mayor sitting here beside me, he has allowed me the honor of bringing this informal meeting to order." He bowed to Xiaoping. "I think it's time the mayor had a break from his many duties."

He leaned over and filled the mayor's glass over a shout of approval from the men and Xiaoping gave a humble nod of his head. Bing paused, looking around the table and smiling. "Gathered here are the most successful men of this small city, men who took risks and learned their business the hard way." There was a concerted rapping of knuckles on the table.

"We are a force for all that is great about the city and for what it has, and will, become. Nothing will stop us. The new Economic Development Zone is just the start of what we can accomplish, and once it is up and running by this time next year, it will be time to look for more opportunity. We are not men who can rest, who are content with what we have accomplished and all that we have. It's not that we are not satisfied," there was a general nod of assent, "it's just that success breeds success. And, regarding how we intend to continue that success, I would like to present to you a proposal that the mayor and I have been discussing recently."

Here Bing rang a buzzer in the outer office and a secretary appeared immediately. "Please prepare the presentation, Ms. Hai," Bing directed. Ms. Hai, dressed in tight, black polyester pants and a cream-colored silk blouse with one too many buttons undone, approached the table with a runway style walk and bent over the projector in the middle of the table. She pressed her thighs against the edge of the teak, swaying slightly left and right the muscles of her buttock with a mesmerizing rhythm. The room went deathly still. Each of them, depending on which side of the table they sat, could see either the outline of the thong beneath the shiny pants, or the tops of a pair of marbled breasts bursting from the blouse. And all shared a covert look of pure envious admiration for Bing.

She took her time loading the projector, clearly enjoying the attention. "Thank you, Ms. Hai," Bing said, unable to hide the self-satisfied grin that spread across his face. "That will be all." The secretary departed with the same runway walk as when she entered only this time a bit slower, a bit more exaggerated, tossing her hair as she went through the door of the conference room. There was a loud exhale of breath when she had gone.

"So," Bing said, all business now, pushing the button on the remote control. A picture of the current Economic Development Zone appeared, followed by a mockup of what the park was expected to look like when complete. "You all have seen the figures for the zone. We are at full capacity with long term leases in place on all available lots." A rapping of knuckles on the table as he clicked again and a blueprint appeared with the parcels marked out and the names of the future tenants. "We need to expand, obviously, and the only logical place to do that is the remaining marshland to the east." Heads nodded in agreement. "There is no sense in building a park elsewhere when we have the infrastructure and systems in place already. And as you know, the mayor and I were very successful in managing to acquire the western half of the marshland from the provincial SEPA recently but the eastern half will be more difficult. It will require more resources." Here the men all exchanged knowing glances at the euphemism. "Although we believe in the end that it can be done, our concern is the timing. There is no longer any doubt that SEPA will soon be a Ministry and that what are now recommendations will soon become law. Any delay to our expansion past the end of winter may prove fatal."

"That means that Tao Lin will hold the power of a ministry official," interrupted Xi Peng. "He is just the one to slow us down, and his negative reports and his snooping will only increase. And now we understand he was given a model worker award in the Capital City last month for his work. His picture is up on the Committee room wall," Peng added with a quizzical glance at the mayor.

"Yes," said Bing. "The award was unfortunate. Beijing has little understanding of how things are run in the provinces and especially in cities like ours. But we all know that Tao Lin is walking on thin ice these days. He is being closely watched and one slip will find him back in jail, and for an extended period of time." There was a satisfied growl from around the table. "Now, before the nightly entertainment arrives from the House of Ms. Wong Sufei," there was an audible and collective sucking in of breath, "if I could just get a show of hands as to who is willing and able to, shall we say, contribute to the resources necessary to make arrangements with the provincial SEPA." There came a rapid and unanimous showing of hands. "Excellent," said Bing beaming. "Obviously, we will contribute in accordance with our means and our unique business situation. My secretary," they all held their breath at the mention of her name, "unfortunately not Ms. Hai who is busy with other projects," a general chuckle from the men, "but another secretary will be in touch with each of you about the details." Bing began to move around the table with a bottle of rice wine, filling the small glasses, placing a hand on the men's shoulders to keep them from jumping individually to their feet, before returning to the head. "So, my good friends," here they all stood together as Bing raised his glass. "Let us drink to our good fortune, to the continued development of Meiyu city, and to our resounding success." Once the toast had been drunk, the bottoms of the tiny glasses tapped in unison against the heavy teak table.

Chapter 27

Xiaoyu sat by the side of her grandmother's new bed, one that her uncle, Cao Xiaoping, had bought and could be raised and lowered in any number of ways. It had shiny rails on the side and wheels and looked very expensive.

"How do you like your bed?" Xiaoyu asked. "It looks comfortable."

Her grandmother sighed. "I used to sleep on a hay stuffed mattress; then, when times were better, on horsehair." She squirmed about, finally putting her head back against the pillow and closing her milky, almost unseeing eyes. "I don't know what this mattress is made of, but whatever it is, it's not horsehair. Goose feathers maybe. No substance at all, like air." Breathing deeply, she rested her clasped hands on her stomach. The table beside the bed was covered with medicine bottles and she shook a pill into her palm. Xiaoyu gave her a glass of water. "Thank you," she said. She had just awakened from a nap and her voice was unusually clear, alertly tilting her head in the direction of her granddaughter. Xiaoyu knew that in an hour or two the arthritis pain would become unbearable and she would need to medicate more but for now she was a younger version of herself.

"I've told you about your father and your uncle and Gao Bing?" she asked as she closed her eyes.

"Yes," Xiaoyu answered, sitting quietly in the chair next to the bed, taking a peek at her cell phone where she had keyed up a game with the sound off. "But you know I always like to hear your stories, especially about my father."

"Well," she sighed, "it was after the war, you know. With Japan. I'm sure they teach you all about that in school."

"They certainly do, grandma," Xiaoyu said, squinting at her phone and zapping a number of intruders with a ray gun in the hopes of reaching a so far unattainable level. The game was better with the sound on, she thought. "But it's only you I get to talk to who survived the war."

"Well, your father and Xiaoping and Bing were quite a little gang. Inseparable. When they weren't at school or at Communist Party indoctrination or doing chores afterward that my husband, your father's stepfather, demanded, they were just wild, always roaming around the lake, exploring the northern hills. Little savages, they were. Well, your father was not quite as bad as the other two. They had sticks they carried with them that were all bloodied on one end from beating senseless whatever creatures they found."

"Disgusting," said Xiaoyu with a shake of her head.

"Well, boys will be boys," said her grandmother. "Your father, on the other hand, was always trying to save something of what the others had killed: frogs, snakes, toads, tadpoles. He would spend hours dissecting them with a small clasp knife he had bought, which he kept very sharp with a soapstone."

"So he always was like a scientist."

"Well, more like a medicine doctor. You know he studied medicine when he first went to university but he didn't like it. Cramped up in a clinic or hospital all day surrounded by sickness. He decided biology and chemistry were better."

"He doesn't talk about the medicine part much," said Xiaoyu, pausing her game and stretching her thumbs up and down. "But he knows how to take care of us when we are sick."

"I guess there are some things he still remembers." She closed her eyes and was silent for some minutes. Xiaoyu thought that perhaps she was asleep until she heard her murmuring. "They were such companions, the three of them. I don't know what happened that separated them so. Money, I suppose: Bing growing rich and Xiaoping as well, despite his lowly mayor's salary, and your father working for the government and the party for little money. And, of course, his crusade on behalf of the environment and the lake. It didn't help that your grandfather was a difficult man, indifferent and distant, always making Xiaoping and your father compete over everything, and tilting the competition in favor of your uncle as he was smaller and two years younger." Xiaoyu listened intently while her grandmother described how the three boys progressively grew older, from loud happy boys to gangly adolescents with changed voices and acne. Well, not Lin, she said, who was the best looking of the three, so tall with clear skin and high cheekbones and thick hair and such a solemn way about him. Girls were suddenly in the picture, of course, and the competition was fierce. She watched them from the window in the courtyard of the house, Lin painfully shy, head hanging, feet tangled as the girls fluttered about. Bing and Xiaoping would do somersaults and walk on their hands and shout jokes at the girls, who remained hovering around Lin until there seemed no use in doing so. They would sigh and give a last longing look at Lin before joining the other two as they showed off shamelessly, which the girls seemed to enjoy.

"The kids at school, you know, all they talk about is money," Xiaoyu said suddenly with a shrug of her shoulders, jolting her grandmother from a prolonged silence. "What this and that costs, and who has what, and how new it is."

"It is still amazing to me that any of you have money. In my day, we had nothing and we were happy with whatever came our way."

"I am happy with what I have," Xiaoyu said with a smile. "Although that new music player that Xi Shi has is pretty cool."

"Maybe your mother will buy you one at Spring Festival."

"I think my mother will be rich one day."

"I've no doubt of that," said Xiaoyu's grandmother before finally falling asleep.

Chapter 28

One morning, a few months after his return from Beijing, as Lin parked his bicycle beside his laboratory, he noticed two vaguely familiar figures loitering by the door. He sighed as they turned and approached him, hands extended. "Ah," Lin said, extending his own hand. "Ms. Ling Su and Mr.—"

"McMillan," the red-headed, sharp-nosed foreigner said as they shook hands. "Please call me Andrew."

"Yes, of course. Mr., uh, Andrew. I see you have managed to get permission to write your story?"

"We have," Ling Su said with a smile. "It took some effort but we have been successful. Would you like to see our documents from the Information Office and the PSB?"

"No, thank you," Lin answered. "You are here so I can only assume you have permission. Why you have gone to so much trouble to see me, is a mystery."

"No mystery at all," said Ling Su. "You are a distinguished SEPA employee with in-depth knowledge of the environmental situation here in the Lake District." Lin nodded cautiously. "We apologize for not getting in touch with you earlier but you are a difficult man to reach."

"I can be, at times. But here you are, so what exactly can I do for you." Lin was concerned to see the PSB officer, who had been parked in the black sedan across the street for many months, get out of the car and begin to take photographs of the three of them with a small camera.

"Perhaps we can go somewhere nearby to talk," Lin said, herding them down the street and away from the municipal building, but not before he saw a curtain on the second-floor shift and a figure step back into the shadows. Across the street and just a block away was a new western-style coffee shop which Lin had noticed while pedaling his bike to work but had never entered. Inside were comfortable chairs and a multitude of young people staring at computers and sipping large containers of coffee.

"What can I get for you?" Andrew asked Lin.

"I don't drink coffee, thank you. Green tea, perhaps? Or water is fine."

"Green tea it is. A latte, Su?"

"Yes, thanks," she said, dropping her oversize bag on a table and sitting heavily in an overstuffed chair. "It's been a long trip. We started yesterday morning from Beijing but the plane was late, as usual, and then we were diverted to Shanghai and had to wait for another flight."

"Air travel in China," Lin said sympathetically but distractedly.

"Yes. Well. I am glad we made it and have the opportunity to interview you."

"I'm not sure I would like this to be a formal interview," Lin said carefully. "You should really be talking to someone at SEPA in the provincial capital. And I should probably clear this visit with someone in the mayor's office."

"Of course, we plan to visit SEPA tomorrow before boarding our flight to Beijing. And we have been in touch with the mayor's office and they have had no objections to our speaking with you. In fact, they have been very helpful," Su said, just as Andrew arrived back at the table and handed her the latte. She gave him a bright smile. "Just what I need."

"And for you, sir." He handed Lin a large, white paper cup. "A green tea latte. I hope you like it."

"Thank you." Lin took a tentative sip and found it surprisingly delicious. Probably full of unnatural additives, he thought. Meanwhile, the table soon became crowded with mobiles and computers and tape recorders. Lin looked at the array of equipment with trepidation. "Is all of that necessary?" he asked. They ignored him as their laptops hummed and they fiddled with their phones.

"Maybe I should ask what you know about our work here so far," Lin began. "Then we won't waste time with questions you know the answers to." They both shrugged their shoulders, and Andrew nodded encouragingly at Su.

"Ok. What we know is that the lake is extremely polluted, mainly from the major industries surrounding it but also from the tributaries. We know that you—"

"SEPA," Lin corrected. She tilted her head slightly and smiled.

"SEPA," she emphasized, "has issued regular warnings to the polluting businesses but with little success. We know that they have little incentive to comply with directives from an administration but that will change once SEPA reaches the status of a Ministry."

Lin nodded his head in acknowledgement.

"You have issued citations numerous times to the Golden Prosper Spice Seasoning factory, the Leather Tannery, the SOE Specialty Cement works, and the Splendid Paradise Textile mill, among the many. You have also discovered a used lead battery smelter in a village northeast of the lake. The smoke from the smelter is affecting the health of the citizens, especially the children. We also know that there is an illegal mining operation at the headwaters of the northwest tributary that is creating a cancer village for the people who live below."

"How do you know this?" Lin asked, his brow furrowed. "Those are official and mostly confidential reports I have filed with SEPA only."

"As you know, a sanitized version of some of your reports has been published on the SEPA website. But actually, we have all your reports."

"You do?" Lin was astounded. "Where did you get them?"

"Mr. Tao," Su said patiently. "We have sources. Cai Jing is obviously a well-known name and we have little problem gathering information. And we do not like to disclose our sources."

"Well, if you have the reports, you don't need to talk to me."

"Personal interest," said Andrew with a shrug. "We need to know something about the man behind the reports. We can make you a national hero."

"I'm no hero. And I don't need or want the attention. It's already gotten me into trouble."

"Yes," said Su. "We know all about that. But then you received your award in Beijing. Anyway, what we were wondering was just how critical is the situation in the cancer village in the northeast?"

"Cancer village?" Lin asked. "Who came up with that description?"

"The fact is, there are thousands, if not tens of thousands of these villages around China. Cancer rates are doubling, tripling. There's a village we have visited near a Petrochemical plant in Shandong where the rate is above seventy percent. Also, an aluminum plant in

Liaoning province where the residents are getting very sick. Any village or town near a rare earth mine in Xinjiang has out of control cancer cases. Mining villages of all sorts are reporting high cancer levels."

"So why don't you talk to someone from those places? Why come to me?"

"Frankly, Mr. Tao," said Su, "there is no one quite like you in any of those places. We only talk to local cadre and party secretaries and mayors who claim that, you know, that they have no idea why cancer cases are spiking but that it surely has nothing to do with local industries."

"So, it's up to me to give you the story?"

"We can make you a national hero," Andrew repeated again. He seemed to like that line, Lin thought, although he failed to consider that he could also land me in jail again. "Besides," he added, "in Beijing you are already well known for your work, and you have the support at the highest level of SEPA." Used to, Lin said to himself, frowning at the thought of Madame Sun's imminent departure.

Lin sighed and shook his head. "You have my reports. You can visit the village in the northeast yourself and see if anyone will talk to you. I am not a licensed medical doctor so I can't tell you anything more than you already know. We are working on having an enforcement team up there as soon as possible. You can bring that up with provincial SEPA when you meet with them."

They stared at him, hands poised over their keyboards.

"Listen," Lin said. "I know enough to know that you will write your stories with or without me. And that you will use my reports for most of your information, and then use my name to fill in the 'personal interest' whether I talk to you or not. So," here he shrugged his shoulders, "the lake is dying. It's, in fact, as good as dead. How it comes back to life is hard to imagine. The wetlands are being developed for industry, and without the wetlands, there can be no rejuvenation. I, I mean SEPA, issue citations to all the polluting industries around the lake which are currently meaningless. In a few months that may not be the case. Now," he stood up quickly, "this is all getting out of control. All this attention is only going to make it harder for me to do my work. I'm sorry if you've wasted you time coming here." They continued to stare at him, this time with what he perceived as a certain amount of empathy. "Thank you for the latte."

He set the half empty cup on the edge of the crowded table and left. Outside, he paused to breathe deeply and wipe a hand over his forehead. It was then that he noticed the PSB officer standing across the street, again with the small camera held out in front of his sunglassed face, looking predatory and satisfied.

Chapter 29

Caijing In-depth Report
The Cost of Progress? Environmental Degradation in China
and a Report on the Environmental Movement
Plus
One Environmentalist's Fight: the Man from Meiyu City
by Ling Su

Lin could barely read past the headline and his hands began to shake. Chen had left the copy of Caijing on the breakfast table and, setting his bowl of rice porridge aside, he picked it up like something alive and possibly lethal. The first page contained graphic photos of people living beside a petrochemical plant somewhere in Shandong province. They were all obviously suffering from thyroid conditions with large tumors sprouting from their necks and faces, not so dissimilar from the villagers Lin had encountered up the northwest tributary. He started reading from a random paragraph.

"We have petitioned the government for relief," said Mrs. Wen, who agreed to talk to us about the conditions outside the Sinopec Petrochemical Works, "but we have gotten no response. My husband died last year from thyroid cancer. I know at least 20 other families who have lost someone. We are scared for our children."

Lin held his chopsticks aloft, unable to eat as he turned the page with trepidation and was confronted with a half-page picture of himself in his waders coming out of the lake, the circle of glass beakers on his vest looking strangely sinister, his cap pushed back on his head, a no-nonsense look on his face. He recognized the picture from one that hung in a meeting room at SEPA provincial headquarters displaying field work being done by various deputy inspectors.

"...the lake is dying. It's, in fact, as good as dead," says Tao Lin, a deputy inspector from the Wenyu Lake district. "How it comes *back to life is hard to imagine." A dedicated, and decorated, inspector, Mr. Tao Lin has been issuing citations and making recommendations to the business community surrounding the lake to no avail. The SEPA enforcement bureau reacts sporadically, if at all, to requests for assistance and their citations are, for the most part, ignored. This, Mr. Tao claims, will change when SEPA becomes a ministry as expected this spring. "In a few months, it will not be the case that these are meaningless citations." Among the many businesses in violation of the environmental laws of the country, are the Golden Prosper Spice Seasoning Works, the..."*

There followed a list of all the best-known factories, mills, tanneries, and workshops that Lin had cited over the years including specific information that could only have been taken verbatim from his reports. He stopped reading, dropping his chopsticks next to his now lukewarm porridge, and closed his eyes. His stomach felt fluttery and he could feel sweat breaking out on his forehead. He turned the page to find another thumbnail picture of himself, the one used for his model worker citation, at the head of a grey box that contained a short biography: his initial training as a medical doctor before moving to biology and chemistry, his work as a soil assessment officer during cultural revolution to assist farmers in increasing farm production; his years in Beijing at SEPA and CASS; his published field studies on water and air qualities in various provinces; and, of course, his recent model worker award. Despite the article being published in China's preeminent magazine, despite Andrew McMillan claiming he would be a national hero, despite his having done nothing wrong other than to do his job, he felt only a gnawing and knowing dread that such attention would bring him grief. On every desk in every town surrounding Wenyu Lake, lay a copy of this magazine, and people would be snarling, clenching their fists and cursing his name. Chen had been right to worry. They would seek revenge, and quickly, before SEPA was designated a ministry. Lin needed Madame Sun now more than ever but she was no doubt mixing compost into her small vegetable garden, contemplating seed purchases, and working on her down-the-line backhand.

His notoriety had some advantages: yes, he was even more intensely hated by the powerful people in the district but they would need to be careful how they treated him. If the central government was truly serious about environmental reforms, then he could use his notoriety to his advantage. If they intended only to pay lip service to the reforms, then Lin would find himself, as always, outnumbered and ostracized, as always on the outside looking in. In the end, he would give anything to be shed of this unwanted attention.

"What do you mean, FASHION!" said Su, slipping into a chair in front of the desk of chief editor Zen. "I don't know anything about fashion!" He looked embarrassed, unlike the communist party propaganda official sitting next to him who watched Su with steely eyes. "I am an investigative journalist. That's what I do. That's what I'm working on. I have another environmental piece that's almost ready for review."

"Yes, well," said Zen. "It's been decided that the one environmental piece was quite enough. It was determined," here he gave a brief glance in the direction of the propaganda official, "that there is too much negativity surrounding the issue. Our focus needs to be more upbeat, more serving the people than giving them impenetrable topics to ponder."

Su looked over at the propaganda official who did not change his expression or lower his gaze. "So now it's fashion?"

"Exactly," said Zen, as if she had suddenly agreed that this was the ideal course of action. "There is a minor fashion show this weekend in Barcelona, a run-up to Paris and Milan, with a number of Chinese labels involved. Here is your itinerary, your ticket, a credit card for foreign use, some material on the show and the participants." He slid a large brown envelope across the desk which she stared at as if it were infected. "Your passport is re-issued and up to date."

She stared at the envelope, and sadly shook her head. "It was good, the environmental piece. Really good. And the second one was even better."

"It was good, Su. No one is doubting your talent, but journalism is political, and the politics of the environment are currently out of favor. At least for now." Here he gave another sidelong glance at the propaganda official.

Zen stood up, pushing the envelope a bit closer towards the edge of the desk. The meeting was over. "Your plane leaves tomorrow night. You have some extra days in Barcelona to get acclimated.

Enjoy yourself. See the sites."

Su stood wearily, slid the envelope off the desk and into her hand. "That's it, then."

Zen nodded his head, affirmatively and affably. "And bring me back some of that Jamon Iberico. They sell it in all the shops at the airport."

"I'll try to remember," she said with little enthusiasm. As she closed the door behind her, she noticed that the propaganda officer had yet to move, or to lower his gaze.

"You're kidding me," said Andrew McMillan, shuffling through the contents of the envelope as he and Su sat at a half empty Starbucks in Beijing's Central Business District. He studied the itinerary and the ticket. "Economy, which is a damn shame, but ten days in Barcelona to cover a three-day fashion show? They must really want to get you out of town."

"Looks that way," Su said, sliding down in the overstuffed chair and putting a hand over her eyes. "What a lot of work I put into that second environmental piece, and for nothing."

"Well, mine's going to be published. It's not Caijing Magazine but it's something."

"What do you have? 600,000 circulation in the middle of America? Not 16 million in the Middle Kingdom. Sorry. No comparison."

"True," said Andrew good-naturedly. "But at least I can publish whatever and whenever I want."

He took a last sip of his coffee and sat back in his chair. "You know, Su, the problem with the central government is they treat everything like a war. They declare war on corruption. Then they declare war on decadent western influences. Then they declare war on the environment. And when you declare war, you inevitably have to declare victory. It doesn't matter whether the war is over, or even whether you won or not. But you have to say you won. And that's where I think you got stuck, right at the time they decided the war was over. Bad timing," he said with a shrug. He reached over and put his hand on her knee. She took her hand away from her eyes and gave him a brave smile.

"Ten days out of the smog, wandering the streets of sunny Barcelona, drinking excellent wine and eating good food and going to bars and shows. Doesn't sound bad to me."

"And you?" she asked. "What are you going to do for ten days without me?"

"I might survive. But probably best we head back to my place for the rest of the day so I can get as much of you as I can before you leave me."

"Well," she said laughing, "if you put it that way."

Andrew leaned over her chair, putting his hands on the armrests, and gave her a kiss. "I do put it that way," he whispered in her ear.

Chapter 30

It was a Saturday, and both Lin and Xiaoyu were visiting Jiang Nan. She was propped up in her bed looking tired, her brow furrowed with obvious pain.

"Can I get something for you, mother?" Lin asked. He rifled through the medicine on the table beside her, studying the labels.

"Perhaps one of those pain killers," she whispered, her throat hoarse. Xiaoyu held a water glass to her lips, and she drank, and then smiled. "Well, aren't I being well taken care of this morning."

"We do our best," Lin said, shaking out a pill into his palm and handing it to his mother. "Better than those worthless Ayi's Xiaoping hired."

"They're not so bad, Lin. It's boring taking care of an old woman, so they play cards and watch television. They keep me company, mostly, and make me move around every few hours."

"The first sign of bedsores and they are going to hear it from me," Lin grumbled, taking a seat at his mother's side. Xiaoyu had moved to a small sofa in the corner, her hands placed carefully in her lap; her phone was on mute and in her knapsack, orders of her father.

"So, mother, what's been happening lately?" Lin asked, stretching his long legs out in front of him.

"Xiaoping came by on Wednesday."

"Oh. And to what did you owe that extraordinary event?"

"Just a visit, Lin. And he wanted to see how I liked the bed."

Lin grunted in response.

"I don't know why you two have to be enemies," she said, sighing. "You were so close when you were young."

"We were always together, mother, but we were never close. We were complete opposites. Getting older just makes that clearer."

"But think how much better life would be if you could get along."

"Unfortunately, we don't get along."

"What has happened between you?" she asked with a hurt expression. "You were always together. Always out by the lake, racing around in the woods and hills."

"Too much has happened between us," was all Lin could answer. What exactly could he say to this old and frail woman who'd had such a difficult life? Yes, he and Xiaoping grew up together as brothers, but they had nothing in common. How could he explain to her what it was like with Xiaoping, how very different they were, how he smashed and tortured things, and how he enjoyed it.

As if reading his thoughts, she said, "He was wild, I know, maybe more than most boys."

Lin gave his head a barely perceptible shake, as the picture of those days passed before his eyes: a live turtle's shell being smashed with a rock until it shattered and how the gore spurted out; what happened to a baited gull after it had strayed to the lake from the sea when it swallowed a crust of bread with a fishhook in it and a line attached, and how Xiaoping played with it like a kite until its intestines were ripped out and it plummeted to its death; how he would throw rocks at the swallows' nests under the bridge by the marshland, then collect the chicks and throw them into the lake and watch as they flapped their wings helplessly until a perch or a large carp would snap them up; the frogs whose mouths he loaded with firecrackers; the tadpoles he popped between his fingers like sunflower seeds. And the deliberate destruction of the specimens Lin managed to save, sneaking up on his worktable and snatching them, holding them aloft with a great cry of victory before grinding them beneath his feet.

And having Cai Chu as a stepfather certainly skewed their relationship as he turned everything they did into a competition. Cai Chu had been made vice Party Secretary of the town after denouncing Lin's father and the departure of Little Deng from the village, then training to become Party Secretary and mayor under the tutelage of an older cadre. Once in power, he was ruthless in his dealings with the village, advancing those who were faithful to him, promoting certain party members in the state-owned businesses under his control, and crushing any descent. Oddly, he was generally fair in his treatment of his son and his stepson, although it was clear which one was favored and expected to follow in his footsteps. It wasn't as if Lin had been forced to live under the stairwell or behind the stove like some poor burdensome orphan. Everyone was poor and lived under the stairwell and behind the stove. Lin had no right to complain; he was housed, clothed, fed, certainly assigned more chores than Xiaoping but allowed to study, eventually even given the opportunity to join the party. But of affection there was none. It seemed that his stepfather was always watching him out of the corner of his eye, waiting for a moment where he would make him stumble, a moment which luckily for Lin never arrived. An early death saved him from whatever plan Cai Chu had in mind, Lin was convinced.

"If only you could all just get along," his mother murmured for the hundredth time, shaking Lin from his thoughts.

"Saying it isn't going to make it happen, I'm afraid," he said. In fact, the opposite was happening. He was at war with Xiaoping, a war he was losing.

Regret tore through him, physically constricting his breathing, and he had to wipe his hand across his suddenly damp forehead. If only he had stayed in Beijing and not returned to Meiyu city then he would not be facing the wrath of his half-brother and his clique of business partners. But then he looked at the gentle woman beside him, whose company he would have missed these dozen years, and at the angelic face of his daughter who would not even exist. He *had* come back, and there was no use regretting it. Now he just needed to figure out how not to lose the war with Xiaoping.

Jiang Nan's eyes had closed as she nestled her head into the pillow. Lin motioned for Xiaoyu to rise and go to the other side of the bed. They each took a firm hold of her hands with both of theirs.

"Sleep well, mother," Lin murmured.

"We'll be back soon, grandmother," Xiaoyu whispered. The old woman's eyes remained closed but there was faint trace of a smile on her wrinkled face.

Chapter 31

Although they had no badminton bags with them this time, Lin and Yang were at their favorite curbside restaurant, sitting on plastic stools and eating their usual cold dishes of spicy peanuts, chicken in hot pepper oil, and smashed cucumber. They each had a hand wrapped around a cold liter bottle of beer.

"So, Yang my friend," Lin said, a peanut balanced between his chopsticks, "to what do I owe the honor of your presence on a non-badminton evening."

Yang sighed and leaned back against the wall. "Listen Lin. I read the Caijing article the other day. My first thought was that such attention would be dangerous. No one in this town wants to be accused in a national magazine, in THE national magazine, of breaking environmental laws and being despoilers of the environment. Even if it is true," he added.

"Believe me, Yang, I know," Lin said in a perplexed voice. "I knew when those people came down that it would be trouble but there was nothing I could do. They had permission to interview me. They had my reports, too, if you can believe it. All of them, complete and in detail. At that point, it didn't matter what I told them when they interviewed me."

"I'm afraid," Yang said with a shake of his head, "the reports were released on purpose by someone in the municipal government, in order to make it look like you did it yourself."

"You know that? How do you know that?" Lin asked. "I mean, I suspected as much. The PSB were always monitoring my reports if not outright stealing them. But you know who it was?" he asked, staring intently at Yang.

"Yes. I mentioned that I had a colleague on the Security Committee. He told me." Yang took a deep breath. "According to him, it was someone from the mayor's office with authorization from the mayor."

"Ha!" Lin exclaimed with a sneer. "It was obvious that my brother and the business community were out to get me but I didn't think he would actually be the one to do it. Like father like son."

"What does that mean?" Yang asked.

"It's a long story." They sipped their beers and dipped their chopsticks into the cold dishes.

"I just have to keep my head down for a while," Lin said, doing his best to be optimistic. "Stay away from anything controversial. Quietly do my job."

Yang shook his head sadly. "It's too late, Lin. That's what I came to tell you. They plan to charge you with divulging state secrets as well as the other charges they already have you for: subverting the power of the state, undermining public order by creating a disturbance in a public place, and the old stand-by, picking quarrels and making trouble. It's serious, I'm afraid, especially anything involving state secrets. That's a capital crime."

"I really am in trouble, Yang," Lin said, closing his eyes and trying to think clearly about the future. "How would I ever convince people that it wasn't me who released the reports? And the other charges are fabricated: I had no intention of subverting state power. We talked about this. Just because I offered people the slightest bit of hope."

Lin leaned back against the wall, then shot up straight on his stool. "What if the journalists confessed to where they got the reports?"

"I thought of that," Yang said. "The question is whether the party or the state really want to know, or whether they are happy pinning it on you."

Lin suddenly looked stricken. "What do I do, my friend?"

"I wish I knew what to tell you. I believe you told me that Madame Sun was out of the picture, unfortunately, although I'm sure she will do what she can as a witness to your character. I will do so as well, Lin, but none of that will save you from what I fear will be a long prison sentence."

They were silent for some time. They lost interest in the beer and the food and simply stared out at the chaotic street scene in front of them.

"My stupidity," said Lin, shaking his head. "My absolute stupidity. Chen warned me but I didn't listen. I was too sure of myself, of my," here he spat out the word, "righteousness. I just could not believe that my being dedicated and committed to my job would get me to this point. How could I have been so stupid, so naïve?" he asked Yang.

"It's not stupid, Lin. What it is, is hard to imagine: the party, and the system, have failed you, and failed you badly. I don't see that there was, or sadly, is anything you can do about it."

There was another long silence while they sat buried in their thoughts.

"You can only hope for mercy," Yang said quietly.

"The party knows nothing of mercy."

"No," Yang said with a sigh. "You're right. Mercy is not something they know anything about."

They stood up, Lin not even making a move when Yang settled the bill, and they shuffled along the narrow street in silence until they emerged near Xiaoyu's school.

"I am truly sorry, my friend," said Yang, putting a hand on Lin's shoulder. "I intend to defend you to the best of my ability but I am a small-town Party Secretary. I am not sure what I can accomplish."

"I appreciate it, Yang. At this point, anything and everything helps." Lin shrugged his shoulders. "I don't suppose they told you exactly when they would arrest me."

"No. But I would suggest you not waste any time getting your house in order."

They shook hands, and Yang, head hanging down, disappeared into the smog-filled night while Lin stayed rooted to the spot for many interminably long minutes.

After talking to Yang the week before, it was no surprise when Lin stared out the window and saw the black sedan pulling up at the gate of the apartment complex in the early morning. Three men got out, regulation black suits, dark t-shirts, sunglasses, and ambled across the street. One stopped at the gate, leaning against the small shack that housed the local security guard and shaking a cigarette from his pack and offering one to the man inside, as the other two headed for Lin's building. What was a surprise was the sudden rush of pure panic: the thought of being incarcerated, the memory of the night he had spent in jail, the three steps of space in the jail cell, the utter hopelessness. For days now he had been resigned to his arrest, writing out and practicing his defense in what was, he now saw clearly, in their eyes an indefensible case. His palms were sweating as he thought of himself before the court, the verdict already determined, the prison sentence handed down. At this realization, he was suddenly moving deliberately into the bedroom, throwing a change of clothes into a bag, toiletries from the bathroom, grabbing a fistful of money from the back of one of his drawers and another fistful from the back of one of his wife's. Think, he said to himself, as he stood immobile in the bedroom. He pulled his phone out of his pocket, stepped into the bathroom, and dropped it into the water tank of the toilet and closed the heavy porcelain lid. Moving quickly now, he stepped into the kitchen and, without thinking, grabbed some grapes from a bowl on the counter. Xiaoyu was still sitting at the breakfast table with a schoolbook and bowl of rice porridge. She looked at him with frightened eyes.

"I need your phone," he whispered, slipping the mobile from the table into his pocket. "Don't try and call me. I will call you." He kissed her gently on the top of her head, then pressed her face against his chest. She reached up and put her hand over his. "It will be ok. I just need to take a trip is all. Tell the men that I went to work very early."

He hoisted the strap of the bag over his head, fumbling with the doors, banging against the outside metal-grated door, and stepped into the hallway just as the elevator was reaching the landing. He stared at the elevator door, then to the end of the landing and the stairs some twenty feet away, and turned to sprint. He would never make it, he thought. They would see his back. To his amazement, the door did not open but continued to the next floor. Of course, it was an even day. He could hear raised voices from the lift as the PSB cops told her to stop and the resident committee woman explained to them that it was an even day and that they were going to the sixth floor and they could walk down to the odd floor and that they were lucky she didn't make them walk up from the 4th floor.

Lin let out a sigh of relief and bounded down the stairwell. At the 3rd floor landing he stopped, his breath coming in short spurts, and surveyed the mass of discarded and haphazardly stacked furniture. He carefully moved two chairs and a dusty rug from in front of a battered television table before sliding his long body under the table, his knees scraping the top. He reached out and pulled the rug against the table and then the two chairs until he found himself in relative darkness. Waiting, trying to slow the beating of his heart, Lin moved his right hip in an effort to find a decent position. As he settled in, it wasn't long before he heard footsteps coming down the stairs, pausing at each landing. Doors were rattled and furniture was kicked in a rather desultory fashion before the footsteps eventually reached the 3rd floor. In the tiny space between the rug and the top of the television table, Lin could make out the legs of the PSB officer as he paused. Lin held his breath, closed his eyes, as the man moved one of the chairs with a loud scrapping sound. He kicked the rug, sending a cloud of dust into the air which made the officer sneeze and curse. He proceeded to clear his nostrils on the landing with a loud snort, one finger on one nostril and then the other, before halfheartedly kicking a few more pieces of furniture and descending to the 2nd floor.

Lin let his breath out and waited until he heard the muffled, metallic slam of the main door on the ground floor. He then moved the chairs and the rug and unfolded his body from the confines of the table. He moved quickly to the window of the landing where he had an unobstructed view of the front gate, the guard house, and the PSB officer now squatting who stood abruptly as the other men appeared around the building. Lin shied back from the window as they pointed, it seemed, directly at him. The man nodded, said something to the local guard in the guard house and also pointed at the top floors. The other two proceeded to the car while the officer turned towards the building, no doubt with orders to stand watch in front of the door to Lin's apartment.

As he heard the distant sound of the front door slamming and then the rumble of the ascending lift, Lin returned to the pile of furniture and climbed back under the television table. With some difficulty, he opened his bag and took out Xiaoyu's tiny flip phone, surprised to find the grapes, having completely forgotten he had put them there. He made sure the phone's mute switch was on, then started slowly chewing the grapes, knowing it might be all he would have to eat for the day, and plotting what his next move would be. Under the circumstances, he had little option but to stay put until darkness. He thought that if he could reach the basement late at night, he could climb up on the heating pipes and possibly knock out one of the narrow windows, make his way to the back wall of the compound and hoist himself over. There was the guard and there were surveillance cameras but hopefully he could get over quickly enough to not be detected. And then what? This thought made him tired, made him contemplate giving up and turning himself in, but remembering his one night in jail was enough to keep his resolve. Lin finished the grapes, wondering inanely whether he had remembered to wash them after he brought them home last night. He pushed his leg back under the table, pulled the carpet and chairs back, put his bag under his head and thankfully fell asleep.

Chapter 32

When he awoke, Lin assumed from the light on the landing that it was mid-afternoon. His legs were cramped and one arm had gone numbingly and painfully to sleep. He carefully pushed back the chairs and the carpet and stood, shaking his arm awake and pacing up and down the landing. He thought about climbing up to the 5th floor and checking the front door of his apartment but it was bound to be watched and he didn't want to take the risk. Lin sighed, gave his body one last stretch before climbing back under the table and pulling the carpet and chairs back into place. And just in time, as a cleaning woman rattled open the landing door, slamming it loudly behind her, and proceeded to sit on one of the chairs. She placed a large bag of garbage not a foot from Lin's nose and began to suck noisily on a piece of fruit. She spat seeds on the floor, reached down and rubbed her legs so that Lin pushed as far back into the shadowed corner as possible. She muttered and cursed about her life in general as she rubbed first one ankle and then the other. After what seemed an hour, she finally hoisted her bag of trash and shuffled down the stairs. Lin knew there would be other cleaning women using the stairway, carrying garbage and taking tiny dogs for walks, although most would be using the lift in the main stairwell. In any event, he put his bag under his head, tried to get his legs into a more comfortable position, and settled in for the long wait.

As darkness came and the building, after the buzz of noise from dinner and after dinner activities, grew deathly still, Lin checked his daughter's phone. Ten o'clock, he saw, and also noted the full battery picture in the upper corner of the screen. Just like her, he thought, one of the few children who would remember to charge her phone before she went to bed. As the next few hours crawled past, Lin told himself to be patient, to not jump the gun, although the desire to stand and stretch was at times too much to bear. But when the building was completely silent, he did crawl out from beneath the table and stretch before descending to the ground floor, pausing to listen for any noise near the main door, and then darting down the last stairs to the dark basement. He turned the phone light on, located the narrow windows at the top of the east facing wall, and climbed up on the water pipes to see if they could be opened but they were sealed shut. He would have to break the one farthest from the hearing of the guard at the main gate and so climbed down to find a brick or rock or piece of wood. Fortunately, there were dozens of bricks scattered about the floor as well as old, oily rags. Lin wrapped a brick in a rag, climbed back up the pipes, and waited for the sound of a garbage truck to roar by, which they did with great regularity late at night. He held the brick in readiness, and a few minutes later, as the sound of an approaching truck got louder, he cocked his arm back and sent the brick crashing through the window. The noise was deafening and he clutched the pipes in panic, sure that he had awakened the entire neighborhood. But after a harrowing few minutes, the deathly silence returned, and Lin climbed down and collected more rags with which to remove the shattered pieces of glass from around the window. He worked slowly, meticulously, waiting for garbage trucks to pass when he had to break the few remaining jagged shards of glass that were imbedded in the window frame. Eventually, he had all the glass out and swept aside so that he could crawl through head first and out into the damp night.

Once outside, Lin made his way along the side of the building until, from the shadows, he could see the guard in the tiny guard house beside the main gate, and the black sedan parked just outside. The guard, who would normally be sleeping soundly in his chair at this hour but was being kept awake by the presence of the PSB officer, thumbed through the pages of a magazine and yawned. Inside the black sedan, Lin could make out the tiny red-orange glow of a cigarette. He crept to the back of the building, picked up the brick wrapped in the rag, and headed to the back of the compound, careful not to trip over the abandoned furniture and mattresses and bicycles that littered the yard. Past another building, he finally came to the back wall, taking note of the surveillance camara on a pole in the corner. The wall was eight or nine feet high, the top spiked with shards of glass set in cement. In a pile of junk leaning against the building, Lin spotted an abandoned three wheeled bicycle with a flatbed on the back. If he could wheel it up against the wall, he could begin to build a ladder to the top. If he moved it just under the camera, he would only be visible for the few seconds, hopefully, that it would take to drop over to the other side.

Lin pulled the bicycle, its wheels rusted and immobile, through the dirt and parked it directly under the camera against the wall. He then darted back to the shadow of the building and waited. So far so good, he thought. He grabbed an abandoned single mattress, its underside covered in mold and slime, and wrestled it onto the bed of the bike. He found another mattress among a pile of junk which he piled on top of that, each time sprinting back to the shadows and waiting. Next, he leaned an old bicycle on top of the mattresses, which gave him enough height to reach the top and begin to clear away the glass shards. He climbed to the wall, resting his feet on the bar of the broken bicycle, and, with the rag-wrapped brick cocked in his hand, waited for the inevitable rumble of a garbage truck. In a few minutes, one appeared and he smashed the brick against the shards as it passed, sweeping the cement clear of the broken glass with the rag. It took two more passing trucks and two more attempts with the brick before he had cleared enough space for his hands and knees to rest on the top of the wall. He climbed down, retrieved his bag which he had left against the side of the building, and put the strap over his head and around his shoulder. He took a deep breath and let it out slowly. The camera would be able to see him once he was crouched on top of the wall so he had to make the leap quickly. What was on the other side was unknown; hopefully he would not land on anything sharp or jagged because there would be no time to look and see.

Lin crept up to the wall, climbed until his feet again rested on the bar of the bicycle. He adjusted his bag so it rested in the crook of his back, took a deep breath, and pulled himself to the top. One of his knees came in contact with a stray shard of glass and he heard his pants tear and felt the cut but he ignored it, crouching for a second at the top before dropping over, feet first, to the other side. He landed with a thump on the top of an abandoned automobile, it's roof swaying slightly under his weight as Lin's feet slipped out from under him and he fell on his rear end. Other than the cut on his knee, he was amazed at his luck. He slid from the roof to the ground, checked his knee to find that the cut was not terribly deep and did not affect his ability to walk, and headed down the street, away from the black sedan, away from the guard at the gate, and away from his home.

    He made his way through empty streets, feeling conspicuous and vulnerable, in the direction of the lake where he knew he could hide in the reeds along the bank until sunrise before joining the throngs of workers and farmers making their way to their factories and fields. He left the streets of the city with a sigh of relief, walked along a dirt road that ran along the lake, and ducked into the first clump of reeds that he came to. The ground was damp and covered in trash but at least, Lin thought, he was not squeezed under a table. He lay down, stretched his legs out, and using his bag as a pillow, stared at the smoggy night and waited patiently for the first signs of dawn.

    In the thin light of early morning, Lin joined the line of workers heading outside of town towards the fields. He was cold and shivering from his night in the open as he ducked into a side street to buy a jacket. The street was stirring with a few early morning shoppers and he found a woman hanging clothes up outside her shop, hooking the hangers onto a square mesh of metal on the wall. He tried a blue nylon jacket on, the sleeves slightly short but otherwise functional. He grabbed a straw hat as well, paid, and headed back towards the road heading east. He ducked into the reeds along the bank of the lake to rub mud and dirt on the jacket. He put the hat on the ground and stomped on it, then found a piece of thick bamboo on the bank which he balanced on his shoulder, and set out heading north and east, blending in with the stream of workers. Only his bag made him look out of place and this he turned around so that it was resting on his stomach and would not be noticed if a police car passed from behind, or could be covered up by his arms if one approached from in front. He knew that it was only a matter of time before they discovered the broken window, the broken glass on the compound wall, and his makeshift ladder, when they would realize that he was not going to go home and give himself up, and then the search would truly be on.

    He began to warm up as he picked up his pace, his long legs carrying him quickly along, his damp clothes slowly drying in the weak sun. He passed the great silos of the MSG plant; already the trucks were roaring in and out, the smokestacks sending out their plumes of greyish-white smoke. Bing would be up there in his throne, Lin thought, smoking and slurping tea and second by second increasing his pile of riches. He walked along the bank of the lake, heading out of the district, feeling a surprising strength in his legs. They would be looking for him in bus stations and train stations near Meiyu city but he planned to walk for days, just as his father had done from Shanghai just before the war. He would sleep in farmhouses or beside the road, if necessary, and eat from street vendors. When he was far enough away, he would stop in some nondescript town and board a long-distance bus, claiming a lost ID and bribing the ticket seller. To Beijing, he thought, where it would be easy to stay lost in the great Capital City while he sought help.

Chapter 33

When the long-distance bus arrived in Fengtai in the early morning after a more than twenty-hour ride, Lin could barely move his body. He had been stuck in the back above the engine with barely enough room to stretch out. All the hard sleep beds had been taken when Lin had boarded; he had been hissed at by the entire bus for not taking his shoes off before going down the aisle. While he struggled to remove his shoes, the other passengers pushed past him, claiming the last of the hard sleeps and he was forced to the back. He noticed that there were a few seats up front but these were stuffed to the roof with cheap bags made of packing material. Lin sat in the back with his bag beneath him, pushing his legs out into the aisle. He tried to rest although each bump in the road was magnified by his location at the way back, and the throbbing of the engine directly beneath him penetrated his body. After four hours, they stopped at a rest stop and Lin got out with the rest but stayed in the dark parking lot. He jogged a bit on the empty pavement and swung his arms in great circles and did some deep knee bends. When everyone had returned and the driver climbed aboard, Lin thought he would not survive the trip in the back on the floor. He shuffled down the aisle to the front and began to remove some of the bags stacked on the two front seats but again he was hissed away, and the driver yelled that the aisle had to be kept clear despite it already being clogged with a multitude of bags. He was tempted to tell them all to go to hell and dig out a seat anyway, but the last thing he needed was to call attention to himself. So for many hours he stood, hanging from the rails of the overhead bin, had even slept standing up for a time, but eventually he lay down in the back, the engine throbbing through his spine, his limbs numb and aching.

When the journey had gratefully ended and he climbed out into the grey dawn, the sound of the traffic was deafening, horns bleating and scooters whining and people scurrying here and there. It was cold, and he pulled the worthless straw hat down around his ears, wrapping his filthy jacket around him and pulling the collar up. Pausing beside a wall outside the bus station to catch his breath, he stretched his tired body and rolled his head on his creaking neck, first in one direction then the other. Lin had had plenty of time to consider a plan of action. Before boarding the bus, he had used Xiaoyu's phone to make a call to Chen. He knew that Chen's phone would be monitored and that they would track all incoming and outgoing calls and that the conversation would need to be short.

"Hello," she answered. He could hear her pushing out of her chair and moving towards somewhere where they could talk.

"Hi," he said.

"No," she said with false enthusiasm. "Not at all. That's fine. I'm sure I can get the document to you by noon tomorrow." A door slammed, and then a fierce whisper through the phone. "For heaven's sake, Lin, where are you?"

"Don't ask," he said. "Don't ask any questions. I won't answer. I only called to say that I'm sorry for all the trouble I am causing. I couldn't face the idea of going to prison although I will most likely end up there anyhow." He paused, could hear Chen's breathing on the other end. "You should denounce me. It will make things easier for you. But don't let Xiaoyu think any worse of me. I just wanted to do my job and to help the lake. Please let her know that." He felt the tears well up in his eyes. "I will miss you both, more than you can imagine." He folded the phone up and dropped his head into his hands. After a moment, he had slipped the battery out of the back before walking a few hundred yards from the bus station and shoving the phone and the battery deep into the first large trash can he had found. Now, although having arrived in the Capital City without a phone and without identification, he believed he was in relative safety. It was a huge city and easy to stay lost in, he had money, and he had his good friend, Hengda, who would certainly help him and give him advice. Lin headed for the subway station and the red line north to Beida. He could not enter the gates of the university without being checked for ID nor could he enter Hengda's apartment block which was also guarded but he would find an inconspicuous place to wait near the apartment until his friend drove by on his way back from work. It would be a long, cold, and tedious day but it was the only plan he had as he turned his bag so it rested on his back and plunged down the stairs to the subway, feeling a grateful rush of warm air.

It was mid-afternoon by the time Lin spotted Hengda's green, Army-style Beijing Jeep sputtering down the road. He had been squatting beside a wall for hours surrounded by itinerate workers, men who moved furniture and anything else that needed moving with their three wheeled bicycles with flatbeds who were playing cards and waiting for work. He was stiff with cold and had difficulty bending his knees as he stood but, with a rush of adrenaline, he managed to sprint beside the jeep and bang on the back window. Hengda gazed into the side mirror with a startled look. The man looked crazed, Hengda thought, with a filthy jacket and ripped pants and a silly straw hat pulled low over a dirty face that showed the beginnings of a sparse and scrubby beard. Does he want to wash my car? Hengda wondered. But where is his bucket and his waving rag? This is not the usual place for car washers. They congregate by the canal further up the street. He wanted to speed up to get away but there was a car in front of him. The man continued to chase after him, and he shouted something in a voice that sounded strangely familiar, shouted Hengda's name so that he brought the Jeep to an abrupt stop. He leaned over to roll down the window. "Lin?"

"My goodness, Hengda. Thank heaven you stopped," Lin said, hanging onto the window and breathing heavily.

"I was tempted to keep going until I heard your voice. Quick. Get in. By the way, you look terrible."

"Yes, well, it's a long story," he said as he opened the door and climbed in.

Hengda stared at the figure beside him, amazed at what had become of his friend. "I figured you were on the run," he said eventually, as he guided the jeep through the chaotic traffic. "The PSB stopped by the office the other day for a little chat. Anyway, here's the gate. Take that hat off and slide down in the seat so the guard can't see you," he ordered. Lin screwed his body up, knees just under the dash and chest and head resting under the window, as they swung into the compound, Hengda bouncing past the guard at the gatehouse who barely looked up from his phone. The place was exactly the same since Lin had seen it a few months ago, the red brick compound with unpaved streets covered in dirt and coal dust and littered with abandoned furniture and bicycles. Hengda jerked the Jeep into a narrow parking space beside a pile of disused furniture and a bent locust tree, and put a hand on Lin's shoulder. "We will need to be careful. Don't leave the car until a minute after I do. There are surveillance cameras everywhere so put my hat on and these sunglasses." Before hopping out, he handed Lin his orange and black Princeton Tigers ski hat and a pair of one-armed sunglasses that he fished out from the glove compartment. Lin waited a minute then squeezed his thin frame out from the door which pressed up against the spindly locust tree. When he entered the building, Hengda was waiting for him just inside and waved him towards the stairs. "Forget the lift. The neighborhood committee woman will certainly report you if she sees you."

They climbed nervously to the 4th floor, praying no one opened a door as they passed, until they reached Hengda's metal meshed entrance, which he opened quickly, and then the main entrance. When they had entered and he had locked both behind them, they let out a great breath of relief.

"Damn spies everywhere," Hengda said, shaking his head. "Police, PSB, neighborhood committee, work unit supervisor, party representative, propaganda officer." He led Lin to the kitchen, sat him down, and turned on the hot water cooker. "It's worse than under the Chairman. At least then they were unsophisticated. Now they have all these electronics. Ah," he paused, looking sympathetically at Lin, "but first a cup of tea. My goodness, you are deep frozen." Lin felt how raw his ears and nose were, and his toes and fingers were numb and tingling.

"I shouldn't be here getting you involved," Lin said with a sad shake of his head. "I'm sorry but I have nowhere else to go, Hengda."

"It's only right that you came here, to your friend in the big city where you can stay safe at least for a while. The thing to do now is to get you warm."

"I was out there for hours," Lin said, shivering. "I didn't want to miss you, and I didn't want to be noticed loitering around so I had to sit quietly beside that group of workers playing cards. Incredible. They sit there all day long doing nothing and don't seem to get cold."

"They are Beijing ren, true Beijingers," Hengda said. "They all come from places much colder than this, and they have about five layers of clothes on." The hot water cooker popped off, and Hengda put a teaspoon each of tea leaves into two large cups and filled them with the boiling water. Lin wrapped his hands gratefully around the cup.

"Careful," Hengda cautioned. "You probably have a bit of frostbite. You should wait until you get the circulation back in your hands before getting them too warm." Lin took his hands away and tucked them under his legs.

"So," Hengda started "let's see. The PSB paid me a visit a few days ago and asked all sorts of questions, although they wouldn't tell me why; you didn't call me to inform me of your arrival; you look as if you've been on the run for a week, at least. They have published the charges against you in the internal People's Daily. You are in trouble, my friend."

"Lots," Lin replied, feeling the steam from the cup reach his face, and finally, for the first time in many days, he let himself sink into the chair, to breathe deeply and relax. "I didn't know they had published charges but a friend was kind enough to warn me beforehand: subverting the power of the state; stirring up trouble; undermining public order; and, most damning, divulging state secrets. That's technically a death sentence, but maybe life in prison, or, if I'm lucky, just a long sentence. Did I miss anything?"

"Well, running from the police would be another," Hengda said, blowing on the tea leaves in his cup. "But that's about it. You know, when I first saw the article in Caijing I thought no good could come from it."

"I did run, Hengda," Lin said, shaking his head in awe of what he had done. "I looked out the window and saw the black sedan and the goons getting out and I ran."

"I don't blame you," he said. "Remember what Sun Tzu said in the Art of War, that of the thirty odd military strategies available, fleeing was the best." Lin smiled and took a sip of his tea, his hands now clutched gratefully around the hot cup as feeling began to flow back into his fingers.

"And this Caijing article, it wasn't my fault, Hengda. It was unavoidable. They had all my reports, everything about me. It didn't matter whether they actually talked to me or not."

"It has made you famous or, perhaps I should say, infamous. That may have an advantage if you intend to deal with foreigners."

"What do you mean, foreigners?"

"Well, what are your options, Lin? I am happy to have you here for as long as you like but eventually one of those cameras or one of those busybodies either in the lift or who patrol the grounds, or even that guard will look up from fiddling with his phone, and himself, and they will see you and ask questions. Of course, you can give yourself up and hope for some sort of leniency," Hengda said, blowing on his tea leaves and frowning, "and spend at least a few decades in jail, if not more. The only other option I can see," he said, taking a large slurp of tea, "is to approach a foreign embassy and seek asylum. Do you have any contacts in the foreign community? I have a few in academic circles but none at an embassy."

"My goodness, Hengda. It seems an extreme solution."

"So is prison. It's going to be one or the other."

"What about Chen? Think of what it would do to her future. And Xiaoyu."

"Difficult, I know," said Hengda with a sigh, "but it's your future we're thinking about here. Chen will self-criticize and divorce you unilaterally and get re-educated or maybe get kicked out of the party but she won't go to prison. Xiaoyu is young. She'll survive."

Lin put his head in his hands and didn't move for many minutes. Hengda could hear the sound of his labored breathing.

"I think you're right. My options are extremely limited," Lin said finally, looking up with red, tired eyes. "There's this foreigner Andrew McMillan." Hengda gave him a quizzical look. "He's the one who was with Caijing when they came to see me, reporting for a U.S. newspaper." Lin laughed bitterly. "He told me he was going to make me a national hero."

"He got that wrong," Hengda scoffed. "And now he owes you. Do you know how to get ahold of him?"

"I kept his card somewhere." Lin pulled it from one of the pockets in his bag. "Andrew McMillan at the Chicago Tribune."

Hengda studied the business card with the impressive masthead of the newspaper printed on the top. "Well, probably best not to contact him with my mobile phone; the PSB have obviously got me on a suspect list. It's safest to send an email from a work computer. I'm going back to the office right now and see about contacting him, and hopefully I get a quick reply. In the meantime," Hengda stood up, "we need to get you into a bathtub. And then you can sleep in the cot in my office. You must be exhausted." Lin nodded. "There's a bathrobe hanging behind the bathroom door. You can use that. I have some clothes you can use. Too small of course, but maybe Qianlu can fix them up. She's still pretty good with a needle and thread."

"Where is Qianlu?" Lin asked.

"She spends her days in supermarkets finding deals: cucumbers for a few fen less; cheap spinach by the pound; dofu that is on special. Seems more effort than it's worth but she enjoys it."

Lin got to his feet, feeling lightheaded but at least his toes and fingers had stopped tingling. "I can't thank you enough, Hengda. You have saved me."

"For now," Hengda said. "And hopefully for more than just now."

Chapter 34

Hengda was surprised to get an immediate response from Andrew McMillan since his email had simply said that he was from Beida and a friend of a friend of the environment who would like to talk to him about some "environmental" issues. Obviously, Andrew McMillan got the connection because he suggested they meet in a coffee shop in two hours' time near the west gate entrance of the university. When Hengda got to the coffee shop there was only one other foreigner there and he was sitting with a group of students speaking loudly in English. He took a seat in an overstuffed chair and began to glance at a newspaper he had brought with him when Andrew McMillan walked in. Hengda raised his hand and Andrew gave him a wave and motioned to the counter. He mimicked drinking from a cup but Hengda shook his head in response. He moved to the counter to order, chatting amiably in Chinese with the girl serving him, who blushed and held her hand in front of her mouth as she giggled at something he said. Hengda went back to his paper.

"So," Andrew McMillan said, setting his bag and his cup down and offering his hand to Hengda. "Andrew McMillan. Please call me Andrew." They shook hands.

"And I am the friend of the environmentalist who I believe you know quite well."

"Yes. An unfortunate story. I would just like to say that I had no intention of getting poor Mr. Tao Lin in trouble. I'm here to follow-up and see if there is anything I can do."

"He's in serious trouble," Hengda said, staring intently into his pale blue eyes. "And you published almost verbatim from his reports which are considered state secrets. You and that Caijing journalist. What did you think the outcome would be from that?"

"Those reports were given to us by a very reliable source in the town government," Andrew replied with a shrug. "You couldn't expect us to ignore them. Plus, Mr. Tao was an award-winning worker at SEPA. I was shocked to hear the charges against him."

"They are serious, serious charges. I don't see that there is any hope for his future."

"It wasn't entirely our fault. The Central Government policies are so obtuse that you never know when a legitimate story becomes a political liability. Ms. Ling from Caijing had an entire series of investigative articles prepared which were suddenly prohibited by her editors."

"Well, that's not something she will go to jail for." Hengda leaned forward in his chair. "What I want to know," he said, rolling the paper up tightly in his hands, "is whether you are willing to help Mr. Tao seek asylum with a foreign embassy. I see no other option for the poor man. It's that or years in prison."

"Unfortunately, I agree. It seems to have come down to that. I'm glad to do what I can," Andrew answered. "I have connections with some foreign officers at the U.S. Embassy. As a matter of fact, I am meeting one of them for drinks later this evening. I'll send him a note now and when I see him, I can ask him what the exact procedure is. A positive is that Tao Lin is well known now since the articles were published and since the charges were made public. That means they will have heard of him at the embassy."

"That may be a positive. At least I hope so. This cannot be bureaucratic," Hengda said. "He hasn't time for that since they appear to be using considerable resources to find him. I've already been questioned by the PSB a few days ago. Anyway, he is currently in hiding in Beijing but I'm not sure how safe he is and for how long."

"They haven't contacted me yet, at least not directly." Andrew took a sip of his coffee, and ran a hand through his hair. "I can tell you from my limited knowledge, as I understand it, once the embassy agrees that he is deserving and qualified for political asylum, and that's the difficult part, then a meeting is organized somewhere at the embassy and they take him in." He shrugged. "Let me talk to my friend and get the specifics."

"Please do," Hengda said. They stared at one another for some moments.

"Again, I am sorry for the trouble that Mr. Tao finds himself in."

"Thank you. I will give him that message when, or if, I see him. Now," Hengda tapped the rolled-up newspaper on the table, "how shall we communicate? I do not believe mobiles are safe."

"Definitely not. Email is better, not completely secure, but better. I will send you a short note once I have some information from the embassy, hopefully with the date, time, and place."

"Good. I look forward to hearing from you." Hengda stood, putting his hand out. "Good afternoon, Andrew." He stuffed the rolled-up newspaper into his back pocket, walked in his rolling gait through the dimly lit coffee shop, and stepped out into the cold Beijing twilight.

"Dude," Jim was saying to Andrew as he held an olive filled martini up to the dim light coming from behind the bar, "my rule is to never make plans in the evening in Beijing. Spontaneity is what it's all about. Otherwise, you may just miss something extraordinary." He took a sip of his martini and turned his eyes to Andrew. "Just last night I was in O'Reilly's and in walks this knock-out Chinese-Canadian girl. Sits right down beside me and starts telling me how she missed a flight and, rather than spend twenty-four hours at the airport, she came into town looking for some fun." His eyes twinkled. Andrew could imagine it: the girl approaching his friend who was tall, dark, handsome and charming. "Well, fun is too weak a word for what we had."

"You made plans to meet me for a drink tonight," Andrew said.

"You don't count. If something else had come along, I would have stood you up."

"Glad to know I'm such a high priority."

"Dude. Last night was high priority. You, I'm afraid, are very low on the priority ladder."

"Well, before another damsel in distress comes through the door, do you think we can discuss the case of the environmentalist?"

"Certainly. Let me just put on my U.S. Embassy First Secretary hat." Here he finished the martini and signaled the barkeep for another. He actually did look serious. "We like it, Andrew. I had a chance to run it by the Minister Counselor on my way out this evening. This Tao Lin is famous enough, he's in trouble enough, and the politics are right. I mean, the central government is all noise about the environment but they never do squat about it. As you well know, it took our air pollution monitoring station on the roof of the embassy to force them into setting up some of their own. I don't have to tell you that this place is an environmental disaster: air pollution index ten, twenty, thirty times higher than what's recommended as safe by the WHO; eighty-five percent of the water is polluted, and forty percent isn't fit for industrial use." He looked over at the barkeep, who was busy shaking his martini, as Andrew swallowed the last of his beer.

"Granting political asylum to an environmentalist," Jim went on, "instead of the usual human rights lawyers and dissidents, has a definite appeal." He gave a satisfied nod of his head. "It would send a certain signal to Zhongnanhai, maybe, that we're interested in protecting the rights of all Chinese citizens who find themselves threatened, etc. etc. etc. blah blah blah." The martini arrived and Jim took a sip, giving a thumb's up to the barkeep. The barkeep picked up Andrew's empty glass and gave him a look but Andrew shook his head.

"Besides," Jim continued, "it would bail you out since you and Su are the ones who got the poor guy in trouble in the first place."

"Not true," Andrew protested, wiping some beer from his upper lip. "He was probably in trouble anyway, but it's this damn obtuse political system. You never know where you stand."

"Yeah, but you publishing your articles at whatever the cost, and protecting your sources didn't help. You guys are mercenary. I understand your profession is a necessary evil, but scruples ain't in it."

"We can't all be high and mighty moralistic Secretaries at the embassy collecting a good salary and all those lovely benefits: no pressure or deadlines or threat of termination. By the way, how much of my taxes go to pay for your swanky apartment?"

"A lot," Jim said with a laugh. "A lot of your taxes. And swanky it is, although a bit of a mess after all that activity last night."

"I'm sure your full-time Ayi will take care of it."

"She's just three times a week, Andrew-my-boy, although I'm thinking of going to five."

"I'm sure you can manage to fit it in your budget."

Jim took a long sip of his drink as they gazed at themselves in the bottle-blocked mirror behind the bar. "When's Su back?" Jim asked after draining his glass and fishing in his pocket for his wallet.

"It was supposed to be early next week but now they plan on keeping her out of the country longer."

"Shame. For your sake, I hope she gets back soon. She's a stunner. What she's doing with you is a complete mystery."

"It's a mystery to me too," Andrew said with a shrug of his shoulders. "A damn nice mystery."

"I'll get this," Jim said, waving his wallet at Andrew and flagging down the barkeep.

"Appreciate it. So what's the next step with Tao Lin?"

"We'll run it by the Ambassador tomorrow. If he agrees, and he should, then I'll send instructions. Pretty simple. We station a couple of marines dressed in civies at the east gate at a prescribed time. He steps out of the crowd and approaches and makes a statement—and this is important—a verbal statement that he is seeking asylum. They grab him and take him in."

"I'm curious: why couldn't you just pick him up in an embassy car?"

"Well, you could. I mean, we did that once with a dissident who was in the hospital and obviously incapacitated. But a car is not sovereign territory like the embassy and can be subject to search and seizure. I remember they loaded that guy from the back of the Sino-Japanese hospital in the dead of night and just made it through the gates with the PSB on their tail."

The barkeep arrived and Jim settled the bill. "What about all the PSB goons and cops watching the embassy? The place must be crawling with them."

"Yeah, well," Jim answered, hoisting a knapsack on his shoulder. "They're always around. Not much to be done about that." Pulling on a hat, a scarf, and a pair of gloves and turning the collar of his coat up, he headed towards the door. "There's a new exhibition at Seven Nine Eight, if you're interested," he said to Andrew. "Always an eclectic crowd. I told you my philosophy is to not make plans, but I don't plan to spend too much time there unless something falls into my lap. Literally."

"With you, Jim, something always does. Anyway, I'll pass. I've got to sit by the phone now that everyone is awake in Chicago and enjoying their second cup of coffee and their third bagel and thinking up things for me to do."

"It's a dog's life," Jim said, grinning and giving Andrew's hand a squeeze. "My best to the inimitable Su. We'll be in touch."

"Will do," Andrew said. "Oh, and thanks," he yelled as Jim flagged down a taxi and disappeared into the smog-filled night.

Chapter 35

Lin slept and slept until he awoke with a rumbling stomach and was fed enormous meals by Qianlu. He stayed in the apartment, reading and trying to keep out of his guests' way. On the third night since his arrival, Hengda came back with news from the U.S. embassy via Andrew McMillan.

"They say tomorrow morning at 9:30 a.m. outside the east gate," Hengda said almost in a whisper. "There is always a huge crowd outside the main gate. You can stay lost in the crowd until you see the embassy personnel appear just south of the main gate. They have your detailed description so you just step out, approach them, say you are seeking asylum, and in you go."

Lin could feel his heart race now that this irrevocable plan was actually going to happen. As he had sat for days waiting in Hengda's apartment, there was always the chance that the embassy would refuse to grant him asylum but now he was certain. He tried to imagine himself in America. What would he do in that strange land? How would he adjust at his age to such a place? And what would they do to Chen? Would Hengda get in trouble for helping him?

"I am worried about Chen, and about you," Lin said somberly.

"Chen will look after herself," Hengda answered, "and as for me, what can they do to a semi-retired professor who lived through the trouble of the Cultural Revolution? If I'm caught, maybe a self-criticism or two. Nothing you need to worry about."

They ate a quiet, somber dinner and Lin went to his cot early. He tossed and turned, unable to sleep, staring at the dark room, barely controlling the panic he felt that made him sit up and shiver every time he was about to fall asleep. When light finally began to seep through the windows of the room, Hengda found Lin sitting motionless on the edge of the cot. "Ok, my friend. Let's get some breakfast and then I will put you in the Jeep and drive you to the subway station which is the safest way to get there." They drank tea and ate porridge and an hour later, Lin was hugging Qianlu goodbye.

She reached up to pat his shoulder, eyes moist and sparkling. "Send us something from the Golden Mountain," she said with a smile.

"I certainly will," Lin said. "Thank you for everything, Qianlu. I will never forget your kindness." They stepped out to the landing and took the stairs quickly to the ground floor. "I'm parked on the right," Hengda said. "Better let me go first. Give me a minute to unlock and get the engine warmed up." After a minute, Lin followed, keeping his head down and feeling the eyes of the surveillance cameras burrowing into his back as he approached the Jeep. Climbing in, he immediately placed his knees under the dash and scrunched down so that his head was below the window.

"Here we go," Hengda said, as he pulled out and headed for the gate. Lin watched the tops of the spindly locust trees and the dusty top floors of the apartment buildings and the smoggy sky flit by until he felt Hengda tense up beside him.

"What the hell is *he* doing?" Hengda muttered aloud. Lin was about to raise his head when Hengda told him to stay down. The gate guard was out of his gatehouse, something Hengda had never seen before, at least not during the long, cold winter months, and was peering near sightedly in the direction of the Jeep. When they were twenty feet from the gate, the guard stepped out and held up his hand.

"Hang on," Hengda said, as he revved the engine and lurched towards the guard, who, at the last second, threw himself against the side of the guardhouse. They swerved out onto the road, weaving between lanes and careening into the path of cars coming in the opposite direction before settling into the northbound traffic. Breathing heavily, they drove in silence for some time.

"Ok," Hengda said, his hands still shaking slightly although there was a certain growl of excitement in his voice. "They're on to us. That idiot guard has no doubt made a call by now but it'll take them awhile to get organized."

"Now I've gotten you into the middle of this mess," Lin said, shaking his head.

"Never mind that. At the light, you're only a hundred yards from the #10 line. Jump out and get lost in the crowd." When he came to a stop, he turned to Lin. "Good luck my good friend. No," he said, patting Lin on the shoulder, "don't say anything. Get out and be quick about it. You're off to America."

Lin gave his friend a fleeting, forsaken look before springing from the car and slipping like water into the masses making their way to the subway.

Lin felt relatively safe among the throngs standing on the platform waiting for the eastbound train, although he kept his head down just in case, knowing that his height made him somewhat conspicuous. When the train arrived, a great crushing wave of humanity rolled towards the doors, those getting out fighting valiantly against the tide and often losing. Lin was carried into the wagon with the wave and managed to grab a strap just as the doors closed and the train lurched forward. He looked at his watch: quarter to nine, with twelve stops before he got to Liangmaqiao and then at least a ten-minute walk to the embassy. He needed to be on time, not late and hopefully not too early. Lin took a series of deep breaths, glad that being tall allowed him to be above the heads of his fellow passenger and to get a bit more oxygen. He surveyed the crowd, noticing that almost all had their faces buried in mobile phones, frowning or smiling, thumbs flying across the tiny keyboards, with the exception of the migrant workers with their big packing material bags and their lunch boxes of boiled eggs and pickled vegetables. They sat atop their bags, eating contentedly, oblivious to the press of people around them. Lin observed everything, trying desperately not to think about what would happen within the hour, that he would be abandoning his country, his wife, his child, his friends, his profession and all that he knew, forsaking it for a great unknown. His thoughts turned towards giving himself up, throwing himself on the mercy of the court and the party, but he knew there was little mercy in either and that, if he was fortunate, the only thing he could look forward to was an interminably long jail sentence.

From his vantage point, he watched a man next to him playing a game on his mobile that had something to do with samurai warriors being trapped or escaping from boxes; they multiplied, escaping from more boxes, swords flying, and then multiplied again until, feeling somewhat dizzy and sick, Lin shifted his gaze to the advertisements for hair color and rice wine and instant noodles until the train finally came to his station. Luckily, many people were getting out and, with concerted effort, they were able to beat back the crowd trying to board. He popped out from the car to the platform as if being delivered from a womb, and caught his breath before lining up for the escalator. Above ground, entering the grey smog that covered the buildings and the street, Lin checked his watch. He was early so he decided to head north and loop around to come at the embassy from the south which should get him there just a few minutes before 9:30.

Approaching the embassy from Lady Street, past the shopping malls and small chinaware shops and flower shops, he again checked his watch. He had five minutes to work his way through the crowd and locate the east gate. There were hundreds of people milling about in front of the main gate; dozens of touts waving reams of papers and shouting their expertise at the filling out of forms for a desperately sought-after visa to the Golden Mountain. One had ingeniously set up a makeshift desk with one end of a piece of plywood balanced on the fender of a parked car and the other on a large cinder block as he scribbled on a great pile of forms, a line of people waiting in front of him. It was cold but no one seemed to notice in the frenzy of shouting and scrambling for assistance or a place in line. Some touts carried signs offering services to improve their chances at passing the interview process for the visa, attracting small knots of people. Lin worked his way through the crowd until he could see the east gate entrance, a massive, closed iron gate for vehicle traffic and a smaller gate for pedestrians beside it. He kept within the fringe of the crowd, glancing at his watch and at the gate nervously, keeping his head down and pretending to be interested in some papers a man had thrust in front of his face.

At 9:30 exactly, the gate opened and two embassy people stepped out of the small gate. They each wore the same dark suits, scarves and gloves and heavy winter boots but no jackets. Their hair was cut short, and they assumed a military stance in front of the iron bared door, hands behind their backs and feet spread slightly apart as they surveyed the crowd and the street. Lin took a deep breath, extricated himself from the crowd and, with a wildly beating heart, walked quickly towards the men. "I am Tao Lin and I am seeking political asylum," he whispered to himself. "I am Tao Lin and I am seeking political asylum," he said aloud. He was 20 steps from the gate when he began to shout, "I am Tao Lin and I am seeking—" at that moment, two muscled PSB goons leapt from a parked sedan on the street and raced towards Lin. Startled, he watched them approach, still moving towards the gate but slowly, suddenly confused. The embassy men watched him, then warily watched the PSB cops. They put their hands out in a welcoming gesture. He was close now, only 10 feet away, when the goons caught up with him. They carried short truncheons beneath their jackets which they jammed expertly, one on either side, into Lin's armpits, painfully lifting him off his feet. They turned, swept back to the car and bundled Lin into the back seat. The door slammed. Lin was lost behind the darkened windows as the men leapt into the front, and the sedan raced away. The Americans disappeared, closing the gate behind them. The whole thing had taken no more than ten seconds.

Chapter 36

As a member of the Chinese Communist Party, the first trial that Lin faced was by a single senior Party official judge to decide whether he would still be allowed in the Party. Obviously, there was no chance that they would rule in favor of Lin but under the law, a Party member was afforded a trial. So it was that Lin found himself very comfortably ensconced in a villa on Qian Hai Lake in the heart of downtown Beijing along with a half dozen other communist party members in various stages of disrepute. Despite the heavy presence of People's Liberation Army soldiers standing guard outside the narrow iron-gated door, they slept comfortably two to a room, with a cook available twelve hours a day as well as a cleaning woman for several hours each morning. Lin was well aware that this would be the last civilized environment he would encounter before being sent to a holding cell awaiting trail and sentencing in Beijing District Court. At the thought of this fleeting respite, he descended into a bittersweet, wordless melancholia which kept his fellow party members at a distance.

From one of the 3rd floor windows, just above the formidable walls that surrounded the villa, Lin, with his height, could stand with his head close to the window and make out the frozen lake and the rows of bare poplar trees along its shore. He stood for hours watching the activity of the lake: there was a swimming group that had cleared the ice to make a pool of water, with ice steps cut through, and they were swimming languidly in the frigid lake, calling loudly to one another, emerging red skinned and joyful as thin towels were passed to them. They were all but naked in their tiny bathing suits, squeezing out the towels and rubbing their raw skin.

Farther out, a group of speed skaters had cleared an oval track on the ice and were skating counterclockwise or chatting on the edges in small groups. Each morning, Lin watched as they dragged a five-gallon bucket of water on a wooden pallet around the oval. The bucket was filled with holes so that the water slowly dripped out, catching in a strip of carpet attached to the back of the pallet that spread the water evenly. As two men dragged the contraption with ropes over their shoulders, others would appear with smaller buckets of water from a nearby hole cut in the ice in order to keep the big bucket topped up. When they finished, Lin marveled at the gleaming glass-like surface and the fine lines their skates made in the ice.

Groups of young people mostly, but also families, walked gingerly on the ice, laughing and shouting, astonished at the view and the novelty of being able to stand in the middle of the lake. They grabbed one another when they slipped, sometimes landing on their backsides to great merriment. Lin watched with envy and a sense of limitless loss.

Other than staring out the window, there were mealtimes, the highlight of everyone's day. Breakfast and lunch were quiet affairs, but dinner was raucous with someone invariably producing a bottle of bai jiu, smuggled in at great profit by one of the staff, which they toasted to its bitter end. Lin was no fan of the liquor and left his glass full so that there was no fear that someone would try to fill it. He listened to the stories of his comrades fall from grace, most told with indignation but some with a cavalier humor. None were in the sort of trouble Lin was in; they would be reprimanded, re-educated, and returned anew to the party with very little learned and a craving to continue as before. There was comrade Ma, who had cleverly foreseen that the big cities of China would need to move their coal fired plants, and the pollution they produced, farther out to the countryside, and had won contracts to build stanchions for power lines between the plants and the capital city of Beijing. He had promised that the stanchions would contain steel and reinforced metal in order to withstand the winds that swept down from Mongolia each winter and spring, but he had mixed in an inordinate amount of cheap tin. One morning after an especially intense wind, the Beijing countryside awoke to the sight of miles and miles of power lines and crumpled metal lying in heaps in farmers' fields. The stanchions had been found sub-standard and Mr. Ma awaiting party review.

Comrade Jie had been tasked with building a section of a highway that would bypass his village some fifty miles northwest of Beijing and connect with a tunnel and ring road for large trucks bypassing the city. The budget he had been given was miniscule, but it was made clear that should he succeed, praise and a promotion would certainly be forthcoming. After consulting with his engineers, the biggest cost was to be the gravel at the base of the road necessary for stability and drainage. Fortunately, or unfortunately, for comrade Jie, not two miles distant was a spur of the Great Wall, abandoned and in disrepair, strewn with weeds and scrub pine, whose walls were made of bricks easily crushed to gravel for the roadbed. The section of the wall was dismantled. All went well until a group of young hikers with influential parents in the Beijing government discovered the missing spur and reported it. It was leaked to the newspapers, and despite the authorities being impressed with comrade Jie's intrepid spirit, he found himself vilified by the people and in custody.

Then came comrade Gu, who's story was told in a gruff, gravelly, somewhat comical voice, and who imagined himself to be at the cutting edge of the advertising industry. He had a business printing flyers for companies all over Beijing, some legitimate but mostly not. They consisted of massage parlors and gambling dens and bathhouses with additional, and not subtly implied, services. He employed an army of immigrant laborers to hand out wallet sized invitations to passerby's and to plaster bus and subway stops with advertisements. He even covered the pavements with his ubiquitous messages using a type of industrial glue, attracting those who kept their eyes downward. His decision to move into the billboard business proved to be his downfall. Having leased a sliver of land on a canal just off Beijing's 3rd ring road overlooking a heavily trafficked intersection, he proceeded to erect a tower to hold an enormous billboard showing a dark-haired gentleman in a red silk tuxedo sitting on a white leather sofa and holding up a bottle of hair tonic. The sign was made of flimsy sheet metal with no ability to ventilate the wind which inevitably plagued the city each winter. Luckily, when the huge sheet metal inevitably crashed down one early February morning around 5 a.m., there was little pedestrian traffic around. Unfortunately, it was the time when the PLA was changing its guards at the nearby embassies. As a troop was marching by, the billboard took out the last two soldiers, killing them instantly. Comrade Gu had paid the families off but the publicity of a badly designed and built billboard killing innocent soldiers and blocking most of a busy intersection during morning rush hour traffic did not endear him to the authorities.

Comrade Chan was one of the last to tell his story. A distiller of fine rice wine liquor, he had become relatively famous not only for the quality of his brand but for its extraordinary thickness and viscosity. A jealous competitor had run tests on the liquor and found that it contained inordinate amounts of finely crushed glass which accounted for its magnificent presentation. Although the communist party had myriad other worries to contend with then the ingredients of certain types of rice wine, this particular brand was beloved by highly placed party cadres and had decorated the tables of innumerable banquets. When comrade Chan was asked why he'd put ground glass into his liquor, his only defense was that no one had told him not to.

Naturally, eyes fell on Lin for his story. Avoiding an explanation for many meals, he eventually conceded that he was in front of the disciplinary judge because he was a dedicated member of the party who wholeheartedly believed in doing his job. Someone quipped that his problem was believing, and, with the exception of Lin, they all had a good laugh at that.

After being summarily and quickly expelled from the Communist Party by the judge, Lin was transferred almost immediately to the Beijing People's High Court located outside the 2nd Ring Road. It was an ugly concrete box with a massive bronze frieze of a flag of China taking up much of its front façade, and it was here that Lin's trial began. The case had garnered a fair amount of attention since the publication of his crimes, his flight, and his capture outside the U.S. embassy, plus a subsequent statement by the embassy in support of Lin's rights. The Party was determined to prosecute Lin as quickly as possible to avoid attention. Although a few foreign journalists hung outside the building in the vain hope of a glimpse of the accused and a statement, Lin was hustled into the back entrance of the court building. No one, of course, was allowed inside. The trial was expected to take no more than a day, according to a spokesperson for the Ministry of Justice, as the evidence against Lin was overwhelming, so overwhelming, in fact, that it would not be necessary to hold the trial anywhere near Meiyu city: no witnesses were to be brought to Beijing in order to give Lin the opportunity to confront them, all evidence had been collected and would be presented through depositions and statements with perhaps a few character witnesses appearing in person. Because the charges involved the passing of state secrets and a possible death sentence, the court appointed a high-level People's Procuratorate to prosecute the case. Lin knew little about the legal system but he did know that the procuratorate made the difference between death, a life sentence, or a lesser sentence.

Lin was brought before the High Court in shackles, both hands and feet, unshaven, disheveled, and dressed in an orange jumpsuit. He was placed in a hard backed chair in front of a tribunal of two judges and an assessor, the assessor's specialty being cases involving charges of espionage and the divulging of state secrets. Behind Lin were a dozen or so communist party officials who would witness and document the proceedings. There were no independent witnesses and no journalists, either domestic or foreign. The trial began with the senior judge reading the charges, the most serious being espionage, then subverting the power of the state, which carried a life sentence, the catch-all picking quarrels and making trouble, a possible five-year term, undermining public order by creating a disturbance in a public place, also five years, refusing arrest, and the newest charge being soliciting asylum from a foreign embassy in order to avoid rightful prosecution.

The second judge told Lin that the People's Procuratorate would be overseeing the trial and, in effect, advocating for both he and the court and would comment as appropriate on the presentation of the evidence. Lin himself would have a chance to rebut the evidence after its presentation was complete. When he asked if he could have access to a pen and paper, the judge impatiently shook his head and began reading the statements, beginning with those from the Public Security Bureau; Tao Lin had organized a protest by numerous villagers from around Wenyu Lake District for the purpose of subverting state power. The accused was heard to promise the villagers access to his classified reports, again for the purpose of subverting state power. He refused to disperse the crowd and was subsequently imprisoned but soon thereafter released due to his standing within the party and his having no previous record as a troublemaker. Photographs were introduced showing the crowd outside the Meiyu City Government Building, with a small red circle around the figure of Lin standing against the door of his laboratory and addressing the crowd. Further, the statement said, it was observed sometime later that the accused met with a foreign journalist as well as a journalist from Caijing magazine for the purpose of divulging state secrets. Here full-blown photographs were presented of Lin outside his laboratory talking with the journalists as well as photos of him entering a coffee shop with the two. Next, the Caijing article was presented, which contained the details of his reports, as prima facie evidence of passing of state secrets. In terms of his resisting arrest, the photographic evidence of Lin's escape from his apartment complex showed the broken basement window, the ladder he had built against the back wall, and the glass that had been cleared from atop the wall. Last, they presented grainy, black and white photos of Lin approaching the east gate of the U.S. embassy which almost doubled Lin over in a wave of pain as he saw so clearly how close he had come to freedom.

The procuratorate rose. "The circumstantial evidence is indeed strong, but is there any physical or electronic evidence showing Tao Lin passing the classified reports to the journalists?"

"Other than the evidence of his contacts with the journalists, no."

The procuratorate sat and began inspecting a liver spot on the back of one of his hands and rubbing it with his thumb.

Next came the statements of various government officials of Meiyu town beginning with mayor Cao Xiaoping who acknowledged that Tao Lin was instrumental in organizing the mob that descended upon the municipal office building for the purpose of undermining order in a public space. He was also involved in undermining the legitimate business of the town government in its desire to provide security and prosperity to its citizens by demanding onerous environmental policies on the business community, the sole purpose of which was to hinder progress. Regarding the passing of state secrets, although the mayor had no first-hand evidence that Tao Lin distributed his reports to the journalists, a mountain of circumstantial evidence indicated that he had. There followed a dozen statements from officials and business leaders in the community condemning Lin's practice of issuing citations without consideration to the business leaders and standard business practices and, indeed, to the considerations of the citizens of the town. There was even a statement from a Ms. Mei who claimed that she had been in the apartment of Tao Lin for the purpose of a job interview as a cleaning woman and had overhead an argument between the accused and his wife in which he stated that he did not want a stranger in his apartment snooping around, that he often brought work home with him and did not want someone looking through his documents. Of all the statements, only two were supportive: one from Yang and another from AGM Hu claiming that Lin was a conscientious worker and an upstanding member of the Chinese Communist Party.

Again, the procuratorate rose. "It is my understanding that Tao Lin's work for the State Environmental Protection Administration involved the serving of citations to the business community. Overzealous as he appears to have been in his duties, this does not automatically imply that he was inhibiting the will of the people. As for this Ms. Mei, it does appear to be a concern that Tao Lin was handling classified documents outside of his laboratory with the intention of keeping it secret." He sat.

There was a further and definitive denunciation regarding his flight from Meiyu city and its clear implication of guilt in regard to the charges against him, the conclusion being that an innocent man would surely have cooperated with the authorities. His ultimate treasonous act, attempting to seek asylum with a foreign power, was further proof of guilt. The procuratorate had no comment on either of these claims.

After a brief pause, a shuffling of papers, and a conference between the procuratorate and the assessor, two actual witnesses appeared in the court, brought in from a side door to stand before the judges and the assessor. Lin was shocked, and grateful, to see that the first was Madame Sun herself who, after giving a brief nod to Lin, stood very erect and with a clear, strong voice gave her name, title (retired), and opinion of the accused: a model worker, well respected, incapable of being guilty of the accusations being made against him, and ending with a plea for leniency. She turned on her heel, and strode towards the door with her head back, leaving the impression that she had done her duty but all too aware it was unlikely that much good would come of it. The second, and last, witness shuffled in, eyes shifting quickly around the room as he stood before the tribunal. Lin was surprised to recognize his colleague from CASS, Mr. *I would if I could but I can't so I shan't* who proceeded to claim that he had personally observed Lin to be in very close contact with a number of foreign delegations that visited the academy throughout the year and that Lin had kowtowed shamelessly in the hopes of an invitation to a foreign land. The man stated with authority that he had overhead Lin tell a friend that if he ever got abroad, he had no intention of returning to the motherland. At the end of his statement, he departed without a look at the accused.

There was a long pause while thermoses of hot water were brought in and teacups were filled. The trial thus far had taken less than three hours. The judge, having finished slurping his tea and putting the lid back on the cup, cleared his throat. "Now, Tao Lin. What do you have to say to the charges brought against you?"

Lin first thought to ask if it mattered but he held his tongue. They obviously wanted to continue the farce that there was a fair and impartial trial taking place. "The charges of passing state secrets, making trouble, and undermining public order are false. I did not pass my reports to the journalists. It seems quite logical that all you have to do is ask them how they got the reports."

The chief judge answered. "The foreigner will not disclose his source which appears to be customary among foreign journalists. In this case, we see no reason to make the issue an international incident. As to the Caijing journalist, she is unavailable for questioning."

"Unavailable?" he said incredulously. There was no answer from the bench. Lin then wondered whether it was worth making an accusation against his half-brother, the mayor of Meiyu city, the hero of the business community, a darling of the communist party, but he knew he would not be believed. It would be his word against Xiaoping's. The disclosure would not come from the journalists; the court had already decided that Lin was to blame. Deflated, he slumped forward in his seat and shook his head slowly. What was the point of all this, he thought? He took a deep breath. "I did not organize the people to gather at the municipal building. They came for information about environmental and health issues and I gave them what information I could. This did not include sharing with them my reports." There was stony silence from the tribunal. Lin sighed. "I have no defense for my flight from Meiyu town other than my very real fear of going to jail for crimes I did not commit. I compounded this mistake by approaching a foreign embassy. For that, I leave myself on the mercy of this court."

"Is that all?" the chief judge asked.

"Yes. No." Lin looked them in the eye. "I have been a committed and dedicated member of the Chinese Communist Party. I have always done my job to the best of my abilities. I have always upheld the environmental laws of the People's Republic of China and worked hard to protect the environment. I do not believe in compromise in this regard. If I stand of accused of being obsessive in my duty, then so be it." He sat back and closed his eyes.

"Good. Well," the chief judge looked around the courtroom, satisfied that the trial had proceeded without delay and that lunch would be on time. "After lunch, the procuratorate will consult with the tribunal and a judgement and sentence will be made."

There was a sudden, excited bustle of people grabbing coats and bags in the happy contemplation of lunch. Two guards led Lin to a small room off the courtroom with a bed, a chair, a tiny table and a squat toilet and locked the door. Lin sat, feeling empty, physically ill and exhausted. The door opened and a guard dropped a bottle of water and a white Styrofoam container of food on the table before slamming the door behind him. The smell of the food made Lin sicker, until he found himself in front of the toilet, his manacled hands against the wall as he retched a stream of sour bile. He wiped his mouth with the sleeve of his coarse orange jumpsuit, drank half the bottle of water in a single gulp before laying down on the cot and staring dejectedly at the ceiling.

Lin had no idea how long he lay there when the door burst open and the two guards heaved him to his feet. With one on each arm, they dragged him into the courtroom and dropped him into the chair facing the tribunal. Everyone had a satisfied and somewhat sleepy post lunch look of contentment as they sucked their teeth and slurped their tea. The chief judge rapped his knuckles on the table and there was immediate silence. "We have completed our consultation and will now hear from the People's Procuratorate."

The procuratorate strode to the middle of the room and, facing Lin, stood with his back to the tribunal. "Tao Lin. You have been accused of serious crimes, some of which carry a death sentence. It would be well within the right of this court to condemn you to death. However, there are circumstances that we, in our judgement, have decided would make such a sentence unjust." Lin let out a breath. *I will not be shot, at least,* he thought. "First, although there is no physical evidence that the state secrets were passed to the foreigner by you other than the evidence proven by your behavior, we are still of the opinion that you did pass these secrets. However, we also agree that you did so not from any desire to enrich yourself but through a misguided belief that some good would come from it. This was bad judgement on your part but not a crime of the highest order. As to the charges of subverting the power of the state, picking quarrels and making trouble, and undermining public order by creating a disturbance in a public place, you are guilty of all of these." Here the procuratorate pointed a well-manicured finger at Lin. "You held yourself above the party and the state, Tao Lin, an egregious charge especially against you, a party member in good standing who has served the party well up until these listed transgressions. No individual should consider themselves above the party and its benevolent policies regarding the governance of its people. You were not authorized, nor were you qualified, to determine what was best for the Chinese people and that is why you have been justly accused of these crimes." He lowered his finger, took a step back to survey the room. "As for resisting arrest and seeking asylum from a foreign embassy, these are crimes for which you have confessed and have been considered in your final sentence." The procuratorate nodded to the tribunal and took his seat.

The tribunal stood. Lin heard a general rustling and scraping of feet and chairs behind him as the officials and court reporters and court witnesses all stood. "Tao Lin," the chief judge intoned, "we have carefully considered your sentence. The charges are clearly enough to justify a life sentence. We have, however, considered your prior behavior, your record as a member of the Chinese Communist Party, various positive statements from party members, and the appearance of a witness on your behalf. With all these factors weighed, and in our supreme benevolence, we now sentence you to twenty-one years in prison. Dismissed."

Chapter 37

The following day, after an uncomfortable night in a holding cell in a local police station, Lin was led out into the cold Beijing dawn to an awaiting police van. He was shackled at the wrists, though his hands were thankfully not placed behind his back; his orange jumpsuit had been replaced by a dark blue one. A large blanket like coat, also blue, with oily grease stains around the collar and sleeves, was draped over his shoulders before he was shoved unceremoniously into the van and the double doors were slammed behind him. Lin stood uncertainly in the gloom; he could just make out the shape of two benches on either side and narrow windows up near the roof which let in barely any light. Once Lin's eyes adjusted, the shape of four other prisoners appeared, two on each bench, all in the same blue jumpsuits with blue coats draped over their shoulders. The van jerked forward and Lin stepped on someone's foot. A man cursed, snarled, and Lin did the same as he went past and took a seat up near the cabin. It was bitter cold and everyone had pulled their coats with their manacled hands as tightly as possible against their bodies. The van jerked one way and then another, weaving into the blare of the morning traffic.

They made many stops throughout the city, Lin lost track of how many, until the benches on both sides were crowded with a dozen men, all similarly dressed and hugging coats awkwardly against their bodies with their bound hands. There was little air in the van and the smell was overpowering: a dozen men all in the same unwashed state with greasy hair and dirty feet and foul breath. Lin thought back to the last shower he had enjoyed at the Qian Hai villa a mere few days ago but seemed like an eternity. In the cell this morning, they had given him a thin, cheap, disposable plastic toothbrush but no toothpaste, and when Lin tried to brush his teeth, the bristles had come loose from the brush and gotten stuck in his mouth or fallen into the tiny sink. He still had bristles lodged between his teeth which he was worrying with his tongue without much success.

After what seemed like hours of lurching in and out of traffic, they could tell that they were leaving the city by the lessening of the noise and the fact that the van moved along at a steady speed. Lin assumed it was north for a number of reasons: because it was the only forested part of the outskirts of Beijing and he could see the tops of the occasional aspen and poplar tree flowing past the dirty narrow windows; what little sunlight there was appeared to be coming from the east; and due to the simple fact that the north of Beijing, not many miles from the shadows of the Great Wall, along the canals that funneled water to the capital city, was where most political prisons were located.

They came to an abrupt stop and Lin heard the creak of a gate being opened and an exchange between the driver and a guard. The van continued on for another minute before halting and shutting the engine down. A fearful silence descended on the prisoners as they stared at their feet, rubbed their eyes, took their heads in their hands. Not a sound was heard for many minutes before the door was thrown open with an alarming crack as it hit the side of the van and two police, pistols in holsters at their sides, waving clubs, ordered them out of the van. They lined the prisoners up roughly in a courtyard, using their clubs to set them a foot apart from one another, until they formed a perfect tight line. "No one move," shouted one of the police as he strode across the courtyard and entered a metal door on the ground floor of one of the nearest buildings. Lin, glancing around him and concentrating on not moving his head, could see three brick buildings, each three stories high, the middle building directly in front of him and one to either side. There was activity behind him and the smell of burned cooking oil but he dared not turn to see what it was. The policeman appeared in the open doorway and signaled to the other cop.

"Now," the other shouted. "Let's move it out. Stay in line." Someone behind Lin stumbled and he heard the club make contact with a body. "In line, I said." They all concentrated on moving their feet in unison and staying as close as possible to the man in front. They stood before the door shivering, only one man allowed to enter at a time. Lin was next to last and, after what seemed an endless wait, he stumbled through the door expecting, hoping, to find some heat after the cold of outside, but the bare concrete room was almost as cold as outdoors. A guard undid his handcuffs and tossed them into a pile of others in the corner. He noticed at his feet mounds of shorn hair as he was pushed roughly into an elevated chair and told to keep his hands at his side. The buzz of electric clippers sounded behind him and as the cold metal touched the back of his head he flinched, feeling the blades break his skin.

"Hold still," growled a guard, banging his club against the side of the chair, "or you'll get plenty more cuts like that." Lin sat rigid, feeling the clippers shave as close to his scalp as was possible, and watched the hair fall in waves down his shoulders and onto the floor.

"Next," came the voice of the barber, and Lin was yanked from the chair by the guard and shoved towards another door. When he entered, the prisoners were sitting on plastic stools in a shower room. They stared at Lin and rubbed the top of their heads. Lin did the same, feeling the bristles of his scalp, and realizing that his shaved head looked just as awful as the others. He was told to sit in a stool beneath a shower head. The last prisoner was brought in, everyone once again rubbed their heads in unison, and they sat in silence in the cold for some minutes. The guard from the barber room eventually returned, grinding a cigarette out on the floor. "Undress," he ordered. The prisoners stepped out of their blue jumpsuits. "Everything off. Put the clothes in the hamper." A canvas basket was wheeled in by another guard, and they stood with their heads hanging down, naked and shivering.

"Sit on the stools and hold your hands over your eyes. Do not open your eyes or mouth. Do not move. If you open your eyes, they will burn, and if you open your mouth, you will be sick. You will need to stay like that for at least ten minutes."

They wheeled the hamper out, and the door closed with a metallic clang. Lin closed his eyes and mouth and held his hands over his eyes. The shower heads hissed in unison, and a thankfully semi-warm water poured out although smelling strongly of benzyl alcohol and what Lin could only assume was polyoxyethylene phenol ether, which, next to the alcohol, was the main ingredient in de-lousing shampoo. Lin found himself thinking about what the poisonous medicine would do to his newly shaved scalp and his skin for the next week, a strange thought considering the fact that he was destined to spend well over seven thousand days of his life, providing he lived that long, in this place. The showers stopped and silence fell as he kept his eyes tightly shut and his hands clamped to his forehead. After ten minutes, the showers started up again, again with lukewarm water but without the chemicals, and they rinsed off. Once the water had stopped, a guard wheeled in a table with towels stacked on it, which they all reached for. The towels were threadbare, as thin as a dishtowel, and worn on the edges. Lin found it necessary to wring his towel out before he could attempt to dry himself off completely.

The next room they were herded into had windows and they could see the identical buildings on either side of them: three story, red-brick, with poplar trees bordering the massive twenty-foot wall that enclosed the compound. Thin, yellow, winter sunlight streamed in through the dirty glass. There were benches stretching along two sides of the room and they were told to take a seat as they turned their eyes to the corner were a man in a filthy white coat sat at a metal desk stacked with papers. He clutched a cigarette in one hand, and a mobile in the other, and he was shouting instructions to someone about a pharmaceutical shipment that appeared to have been delivered to the wrong location. He slapped the phone down on one of the stacks of papers and sighed, stubbing his cigarette out in an overflowing ashtray and reached for a stethoscope. He did not stand up but wheeled his chair over to the prisoners with powerful thrusts of his feet and began to examine them. He looked in their eyes for signs of jaundice, checked their tongues for strep or other viruses, tapped their chests and back, and had them breathe in deeply while he held the ice-cold stethoscope to their chests. He took no more than a minute or two for each prisoner, although he paused at the last, an emaciated man who appeared to be on the verge of weeping at any given moment.

"I don't like the sound of this one," the Doctor said, removing the stethoscope from his chest. "Extremely congested. Put him in quarantine and have him checked for TB just in case. Probably he just smokes as much as I do." The guards chuckled. "Do you smoke?" he asked. The man nodded. "Well, naturally you smoke. There are half a billion smokers in the People's Republic. The question should be: do you smoke heavily?" The man nodded again. "Quarantine and a TB test anyway," he said as he wheeled himself back to his desk with a push and began to fill out a stack of papers.

Naked still, they were herded into yet another room, this one bigger than the others with a counter against the far wall with a half wire-mesh cage covering the top half where they could see behind the cage rows of shelves containing dark grey clothes. They were placed standing with their backs flat against a wall marked with measurements for their height and their width and footprints with measurements for their feet. A guard stepped forward and sized up the first prisoner. "Five seven, wide, eight and a half," he yelled over his shoulder towards the counter. There was a scurrying sound of activity before a stack of clothes with a pair of Mao slippers and a nylon net bag on top appeared miraculously beneath the wire mesh. He ordered the prisoner to pick up the stack before turning to the next man. "Five five, medium, seven and a half." On down the line he went until he came to Lin, who towered above the other prisoners as well as the guard. He grunted, muttered something about doing him last, and continued. "Five three, wide, seven and a half." Lin was last, standing shivering against the cold cement wall while the scurrying sound came from the behind the cage and a face appeared below the wire mesh. He eyeballed Lin, shook his head, and disappeared. After a few minutes, a stack of clothes appeared. "It's the best I can do," the face said with a sigh as he lit a cigarette and leaned his elbows on the counter.

Into the next room they went which contained benches and long, wooden tables. One of the prisoners, shivering violently, had searched into his pile of clothes for his underwear which he began to put on. A guard strode over and gave him a jab in the stomach with his truncheon. "Did I say to get dressed?" the guard snarled at the doubled-over man. "You'll get dressed when I tell you to get dressed. Now, sit at the table and put the clothes in front of you." They did as they were told. The guard, chubby and short, with squinting eyes and a sparse mustache, strode up and down between the tables. He held in one hand slips of white paper and in the other a black marker, stopping before the first man and slapping a piece of paper and the black marker down in front of the stack of clothes.

"This is your number. This is who you are from now on, for as long as you are imprisoned here. You no longer have a name, just the number." He tapped the paper in front of the first prisoner. "Read it to me," he said.

"One one four one."

"Right, number one one four one. Use this marker to put your number on the tag of the net bag. This is your laundry bag." He held up the net bag, showing the tag sewn to the bottom. "You have two sets of clothes. Your dirty laundry gets washed once every four days. It is distributed by the tag and number. If you do not write the proper number, or the number cannot be read, you will receive no clean laundry. Now write," he ordered, pointing a stubby finger at the tag. The prisoner wrote his number on the label and passed the pen on to the next. Down the line they went. "Read it to me."

"One one four two." The prisoner wrote his number on his laundry bag tag.

"One one four three," said the next man.

"One one four five," said the next. Lin's ears pricked up at this: even in a Chinese prison, a place that reeked of hopelessness and mortality, the authorities, with their obsessive superstition, shunned the number one four four, which brought bad luck and death.

Lin was next. "One one four six," he said, repeating it again in his head, and again, his identity, all that he was, a number which he would use for the next seven thousand six hundred and sixty six days. The last prisoner said his number, wrote his name.

"Now get dressed."

Chapter 38

The Shunyi District People's Political Prison was located on a quiet, tree-lined street surrounded by small farms and villages and beside a canal that brought water from the Miyun reservoir to the Capital City. In this bucolic setting, behind the towering walls topped by barbed wire, the prison housed three hundred party members, ex-party members, and mid to high level businessmen who had fallen afoul of the Communist Party. Tao Lin, sometimes Tao Lin but mostly number one one four six, resided in Building three, a building exactly the same as the other two buildings, the upper two floors consisting of two rows of twenty-five iron beds on which rested a wooden board, a mattress no thicker than a wool blanket, and a metal tag stamped onto a small footlocker with the prisoner's number. Attached to the ground floor of each building was a cramped mess hall with what were once bright colored plastic chairs attached to an aluminum rail and attached to long narrow tables, all bolted to the concrete floor.

Large, slashing red characters adorned the walls exhorting the prisoners to adhere to party principles and to conform to the party line. The only difference between the buildings was that the ground floor of Lin's housed re-education classrooms, the laundry, and a small sickbay with a dozen beds and a dentist chair; building two housed the induction center and showers; and building one the administration offices and guard quarters as well as the infamous cellar where the solitary cells were located. Atop each of the thin mattresses of the hundred beds per building rested either a sheet in summer or a thin down blanket in winter. The sheet or blanket was swapped not because of what the actual weather conditions might be, just like the coal fired heaters, but by a pre-determined official date, a date that so far claimed it was not yet winter. So it was that, in mid-October, during a particularly severe cold snap, Lin found himself awake early and shivering beneath his sheet rather than relatively comfortably burrowed beneath his down blanket. This was his ninth year of incarceration, close to halfway through his sentence, which, instead of giving him some small solace, only left him with the same hopeless dread that he felt every morning, the same despair at the endless monotony of his days, the sad frustration at being pressed on all sides by fellow prisoners, all suffering their own ceaseless depression.

He listened to the snoring, muttering, flatulent, sometimes carnal grunting of his fellow inmates, sounds now so familiar he hardly noticed them, even when, as often happened, someone cried out in their sleep in a strangled voice. He was thinking bleakly of the day ahead as the loudspeaker began blaring the Chinese National Anthem, the call to rise up at 6:00 a.m., and the figures in the grey light began to stir from their sleep. There was a general shuffle to the bathroom which consisted of a dozen sinks, each with tooth powder and soap dispensers hanging on either side, and a dozen open squat toilets, quickly occupied, facing one another. There were no showers; showers happened once a week in the induction center along with checks for lice, bedbugs, tinea pedis, or athlete's foot, and any number of skin related conditions. They'd had their shower yesterday and Lin could still feel the skin of his infected feet burning from the painful soaking in the terbinafine solution. They dressed in the feeble light from a half dozen naked bulbs hanging from the ceiling, always in the same dark grey jumpsuits with black borders on the sleeves and cuffs. They grabbed their iron bowls with iron chopsticks from the lockers at the foot of their beds which contained all that they owned, descended the stairs while being prodded and yelled at by bad-tempered guards with sleep-filled eyes and unruly hair, and into the mess hall where they stood in a line patiently, belly to back, along the wall.

Lin did not join the line of inmates for meals but instead, with his friend Guo Bocheng, crossed the prison yard to the kitchen in order to carry the great, steaming cauldron of food to Building three's mess hall. For years they had volunteered for this duty, a job no one else wanted. Bocheng and Lin greeted each other warmly in the dark and chill dawn. "Another day just like yesterday," said Lin, and gave his friend a smile.

"Not exactly," said Bocheng. "You are now almost halfway through your sentence, and I am one day closer to freedom at the end of this winter."

Lin sighed, rubbed his cold hands together. "Only one more winter to go, Bocheng. That is a good thing."

Bocheng had arrived at the prison a few years after Lin. A chief editor of an influential party newspaper, he had made the mistake of failing to see the end of the war against corruption and had continued publishing articles about corrupt officials. His last investigative series, which triggered his seven-year sentence, involved a corrupt party official in charge of procurement and contracts for the three gorges dam. It turned out his basement contained stacks and stacks of tightly packed hundred-yuan bills that were beginning to mold, a room full of Ming dynasty antiques stolen from tombs outside Beijing, and a piece of raw jade the size of a compact car. He had transported the jade from Burma and needed to use a construction crane to lower it through a hole in his roof, a hole in a second-floor bedroom, another hole in the living room, and into the basement. Bocheng ran the story despite the fact that the official was very highly placed and influential. Last he heard, the official was reprimanded and serving a three-year sentence under house arrest, presumably without the cash, antiques, and jade to keep him company, while Bocheng got seven years in prison. Part of the sentence was for the usual subverting the authority of the state, picking quarrels and making trouble, and holding himself above the power of the Chinese Communist Party but a much larger part was due to the fact that the BBC had managed to get not only footage of the decaying cash and the jade but a garage containing a Porsche Targa Carrera, a Ferrari, a late model Mercedes, and a Harley Davidson. And most damning of all for Bocheng was the broadcasting of an ill-advised interview with the BBC where he exclaimed that this was only the start of rooting out the corruption within the CCP. It was, in fact, the end, unbeknownst to him, and thus the lengthy sentence.

As they crossed the dusty courtyard to the kitchen, Bocheng stared at Lin. "As I tell you every morning, Lin, don't lose heart. Stay strong. Otherwise, you will become weak and hopeless like all the others. And that will lead to sickness, and possibly death."

"Keep telling me that, Bocheng, and I will keep trying. I don't like to think of the day when you are gone and I am alone in this nightmare."

"I'll do my best to keep you well supplied from the outside,"

Bocheng said.

"I'll need all the supplies I can get."

They arrived at the door of the kitchen, enjoying what little heat escaped. and greeted the four Ayi's who worked there by name. They greeted them by number as they were required to do before motioning them inside where they were directed to one of the massive gas stoves to remove the lidded cauldron. They each grabbed a handle which was wrapped in a kitchen rag, and grunted at the weight as they lowered it almost to the ground and started out the door, shouting a goodbye to the Ayi's.

As life for the inmates was a never-ending, often desperate, search for nutrition, over the years Lin and Bocheng had developed a system to pilfer food as they crossed the prison yard. On the pretext of changing sides and shifting the weight to their other hand, they would rest the cauldron on a bench. As they rearranged the kitchen rag from one handle to the next, they reached under the lid with three skin-hardened fingers and scooped up whatever food was within. It was scalding hot but as the years past, they found they could scoop up quite a mouthful without the least discomfort. There were security cameras, of course, but no one noticed the two old men who for the last countless years had carried food from the kitchen. They were also adept at swallowing without chewing and never leaving any traces of food on their mouths. Breakfast was problematic as they couldn't get much porridge to rest on the shallow spoon their fingers made but for lunch and dinner, they usually managed to get a chunk or two of treasured tofu.

Prison food consisted almost exclusively of tofu, over-cooked or pickled vegetables, porridge or rice, a preserved egg every few days, and canned fruit. Sometimes, perhaps once a month, there was a non-descript minced meat added to the tofu which caused great excitement among the inmates. They were all obsessed with food; it was all they talked about, all they dreamt about, and there was never enough. They suffered from a lack of essential vitamins and minerals, especially vitamin C and calcium and iodine. The lone dentist chair in the prison was occupied all day, every day, with prisoners suffering from gum infections and sores and loose teeth. Of course, almost every prisoner smoked at every given opportunity, which was permitted for half an hour after each meal and for an hour before lights went out. The prison authorities could not imagine banning the use of tobacco unless as a punishment, despite the fact that it contributed so heavily to the poor health of the inmates.

Once Lin and Bocheng had entered the mess hall, the line of men along the wall straightened up noticeably and began to ready their bowls. They set the cauldron down on a tin table in front of an Ayi with a ladle. The only benefit other than the pilfering was that they got to be served first, and so they retrieved their bowls from a table and received a ladle of porridge with pickled vegetables and bits of smoked tofu and took a seat at the back. They talked in whispers between mouthfuls.

"It's cold this morning," grumbled Bocheng. "Below freezing at night. I saw ice on a puddle in the courtyard."

"Another winter for you," said Lin, "but it will be your last."

"More chilblains, more flu and strep and fevers and cold sores." Bocheng shook his head sadly as he scrapped the last of his porridge into his mouth, holding the bowl near his chin and using the chopsticks in a shoveling motion. "I know I shouldn't complain, Lin, especially to you with so many more winters to go, but the thought of another winter is depressing."

"As you always tell me, my friend, stay strong," Lin said, also shoveling the last of his porridge into his mouth. "No sense in getting a fatal sickness now that you're so close." The winter sickness they most feared was influenza, easily spread and not easily controlled without an expensive vaccine which the prison authorities had no intention of providing. They had also seen plenty of cases of Hepatitis C, a virus contracted mostly from dirty needles used for antibiotic drips the "nurses" insisted on giving patients with severe colds or flus. Then there was the usual cases of arthritis and hypertension and heart conditions and asthma and cancer which, in the cold months, with the lack of adequate heat and nutrition, could turn to death. Lin saw at least a body a month transported from the prison in the brutally cold winter but hardly any during the summer.

The loudspeaker blared out the end of breakfast and they stood in line to rinse their bowls in tepid water and climbed the stairs to straighten up their beds and clean their barracks. Lin folded his sheet and then sat on the metal locker at the foot of his bed. He was excused from cleaning duties because he volunteered for so many other chores: the daily food carrying, the carrying of buckets of coal in the winter from the shed located in the corner of the prison to the furnace, as well as shoveling coal into the furnace. In the warmer months, he carried buckets of water for the guard's vegetable garden located, unfortunately, just outside the gate of the prison and inaccessible to pilfering by Lin. He could only glance longingly at the garden as he handed the buckets through a small opening in the door of the gate to a waiting guard. He also swept the courtyard and the grounds daily with a bamboo handled broom made of dried willow branches which he also used on the few occasions when it snowed. He did whatever heavier outside activity the guards wanted done and was therefore left alone in the after-breakfast hour relegated to the cleaning of their barracks.

Lin sat cross-legged on the locker, the prisoners apathetically dragging buckets of dirty water and pushing dirty mops under the beds and around the boxes, and re-read a letter he had received last week from Hengda. It was heavily censored, as was all the mail, with thick dark lines drawn through a third of the text, and Lin was forced to speculate about what exactly Hengda was trying to tell him: he was living comfortably at home and staying close to his apartment, meaning he was probably not under house arrest but still being monitored by the police. He was not needed at the Beida office anymore and was home, still working on his translation of his book, <u>Huckleberry Finn</u>. The title, in English, was blotted out by the security personnel; everything foreign was censored and considered inherently harmful to the state. Lin understood that Hengda had been forced to retire and was persona non grata at the university. He remained cheerful throughout the letter, never showing the least sign of regret at having helped Lin in his attempt to escape.

The more interesting part of the letter was about Chen, who, according to Hengda, had been accepted back into the party after a few years of intense re-education and self-criticism. She had denounced Lin as soon as he was arrested, and filed unilaterally for divorce upon his incarceration, something she had a right to do under the divorce laws of the People's Republic. Lin never received any mail from Chen, and only an occasional letter from Xiaoyu, full of trivial news of her schooling and her friends and never a mention of his situation. And these had stopped rather abruptly some years back. As for Chen, after her reinstatement, her real estate investments had grown right along with the boom experienced by the rest of the country. Having served as vice-president for five years at a private, provincial government-supported real estate investment company, she had started her own firm whose shares were returning fantastic profits for her investors. Hengda had enclosed an article from the Provincial China Youth Daily highlighting successful women business leaders and entrepreneurs which included a biography and a full photo of Lin's ex-wife. Gone was any trace of the peasant farmer's daughter, he thought, dressed as she was in a dark grey skirt and jacket with a silk blouse, in a massive gleaming office, leaning on a rosewood desk. The desk was dark, reflecting a glow from the light coming through the floor to ceiling windows so that it resembled a cloud upon which Chen floated; he wanted to crawl on top of it, to curl up on an unused corner of it, and sleep forever.

As for Xiaoyu, Hengda reported that she was studying at a university abroad and despite the reference to exactly where she was studying being blacked out, he had managed a line elsewhere in the letter about his own daughter taking a vacation to Australia, a highly unlikely event considering the distance from the U.S. east coast and the fact that his daughter loathed vacations, was a workaholic, and was never away from her hospital for more than a few days. This would explain why Lin had stopped hearing from Xiaoyu as the censors would never although mail with a foreign address and foreign stamp to get through to the prison. Lin refolded Hengda's letter and stood to slip it into his box, happily picturing his daughter on some manicured-lawned, tree-lined campus in Melbourne or Sydney surrounded by healthy, handsome, energetic Australians.

The first letter Lin had received, and which he kept buried at the bottom of his footlocker and tried not to look at again, was from his 2nd week at the prison, from his half-brother Cao Xiaoping informing him that their mother had died. Surprisingly, they had allowed Lin to read the letter in the relative privacy of the hallway of building 3 outside the guard quarters rather than in the barracks, meaning they were aware of its contents.

"Dear Lin:

Our mother died peacefully in her sleep yesterday. It was her time, and considering her arthritis and failing eyesight, a blessing that it came when it did.

At the time, Lin buried his head in his hands and let out an audible groan. To have lost his mother while he sat in prison in Beijing was more than he could bear.

As you know, she was experiencing pain but was recently given morphine to ease it.

So, those inept nurses you hired on the cheap probably upped the dosage enough to kill her and then went back to playing cards and watching television, Lin thought. Hardly a peaceful end.

I am sure that your dramatic fall from grace within the Party contributed to her death; she mentioned as much to me.

Lin had to choke back tears at that. Not that he believed for a second that she would have said such a thing, but he knew that his predicament must have caused her enormous mental anguish if not an earlier death.

She was a good mother to us both. She led a difficult and challenging life, in many respects, due to her disability and to her circumstances but she never complained and she was always there for us.

Her unhappiness stemmed from the fact that your father treated her like part of the furniture and never let her forget that she'd had me, a bastard child before he married her, and that he had rescued us from ignominy and ostracism and probable starvation.

I would just like to add that I hope you will take the time during your prison sentence to reflect on all that you have done wrong in your treatment of the Party and the people of China. You were given a golden opportunity by my father to be a faithful and productive member of the Party and your own selfish ego led you to where you are today.

And my inability to be as corrupt and unscrupulous as you has led me to where I am today, Lin thought as he ground his teeth in frustration.

Your passing of state secrets to foreigners was a horrific crime punishable by death and you should be thankful that you were spared by the benevolence of the Party.

And it was you, or one of your henchmen under your direction, who passed the supposed state secrets on to the foreigners.

Our mother was cremated, as was her wish; her ashes were scattered on the island where she met my father.

And mine.

Sincerely, Xiaoping

Chapter 39

The loudspeaker blared, shaking Lin from his reverie as he climbed off his footlocker and stretched his legs. The inmates stored their cleaning gear in a corner of the barracks and descended the stairs to the courtyard outside their building. At least a dozen prisoners peeled off to stand in line at the back to the door of the infirmary as the rest took their place in four lines for morning calisthenics. Standing in the dawn light in their thin summer clothes, seeing their breath and shivering, they went through the ritual of raising their arms over their heads, marching in place, and touching their toes. The guard in charge sat on a bench reading a newspaper and simply shouted out three words: arms, march, and toes, over and over again in a bored, monotonous voice. Lin was one of the few who actually concentrated on the exercises while the majority of the inmates stood in place until the guard raised his eyes which forced them to make some deferential movements. After fifteen minutes, they filed back into the barracks, half of them trudging up the stairs while the other half continued straight ahead to the education center, another bare concrete room but with chairs attached to desks like those found in a middle school classroom. On each desk was a pencil and a few sheets of paper which meant they would be spending the first hour writing self-criticisms before a lecture would begin on CCP thought and policy, or perhaps yet another viewing of endless war films showing stupendous heroism and self-sacrifice on the part of Chinese communist soldiers against evil Imperialist Japanese and Chang Kai-shek forces, or perhaps a film on the wonders of the workings of the Chinese Communist Party.

Lin looked nervously around for guard Kao, glad to see that he was not here this morning. Last week, there had been a very unpleasant encounter with guard Kao and Lin when the guard had arrived at the classroom late, lugging a large cannister of film. He had looked terrible, his eyes bloodshot, sweat pouring from his forehead despite the cool weather, his hands shaking. He was known for his hard drinking, his ill-health, his hatred of the job, and for broadcasting endless complaints about his shrew of a wife, and he had cursed repeatedly as he wound the film through the complicated innards of the projector. He had turned the lights out, turned the projector on, ran the first segment until numbers appeared counting down from five and the opening credits began to run. He paused the film, moved to the front of the room, and stared gloomily out at the inmates.

"This is a film about the great Chairman Mao's public works projects in and around Beijing in the 50's. We were fortunate to get one of only a dozen copies from the propaganda department of Beijing City. It is a very important film, highly prized for having captured the Chairman in an outdoor, natural setting and so faithfully serving the people. I want everyone," here he glared around the room and passed a hand over his sweaty forehead, "paying the closest attention. No talking. If you are found sleeping, you will get a week in solitary. If you make one move from your seat, you will get the same. Is that understood?"

"Yes, guard Kao," they all answered in unison.

"Good." He moved back to the projector, and flipped the switch to begin the whirring, clacking sound of the projector, and slid out the door, slamming it behind him.

"Off for a little hair of the dog," someone mumbled as they all watched the opening credits and then a long shot of a reservoir, probably the Miyun, and an ancient tractor rumbling along an embankment followed by an army of cheerful, Mao jacketed workers with shovels on their shoulders. The scene cut to a tent beneath a grove of beech trees, the flaps opening and the smiling, rotund figure of the Chairman appeared, a cigarette clutched in his hand. The camera followed him marching about, grainy and jumpy footage but extraordinary shots of the Chairman in action. Here he was, huddled around a table surrounded by engineers and staring at a set of blueprints, now picking up a shovel and hefting it like a club, then addressing a mob of workers standing in a gulley. There was no sound.

"Isn't this supposed to be a talkie?" someone whispered.

"I'm sure we're supposed to hear the words of the Chairman," another said in a hoarse voice.

"Hey Lin," a man beside him said. "Don't you think you ought to tell guard Kao the sound's not working?" They all turned to Lin, the designated spokesman as one of the longest serving inmates.

"You heard him," Lin answered. "He said not to move. Or it's a week in the pit. The fact is, we're in the wrong whatever we do, but I'm not risking stepping out of the room, especially considering his present mood."

They sat some more in silence, and tried to imagine what the narrator was saying. Someone offered to fill in the silence with a made-up dialogue, and began a speech which included famous Mao sayings and communist party catch words, sarcastically twisted through false tons and innuendo. There was quiet laughter all around, and then more silence as the film appeared to be reaching its conclusion. Just then guard Kao pushed the door open and stood in the gloom, rubbing both hands through his thick cropped hair.

After visibly choking back his anger, he finally screamed. "Just what in the hell do you think you are doing? What kind of melon head idiots sit watching a film with no sound?"

There was tense silence in the room, everyone staring at their feet, as guard Kao flicked the lights on, strode to the projector, and snapped the off switch. Mao, who had been waving to a crowd of workers, slowly ground to a halt, his hand permanently raised in a fascist salute.

"Lin, number 1146," guard Kao barked, again pushing both hands through his hair until they were clasped behind his head. He let out a long sigh and stared at the ceiling.

"Yes, guard Kao," Lin answered, standing by his chair.

"Why don't you give me an idea of just what the hell you were thinking."

"I was simply following orders, guard Kao. Your last words were that no one was to speak, sleep, or move. I apologize if there were more to the orders than I realized."

"And no one in this room thought to come inform me of the fact that the sound was not working?"

Lin paused, wondering how far he could push the guard. "It's not something we discussed. You ordered us not to talk."

Guard Kao shook his head. He appeared to be on the verge of making a pronouncement but then shook his head again.

"OK. You will now watch this film *with the sound* for the entire week. Do you understand?"

"Yes, guard Kao," they answered in unison.

"And you will write a lengthy essay on just what it was like to see the Chairman in such a setting, and to *hear* what the narrator had to say about the great actions of the Chairman."

They all stared at their feet until the loudspeaker had blared out the time for lunch, and they had shuffled out the door under the glare of guard Kao.

That was last week, a narrow escape from what could have been time in solitary or half rations or extra cleaning duties. This week, Lin thought, sitting quietly at the tiny desk writing his self-criticism and extolling the virtues of the Chinese Communist Party, was a relief. A guard entered with a slam of the door and the writing papers were collected, to be returned after comments and corrections from the Communist Party Propaganda Official assigned to the prison. This was followed by a recording of a series of famous speeches by Deng Xiaoping, beginning with his pronouncement that "It doesn't matter whether the cat is black or white as long as it catches mice." Thankfully, just as the inmates were slipping into a somnambulant state, the loudspeaker blared the call for lunch and they all rose, shuffled out of the classroom, up the stairs to collect their bowls and chopsticks, and back down to stand in line in the canteen. Lin and Bocheng left their bowls on a table and headed across the courtyard in the now relatively warm autumn sunshine to the kitchen.

"It doesn't matter if the food is black or white as long as there's plenty of it," Bocheng said with a grin.

"It doesn't matter if the prison is black or white as long as we get out of it," responded Lin.

"It doesn't matter if a guard is black or white as long as he can be bribed."

"It doesn't matter if a party official is black or white as long as he is corrupt."

They continued in this vein, smiling, until they came to the door of the kitchen, greeted the Ayi's by name, were directed to the stove, grabbed the cauldron, headed back across the courtyard, and performed their ritual of changing hands while dipping their fingers into the boiling food. They grunted with approval as they tasted tiny flecks of meat for the first time in weeks. After so many years, Lin was still amazed at the small pleasure this afforded, and he knew that once no pleasure was to be found in the small ways pleasure came to him, he was doomed.

Chapter 40

The years went by, and hard as Lin tried to stay healthy, he began to lose the fight. First there was a particularly brutal winter in his fifteenth year where the wind whipped down from Mongolia, seeping through the cracks between the windows and the red brick. Everyone caught influenza. Outside exercise was cancelled, the food had to be brought the short way from the kitchen in an army jeep in order to protect it from the bitter cold, and the prisoners were confined to their barracks where they stayed balled up in their beds beneath their single down blankets, getting up only to relieve themselves and to fill their teacups with hot water. Lin fought it as long as he could but the influenza had collected in his lungs and he was having difficulty breathing. When he did arrive at the door of the infirmary, he was pale and wheezing and barely able to stand. They put him on an antibiotic drip and from the needle he contracted Hepatitis C which, as the years wore on, effected his liver. He was quite healthy for a prisoner, until he was not. For the last six years of his sentence, he spent most of his days curled up in his bed in winter, or leaning against a wall in the sunlight during the warmer months, not moving much, conserving what strength he had left. The longest serving prisoner in anyone's memory, he was left alone by the guards and shown a certain measure of respect. By the time his time was up, after twenty-one inhumane years, he was a broken man, stooped and shaking, with a perpetual cough and a liver and spleen that barely functioned.

Incredibly, miraculously, at his release he was given a plastic box smelling of camphor and filled with his possessions that had been taken from him at the time of his sentencing including his watch and a wallet still filled with hundred Renminbi notes. He was astonished when he felt the soft cotton of the clothes he had gotten from Hengda all those years ago, the cuffs and hems let out so expertly by Qianlu, after twenty-one years of wearing only a rough grey jumpsuit. When he stepped into the courtyard in the winter sunshine in his civilian clothes, his belt pulled in a few notches, there were a few guards milling about who extended their hands and wished him well before he boarded the van to Beijing, and the Ayi's from the kitchen came out to see him off. He could barely control his urge to weep, avoiding catching anyone's eye as he climbed unsteadily into the passenger seat and stared into the dirty windscreen before him.

As the van hummed quietly through the gates of the prison, he noticed at once how the space opened up all around him, no longer contained by the great, red-brick walls that had towered over him for so long. With a feeling of anxious wonder, he stared at the crowds and lines of cars and the ubiquitous high-rise buildings that had now reached out as far as what had once been rural countryside. Lin noticed how the cars had become rounder, sleeker, the tires smaller, the colors softer and more varied, the brand names unrecognizable although clearly Chinese. The people hadn't changed at all but the city was so much bigger and more crowded and there were signs for new subway lines that hadn't existed when Lin had been incarcerated. From the passenger window, he noticed with astonishment that the taxis had passengers but no drivers. He questioned his driver who told him all the taxis were now auto drive as well as most of the privately owned cars. He showed Lin how the automatic drive worked, taking his hands from the wheel and his feet from the pedals on the floor, but quickly turned it off, telling him he was old fashioned and liked to do the actual driving himself. They passed at least two new ring roads on their way to the city center which confused Lin as to where exactly he was until he saw from an overpass a tree-lined street leading to the east gate of Beida. The university was completely surrounded by development, a small oasis in the midst of eclectic architecture and traffic and masses of people.

His first stop would certainly have been to see Hengda but he was dead, a heart attack in his sleep, according to the letter he received from Qianlu. She said she was posting the letter into a mailbox at the airport on her way to see her daughter in New York, a trip he guessed was one she didn't return from since for years he had heard nothing from her. He had no contacts in Beijing anymore, other than Hengda and Qianlu, and Madame Sun who, he had heard from an inmate who knew her husband, had had a stroke and now sat only half mobile in her courtyard house, unable to speak but with those sharp, alert eyes glaring at the relatives who fussed about her. Lin had requested to be dropped at the train station, surprised to find that he was not taken to the station he remembered just off Chang An avenue in the heart of the city, but to the far south, a massive metal and glass structure housing three stories of shops and restaurants and tracks where sleek bullet trains sat buzzing like tethered animals.

"What happened to the old East Station?" Lin asked, staring out at the huge entrance hall and the trains pulling in and out. The driver shrugged his shoulders indifferently. "You said the train station. Well, this is it. I don't know anyone who goes to the East Station anymore, unless you're taking a local."

Clutching the handle of a sturdy plastic bag holding all that he owned, a change of underwear and socks and a wool sweater and his toiletries, Lin shuffled through the doorway into the regal entrance hall and was instantly overwhelmed. He found the first available seat and tilted his head back and stared at the glass roof two hundred feet over his head, at the maze of escalators that crisscrossed the three floors of shops, and at the people who moved confidently around with their bundles of goods and loud voices, many wearing strange complicated-looking glasses. He shifted his buttock, amazed to find how comfortable a train station seat could be after so many years of sitting on wooden benches and chairs. He coughed, felt the sensitive swelling in his liver with his fingers before checking his wallet for the fifth time for his identification card, freshly printed and giving an address back in Meiyun town where a room was waiting for him. This was courtesy of his former position, and time served, at SEPA, now the Ministry of Environmental Protection. The Chinese Communist Party was not quite cold enough to throw a former Party Member, even a disgraced one, out on the street with nothing, but it would be hard to call what would certainly be a tiny room in an undoubtedly decrepit high-rise on the outskirts of town and a pension of seventeen dollars a month much of anything. Lin studied the gigantic electronic departure board to his right, seeing a train departing for the provincial capital in mid-afternoon. It gave an arrival time of some six hours after departure which seemed incredible to Lin since before his incarceration the train was an overnight sleeper that took the better part of a day. He leaned his head back on the plush leather of the chair, luxuriously moving his hips from one side to another and stretching out his long legs before falling into a half sleep.

The train had been a miracle, hitting speeds of two hundred m.p.h. and flashing past a countryside filled with high-rise developments and small cities that hadn't existed twenty-one years before. A man beside him had been fiddling with a pair of glasses that had what appeared to be sensors all around the lenses and small pods at the end of the arms. Lin quietly asked him what kind of glasses they were. The man had given him a curious, somewhat distrustful look, telling him they were the latest version of specs before putting them on and ignoring Lin until he got off at the next stop.

Lin stared with wonder out the window until darkness fell and he nodded off to the humming of the train cutting through the countryside. He had arrived as scheduled, taken a regional train to Meiyun town, a train that now ran faster than he could ever have imagined, and was home in the late evening. He had taken a taxi, one he could ill afford but it was dark and he was tired and he had no idea where, exactly, his new room was located. The taxi driver pulled up in front of a non-descript ten-story building surrounded by small shops and bicycle sheds and piles of construction material, who then became very upset when Lin presented him with a handful of paper money. He eventually accepted it, with much grumbling and cursing. Lin had had to wake the apartment manager to get a key, a severely unhappy man who unceremoniously directed Lin to a 3rd floor room with a wave of his hand and slam of his door. The lift was out of order, it looked as if it had been for some time, and Lin climbed the cluttered staircase, fitted the key to his room with some difficulty, and took only a cursory glance around before undressing and dropping immediately onto a single bed pushed against the wall. The mattress, thin as it was, was heavenly after so many years on his prison bed. Yawning, lying on his back and rubbing his sensitive liver and spleen, Lin fell into a deep sleep.

When Lin awoke late in the morning, the sunlight streaming through the lone window above the tiny kitchen sink, he was dazed and confused. On one side of him was a wall, not rows of sleeping men, and on the other a wooden chair and a narrow desk, a two-burner stove resting on a cabinet containing a refrigerator no bigger than those found in hotel rooms, a shelf on the wall with two water glasses, two plates, and two bowls, and a glass door which he could see contained a squat toilet with a shower head hanging nearby.

Maybe altogether twenty feet by ten, the bathroom perhaps four feet by four, he thought, but all his. He would not have to share it with fifty disgruntled inmates, cursing, farting, spitting, grumbling, and sighing in unison. Lin shook his head at the wonder of it before getting up, gathering his clothes and leaving them on the bed, and stepping into the tiny bathroom. There was just enough room beside the toilet to stand and direct the water onto his head. The water was hot, and stayed hot, a wonder that brought tears to Lin's eyes. He stood beneath the stream for as long as he liked, no one jostling him, pressuring him to hurry up, the water not going from lukewarm to cold to ice cold in a matter of seconds. It seemed too extraordinary to be true.

There was a soap dish attached to the wall but no soap. He would need to buy some, he thought, as he dried himself off with a thin towel, stepped out of the bathroom, and found his bag leaning near the door. He unpacked his meager belongings, changed his under clothes, brushed his teeth in the kitchen sink, and then sat down on the bed and stared out the lone window at a relatively blue sky that appeared to contain traces of clouds, clouds being an extremely rare sight to see twenty-one years ago in Meiyun town. It seemed there was so much for Lin to do, to walk around the town, to see the changes, do some shopping, revel in his freedom, but it all frightened him. He wasn't sure he would even know how to buy things, having been handed everything he needed for the last twenty-one years: a new grey jumpsuit when his had become unmendable, a toothbrush when his had no bristles, a haircut which required no exchange of currency, shoes when his had disintegrated. He sat on the bed in a semi-trance, unable to move, staring at the thin clouds drifting past his window until he felt a great thirst and he got up to fill one of the glasses with tap water. He returned to the bed, curled up in a tight ball, and closed his eyes. Overwhelmed, he put off all he could and would do for another day.

It was a week before Lin made his way out of his room in daylight. He had crept out a few times late at night to shop at the local Jinkelong, stocking up on fruit and vegetables and tofu and even the occasional piece of pork. His first daytime excursion was to the market to buy a small, wooden handled cane which he used to make his way to the lake a half mile away. He sat on a bench on the bank and caught his breath, seeing himself from afar, an old and bent man with whitish grey hair and a limp, a distinctly yellow, jaundiced tinge to his skin from his stressed liver, rubbing his side and looking myopically at the water. As he surveyed the lake, what surprised Lin was that both the north and south banks were visible. They were hazy, yes, with a thick layer of pollution hugging the surface and the shores, but in all the years before his incarceration he had never been able to make out those shores from where he sat. It appeared that the air quality had improved but whether there was any improvement in the quality of the water, he couldn't tell. He would need to make inquiries before reaching any conclusions about the environmental condition of the lake.

He stood and made his slow way along the bank of the lake until he came to the island where the Great House of the Chief Magistrate had once stood, since destroyed and taken over by the fertilizer factory which itself had been bulldozed; the land was now dotted with abandoned villas and a few low-rise apartment complexes, all consisting of bare cement walls and roofs and lawns and gardens overrun with weeds and piles of construction trash. Lin crossed the original, narrow arched bridge and paused beneath a metal framed gate which welcomed him to the Millionaire Villa Mansion Gardens in faded characters. Whomever had abandoned such prime real estate must have been very high up in the government and the communist party and suffered a spectacular fall from grace, he thought. The fact that it now lay undeveloped pointed to a toxic political situation that no one risked becoming enmeshed in.

Lin picked his way through the cluttered street to one of the low-rise apartment complexes and began to climb the bare cement staircase with no banister, staying close to the wall and pausing frequently to catch his breath. When he reached the floor above, he went through an empty apartment until he found a balcony. Leaning his cane against the concrete railing, he gazed out at the town, amazed at the sprawl of high-rises and factories and shops that spread out before him. The hills to the northwest were no longer covered in fruit and nut trees but in villas and apartments and small factories, and Lin could see where the marsh had been completely drained and replaced with large industrial buildings tightly clustered together. Atop one of the highest buildings in the industrial park was a massive billboard featuring the dancing, smiling carp with the green and red background which advertised Wenyu Lake beer. His ex-friend Bing had obviously done well for himself in the highly competitive beer market. On the few occasions when the inmates had been allowed access to a television, either to view a major sport's event with Chinese athletes, or to see the Great Leader and Mao Zedong personification, Xi Jinping, greeting or visiting foreign dignitaries, he had seen commercials for Wenyu Lake beer and even seen Bing's smiling face handing a trophy and a cheque to a grateful player.

Lin backed away from the railing to the bare concrete wall and began to scavenge the scraps of construction material, assorted abandoned bricks and pieces of dried out plywood. These he used to build a rickety bench where he sat, a bit unsteadily, out of the wind, his hands resting on the handle of his cane, enjoying the view and the warm winter sunshine.

Chapter 41

After many years absence, Chen found herself back in Meiyu city. She'd had little reason to return: no projects which needed her attention and most of her relatives dead and buried. There was her old friend Bing, of course, but she had outstripped even him with the wealth of her real estate firm and she no longer needed him as she used to. Oh, he had served his purpose in the beginning, lending her enough money to get her first development off the ground, at a handsome profit to himself. In fact, Chen had made nothing on that first development; she knew very well how to generously distribute the profits, how to pay the right people off. The next deal had been easier, and all the ones that came after, and now she had them all eating out of the palm of her hand, banks and money managers and venture capitalists pouring money into her firm. There was buzz from her specs on the seat of her Mercedes Maybach X Class limousine. She picked up the glasses and in the far right corner of the screen saw the name and number of the caller, the new mayor of Meiyu city, hopefully with a better offer than the last one, she thought. It had been easier dealing with Cao Xiaoping when he was mayor, a simple matter of him stating the price and a bank transfer to a Hong Kong account, and all was taken care of. But this one was slippery, always grasping for more after the terms had been settled. She dismissed the call, and dropped the glasses onto the plush, white leather seat. Let him stew for a bit.

She was parked outside the bridge to the island where the abandoned villas and apartment complexes were located. She had a good view of it through the tinted windows, of the dilapidated gate and the bare concrete structures, although her view was often obstructed by the faces of peasants walking around the limousine, giving appreciative nods of their heads before pressing their noses grotesquely against the darkened windows. Chen told the driver to get out and keep them away; they were smearing the glass. When he opened the door, the sounds of the city poured in, jarring her ears, before the door closed and she was once again hermetically sealed, left with only the gentle hum of the batteries and the air conditioning.

It was a tricky deal, this one. The development had belonged to the son of a very high-level cadre in Beijing who had absconded with the 2nd tranche payment and was now being hunted by the international arm of the PSB somewhere in Latin America. The high-level cadre father wished to keep the investment in the family and pass it on to a daughter-in-law, but the behavior of the son had made this transfer problematic. Other higher-ups in the provincial capital were interested in unloading the property and it appeared that they had come to an agreement with the Beijing cadre father. For Chen, the terms of the agreement were of paramount concern for it would determine just how much might be left to actually develop the property. She had an idea of what the Beijinger wanted and expected, but the eel-like local mayor kept shifting his position, bringing more parties in, more mouths to feed. Her idea was to develop the island as an amusement park, water-themed and complete with water slides and rides and great pools of carp and fish restaurants. A floating Disney. The benefits to the city would be enormous with rich Chinese tourists arriving by the tens of thousands, flinging their ready cash everywhere. But this new mayor was short sighted and could only grasp the small picture. Ah well, she thought, let him stew. I've got plenty of other irons in the fire. He'll come around once he stops long enough to consider his limited options.

She leaned back, pulled a silver case from her purse and took out a hand-rolled cigarette in greenish-white paper. It was pure organic tobacco from America, grown without any chemicals or additives, and rolled in the finest and purest paper. She kept eight cigarettes in her silver case, always eight and only eight, rolled by a maid each morning, and if she was traveling, delivered by courier. She smoked only after noon, and if she smoked more than eight before the end of the day, she smoked no more. She was very disciplined, never accepting the offer of cheap Chinese tobacco at the endless banquets she attended. She lit up, leaned back, let a thin stream of smoke drift to the roof of the car, and in the stillness that the cigarette brought her, she thought of Lin and Xiaoyu and how they haunted these streets, which was another reason she so rarely returned. Xiaoyu was an especially painful subject, Chen's innumerable attempts to send money and to make bank transfers to Sydney rejected, attempts to visit put off by weak excuses, communication consisting of a few emails a year with photos of the baby. The large sums of money Chen kept trying to send were, Xiaoyu had told her a few years ago, not only unnecessary and unwanted but, even worse, somehow tainted; she didn't want it to corrupt her marriage, her work, or her daughters which Chen completely failed to understand. What could possibly be wrong with giving an advantage to her granddaughters: the best private education and perhaps a prestigious university in America. Xiaoyu wouldn't hear of it, said the local schools were fine. An idealist, of course, like her father. Well, her father had paid the price, she thought. At least Xiaoyu was in a country where idealism appeared to be accepted and didn't land you in prison.

Something drew her eyes to the people streaming past her windows, and the sight of a tall man, somewhat stooped, hair gone white, thick framed glasses of the sort favored by cadre engineers, a bag hanging from his shoulder and using a cane to work his way through the crowd. She had heard from someone at the Ministry of Environmental Protection that Lin was out of prison and back in Meiyou city but she had not expected him to appear like a ghost before the windscreen. She shrank back into the shadows of the plush seat although it would have been impossible for Lin to have seen her through the dark windows. He looked so old and decrepit, she thought, then gazing at herself in the rearview mirror, her perfect skin, thick coifed hair, rounded eyes (a simple procedure), gleaming teeth. Well, that's what he did to himself. She watched as he turned and crossed the arched bridge, shuffling slowly on the ascent, picking up a bit of speed on the way down, and disappearing beneath the crumbling gate. So extreme, she thought, always going too far, with his inability to compromise. It was incomprehensible, she thought, when he could have been sitting here beside me all this time in absolute splendor. Maybe Xiaoyu would have stayed with them. Maybe. . . She tapped on the window and the driver climbed back and turned his fat head in her direction. "Back to the capital, as fast as possible," she said. "I've had enough of this dump."

Chapter 42

When he was not shuffling from food market to food market looking for bargains to stretch his pittance of a budget, Lin spent a good part of each day climbing to his bench on the abandoned building on the island to gaze out at the city and the lake. He had been to the municipal offices to register his address and to fill out an endless array of forms in order to receive his mail and his pathetic pension and his pathetic health insurance of twelve dollars a month. He had been thrilled, and extremely grateful, to find that a kind government employee had kept a handful of letters from Xiaoyu that she had addressed to the town municipal office. Although obviously opened by some grubby-handed, officious PSB officer, he had carried them excitedly back to his room, marveling at the beautiful foreign postage stamps, and, with shaking hands, sat on his bed to read them.

They were short and chatty, full of basic information about her life in Australia, that showed that they were written with the censor in mind, and with the knowledge that he may never receive them. She had completed a degree in education and social work and had spent a year in the outback at an aboriginal settlement. By the end of the last letter, written three years earlier, she was in Sydney teaching at a daycare center part-time and caring for her just born baby girl, Sofie. Her husband, Peter, taught history and sports at a primary school. There was a snapshot enclosed, which he stared at for hours: Xiaoyu, a pretty woman in her late twenties or early thirties now, tall even by Australian standards, a dark-haired smiling baby balanced on her hip and grabbing at one of her dangling earrings, and Peter with his arm around her, tall, blond, with gleaming teeth, looking happily down at Xiaoyu, a hand around her shoulder and the other squeezing the baby's foot. Behind them was a tiny white bungalow house with blue shutters and a red-tiled roof. There was a return postal address, and an email address, and since Lin had no computer and no mobile, and no chance of acquiring either, he set about with conventional pen and paper getting back in touch with his daughter which was an incredible comfort to him.

Paying a visit to the municipal office one day, he had noticed that his laboratory had long since been torn down and replaced with a non-descript, rusty and stained six-story office building. He met an acquaintance outside the entrance to the administration office and inquired about his half-brother, Cao Xiaoping, whom, he could see from the large, framed picture of the current mayor hanging conspicuously on the wall, was mayor no more and would be well past his mandatory retirement age. He was told that Cao had moved up to the provincial capital ten years ago to assist his wife with the marketing and government relations surrounding her plastic surgery business. The business had grown beyond all expectations, women storming the doors of the clinics with shopping bags full of cash and demanding all manner of procedures. Cao was rich, lived in a massive villa outside the capital, drove a Mercedes Sedan and a Porsche sports car. That is, he was told, until his death just last year of lung cancer. Lin was surprised by how little he felt at hearing the news. "You can't take it with you," the man had said with a schadenfreude shake of his head, as if perhaps the money had been the cause of Cao's death rather than the three packs of cigarettes he had consumed daily throughout his life.

It seemed that there was no one else left that Lin might inquire about other than his friend Yang who had been kind enough to stay in touch with him while he was in prison, sending environmental magazines and technical journals once or twice a year along with gossipy news from around the lake, most of it heavily censored. But Lin kept putting off getting in touch, remembering their athletic evenings, and thoroughly ashamed at what a pathetic figure he now cut. He was surprised, therefore, one early morning to find Yang outside his door, leaning against an electric three-wheeled tricycle, his arms ensconced in a set of metal crutches, his salt and pepper hair much saltier but otherwise looking incredibly healthy and not much changed.

"Did you think you were going to avoid me forever, my old friend?" he said, smiling and propelling himself expertly with his strong arms, as he closed the gap between them with two swings of his crutches. He disentangled himself from a crutch and stuck his hand out. Lin grabbed it with both his hands and felt the tears well-up in his eyes.

"Yang," was all he could manage to say. "Yang, my friend. I was meaning to get in touch."

"Yes, yes. But I have beat you to it. I asked around at the municipal office and, after some initial resistance, they agreed to give me your address. By the way," Yang said, looking at Lin carefully, "you look terrible. Your skin is yellow, and you are way too thin. We need to get some meat on those bones of yours."

Lin looked embarrassedly at his feet before looking up with a shrug. "And you? You look extremely fit but I'm sorry to see you have crutches."

"Ah well. All those operations, you know, and then, stupidly, I opted for one more which they botched and my knee finally gave out. But as you can see, my upper body has compensated." He flexed his biceps and his abdominals, holding the crutches above his head and grinning.

"Very impressive," Lin said, a smile spread across his jaundiced face.

"Now, exactly where were you headed? Shopping no doubt." Lin nodded. "Well, let's do that together. You can climb aboard my sleek machine here," he said, banging one of the dented fenders with a crutch. "I have a shopping basket in the back which turns into a seat like so." He flipped a cushioned seat onto the top of the basket. Lin climbed tentatively aboard, facing backwards, happy to see that there was even space enough for his long legs and his cane, his feet resting comfortably on the rear step. Yang put his crutches in a specially built round cylinder attached to the frame and swung his good leg over the seat before hefting the other onto the running board with his powerful arms. Turning his head slightly, he shouted, "I promise to drive carefully," before shooting out into the street and proceeding to weave between automobiles and other scooters, at one point heading into oncoming traffic and turning onto the sidewalk at the last minute, crossing wildly again to the proper side of the street.

Lin grabbed the handrails for dear life. "I know I look terrible," he shouted, tilting his head back so Yang could hear him, "but I wouldn't mind living a bit longer."

There was a loud laugh which was soon lost in the chaos of car horns and screeching breaks and shouts from other scooter drivers. Eventually they slammed to a halt in front of a shiny glass store front that advertised health foods and products from the United States, Germany, Australia, and New Zealand. Lin dismounted and stood staring at the bright shelves and the colorful advertising.

"What have we here, Yang?" Lin asked.

"I've become a bit of a health nut since you were gone. I buy my protein powder here and various vitamins that help me build up my muscles as well as my immune system. All the products are certified organic and produced abroad."

"You wouldn't have seen such a place in the old days. And it sounds expensive," Lin said with a frown as they made their way up the front steps and into the white-tiled store with shelve after shelve of glass jars, plastic bottles, protein bars and drinks, and packages of pills.

"Never mind that. First, we need to fix you up a bit. Judging by your skin color and the way you keep a hand on your side, your liver is acting up. Am I right?" Lin nodded. "Ok, let's start with a glass of almond milk, banana, kelp, wheat bran, brewer's yeast, and maybe a little molasses." They approached a juice bar where Yang was greeted warmly by a young, heavily pumped-up man with a crew cut, two shiny gold earrings, and a pock-marked face. "Yang," he reached across the counter with an extended fist on the end of a massive arm and they exchanged a fist bump. "What brings you back here so soon?"

"Not for me, Jian. I'm shopping for my friend here who needs to get back into shape." Jian nodded amiably at Lin, resting his arms on the counter in front of the endless array of ingredients, arms that were easily bigger than Lin's legs. Yang placed the order for Lin while the man looked Lin over and nodded affably. "And the usual for me."

"You bet," he said as he began to fill two blenders with strange substances. Meanwhile, Yang took Lin on a tour of the rows of shelves, pointing out the power-drink powder he favored as well as jars and jars of vitamins with foreign script. He stopped in front of a jar and lifted it off the shelf. "Coenzyme Q10. Supplies oxygen to the liver." He put the jar under this arm. They moved on until they came to another jar. "Free-form amino acid complex. Gives you solid amounts of protein without straining the liver." This he also put under his arm. The blenders stopped whirring and they picked up their drinks before settling into two aluminum chairs around an aluminum table by the window. They sat and sipped, Lin surprised at how good it tasted.

"That will fix you up," Yang said with a satisfied nod of his head. "Plus raw vegetables and fruit every day."

"How did you get so knowledgeable about this stuff?" Lin asked.

"As I said, I've become a bit of a health nut. I've been retired for almost ten years now, with a bum knee and plenty of time on my hands. I advise a lot of the youngsters at our local gym on health issues, the importance of diet, various vitamins that aren't available in a normal diet because of modern agricultural practices. They like to hear advice from an old man, and it keeps me busy," he said, smiling and finishing the last of his juice. They were silent for a time. "And you, my friend," Yang whispered, "have had a rough time of it." Lin lowered his eyes, nodding ever so slightly.

"It was all you can imagine, Yang, and worse. The boredom, the endless boredom, and the lack of food and heat during those Beijing winters. I got influenza a few years back, and then an antibiotic drip with a dirty needle gave me Hepatitis C."

"All too common in Chinese prisons," Yang said with a shake of his head.

"So, of course, my liver and spleen are weak and I have a hard time eating. Sad, really, after all those years of being fixated with food, and now that I have a chance to eat again, I can't." Lin sighed, saw that he was making his friend depressed. "Probably best to not think about it," he said, tapping the flat of his hand decisively against the aluminum table.

Yang brightened immediately. "Exactly. Why dwell on what is past? You have a future to think about. It may not look like much of a future at the moment but just give it some time."

"Thank you, Yang. I will try my best to take your advice."

"Excellent," he said with a great show of bravado. "That's the attitude. Let's start with a promise to meet here every week for a health drink."

"With pleasure." They stayed by the window, watching the crowds move up and down the tree-lined street, sharing bits of gossip about the towns and cities surrounding the lake, and about the lake itself. Lin was curious about the textile mill and whether the water had improved. Yang said that they had in fact installed a filter system at the mill but since it had grown to three times the size it was fifteen years ago, it meant the water was just as dirty as before. He wouldn't know just how dirty, of course, because the Environmental Ministry did not publish the data and considered almost everything a state secret. But there were inspectors around who appeared to be issuing citations through the authority of the Ministry of Ecology and Environment and getting some results. They are doing now, Lin thought, exactly what I was doing twenty-one years ago and not going to jail for it.

"And has it improved the lake, Yang? What do you hear about the lake?" Lin asked.

"Again, difficult to get any information, but I would say it's dead, just as you said it would be. You know, of course, the marsh has been completely drained off and there is a lot more development on the tributaries."

"So I noticed," Lin said with a shake of his head.

"Factories are required to install pollution mitigation systems but they are stopgap. They even have a name for them: they're called the ON/OFF. When the inspector shows up, they turn them on, and when he's gone, they turn them off." Lin shook his head at that.

"The air quality has improved since they closed the old steel mill in the northwest and a number of outdated coal plants," Yang continued.

"Yes. I noticed that too. I could actually see across parts of the lake from town."

"So that's something, at least," Yang shrugged. "Of course, I don't see boats out on the lake pulling up great schools of Wenyu Carp." They both smiled at the thought of that.

They finally stood, Yang insisting on paying for the jars he had collected for Lin, and Lin rather sheepishly accepting, shoulders bowed under the reality of his meager finances. As they departed, they gave a friendly wave to Jian who looked out from his specs with a smile and a wave.

On the street, despite Yang's protest, Lin insisted on taking a bus back to his room, and the two clasped hands and agreed that they would meet next week, same time and same place. Lin waved in wonder as Yang lurched out into the street, weaving impossibly in and out of the traffic, a certain fierce competitiveness showing in the thick, bunching muscles of his neck.

Chapter 43

Cao Xiaoping sat at the wheel of his shiny canary-yellow Porsche 911 Carrera convertible, the latest hydrogen fuel cell engine humming with barely contained force, letting the early summer breeze blow through the open windows as he cruised through the streets of the villa compound. He thought that a cigarette would make this moment perfect, but then thought maybe not having a body completely riddled with cancer would make it perfect. The timing was tragic; just as he had stopped working so hard, begun to enjoy the fruits of his labor, begun to enjoy the exclusivity of this villa compound he and his wife lived in and the interesting people they were surrounded by, he was dying. He felt another kick of the morphine that his nurse had shot him up with before he left the house making everything cartoon like, the leaves on the trees shimmering, the manicured lawns turning an emerald green, the uniform white exterior of the houses so warm and inviting like pillows. It was beyond belief that in a matter of weeks, probably days, he would not be around to enjoy this life. Despite the euphoria of the morphine, the sadness swept over him.

With the car on auto drive, he passed the club house, children racing about the pool with their piercing screams and their hovering Ayi's, past the tennis courts, quiet this time of day although at the near court he could make out the figure of Maria hitting a basket of balls to a pair of kids. He pulled the car over, climbed slowly out, using all the strength left in his arms to raise himself from the seat, and made his way to the court's chain-link fence. He walked with a hitch, his hips dragging, his knees locked. He knew he looked like a skeleton, the skin tight on his skull, exposing his yellowed teeth and bulging eyes, but he wanted to see Maria, to say goodbye. They had become close over the last few years as he had started taking tennis lessons and had done some business with her husband, a Siemens executive and an arrogant man who spoke perfect Chinese but was contemptuous of Chinese people and their government. Arrogant, yes, but not too proud to sell Xiaoping some very expensive, very high-end medical equipment for the clinics, and at a very handsome profit for Siemens. He couldn't see what Maria saw in the man. Xiaoping had imagined that perhaps his own relationship with Maria could have gone past the friendship stage. After all, one summer, when she was in Germany with the children and her husband was alone, he had been out in the very early morning, unable to sleep, cruising around in his Porsche, and had seen a slender Chinese girl, her sandals dangling from one hand and a tiny Gucci bag in the other, sprinting out of their villa towards a waiting taxi. He thought it would be a very useful piece of information at the time.

He approached the fence, hooked his fingers through the wire. The kids paused to look at him, and Maria followed their eyes to look behind her.

"Xiaoping," she said warmly, waving to the boys to pick up the balls, and moving towards the fence. He marveled at her short white skirt, her strong legs, the blond ponytail pulled tight against her scalp, her gleaming teeth and perfect skin, but he couldn't avoid seeing the startled look in her eyes. She linked her hands with his through the fence, saw the tears welling up. "How are you, Xiaoping?"

"Just as you see, Maria. Not well, not well at all. But I wanted to stop, to see you, to say goodbye."

"Oh, there will be time for that," she said with a brave voice but she couldn't hide the truth from her eyes.

"Well, hopefully. We'll call. Maybe towards the end of the month…" his voice trailed off. He'd be dead by then.

The kids had taken a seat on the bench facing one another, their eyes covered by specs and their hands flying across a virtual reality game map only visible to the two of them. Occasionally they glanced furtively in Maria's direction.

"I'll let you get back to your lesson," he said, attempting a smile but, with the tightness of his skin, feared it was more like a grimace.

She waved distractedly at the boys and at the court. "Maybe dinner at our place? Next week is best. Friedrich is in Shanghai until then."

"Maybe," he said, again with what he hoped was a smile. "Let's text."

"Good," she said, releasing her hold on his fingers through the fence. "Take care, my friend."

"You too, Maria," he said before turning and, with his stiff-legged, hitching gate, made his way back to the car. He thought about shouting over his shoulder: your husband has some Chinese girl on the side. I saw her coming out of the house last summer. But he didn't have the energy, couldn't see, at this stage, what advantage it might bring him.

He slipped gingerly down into the driver's seat, resting his head against the headrest and staring up at what he could see of the sky through the haze. He forgot about Maria, just another regret, another missed opportunity, and went back to a thought that truly galled him: the fact that his half-brother Lin would outlive him. Even with such a long prison sentence, Lin would be around after he was dead. So unfair, he thought, since the passing of those state secrets should have been as good as a death sentence. At least, that's what he thought when he had his office turn them over to the journalists, but Lin had been spared and, in a short time, would be free. How could life turn out that way? Xiaoping thought, as the car pulled out into the quiet tree-lined street, the fuel cells magically humming. He tried desperately not to think about his own unreasonable death sentence.

Chapter 44

So Lin had his weekly meeting with Yang to look forward to. Yang had instructed him on the use of his specs in order to get in touch with Xiaoyu, and Lin was thrilled that he could actually see her and the children. There were two now, and occasionally husband Peter would appear with a waving hand and a smile. Lin kept the camera off himself, and Yang had set up a single photo of him in place of the camera, doctored to take out the yellow pallor of his skin and the deep wrinkles in his face. Each time Lin and Xiaoyu talked, she invited him to Australia but he refused, thanking her profusely but telling her he was happy where he was, back in his hometown, and had no desire to travel to a foreign land. He knew that Xiaoyu was expecting yet another child and that she lived in a small house and having a father around whose health was precarious would be an unwanted burden. She sent small amounts of money, for which Lin was extremely grateful. Vaguely, and not often, she mentioned a visit to China, but nothing ever came of it. No doubt she wished to avoid the clutches of her mother.

Despite the best efforts of Yang's vitamin regimen, Lin's health did not improve although he couldn't say it got worse. He continued to have trouble eating, his swollen liver and spleen pressing against his stomach and making him lose his appetite, but he was able to make his almost daily pilgrimage to the island and the 2nd floor of the abandoned building to gaze out at the city and the lake and even the distant hills when a fortunate breeze blew the smog to the southeast. The winter and spring passed quite pleasantly until the heat bore down on the town and Lin found his small room unbearable. He bought a fan with some of the money that Xiaoyu had sent but it only seemed to push the hot air about. He took to spending whole nights on the island in the abandoned apartment building, where there was always a slight breeze, and where he had rigged up a thatched roof covered with canvas packing material to keep the sun out; no need to keep the rain out as not a drop had fallen in months. Even the water in the lake had begun to recede, something no one had ever seen before, exposing slime covered boulders and all manner of rusting trash: toilets and refrigerators and stoves and bicycles and even the back end of a few cars.

Wildfires broke out in the hills and farmers talked of a complete loss of their spring crop. It seemed impossible that it could go on with the sun blazing down each day, but finally the rains came. The problem then was that they never stopped. They hit the concrete-like soil with the force of bullets, causing mud slides and washing away whole villages, and the rain never let up. The sky remained an angry grey, spilling out water of such a magnitude that not only did the lake fill up again but it began to burst its banks. The tributaries flooded, taking out the tannery in the northwest and leaving streaks of yellow, red, and light-brown dye floating on the lake, the equipment and buildings all under water. The industrial park flooded, the marsh no longer there to absorb the excess, the mass of concrete parking lots funneling water furiously to the lake and to the city, which was now three feet under water.

And still the rains came. The last time Lin had managed to make it back to the island from his room, wading hip deep through the flooded streets with groceries and a change of clothes, it was a scary journey as he used the tip of his cane to locate submerged obstacles in the fast-moving water. He had barely made it back, the bridge being all but covered, and climbed to his perch on the balcony of the abandoned building knowing that, should the rains continue, he would be unable to move again. Lin crouched on his bench beneath his small roof, nibbling on his provisions, watching the relentless wall of water crash down. When he ventured out from beneath his lean-to, he could see that the island was no more, that the water had almost reached the 2nd floor. Boots and rafts began to appear, rubber, wooden, whatever would float, carrying starved and weary families. They shouted news to Lin as he hung over the balcony a mere ten feet away. Sometimes they threw a rope and he shared with them what little food he had left as they told him about the locks and dikes on the Yangzi giving way, the power station on the Three Gorges crumbling due to the rains, and to inferior cement, it was rumored, and inadequate and sub-standard steel rebar. Buildings were toppling over. Half the country was under water. Water buffaloes floated by, their hooves slashing the water, their eyes rolling in terror, but soon many dead animals were to be seen, and bodies, drifting by in clusters.

So went the news as the dwindling fleet of the living went past, heading south with no plan and no hope. He watched them disappear, shouting their despair, weaving between the great silos of the MSG factory and down to the tributary that passed the textile mill, a river now so swollen it would undoubtedly capsize such fragile craft. They shouted that the provincial capital had been abandoned and that the people who fled in their cars had drowned in the long lines of traffic. People on foot were swept from roads by the force of the water. A million were dead, it was reported. Two million. Ten. Lin had not eaten for days, his vision and thoughts becoming blurred and unstable. The rain did not let up; the boats stopped coming, and Lin watched the water reach the floor and climb steadily towards his bench. He woke one morning to find not only that the water was soaking his bedding, but to an extraordinary scene of great beauty: rafts of ducks appeared floating gracefully on what was once a churning brown mass of water but what had suddenly become clear on the surface. Thousands of birds covered the tops of submerged trees, and Lin saw a shimmering school of carp creep by, their tails languidly propelling them through the current, their mouths occasionally breaking the surface. His heart soared, and he laughed aloud as the water reached his waist. What a miraculous cleansing, he thought.

His bench was now completely submerged and he pulled it from its place on the bricks. He put it between his legs and rested his chest on it, like a surfer, and floated gently over the balcony and into what was now quite suddenly, quite incredibly, clear water. He moved easily with the current, marveling at the flocks of birds that kept landing, wood ducks and mallards and seagulls and coots. Pelicans! He was sure he saw a half dozen mud-brown pelicans, their prehistoric beaks extended, skimming the surface of the water. He shouted with pleasure as a log floated past, a dozen emerald green frogs resting on its bark. A large black snake followed, making S shapes in the water as it moved. And most wonderous of all, a school of Baiji, Yangtze River dolphins, said to have been extinct for decades, gamboling through the water with an occasional leap of their pink backs into the air, mouths in that permanent smile that looked like unadulterated glee. Lin was traveling faster now as he headed towards the southern river, steering around the tops of buildings and approaching the MSG factory. A single, monstrous carp surfaced lazily beside him, rolling and gleaming a deep red and brown, expanding its perfectly round mouth in greeting. In his shear happiness, Lin banged the water with the palms of his hands and carefully rolled over on his back to take in the flocks of birds that were now everywhere. Speeding towards the MSG silos, he passed beneath Bing's gleaming, glass office tower. He caught a glimpse of his ex-friend staring gloomily out at the water, his hands grabbing what was left of his hair. Bing's eyes widened incredulously as he recognized Lin floating by on his board, laughing and smiling and waving. Lin threw his head back, raising both arms triumphantly in the air, before crashing head-on into the concrete mass of a silo and sinking beneath the crystal-clear waters of Wenyu Lake.

THE END

John H. Zane

About the Author

John H. Zane, born in 1957, is a lawyer and China Business Analyst who was first sent to the People's Republic of China in the 1990s for a Venture Capital firm out of Manhattan. His first project was investing in cement plants throughout northeast and central China. He then spent over a decade and a half in the PRC consulting foreign businesses and advising NGOs. He worked as a Dean of Academics at an American Study Abroad program at Beijing's Jing Mao daxue, the University of International Business and Economics. He currently spends time in New Bedford, Massachusetts and in the mountains south of Munich, Bavaria with his family and their Chinese rescue dog.

Printed in the USA
CPSIA information can be obtained
at www.ICGtesting.com
CBHW031643011024
15215CB00055B/1587